NORTH PACIFIC

*A Story
of Life,
Love,
Suffering,
and Grace*

Michael Steffan

Copyright © 2023 Michael Steffan

All rights reserved.

No part of this book may be reproduced, stored in a retrieval system, or transmitted in any form or by any means, electronic, mechanical, photocopying, recording, or otherwise, without express written permission of the author.

ISBN: 979-8-9875921-1-3

Printed in the United States of America

Cover Art by Michael Steffan. The photo, showing Commencement Bay from Tacoma, Washington, was taken by the author and digitally enhanced using Prisma "photo editing" software.

For Becky

Acknowledgments

I warmly thank William Parrett and Mary Smith for reviewing the novel's text and offering me advice.

I was greatly helped by William's pertinent questions about the storyline and his perspective and thoughts on different parts of the narrative.

Mary also critiqued and challenged aspects of the story and, most importantly, held me accountable to the faith of my upbringing with her steadfast and admirable traditional Catholic views.

Their help resulted in many improvements to the story. May God bless you both.

A final thank you goes to Jonathan Sun, a young friend of mine and student at Washington State University. Jonathan helped me to format the book. Without his help, this story would not have been published.

Contents

I. Unus Vultus (One-Look)	1
II. Fundamentum (Foundation)	29
III. Peccatum (Sin)	109
IV. Bellum (War)	173
V. Vita (Life)	223
VI. Delorem (Sorrow)	305
VII. Deus Sitas (God-Centered)	355
VIII. Confido in Deo (Trust in God)	397
IX. Gratia (Grace)	437
Author's Note	459

*"For me, prayer is a surge of the heart.
It is a simple look turned toward heaven,
it is a cry of recognition and of love,
embracing both trial and joy."*

- St. Therese of Lisieux

UNUS VULTUS

(One-Look)

"…for she was exceeding(ly) beautiful."

Esther 1:11

Douay-Rheims

North Pacific

1.

Joseph's view of Commencement Bay in southern Puget Sound spread magnificently before him. High above the water on a steep hill, his house's living room windows provided an unmatched panorama. He could see Vashon and Maury islands to the northwest, with Quartermaster Harbor between them. East Passage connecting Tacoma with Seattle lay directly before him to the north. While to the east, the port of Tacoma beckoned with its naturally deep, welcoming harbor. To top it off, there were the Olympic Mountains to the west and Mt. Rainier and the Cascade mountain range to the east to add to the unparalleled vista. How many times had he taken in this sight over the years? Yet, he never failed to appreciate the immeasurable beauty. This morning the surface of the bay was gray, reflecting the cloudy sky above and what looked like the possibility of a rain shower.

He observed a merchant ship coming south through East Passage turn to port as she reached the bay. The faded paint denoting the vessel's name on the starboard bow became almost decipherable through the overcast Sunday morning sky. Joseph picked up the binoculars from the side table and tried to make out the lettering.

Failing, he panned the binoculars to the right. He saw another much smaller vessel, 30 to 40 feet long, moving in the opposite direction. The fine-looking enclosed cabin cruiser, probably a Chris Craft, passed within a couple of hundred yards of the Browns Point lighthouse, located about three miles NNW across the water on the north side of the bay.

The sight of both vessels prompted the question, where are they headed? Would it be a long or a short trip? What was the purpose? Boats and ships of every size and description moved through these waters daily. They reminded Joseph of a prayer he had learned when he was younger. "O God, watch over thy servants in these vessels, ward off all dangers, favor them with a tranquil passage, and grant they attain their desired port."

Finally, he set the binoculars back on the side table and walked toward the kitchen, where he turned off the radio. His thoughts shifted to what he had just heard on the news broadcast a few minutes before. The war in Europe continued to rage. How long could it be before the United States would become entangled in the burgeoning world conflict? Yet, it was the Pacific that most occupied his thoughts. In the largest of oceans, war appeared to be on the brink – a conflagration waiting for a spark.

Joseph walked over to the hall closet. He put his jacket on while looking at his image in the mirror that hung on the inside of the closet door. Was it really possible that he was now 34 years old? Is it actually 1941 already? Where did the time go? Then looking out the front window one more time at the sky hanging somewhat oppressively over the bay, he reached into the closet on the small shelf above the coat rod and grabbed a lightweight stocking cap - just in case.

Joseph left the house and began his 20-minute walk to morning Mass. Looking at the threatening skies overhead, he sighed and retrieved the cap from his coat pocket, pulling it onto his head. The muffling silence of the cloud-covered early morning sky settled over him.

By the time he had gotten to within two blocks of the church, a light rain had begun falling. Joseph unconsciously picked up his pace. Why didn't I drive this morning? Old habits die hard, I guess. The weather has been great for the last few days. Why couldn't the rain hold off until this afternoon? He patted his other jacket pocket and sighed with relief, thankful that he had at least remembered to grab his missal before he had left. Hustle though he might, the

North Pacific mist-like rain had thoroughly doused Joseph by the time he arrived at the church's front doors.

2.

St. Dominic Catholic Church, with construction completed in 1908, was a modest-sized gray stone structure with exceptional windows. The sizeable leaded stained-glass panes on either side of the church allowed natural light to brighten the individual Dominican saints depicted inside each casement. Looking up at the portrayals from within the church reminded one that the saints were blessed but even more so totally and utterly dependent upon God - as the light pouring through the vitreous glass attested. The church was found close to the top of the slightly sloping topography high above Commencement Bay in Tacoma's "North End," a few blocks from the campus of Rainier College.

Joseph opened one of the large front doors of the church and entered. He paused in the vestibule, removing the damp stocking cap from his head. He pushed the cap down into the empty pocket of his jacket as he walked forward into the church's nave through the second set of smaller, propped-open doors. Upon entering the nave, he paused at the holy water font. Pursing his thumb and first two fingers into a triangle, symbolizing the three persons of

North Pacific

the Blessed Trinity, Joseph dipped them in the water and made the sign of the cross. He continued down the middle aisle reaching roughly the midpoint in the nave, where he stopped, genuflected toward the Blessed Sacrament, reserved in the tabernacle that sat on the high altar, and slipped into a pew on the left-hand side of the church. Sitting, he pulled down the kneeler, slid off the seat, and knelt. He reached into his right-hand coat pocket, withdrew his worn matte black Sunday missal, and began arranging a ribbon for the readings for that Sunday as per the liturgical calendar.

As Joseph looked toward the altar, he became aware of the red sanctuary lamp. The sanctuary lamp candle was enclosed in red glass and suspended by a chain from the back wall behind the high altar. It seemed to burn more deeply and intensely than usual as he began his prayers before Mass. He tried to concentrate on his preparatory prayers but was unable as his eyes were drawn to the small crimson flame that seemed to burn so intensely and powerfully this morning. Always kept lit, the flame, for Catholics, signifies that the tabernacle on the high altar held previously consecrated hosts. The "real presence of Christ" in the Blessed Sacrament reserved in the tabernacle was second only in importance to receiving the Lord in communion.

Did anyone else see the flame's intensity today as he did? What was going on? His eyes went from the flame to the tabernacle and back. And then, his gaze rose decisively above and behind the tabernacle to the back wall where the commanding 15-foot-tall crucifix depicting Christ nailed to the cross seemed to be looking right at and right through him.

For a moment, he contemplated the face of Christ. Then, unable to stare down the Lord, he shifted his view to Jesus' wounds in his hands and feet where the nails had been driven into the wood. As he thought about these things, the lights came up in the sanctuary, and Father Etienne Sauveterre and two altar boys entered from the doorway to the right of the altar. All in attendance stood. The priest ascended the altar and adjusted the position of the lectionary with the readings for the day in it. He returned to the middle of the altar, descended its steps, turned around, and knelt with his back to the parishioners. He began by making the sign of the cross, "In Nomine Patris et Filii, et Spiritus Sancti" (In the name of the Father, and of the Son, and of the Holy Ghost). "Amen," responded the altar servers.

The liturgy continued until the reading of the epistle and gospel for that Sunday was completed. Then the priest walked over to the ambo and began his prepared homily. Near the end of his discourse, Father Etienne, a renowned Dominican homilist (the parish had been blessed to have him residing there), referred to a phrase from the book of Ecclesiasticus that noted *All flesh shall fade as grass…"* (Eccl 14.18). The French priest then stated the obvious, that life was fragile and fleeting. He summed up his oration by quoting a verse from one of the Psalms, *I spoke with my tongue: O Lord, make me know my end. And what is the number of my days; that I may know what is wanting to me"* (Ps 38:5). What Joseph heard were the same things he had mused about several times before in his life about the swiftness and sometimes seemingly meaninglessness of human existence. His mind kept returning to the notion that life is truly short, and he asked himself, do I have a purpose more meaningful than the one I'm living now? Finally, Father finished with the final verse of the same psalm, *O forgive me, that I may be refreshed, before I go hence, and be no more"* (Ps 38:14). The last phrase stung Joseph.

The Mass continued, eventually approaching the communion. Father Etienne turned toward the people and elevated the gold chalice in his right hand and a particle of the consecrated host above the chalice with the other while declaring, "Ecce Agnus Dei, ecce Qui tollit peccata mundi" (Behold the Lamb of God, behold Him who takes away the sins of the world) to which the faithful responded "Domine, non sum dignus…" (Lord, I am not worthy…) Moments later, those who were going to receive communion began moving toward the middle aisle to approach the altar rail that separated the sanctuary from the nave of the church.

As Joseph stood up, he noticed an older woman who appeared to be of Japanese descent coming out of the pew directly across the middle aisle from him. As the woman turned toward the front of the church and started down the aisle to the communion rail, his eyes were drawn to a younger Japanese woman following her. Her presence at once and forever struck him. She was physically slight and around 30 years of age, with long black hair held together loosely in the back by a black ribbon near the top of her shoulders. She carried herself with grace and assurance. No more than 5' 2" with big dark eyes, she roused his consciousness to such a level that he lost focus on his imminent reception of the Most Blessed Sacrament. Joseph struggled mightily to regain a single-mindedness about what he was supposed to be doing as he went ahead toward the altar. Try as he might, he could not help glancing one more time over at this woman as they approached the altar railing on either side of the middle aisle. He mentally proclaimed to himself that she was utterly captivating.

After kneeling and receiving communion on his tongue, Joseph returned to his pew by way of the outer aisle on the left side of the church. He knelt and immediately begged God to forgive him for his lapse of concentration. He then tried to say his customary post-communion prayers beginning with the *Anima Christi* (Soul of Christ) but failed wretchedly, with the image of the woman completely disrupting his train of thought. Joseph strained to keep his eyes looking directly at the tabernacle on the altar. The priest began the prayers after communion, and Joseph continued to be distracted.

As Mass ended, Joseph again turned to see if this woman, this vision, who had so stirred his feelings, was still there. She was. The Mass attendees who did not remain to kneel and pray, began moving slowly toward the back of the church. Joseph managed to time his departure in order to hold open one of the large outer church doors for the two ladies. The older woman gave him a slight bow of her head of deferential courtesy and went ahead down the three steps to the wide sidewalk in front of the church. Her younger companion followed close behind her. As she descended the steps, she glanced ever so slightly back at Joseph.

Joseph continued holding the door as more churchgoers filed out. He wondered to himself if this woman, the object of his disorientation, might, just might, have given him a second look as she had gone out the door. Time seemed to come to a halt, and after a confusing moment or two, Joseph finally let go of the door. Time, however, had not halted for the two women. They had rounded the corner of the church and were walking briskly down the street. Joseph made his way through the milling parishioners to the corner and glimpsed them, walking toward the bus stop. After nodding unconscious greetings toward a few familiar faces, including Father Etienne, he saw the City bus arrive. The new center of his world boarded the bus, and a moment later, it pulled away, heading downtown.

Standing there like a fool, he realized it was still raining. Buttoning his jacket and pulling his stocking cap back on, he checked to ensure he had put his missal back into his jacket pocket. Joseph then started for home, putting one foot in front of the other, lost in reflection.

3.

Between the rain and his scattered thoughts, Joseph stopped about a half-mile from the church at 3 Bridges Café to grab a cup of coffee, get out of the misty drizzle, and, most importantly, collect himself. He entered the café and sat at the last seat at the counter closest to the wide window that opened onto the street.

The waitress, an attractive brunette in her mid to late 30s, came over from the other end of the counter and offered him coffee and a menu. At length, her customer, whom she could see was mentally somewhere else, noticed her and said, "Just coffee, please, black." She smiled, walked over to the large pot of coffee sitting on a burner on low heat, poured him a cup, returned, and said, "Here you go." Again, he hardly noticed her, prompting her to genially ask, "You okay?"

Joseph, clearly hearing that, embarrassed, replied, "Sorry, I was just thinking about something. Forgive me." She gave him a quizzical smile and moved down the counter to greet a gentleman who had occupied another stool. Joseph took a sip of the coffee. It was hot, slightly burning his tongue.

North Pacific

Looking out the window, thinking of the woman at Mass, Joseph asked himself, wasn't she breathtaking? I've never seen anyone like her. Everything about her was perfect, or at least what he had observed and remembered. I swear she looked at me. Well, I can't be sure she did, but I think she did. Listen to yourself. Calm down. He took another sip of the coffee.

The black coffee in the thick white mug had cooled down just enough that he could taste the dark roasted flavors and let the heat of the cup warm his hands. Joseph remained at the café for about half an hour, receiving one large refill from his waitress, smiling at him again. He noticed her name tag and said, "Denise, I'm Joseph, and I'm sorry for being, well, me, I guess." She smiled and said, "You're fine. You just looked so lost in thought. It happens around here more than you might think. I hope the rest of your day is less complicated." Joseph smiled for the first time and was about to ask her how her day was going when a couple at a table over in the corner gestured to her for their bill. Joseph and Denise smiled at each other as she started moving toward the couple while hunting through her apron pocket to find their ticket. Getting up to leave, he reached for his wallet and paid for the coffee, leaving a tip for his waitress twice what he usually would for being somewhat less than an attentive customer.

The rain had stopped. Gathering himself, he stepped out of the café and headed home—no need now for a stocking cap. Joseph backtracked a few blocks west, veered off the main bus line route, and continued north on a side street.

As he walked, the gray cloud cover that had stilled and dampened the morning had moved to the northeast, giving way to a sunny day. He unbuttoned his jacket. Ten minutes later and almost home, Joseph shook his head in wonderment and thought that the stunning discovery of this woman that overpowered his mind and senses to such a degree was all a bit much for a simple Sunday morning low Mass.

4.

It had been three days since Joseph's remarkable experience at Mass. He could not get that beautiful woman out of his thoughts. After parking his gray 1936 Studebaker "Dictator" two-door coupe on the street out in front of Carr's Diner, he entered the establishment, looked around, and not seeing his friend Martin, slid into a booth and ordered coffee.

Carr's Diner was located in the two-block long row of buildings and shops that made up the commercial section of "Old Town," the site on Commencement Bay in southern Puget Sound where Tacoma had been founded in 1864 by Job Carr.

In the 1870s, the Northern Pacific Railroad selected Tacoma as the western terminus for its cross-country operations. It built a rail hub two miles east of the original settlement, thus creating "New" Tacoma. Over the years, as the town grew, the "new" was dropped as it became the heart of the growing city and busy seaport. The original settlement for a while was known as "Old Tacoma," and then eventually and affectionately became "Old Town," a neighborhood among others forming the city's sprawling North End. Just a block up from Commencement Bay's southern waterfront, the Old Town businesses were at the base of a semi-circular naturally carved-out slope rising hundreds of feet for over three-quarters of a mile. The neighborhood, marked by blocks and streets and populated with homes, swept upward from the bay to the top of the slope and beyond.

Joseph received his cup of coffee at the same time Martin walked in. It was their weekly lunch, and Martin Linart was Joseph's closest friend. Martin was tall and lanky with light brown hair that he combed straight back. He had always insisted his family was of Walloon descent from eastern Belgium. Joseph always suspected Martin had gotten his 6' 2" height from some possibly indirect Dutch ancestry. Four inches shorter, with dark brown hair and hazel eyes, Joseph had always been slightly envious of Martin's larger stature. Martin was an engineer with the Commencement Bay Boat Building Co., helping design fishing vessels for the waters of Puget Sound and Southeastern Alaska.

North Pacific

Martin slid into the booth across from Joseph and said, "Well, have you figured out a way to keep us out of the war?"

Joseph smiled and replied, "Not yet."

This week they discussed the sinking of the pride of the British Navy, *HMS Hood*, with the loss of 1,400 sailors and, three days later, the sinking of the German Battleship *Bismarck,* taking 2,300 souls to a watery grave. It was hard for them to believe how quickly these things were happening. Less than a year ago, the French had signed an armistice with Germany after a humiliating defeat at the hands of Hitler's Panzer tank divisions.

Then the conversation shifted as Joseph spoke about Japan and how they had occupied French Indochina and called up one million men just a few weeks before for military service. Joseph believed the issue there seemed to be all about oil and whether Japan could secure enough for their Army and Navy as they continued their war against China.

Joseph and Martin went back and forth on these topics until their food arrived. They both had ordered the pork chop, mashed potatoes, and green peas special and with forks and knives in hand, they proceeded to eat.

After lunch, which seemed more like dinner, Joseph sat back in the booth, sipped his coffee, and asked Martin how the family was doing. Martin had now been married for eight years. He and Colleen, his generous and mission-driven better half, had two children, Mark, age seven, and a daughter Darcy, five.

"They're good. Mark has discovered baseball. I swear that's all he wants to do. I am forever playing catch with him and pitching the ball for him to hit. He wears me out. Darcy loves the swing I built in the backyard using that big low-hanging branch on our maple tree."

There was a pause in the conversation, and Martin looked at his friend and patiently said, "Where'd you go? We were talking, or at least I was, and you drifted away, looking out the window. What have you got going on in that gray matter of yours? You seem a bit distracted."

After pausing, Joseph looked at him sheepishly and said, "I'm sorry, Martin. Last Sunday, I saw a woman at Mass, and I can't get her out of my head."

"You're kidding me, right? It's been a while for you, buddy."

"I know, I know, but it's true."

"Tell me about her," Martin good-naturedly pressed.

"Well, I didn't notice her until near the end of Mass. I held the door for her on her way out and watched her catch the bus heading downtown. I think she's Japanese,"

"Japanese," Martin mused. "So why didn't you talk to her? Why didn't you walk up to her and introduce yourself?"

"Yeah, well, you know I'm not good at that sort of thing. I don't know. When I held the door for her, she smiled, I think. I didn't want to make a fool of myself. Besides, she was with another woman, maybe her mother, I don't know."

Joseph started staring out the window again. Even though Martin knew Joseph was prone to losing himself in his thoughts, he realized that this woman had made a big impression on his cohort. Trying to get hold of the situation, Martin tilted his head and asked, "How is she different from Diane?"

Martin and Joseph went way back. They had grown up together and attended the same elementary, junior high, and high school. Even though Martin had married his high school sweetheart Colleen and had two children, he and Joseph still found time to get together and sort out the world's problems as all men are prone to. Both were thirty-four years old, not old, of course, but with the world crumbling around them, they were starting to ask questions regarding the meaning in their lives that they had only touched on when they were younger. It was the stuff that everyone asked at one time or another. Joseph related to Martin the crux of the homily Father Sauveterre had given about the shortness of life and his own ongoing struggles with his existence. Each had a different view of the age-old question. It was true that Martin had attended catechism classes with Joseph when they were young, but he had slowly drifted away from the faith. On many occasions, they would discuss matters related to the "Why" questions of life and, of course, resolve none of them.

North Pacific

Martin's reference to Diane got Joseph's attention. Joseph and Diane had been an item for some time coming out of college. Most had assumed the two would marry, but the relationship had run its course for complicated reasons - though some strong feelings persisted.

"You know, Martin. There has been nothing compared to what I felt seeing this woman the other day. With Diane, I noticed her for sure, but not like this. This was different. It was one look, and wham was already there. What was it like for you and Colleen?"

"Colleen and I first became great friends, and over time I realized I had feelings for her and wanted to be with her." He began to laugh, "Buddy, I think you're a train wreck right now. Maybe if you see her again or actually meet her, you'll come back down to earth and be less enamored than you are now."

"I tell you, Martin, this woman really got to me."

The conversation continued for another ten minutes, and then both realized it was time to get going.

Joseph lived near the top of the hill on the west side of Old Town. You would drive a couple of blocks from Carr's Diner and ascend "30th Street hill." The hill rose more than 200 feet in less than a half-mile covering six city blocks. This dramatic elevation change accounted for Joseph's commanding view of Commencement Bay.

Martin's home was almost a mile further into what was known as the North End of town near the Proctor shopping district. His house was closer to the neighborhood businesses and the bus line, which had replaced the venerable electric streetcar system just a few years before. Buses now plied the old streetcar routes between Tacoma's downtown business district and the other city neighborhoods.

As they exited the restaurant heading for their vehicles, Martin asked the obvious question, "So what are you going to do about this mystery lady?"

Joseph slowly looked at Martin, then, with a slight smile and shrugging his shoulders, said, "I don't know, but I will tell you that I'm not going to miss Sunday Mass anytime soon."

~~~~~

On Saturday morning, Joseph made himself a fried egg, toasted two pieces of bread, and brewed a small pot of Folger's coffee for breakfast. Over his meal, he pondered the moments from his week. Yes, he was still astonished by his feelings about that woman. Yes, going to Mass tomorrow was going to be a big deal. He tried to come up with something to say to her if the chance presented itself. As Martin had pointed out, he needed to be more assertive than was his nature. He pictured how it might play out, what he might say, but nothing special came to mind. Frustrated, he attempted to put the subject out of his thoughts.

Interestingly, Martin had also raised the issue of Diane. That she had left a mark on Joseph, there was no doubt. He thought about the circumstances that had led to their relationship ending more often than he probably should have, but there it was. Others had said what happened to him and Diane was fate. Yet Joseph believed decisions made and unintended consequences played a more significant part in his and Diane's past.

It was a beautiful day, and he had promised himself that he would wash the car that morning. He needed to do his grocery shopping and straighten up the house. Joseph finished his meal. As he moved the dish, utensils, and cup to the kitchen sink and added the frying pan and spatula, he realized how apprehensive he was about how things might go the next day.

5.

Sunday morning finally arrived. Joseph rose, showered, and dressed quickly. Even though the weather was perfect, he decided to drive to Mass. He sat in the church parking lot for a few minutes, hoping to see "that woman" walking up from the bus stop. He did not. He went into the church. He sat in his usual spot and glanced to his right, but again, she was not there. And though Joseph was willing to wait for her arrival, the Mass did not. Father Louis Simone, the older pastor of St. Dominic, during his homily, as Joseph remembered it later, told everyone that basically, life wasn't fair, so get over it. It was classic Father Simone. The problem was that Joseph kept looking for his mystery woman and could not find her in attendance. His head was on a swivel, and he was self-conscious of it. He tried to restrain himself. After receiving communion, his post-communion prayers included a "mea culpa" for not concentrating on the Mass as much as he should have, and then it was over. He got up quickly and went outside. He watched as the parishioners exited the church. Again, there was no sign of her. Joseph was crushed.

~~~~~

He drove home. Joseph sighed as he stood in the living room, looking out over the bay. He wasn't sure of what to do. However, he was aware of how unbearably quiet it was in the house. He dropped his head, stared at the floor for a few seconds, then, raising it again, exhaled. Out of habit, he turned toward the kitchen to prepare breakfast and then realized he was not hungry. Over the next two hours, Joseph changed clothes, did household chores, and eventually made a sandwich and a pot of coffee for lunch.

Over the last few years, he had come to dislike Sundays. Too many Sundays he spent hanging out around the house. For him, the place on Sundays felt too quiet and lonely. After finishing the sandwich and drinking a couple of cups of the dark brew, he decided he needed to get out of the house for a while. He formulated a plan to go to a movie to forget his disappointment.

Joseph did not make it downtown until 1.30 PM. He parked on St. Helen's Street and walked down the block to Broadway. He looked at his watch and the movie's start time on the marquee over the entrance to the Roxy Theatre. Joseph wanted to see *The Sea Wolf*, starring Edward G. Robinson, Ida Lupino, and John Garfield, but it had started 45 minutes earlier. The next showing would be in about an hour and a half. This was not his day.

Tacoma, for a time, was known as the "Lumber Capital of the World," a place where indeed, rail met sail, as the saying went. Tacoma's downtown area was set on the side of a steep hill that climbed five blocks from its main street at the bottom, Pacific Avenue, up to Tacoma Avenue near the top. Joseph was standing at 9th Street and Broadway.

He knew that Japan Town, known to those of Japanese heritage as "Nihonmachi," occupied slightly less than a half-square mile, inter-mingled with other shops and businesses, just to the south of the heart of the downtown area starting on 13th Street. Between a thousand and two thousand Japanese had immigrated to this area and called Tacoma home. Occupied with thoughts of "her," Joseph decided to take a walking tour of sorts through that part of town. It was a beautiful late spring day. He began wandering down Broadway to 13th Street, then turned right and went up the hill to Market St., turned left, and took in the sights and sounds of the area. Joseph thought about what he was doing. Am I hoping to run into her down here? God, I'm pathetic. He also realized that finding her would be akin to the proverbial needle in a haystack affair.

He walked by laundries and meat and poultry shops with white tile floors, marble countertops, and porcelain butcher scales. He also saw many fruit and vegetable sellers with workers wearing long white coats. It was surprising, to him at least, the number of hotels he discovered. Many Japanese at that time lived in hotel rooms without kitchens or refrigerators and shopped for fresh food daily or ate at small local restaurants and cafes. Joseph had grown up here. This was his town. Yet, he realized he had never really studied Japan Town's businesses and other establishments.

He did remember that in the summer of 1929, he had toured two Imperial Japanese Navy cruisers, *Iwata,* and *Asama,* that had visited the city.

He saw a Methodist church and a Buddhist temple as he continued his walk. Based on a journal article he had previously read, it struck him that Japanese Americans, if they were religious, overwhelmingly attended Buddhist temples or were members of the Protestant Methodist church. The number of Japanese Americans that practiced Roman Catholicism was minuscule by comparison. Joseph wondered how the woman of his interest had found her way into the faith he practiced.

Feeling the futility of his hastily conceived effort, Joseph decided he was ready to pack it in and head for home. He walked down 17th Street until he reached Broadway, then headed back toward his car. His heart was no longer into seeing the movie. As he approached 9th Street and Broadway, the site of the Roxy Theatre again, he thought he glimpsed her. As he got closer, but still half a block away, he realized she was conversing with some man in front of the theatre. Damn, Joseph thought, it was her. He had found her.

In his excitement, it took Joseph a moment to comprehend that she was with a guy. Joseph stopped walking. No, he thought, this can't be, and then he thought, well, of course, it could be. She's beautiful. The two figures in front of the theater finished their conversation, and then, as Joseph watched, they walked over to the glass window of the booth in front of the cinema and bought tickets. As Joseph stood there, his shoulders slumped forward, as the couple disappeared into the movie house.

Disheartened, to say the least, Joseph looked down at the sidewalk, blew what little air he had left in him out, and then began walking again. He walked by the theatre, no longer thinking about much of anything, finally getting in his car and driving home. By the time he reached the house, he had concluded that he felt like a clown for having tramped around downtown looking for her. Beyond feeling foolish was the awful realization that he had found her with another man.

~~~~~

North Pacific

Generally, on a Sunday afternoon or early evening, Joseph might go over to Martin and Colleen's for dinner or grab a bite at one of the local restaurants. But tonight, he was deflated and had no appetite. He did some rote tasks around the house. However, his mind would not engage. He refused to let it. At about 7 PM, realizing he was hungry, Joseph ate some raw vegetables that were in the refrigerator and washed them down with a reheated cup of coffee from lunch. He turned the radio on while eating and listened to "The String Quartet No. 6" by the Hungarian composer Bela Bartok. It was a four-movement piece with an incredibly sad ending that did not help Joseph's disposition. He turned the dial on the radio and found a station playing contemporary music. The music seemed to help him rally a bit from his moodiness.

~~~~~

Later that evening, he built a fire and sat on the old brown leather sofa, staring out the large window in the living room at the darkening skies over the bay. This time of year, in the northern climes, it didn't really get dark until closer to 10 PM. As Joseph stared at the Browns Point lighthouse across the water, he considered the state of his existence. For obvious reasons, an old testament verse recited by Father Etienne at a talk he had given a while back came to mind. *"It is not good for man to be alone"* (Gen 2:18). He remembered the verse because Father Etienne had delivered it with such solemnity. It was a passage that kept returning to him. It resonated with his mood that evening, one of a newly discovered depression.

In that same talk, Father had said that man is aware of his aloneness. Man, he said, grasps the concept, for the most part, because if you have experienced loneliness, you never forget the visceral feelings it stirs deep within your soul. Didn't he know it.

He thought he had done much to enhance his chances of living a life full of happiness. But the personal effort he had put forth had not brought him happiness as he had imagined. Wasn't that clear? As it was, as 10 PM arrived, he sat alone in his living room in darkness other than the dying fire and the lighthouse. He had no one to talk to, to take care of, to plan something together, to laugh with, or even cry with. He thought the "things" we do in life are important, but all seem incomplete without a companion to share them with. Joseph, openly struggling with uncertainty about his own life, stared into the fire and thought spiritually that something was missing. Physically, someone was missing. And to top it off, this woman, the woman of now even his dreams, although he had never even met her, was with some other guy. Man, he just couldn't shake that thought.

FUNDAMENTUM

(Foundation)

"Built upon the foundation of the apostles and prophets, Jesus Christ himself being the chief cornerstone...."

Ephesians 2:20

Douay-Rheims

North Pacific

6.

Alexandr and Maria Vaenko were immigrants to the United States from the expansive Austro-Hungarian Empire in Central Europe. They married and came to America in 1896. Learning English was their priority and an absolute necessity to obtain work and get by in their newly adopted country. Both Alexandr and Maria achieved this goal with serviceable, though accented English. After learning English and performing menial tasks for a few years on the East Coast, the Vaenkos, using a small gift of money they received from Alexandr's father in the "old country" and their own scant savings, put their meager possessions into one bag and "took a chance."

Alexandr had seen a brochure promoting the city on Commencement Bay and liked to pronounce the name Ta-co-ma. He would tell Maria it sounded perfect for them. Looking at her and pointing to the pamphlet from speculators trying to entice people to move to this remote corner of the country, he would say, "This is where we will make our home." They traveled west by rail to the Pacific Northwest and arrived in Tacoma on Puget Sound in what was then the 11-year-old State of Washington. The year was

1900, and after a few desperate months, Alexandr was, much to his delight, able to land a job at a sawmill on Commencement Bay.

Tacoma, in 1900, had finally recovered from a depression that lasted from 1893 to 1897. The population of the city was close to 40,000. There was a 2-mile stretch along the south shore of Commencement Bay that, at its peak, had close to two dozen privately owned sawmills operating twenty-four hours a day. In the first half of the 20th century, millions of board feet of lumber would be cut and shipped to ports all over the world. This stretch of sawmills along the shoreline also fronted what then was known as "Old Town."

Alexandr took to working at the sawmill on the bay like a fish to water. He learned to be a fireman, sweeping and shoveling sawdust and tossing short pieces of wood into the steam-fired boilers to run the mill. He quickly learned other jobs, including lumber trucker, log tumbler, and block setter.

The mill owner, Harold "Harry" Phillips, impressed by Alexandr's efforts and demeanor, took a liking to him, and the two became great friends. Harry, who had just turned 70, would always seek out Alexandr, who would entertain him with funny stories from the "old country." In 1902, Harry, who lived alone in a good-sized house straight up the hill from the sawmill, had a small 1,200-square-foot house constructed next to his, intending to give it to his niece, whom he hoped would help take care of him as he aged. But his niece had other ideas, and the house remained vacant. One day, Harry and Alexandr were walking around the mill's sixty-foot-tall wood waste burner, or as they called it, the "slash" burner. The burner looked like an inverted cone with a round steel grill screen cap on top. A conveyor belt would deliver wet sawdust to an opening near the top of the burner. Against the night sky, smoke, ash, and hot embers would emit from the steel mesh on top of the wood burner, creating an unearthly glow.

During their conversation, Alexandr said something about how his wife, Maria, was deprived of light in their accommodations. Harry asked Alexandr where he and his wife lived. Alexandr told him they rented a space in the basement of a home in Old Town. Harry pulled Alexandr aside a few days later and said, "How'd you like to rent a house?"

Alexandr stammered at first and said, "Thanks, Harry, but I'm not sure I have enough money to afford whatever you might have in mind."

"Hell, Alexandr, don't you think I know what you make? I'm the one who pays you. We'll make it work." In return for Harry's generous rental agreement, both Alexandr and Maria agreed to help Harry with favors he asked, such as doing his laundry, cleaning Mr. Phillip's home, and helping him with some house repairs. Alexandr was thrilled to move Maria out of the dark, cramped, and damp basement space they had been renting and put her into this new little house with a spectacular view.

North Pacific

The rented house consisted of an entryway, living room, kitchen, and bathroom on the main floor and a single bedroom on the upper level connected by an open set of rather steep stairs. The house had been constructed on the side of a declivitous hill, leaving an almost non-existent yard, save for a small patch of grass between the front porch and the sidewalk. However, it did have a spectacular view of Commencement Bay. Maria could not have been happier.

Though the work at the sawmill was hard, the Vaenkos loved their new life in America. After years of near poverty, the couple felt that even though they were not well off – by any means – they could finally enjoy life together without fear of destitution. The couple lived in the little house near the top of the hill overlooking the bay enjoying each other's company and feeling blessed by God that they could have this life together. A few years later, Harry, their benefactor and now remarkably close friend, passed away after a short illness. To their complete surprise and forever in their prayers of gratitude, Harry, in his will, bequeathed Alexandr and Maria the little house. They openly wept at Harry's funeral and were awed by his generosity.

North Pacific

7.

After years of trying, Alexandr and Maria's first child, Joseph, was born in the house with a splendid view in 1907. An Old Town midwife had helped Maria deliver her son. Alexandr was an incredibly proud papa. Though the couple dreamed of having more children, it did not come to pass. Joseph enjoyed the elevated level of attention that an only child often receives, especially from his mother.

As time passed, the family would faithfully walk the mile or so to Mass at St. Dominic on Sundays. After Mass and breakfast, the family would ride the electric streetcar to Point Defiance Park when the weather was good. Point Defiance was a sprawling and unique municipal park situated at the northwest tip of the city on Commencement Bay. The Vaenkos would often take and enjoy a picnic lunch.

When Joseph was old enough, he began sleeping in the living room. The house only had one bedroom, and it was upstairs. His single bed was set lengthwise against the house's east wall, with the head up against the side of the staircase. He kept his clothes in a low wooden box with some material affixed to the underside, allowing the box to slide under the bed frame on the fir floors. The bed and the box that held his clothing constituted his "bedroom." On many a night, when Joseph could not sleep, he would prop himself up on his pillow and stare out the front window at the lights around the bay.

Growing up, Joseph attended the local public schools because of distance and financial considerations. He was a good student. He met and fit in well with his classmates. Joseph became good friends with Martin Linart. They were inseparable on the playground and engaged in sports together as they grew. Both Joseph and Martin liked football and baseball. Later, Martin gravitated to basketball as he became taller than most of his school chums.

Concerning religion, the Vaenkos, before coming to America, had practiced Eastern Rite Catholicism. There was nowhere in Tacoma to attend the Eastern or orthodox-like liturgy to which they were accustomed. They talked to some people and decided to attend the Latin Rite Mass, said by Father Louis Simone O.P., a French Dominican priest who had just begun working in Tacoma.

Father Simone said Mass on Sundays in parishioners' homes for the first few years while the construction of a church proceeded. Then in 1908, the newly built St. Dominic opened its doors to excited parishioners. The clincher for the Vaenkos had been that Father Simone, before coming to the west coast of the United States, had worked for many years in Central Europe and could converse to a high degree with native speakers from all over the Austro-Hungarian Empire. Father Simone had experienced the Eastern Rite Liturgy firsthand. He knew how to help the Vaenkos understand the differences and nuances between what they were used to and the Latin Rite Mass.

Once Joseph began schooling, every Saturday morning, Maria would walk Joseph and his buddy Martin to the church - until they were old enough to walk on their own - to be catechized by Father Simone. During those Saturday catechetical sessions, Joseph was introduced to the Catholic practice of "eucharistic adoration." Father Simone would march the little troop of children from the library within the rectory to the church. He would explain that praying to the Lord, who was, in a most extraordinary way, present in the consecrated hosts reserved in the tabernacle on the high altar, was about as good as it gets in this life. He told them to pray and talk to Our Lord. Father's goal was to build a strong attachment to this practice. Father Simone would say, "Bring your problems here. Pray and speak to the Lord about them." Young Joseph took this aspect of Church life to heart, to his mother's delight.

With dark hair and high cheekbones, Maria was about the most comely and pleasant person you would want to meet. She was attentive, selfless, and a great listener. Her family meant everything to her. She and her husband had performed thankless work as they created a niche for themselves and their son in this place so far from their native land.

Nothing was more enjoyable for Maria than to sit in front of the large living room window and take in the activity, the growth, and the beauty of the view presented to her in her own home. She remembered, by comparison, the most primitive dwellings she and her husband had experienced when they were young.

Lastly, Maria practiced her Catholic faith with a certain Central European piety focused on the Cross of Christ and a strong Marian devotion. It was this faith that Maria passed on to her only child.

Alexandr worked long hours at the sawmill, and when he came home, he would eat dinner and then usually collapse in the big chair in the living room. Maria would eventually wake him and tell him it was time to go upstairs to bed. Many times Alexandr had to work on the weekends. The extra money helped, but it meant that he would spend less time with his family.

Maria and her son had a special relationship. The two became as close as any mother and child could be. They would sit for hours in the living room, looking out at the bay while discussing everything under the sun. Joseph would come home from school on weekdays and do his chores around the house as Maria prepared supper.

He would sit at the table that separated the kitchen from the living room and tell his mother about everything he was thinking. She would always wait until Joseph had exhausted every possible way of relating to her what was on his mind and then query him about certain aspects of whatever he was discussing. The questions would make Joseph pause and rethink his thoughts and assumptions. Then he would incorporate her insights related to what was on his mind and restate his original idea with new thinking applied to it.

This loving back and forth was the cornerstone of their relationship. Later in life, Joseph would never forget that his mother's thoughts made him think more clearly, and if he were troubled about something, her thoughts would always calm him down so that he could view his problem in a more considered manner. These endless and thoughtful discussions made Joseph a much better student and prepared him for his later higher education.

8.

Joseph's life changed on the day that Alexandr told him that his mother was sick. He remembered his father had never seemed so devastated. At 44, Maria had always been a healthy woman who rose early and worked late to keep her home spotless. She loved her husband and son unconditionally.

Joseph began praying every night for the Lord to heal his mother. During her sickness, he would overhear Maria praying to God to watch over her husband and child. Her plaintive cry to God broke his heart. Joseph shared in Maria's year-long struggle. Near the end, when Maria could no longer climb the stairs to the bedroom, she would sleep in Joseph's bed. Joseph moved over and slept on the sofa, watching his mother endure the long nights.

North Pacific

One day, while suffering through her trial, Maria gave Joseph a medal on a chain she had always worn around her neck. Maria told him that she had received it from a priest in New York City after she and Alexandr had first arrived in this country. The priest had given it to her after Mass one day on the feast of the Exultation of the Cross. The kind priest had also given her a holy card that remembered the feast day and featured a Cross on the front of the card and a prayer on the back that read:

> "We ought to glory in the Cross
>
> of our Lord Jesus Christ,
>
> in whom is our salvation,
>
> life, and resurrection,
>
> and by whom we are saved."

Maria explained to Joseph that it always reminded her of an expression she had learned growing up. "Your salvation is in the Cross." Finally, she told Joseph that having this medal always reminded her of the wayside Crosses found just outside of so many villages in the "old country." As a young girl, she would pick flowers and lay them at these shrines. Joseph told his mother he would always wear it.

On another day, she taught him that Jesus, while hanging on the cross, entrusted his mother, Mary, to St. John and, likewise, the apostle to Mary. After that, St. John took Mary into his home. Shortly after Maria had received her prognosis, she told Joseph, "You must promise me you will always keep the Blessed Virgin Mary in your prayers. Remember, Mary, is "blessed with grace." Jesus so loved his mother that he would do anything for her. Pray that she might plead on your behalf with her son during your life."

He was there when she bravely succumbed to the ravages of the disease. It was the late summer of 1921 when Maria died. Joseph's happy family life was cut brutally short by the shattering loss of his mother to cancer. Joseph shared in his mother's year-long battle with the illness, which took much of the joy out of his young life.

~~~~~

The funeral was an incredibly hard affair. Father Simone met the pallbearers and the funeral casket in front of the church. He took a hyssop branch from a container held by an altar boy filled with holy water and sprinkled the coffin as he recited aloud, "Come to her assistance, ye saints of God! Meet her, ye angels of the Lord. Receive her soul and present it to the Most High. May Christ who called thee, receive thee; and may the angels lead thee into the bosom of Abraham." The priest again sprinkled the casket with holy water and said, "Eternal rest grant unto Maria, O Lord! And may perpetual light shine upon her."

Then the funeral casket was carried into St. Dominic and brought to the front of the nave before the communion rail. At the end of the funeral Mass, Father Simone descended from the high altar to the casket and, in a loud voice, made supplications including "Deliver, O Lord, we beseech Thee, the soul of the Thy handmaid, Maria... Eternal rest grant unto her O Lord" to which the congregants responded, "And may perpetual light shine upon her." Father finished by saying, "May her soul and all the souls of the faithful departed, through the mercy of God, rest in peace." Later at the cemetery, Joseph remembered trying not to cry. After all, he was 14 now and wanted to act like a man. However, when he looked at his father grieving at the graveside and saw his tears, Joseph also broke down. It was too much. She was gone.

~~~~~

After Maria's passing, Joseph and Alexandr struggled to reestablish a semblance of home life. Alexandr, not exactly a conversationalist to begin with, was even less conversant now. He would return from the sawmill in the late afternoon. He and Joseph would eat whatever they could put together for dinner, mostly sandwiches. Sitting at the table without Maria was painful for the Vaenko men. After dinner, Joseph would do the dishes, and Alexandr would sit in the big chair in the living room. Soon, he would say good night to Joseph and go upstairs. Joseph would do his homework at the kitchen table and then stand in front of the living room window, wondering what had happened to his life.

North Pacific

They would go grocery shopping on Saturdays, riding the electric streetcar to the market, and then riding it back home with boxes full of staples for the coming week. Sundays were somewhat normal with the early rising, walking to St. Dominic, and returning home after Mass. Alexandr had his friends at the sawmill, while Joseph had his schoolmates. It took a long time for them to get past the tragedy, but, bit by bit, they began to put together a modicum of life without Maria.

The experience of his mother's suffering and death led Joseph to question God for the first time in his life. How could God allow his dear mother to experience that horrible death if He was all good?

In one of his homilies, Joseph remembered Father Simone explained the question it in terms of God's will. The priest spoke of how God's will was both the good and the bad that happened in one's life. Yet they were different in that God gives us the good and allows the bad. Father explained that God could not will evil, which was opposed to his nature and thus not possible, but he could and did "allow for evil" to protect man's ultimate freedom of choice.

He was at an age where he was no longer a child yet not truly a man. His relationship with God was subjected to tentative doubts for the first time when he received no direct response from on high. The experience had shaken him. He often went to St. Dominic to pray in front of the Blessed Sacrament. And many nights at home in bed, he engaged in intense "one-sided" conversations with the God of his upbringing. Her death took away the person closest to him.

A month or so after Maria's passing, at night, in bed, great loneliness would often overcome Joseph. It frightened him. He would wake up in the middle of the night almost trembling from a dream where he was floating and slowly tumbling into a great dark void.

9.

With his mother's death, Joseph's relationship with his father deepened over time. With Maria's passing, ever so slowly, Alexandr and Joseph began talking more in the evenings. It was not the same as when Joseph would speak with his mother. Those unique, wide-ranging free discussions were a thing of the past. The exchange of thought between father and son was a bit more guarded, as many men are predisposed to be. However, the two of them managed to convey to each other what was necessary and sometimes even opinions and views they might not have shared in the past. As Joseph grew, they discovered they had more interests in common, and a genuine father-and-son bond developed.

Because of Alexandr's tenure with his work, he was able to get his son a few odd jobs down at the sawmill. Joseph would finish school and head down the hill to the sawmill, at first a couple of times a week, and sweep and clean up anything necessary. He would be paid a small remuneration "off the books." As Joseph approached manhood, he was given more work to perform, now, of course, "on the books." Alexandr made Joseph save half of everything he earned, telling him he would thank his father for teaching him to be prudent with his money.

It wasn't all work, though, for the Vaenko men. The summer after Maria's death, Alexandr and Joseph bought fishing poles and put them to use in Commencement Bay. Sometimes they would fish for petrale sole from the docks surrounding the sawmill, and at other times they would rent a boat and fish in deeper water. Over the years, they mainly caught coho salmon, or sometimes "humpies" (also known as pink salmon) off Browns Point, but once in a great while, they would hook a king. Those big chinooks were the stuff memories were made of, and the two shared their fish stories with whomever they could. They both enjoyed the fishing and the time together. In Old Town, there was much interest in fishing as a large segment of those who had settled there were immigrants of Slavic Croatian ancestry. They fished Puget Sound and later Southeastern Alaska for a living in their distinctive salmon purse seiners.

Alexandr especially enjoyed sitting out in the bay fishing with his son while viewing Mt. Rainier to the east. The magnificent snowcapped peak rising well over 14,000 feet into the morning sky and the rest of the Cascade mountain range and the Olympic mountains to the west reminded him of his homeland's beautiful southern Carpathian mountains. He remembered well walking in the Carpathian foothills with Maria while courting. He was quick to wipe his eye with a sleeve whenever a hint of a tear appeared.

~~~~~

It had been almost a year since Maria's death. One morning while walking down the steep incline to the sawmill, Alexandr began thinking seriously about his boy's future. As the days passed, his concern about his son's outlook increased. He knew that his son was an excellent student. Joseph's report cards were nothing but good grades. Conversations with his son at the dinner table and on other occasions convinced him that Joseph had a chance to make something of himself in this country, this land of opportunity, as he remembered the saying went. Despite Maria's death, Alexandr believed this great country had been the best thing to happen to him, and he knew, in his heart of hearts, that his boy could be successful.

Yet he also knew that life could be extremely hard and unforgiving. There was so much uncertainty, things he could not control. What else could be said of the cruel loss of Maria? Every time he thought of her, he involuntarily started to tear up. What if he had never gotten the job at the sawmill when he and Maria arrived? Where would they have lived had he not received the gift of his home from his good friend Harry Phillips? Yes, I must do something,

North Pacific

Alexandr thought to himself. I must do what I can to help Joseph with his future. But what?

Try as he might, Alexandr had only come up with the idea of getting him work down at the sawmill. But that was precisely the reason he started contemplating Joseph's future in the first place. In the big scheme of things, working at the mill was no idea at all for a better future for his son. So he continued to think about it every day. Yet, nothing came to him as to a solution for his boy.

~~~~~

It happened while he sat with Joseph at Mass one Sunday morning, listening to Father Simone's homily when it struck him. Father Simone, that's it! Why didn't I think of that to begin with? I will talk to Father Simone about my concern for Joseph's future. This is the answer to my prayers. I will arrange a time to meet with him, and yes, he will help me. I know he will. Alexandr placed both palms to his forehead and said to himself, "Slava Isusu Khrystu!" (Glory to Jesus Christ!). He displayed a broad grin for the rest of the Mass.

When Mass ended, and the parishioners were filing out of the church, Alexandr tugged at Joseph's jacket sleeve and said, "I want to speak to Father about a matter. I'll be back in a minute. Until I finish, why don't you say hello to one of those nice young ladies, gesturing toward a group of teenage girls chatting." Joseph rolled his eyes and moved away from the young women toward a friend he knew from school.

Meanwhile, Alexandr made a direct path to where Father Simone was shaking hands with those headed for the parking lot and those walking home. As Alexandr approached the priest, he heard him talking to an older couple about a new priest arriving in a few days. "Oh, he is an excellent priest," Father Simone said proudly. His name is Father Etienne Sauveterre. He is French like me. You will be very pleased with him. He's coming from Seattle, where he's been in residence for a few years. I guess they decided I needed some steady help down here rather than a fill-in when I'm gone or sick. Maybe the Provincial General thinks I'm getting old." He and the couple laughed. "All I know is I am pleased that there will be two of us to manage all that is happening at the parish. It can be overwhelming." He told the couple, "Have a good day now." Another parishioner passed by and shook Father's hand.

Then the priest turned and said, "Alexandr, how are you?" Alexandr wasted no time and launched into his thoughts about Joseph. The two men talked for a few minutes, and Father Simone nodded. "Yes, I get what you're trying to do. I'm glad you're thinking about Joseph. He's a seriously bright young man. How about if you give me this week to mull it over? I will also add your petition for a plan for your son to my prayers before daily Mass. Then we could get together next Sunday and have a proper discussion in the rectory.

"Thank you, Father," Alexandr said respectfully. "I know you're busy. Thank you again." The two men shook hands.

Father took his hand, placed it on Alexandr's shoulder, and said in a low but serious voice, "Your dear wife Maria, truly a saint, must be guiding your thoughts from heaven. I'll see you next week."

Alexandr nodded, and Father turned to greet yet another late-leaving parishioner. Alexandr looked around to find his son. Joseph was standing out by the street. When he saw his father surveying what was left of the crowd, he raised his hand slightly, and Alexandr finally caught sight of him. They headed out, walking home without speaking much, Joseph enjoying the warm morning sunshine while Alexandr maintained his broad smile.

~~~~~

Dinner that night was leftover beef soup, consisting of stew meat, beef stock, celery, and carrots "seasoned" at the kitchen table with catsup. "Joseph," Alexandr queried as they ate the meal, "Do you have any ideas about what you want to do when you finish school in a few years?"

Surprised by the question, Joseph looked up and replied, "I really haven't given it that much thought."

"Well, you should, young man. We're talking about your future. What could be more important?"

This startled Joseph. He wasn't expecting this conversation or the importance his father seemed to attach to it out of nowhere. But there he was, his father, with a cloth napkin tucked into his shirt at the neck, looking as intense as he could while holding a soup spoon in his large hand.

"What's going on, Dad?"

"Joseph, since your mother's passing, I've been thinking about you and what you may want to do with your life. I know she would be worrying and prodding you to make good choices and follow your dreams. Do you have dreams for the future? Isn't that what this country is all about? When your mother and I came to America, we had heard stories of people like us, making lots of money and enjoying the "good" life. Of course, once here, we discovered the streets were not paved with gold. Yet this country held the opportunity, with hard work and determination, to make a much better life than back in the "old country." As you know, we were not able to make lots of money, but we made enough money to have this life, and I wouldn't trade it for anything. America has been good to us. Truly, God has blessed us."

Joseph focused on Alexandr. He could clearly see that this was rapidly becoming the most important conversation he had ever had with his son.

Alexandr continued, "I know you are only 15, but the world is a very rough and tough place. It comes at you amazingly fast, and life can and will wear you down if you're not prepared for it. Without your mother's steady influence, I fear you could fall in with the wrong crowd."

"Oh, Dad, that won't happen to me. I know right from wrong."

"You may think you know it all now, but, as I just told you, life can be hard and sometimes tricky. I've made bad decisions. I've seen guys make some terrible mistakes during their lives. Many times they make these wrong decisions to get by or get ahead."

Joseph realized his father was trying to make a point with him but didn't grasp where this conversation was heading. So he took a page from his mother's reasoning skills, "What are you thinking about, Dad? What are you trying to get at?"

Alexandr swallowed a spoonful of soup and then took a bite out of his piece of bread. Joseph could see that his father was thinking about what he wanted to say to him next. Alexandr took a sip of water, looked hard at his son, and spoke. "Joseph, other than losing your mother, God has blessed me in my life. I married the girl of my dreams. We came to America with high hopes. Those hopes were realized when I met Harry Phillips and proved my worth to him at the sawmill. Joseph, you were the most important gift God gave your mother and me. Your mother is gone, and I know she would want the best for you. I do too. You are a smart boy, and I don't want you to have to work at the sawmill all your life. The sawmill is good honest hard work but look at me. I've had bones broken. My fingers are now all crooked. My back hurts all the time. Somedays, I can barely walk. You can do better. I want that for you, and that's why I set up an appointment to meet with Father Simone to talk about how to take advantage of your – how do I say – abilities. We need a plan."

"A plan? What kind of a plan?" Joseph could tell by Alexandr's deportment and expression that this was extremely important to his father.

"Why do you think I am meeting with Father Simone?" Alexandr exclaimed.

"I'm sorry, Dad, I didn't mean for that to come out the way it did," Joseph was now fully aware of the significance of the conversation and what it meant to his father. The two of them continued to talk at some length. Joseph, a 15-year-old, with possibly a bit of trepidation, agreed to his father's wish.

Walking to work the following day in the rain, Alexandr was still "worked up" over the dinner conversation with Joseph. He thought the talk had gone okay. He shook his head and wished his wife had not left him with such issues. But he knew it was the right thing to do. He would see this through. He thought to himself, "I know my Joseph is smart. It's just that sometimes, maybe not so much. Oh, Maria, you should be here."

North Pacific

10.

It had been a week since Alexandr had spoken to Fr. Simone about his "plan." Now, it was time to go ahead and finish what he had started.

The new priest, Father Sauveterre, said the Mass. This surprised Alexandr. He had thought he would see Fr. Simone on the altar that morning, and this "changeup" threw him off his game a bit, but he persevered, and by the end of Mass, he had settled down somewhat.

Joseph already knew that Alexandr was going to stay after Mass, so after saying good morning to a few parishioners, he told his father he was going to head home. He also said, "Good luck this morning with your meeting." Alexandr gave him a bit of a forced smile and nodded. Joseph headed home while Alexandr made his way to the rectory across the parking lot from the church.

Alexandr knocked on the door and waited. He began to think, what if Father Simone is not here when there was a click, and Father Simone opened the door. Alexandr was immensely relieved, and the two shook hands and greeted one another. The Dominican let him in, and they walked through the large library room. Father explained that the room served many purposes, including a meeting room, a place to study, and a library. Toward the back of the room was a hallway, down which they continued until reaching the priest's office. With a comforting smile, the 50ish, short, solid, and balding priest offered Alexandr a chair, and both sat down. Alexandr could hardly contain himself, so he didn't, "Father, what is the plan?"

Father Simone chuckled, "Alexandr, I can tell you are eager to see to your son's future, which is commendable, but no plan will work unless everyone involved is 100% committed. Alexandr, I have given your request much thought. I know your son. He was one of my better altar boys before his mother died. I have talked to him many times and know he is particularly bright. I know that with the loss of Joseph's mother, there is a greater chance that he might not apply himself as he would if she were alive and interacting with him daily. After we talked last Sunday, Alexandr, I returned to my office and put our meeting on my calendar and my list of projects. I have to tell you that my list is pretty long. I always carry it with me, and I look at the list when I have a moment to assess how I'm doing. Well, I found some time on Wednesday night to write some things down about how to approach what you call the "plan." I thought about it, prayed about it, and decided that this would not be a one or multiple-page document with words of wisdom and a detailed schedule with a goal, objectives, and tasks for Joseph. Rather, Joseph's 'plan,' as I see it is a person."

Up to this point, Alexandr had been sitting erect and motionless, listening raptly to Father's words. Now, he shifted in his chair, cleared his throat, and with some bewilderment, exclaimed, "I'm sorry, Father, I'm a little confused."

"Of course, Alexandr, I'm just explaining my line of reasoning that got me to what I believe will be a satisfactory solution to your request."

Alexandr raised an eyebrow and started to say something but stopped and then started again, "Okay, Father, maybe you should go ahead and tell me about this 'person.' You know, the one you mentioned."

"Alexandr, the person I'm alluding to is our new priest Father Etienne Sauveterre." Fr. Simone smiled with satisfaction. Mr. Vaenko's eyes widened, and he started to speak, but again, for the second time, nothing came out. Father Simone seeing Alexandr's slight confusion, said, "Let me explain. After thinking and praying about your request, I finally hit upon what I thought would be a wonderful solution. As I've already said, we could whip up a plan on a piece of paper, which might or might not work. I thought if Joseph were going to excel in his studies, he needed to be mentored." Father Simone paused to let that thought sink in. "But then I thought, it can't be me. I'm just flat-out too busy at this point to help Joseph achieve his educational goals. It is certainly not that I wouldn't want to, but I'm swamped with parish work and our efforts at the college. Then it came to me. We have Fr. Etienne now. If willing, he might be the perfect choice to take on this role. Alexandr, I spoke to Father Etienne. He said he would have to meet with Joseph and assess him. If Joseph makes a good impression, he will mentor him. Alexandr, Father Etienne is a scholar of some renown. He trained under Hyacinthe-Maria Cormier, the former Master General of the Dominican Order."

Now engaged in the conversation, Alexandr interrupted Father to ask, "Why would, as you say, such a 'scholar' come to Tacoma?"

"After Father Etienne was ordained, he continued his studies in Europe, but a few years ago, he was assigned to the Province of the Most Holy Name of Jesus here in the Western United States. From there, he was sent to Seattle, where he worked at Blessed Sacrament Parish. He loves the region. Father Etienne writes homilies like nothing you've ever heard. As I say, he has a God-given gift for it. He is so good at it that the Order has asked him to share his discourses with the other Dominican priests. He's even published a book of them in French. Anyway, the Order thinks so highly of him that, at his request, they have allowed him to stay in this Province as long as he continues to write homilies and share them with the rest of the Dominicans around the world. Since he's been in the United States for a while, he now speaks excellent English as well as his native French, and, of course, he's quite good with Latin. Alexandr, I tell you, this is a great opportunity for Joseph."

Still a little overwhelmed but also caught up in the excitement generated by Father Simone's story about Fr. Sauveterre, Alexandr said, "Yes, Father, this sounds like a great opportunity for my son. I hope he is up to the task.

What am I saying? I know he is up to it." A satisfied look now spread across Alexandr's face as he stood up from the chair. "When can Joseph meet him?"

~~~~~

The elder Vaenko walked home slowly after finishing his meeting with Father Simone. Well, he thought to himself, I've gone from having Fr. Simone create a plan of some sort to a Dominican scholar from France possibly mentoring my son. I think I need a drink. Upon arriving at the house, he went straight to the kitchen, opened the cupboard beneath the sink, lifted out a half-empty bottle of plum brandy, grabbed a shot glass from another cabinet in the corner, filled it, and swallowed it in one gulp. He grimaced and stood there momentarily, wondering if life without Maria would always be this hard and complicated. Then he poured himself one more shot and downed it. He looked at the clock. "Bozhe moi!" (My God!), he said to himself. It was only 10:30 AM. He at once put the cork back in the bottle and returned it to its place under the sink.

~~~~~

That afternoon, Joseph returned home from a pickup football game he and some friends had planned the previous Friday while at school. Approaching the house,

Joseph noticed Alexandr sitting on the top step of the small front porch with his face pointed toward the warm sun.

"Hello, Joseph," said his father.

"Catching some sunshine, Dad?"

"It feels so nice and warm. Where have you been?"

"Playing ball with some of the guys. How did it go this morning with Father Simone?"

"Good, I think."

"What does that mean?"

"It means you are going to meet with the new priest, Father Sauveterre (he struggled somewhat with pronouncing the new priest's name). You will be meeting him on Wednesday afternoon after school."

"What happened to me meeting with Fr. Simone?"

"He's busy right now, and he thinks the new priest will be a better, umm, "fit" for what we're asking of him. Fr. Simone tells me Fr. Sauveterre is a scholar, you know, really smart."

"Oh brother," thought Joseph, "What am I getting into?"

"The new priest wants to meet with you to see how smart you are."

Great, thought Joseph. "He wants to, what, size me up?"

"Yes, Joseph, that's a good way of putting it. He wants to know if you are smart enough and committed enough to take on this plan we have discussed. You must convince him that you, Joseph Vaenko, can do the work necessary to have a better life, you know, the 'American Dream.'"

Joseph saw from the look on his Father's face that there was no way out at this point, even if he wanted to, and so said, "All right, Father, I'll do it," while thinking to himself, good grief, what have I gotten myself into?

11.

Joseph thought he would be lying to himself if he believed he was not nervous as he made the walk from school to St. Dominic on the following Wednesday afternoon.

Alexandr encouraged him to dress well, comb his hair and be a gentleman in the priest's presence. He repeated how important this meeting was and that Joseph's future was, as he saw it, riding in the balance.

"No pressure here," he mumbled to himself. Then there was the matter of Father Sauveterre. Who is this guy? What questions will he ask me? Will there be a test of some kind? As he exhaled the spent oxygen from his lungs, he arrived at the church's rectory.

Joseph rang the doorbell. A few moments later, the door opened, and there stood the parish's new Dominican priest, Father Etienne Sauveterre. He looked to be around forty, a slight man, standing no more than five feet eight inches tall with an aquiline nose and black hair combed straight back. He said, "Hello, you must be Mr. Vaenko."

"Hello, Father," replied Joseph. As he said this, he realized how nervous he really was.

Father smiled and stepped back to allow Joseph in. He closed the door and led Joseph to a table in the good-sized library room, where they sat.

Father Sauveterre saw that the young man was anxious and said, "How about we begin this discussion by telling each other a little bit about ourselves?"

Joseph noticed that the priest's English was quite good.

Father Etienne said, "I'll start. I grew up in a city in France known as Orleans. It is about seventy miles from Paris in the Loire River Valley. The valley is famous for its castles, wine, and sunflowers. The city itself possesses the Orleans Cathedral, a magnificent Gothic structure. Orleans was the site of Joan of Arc's first victory over the English in the Hundred Years War in 1429 when she relieved the city from the English army's siege. Before he died, my father was a minor city official, and my mother still lives there. I am, what is the word, ah yes, an 'avid' reader of books mostly dealing with theology, of course, but also philosophy and literature. I have many books, most of which are in that, you would say, 'alcove,' over there," pointing towards the recessed wall filled with books by the windows on the far side of the library. "As to what I do, besides being a priest, I write homilies, which I must say I enjoy very much. Finally, I have a deep, umm, fondness for this part of your country. The views are spectacular. The weather is mild and comfortable, neither too hot in the summer nor too cold in the winter. The rain is light and rarely oppressive. It always smells so fresh outside, and even on the days when the weather is cloudy and gray, it feels quiet and restful."

There was a pause. Joseph recognized that Father's biographical sketch and random thoughts were now complete. So now it was his turn. "Well, Father, my name is Joseph Vaenko. I've just turned sixteen. My parents came to the United States from the Austro-Hungarian Empire years before the Great War in Europe. I asked my father where we were from in the empire, and he told me we were from the beautiful southern Carpathian Mountains. As for me, I'm from the house I was born in and still live in, and I am an American."

Father smiled.

Joseph continued, "My mother died over a year ago now, and I live with my father. I have no brothers or sisters. I miss my mother beyond words." He paused slightly, then regaining his composure resumed. "I have done well at school and have an A average, but it has been hard work. My mother was always after me to do my homework." Smiling, Joseph said, "You know how moms can be. Anyway, my favorite subject has always been history. I can't get enough of it. I especially like military history, naval history, to be specific. I even know something about the French Navy. During the Great War, I can tell you that

French naval units were highly concentrated in the Mediterranean Sea to keep an eye on the Italian Navy before Italy switched sides. Then they helped contain the Austro-Hungarian Navy in the Adriatic. I can also tell you that my favorite French battleships are of the Bretagne class. They are great-looking ships with those tripod masts. I also know all about the British and German navies. I've read about the naval actions in the North Sea at Dogger Bank and the Battle of Jutland. However, the most interesting naval action I have read about is the battle of Tsushima between the Russian and Japanese fleets in 1905. The only problem is there is not much information in English about the battle, say, compared to the Great War in Europe." Father Etienne listened to the young man with interest.

"Besides reading, I like to play sports, especially football and baseball. I'm fairly good at both, but I've discovered this year that when they pitch me inside, I tend to bail out too quickly." He smiled at Father before deciding that the French priest probably didn't know what he was talking about as to the inner workings of baseball, or maybe baseball at all, so he switched subjects.

"I was an altar boy, starting in about fourth grade, but have not served since my mother died. I've had a hard time doing anything, for that matter, since she passed away." His voice trailed off.

Father Etienne perceived Joseph's pain about the loss of his mother. "Joseph, you seem to be a young man with much going on in your life, and, yes, losing one's mother can be so exceedingly difficult. Let me ask you, how are you when it comes to the state of your faith?"

Starting to warm to the priest, Joseph said, "Well, Father, I'm not certain what you mean by that question?" He paused, "I accept and can recite the Creed, both the Apostles' and the Nicene. I know the basics of my catechism, I sometimes get mixed up with the different kinds of grace and other distinctions and terms, but overall, I think I'm okay. I never miss Mass on Sundays. I say my daily prayers. If you're relating my mother's death to my faith, to be honest, yes, it has, I don't know, shaken me," he looked down, feeling slightly uncomfortable.

"It has tested my faith, Father. What I mean by that is, well, it scared me, Father, and it still does. It is one thing to learn about God from a catechism and the readings from sacred scripture during Mass, but having your mother taken away from you for the rest of your life is quite something else. She's gone. I mean, she's really gone. Is she truly with God? Why can't I feel more confident about that? I mean, If anyone were going to get into heaven, it would be my dear mother, but I guess the real question became for me, is there truly a God? Why can't I have a sign of some kind from him that assures me everything is all right? I'm sorry, Father, you may not want to have heard that, but I have to tell you the truth."

Father Etienne looked at Joseph, exhaled, and said, "I am deeply sorry about the loss of your mother. It is abundantly clear to me, from listening to you, that you so loved her. I'm certain you've heard or read about the story in St. John's gospel where he tells of the time Christ appeared to the apostles after his resurrection, but one of them, Thomas, was not present?"

Joseph weakly nodded assent. "Yes, Father, that's the story of Thomas, the doubter."

Father Etienne continued his thought. "So, after the other apostles told Thomas what had happened, Thomas said that he would not believe what they had told him unless he could see and touch the mark of the nails in the Lord's hands and touch the spot where the soldier's lance had pierced Jesus' side. Eight days later, Jesus again appeared to the apostles, now with Thomas in their midst. The Lord told Thomas to see his wounds, touch his hands where the nails had been, and place his hand where the lance had entered his side. Thomas replied, *'My Lord, and my God,'* to which Christ said, *'Be not faithless, but believing.'* Jesus then added, *'Because thou hast seen me, Thomas, thou hast believed: blessed are they who have not seen and have believed"* (Jn 20:29). Father Etienne stopped for a moment and then continued, "So, not only is Jesus, in his response, talking to Thomas, but also to all of us today. Yet, doubt can also take hold of us during the pain of sickness or the loss of a loved one. He is telling us that there is a reality beyond the natural laws of this world. There is a supernatural reality that we know of through the patriarchs and prophets, and lastly, through Jesus Christ, whose word is the way, the truth, and the life. Thus we arrive at faith."

Joseph closed his eyes for a moment and then reopened them. "It's just so hard, Father. I miss her."

North Pacific

"Of course you do, my son, of course you do." Father Etienne had been impressed by Joseph's general knowledge and esoteric interest in naval history. His love for his mother was heartbreaking and poignant. Father Etienne thought for a moment interlocking his fingers as they supported his chin. "Joseph, I think we can work together. If you are willing to make the necessary effort, I would be pleased to mentor you."

"Well, thank you, Father," a surprised Joseph replied. "My dad wanted this to happen. Since my mother died, he has been increasingly concerned about my future. It really has him wound up. He will be so relieved," Joseph paused and then added, smiling, "Actually, I'm pretty relieved and now excited myself."

That evening, after Alexandr had arrived home from work, Joseph greeted him with, "Father Etienne is going to be my mentor." Alexandr tilted his head, and Joseph continued. "Father said he would teach me how to study to go to college and get the most out of it."

Alexandr's face lit up. "Bozhe moi! (My God!), that's great. I knew we could do this. Your mother would be so proud of you. I know I am," he said, his voice slightly cracking. His head dropped slightly as he grabbed his forehead with one hand, momentarily covering his eyes. Joseph walked over to him, and they embraced. When the elder Vaenko had composed himself, he took a deep breath and looked at his son. "When do you start, Joseph?"

12.

The routine was established. Mondays, Joseph would show up after school at the rectory, where Father Etienne would meet with him in the library. There, Father would set the schedule for the week. Initially, The Dominican priest explained that Joseph must attend to the basics, pay attention in class, do the homework, study, and score high on all examinations. On Fridays, Joseph would return to the rectory, and Father would ask him what he had done at school that week, and then they would discuss it. After a month or so, Father Etienne started adding topics to Joseph's studies.

After establishing a friendship, and it indeed was just that, Joseph and Father Etienne, throughout many sessions, talked about what Joseph might do with his life. Education was crucial, Father Etienne stressed to his young charge. Joseph understood this and confided to the priest that even though he very much respected his father's work, he hoped that he might pursue a vocation more aligned with his own budding interests. He shared with the good Father his love of history. Father Etienne, already aware of Joseph's interest in naval history, quickly discerned that Joseph would like to research, write, and teach history someday. It was settled. Father Etienne and Joseph agreed his goal should be that of a historian. Father emphasized that attaining this goal would be no easy matter and would require much study, a college degree, and serious graduate work. Some problems would need to be addressed. Given Joseph's family circumstances, the goal could create financial issues. But now was not the time to dwell on the money aspects of the endeavor but rather to accept and work toward that end.

Joseph wholeheartedly agreed with Father that a future that focused on the research and writing of history was to be the goal. The meetings and mentoring focused more and more on the teenager's progress toward his aspiration. Additionally, they would converse about a wide range of subjects, from living in France to the meaning and usage of American words and catchphrases. Father Etienne also encouraged Joseph to develop a prayer relationship with his namesake patron saint. Father provided him with a few holy cards with prayers on the back. Joseph recited the prayers daily, asking St. Joseph to pray for him to be the man God expected him to be.

Alexandr came home one day and was all excited with the news that there had been a part-time opening at the sawmill that he had secured for Joseph. His Father saw this as a way of earning money Joseph could use to help pay for his education.

It was hard work. The lumber cut from a given tree trunk would result in up to fifty percent of the tree becoming waste wood of one form or another. Joseph worked all ends of the process to get this wood scrap and sawdust onto the conveyor belt that carried the waste up and then dumped it into the wood burner. This work took up many of Joseph's afternoons after school. It didn't pay much, but it all counted. On those days he worked at the sawmill, Joseph would get home around dinner time, eat, and then hit the books. Of course, after cleaning up scrap wood all afternoon, he would become exhausted trying to study. This resulted in falling asleep at the kitchen table at night, waking and finding himself working for another hour or two to finish his assignments, getting a few hours of sleep, and then off to school in the morning, dead tired.

Another casualty of the new study and work regimen was the lack of time to socialize and play sports. Joseph slowly lost close contact with his school buddies between meeting with Father Sauveterre a couple of times a week and working down at the sawmill. At first, Joseph tried to make up for the lost weekdays by playing ball and meeting with friends on the weekends. But even this strategy began to falter as Father Etienne assigned more challenging work to him. Finally, Joseph had to give up sports at school. He was a good athlete who, at that age, thrived on competition. To forego organized sports was probably the toughest choice he had to make during high school. He discussed it with Father Etienne, privately hoping to persuade the priest of his ability to succeed in both endeavors. Father Etienne convinced him otherwise. In just a little over a year and a half, precipitated by the death of his mother, Joseph's life had changed markedly.

North Pacific

At the Vaenko home in the evenings, Joseph and his father would eat meals that had them both longing for Maria's cooking. Then he would do his homework for school. Late in the evening, he would crawl into his narrow bed, pushed up against the living room wall, and fall asleep at once. On weekends, the Vaenko men would do the routine shopping and work on household projects, including cleaning the house, fixing leaks in the roof, or cutting and weeding the front grass. As always, on Sundays, it was a walk to Mass in the morning, but they no longer, in the afternoons, traveled to Pt. Defiance Park. Without Maria, that diversion had lost its meaning.

13.

The large front door creaked as Joseph entered the church. The sun filtering through the tall stained-glass windows on the west side of the stone edifice produced a remarkable dappled lighting effect in the otherwise unlit interior. He saw he was the only visitor as he walked into the nave listening to his footsteps as they fell one after the other and faintly echoed in the silent space. Joseph genuflected toward the tabernacle and then entered a pew and knelt. He said a short prayer and slid back, sitting in the pew. He stared intently at the tabernacle. The stillness inside the church contributed to a hushed experience. He noted and was assured by the sanctuary lamp that burned a deep red that he was in the presence of Christ in a most extraordinary way. I suspect Father Etienne would describe it as how the two travelers in St. Luke's gospel recognized Jesus "...*in the breaking of the bread*" (Lk 24:35).

Spending some time with the Lord became a regular practice. He would go there looking for answers to his mother's loss and pray about other things going on in his life. Joseph prayed and remembered his mother. Whenever he thought of her, he would touch the medal over his heart and implore the Lord to help him come to terms with her death.

During his struggles with the amount of work associated with Father Sauveterre's mentoring, Joseph prayed for the ability to keep up with the demands of school and the French priest. Was this what he was supposed to be doing right now in his life? Why couldn't he have a social life? What about the idea of a girlfriend? Why did God create me? That was the big question. He realized that he mostly complained to God about the lack of time to pursue personal enjoyment. When he put it that way, it always struck him as not much of an argument on his part. Yes, he knew that if he continued to pursue his education, good things would, or at least should, come his way. He said a small prayer. "Help me with my life Lord. Show me the way to happiness."

A cloud drifted by outside, momentarily dimming the sunlight penetrating the church's windows. Then, just as rapidly, the sunshine returned, pouring in the windows as the cloud continued its relentless easterly journey. He closed his eyes and prayed to God that he might understand his life and purpose. He asked that he make the correct decisions at the right times to do the Almighty's will. He had been taught that during his catechism classes on Saturday mornings. Everything he had learned in those classes he had thought deeply about, and to him, at the time, had all made sense. But his Mother's death was hard for him to reconcile. He felt his mind beginning to wander. Joseph realized he had probably spent about 45 minutes there and needed to get going.

It was Monday afternoon, time to meet with Father Etienne. Joseph left the church and crossed the parking lot to the rectory. When Joseph wasn't worrying about whether or not his assignments were completed, he looked forward to talking to the French priest. The meetings were a diversion from his daily routines. The priest had a relaxed way about himself that put the young man at ease. They genuinely enjoyed each other's company and would digress into conversations unrelated to Joseph's immediate assignments. Joseph remembered, for example, that Father Etienne was a prodigious reader. On this occasion, Father asked Joseph if he had ever heard of Blaise Pascal.

"Yes, Father, I've heard the name, but I must admit, I don't know much about him."

"Oh, you must know about this man," Father said, rising from his chair and walking over to the alcove where his books were shelved. He looked for a moment and then removed a volume, returned to the table, and placed it in front of Joseph. "Here is his most famous book, *Pensées* (Thoughts)." Father stood across the table from Joseph, waiting for him to react.

Joseph, for his part, grinned as he turned the book about and looked at the first few pages. "Father, the book is in French."

"Yes, it is," the French priest proudly smiled. Again, Father returned to the bookcase and, this time, retrieved a much larger book from the bottom shelf and placed it on the table facing Joseph as he had with the first. "This is, what I presume, you are asking for?"

Joseph studied the cover. "It's a French-English Dictionary."

"Indeed, it is," replied the smiling priest. "Joseph, I believe it would tell me a lot about your mental, what's the word, 'acuity' to apply yourself and read what Pascal wrote about in this, his most famous work, in his native tongue."

Joseph, taken off guard, stared at the priest and finally stated the obvious, "You want me to read Pascal – in French?"

"I believe you can do it, Joseph. Would you be willing to attempt it?"

Joseph looked at the priest standing there smiling at him and said with a detectable hesitancy, "I can try."

Father Etienne was delighted. "Well, let's not waste any more time. I will be in Seattle this coming Friday, so we'll meet a week from now again at our usual time. Sound good?"

"Uh, yeah, sure, Father," Joseph said, still somewhat dazed at the rapid turn of events that had just transpired.

They both stood. "I think you'll be impressed with the *Pensées* of Monsieur Pascal."

With that, Father Etienne said goodbye and retreated down the hall to his office. Joseph looked again at the book and the large dictionary lying on the table and thought, "What just happened?" He gathered his things along with the two volumes and headed out of the rectory. Halfway home, he realized the dictionary was kind of heavy.

~~~~~

School slowly changed for Joseph. He had started high school feeling like one of a large group of friends but gradually began to see less and less of them. First, he had gotten the part-time job down at the sawmill and now he had Father Sauveterre mentoring him a couple of days a week after school. Joseph found that he had no time for friends or friendships. It wasn't that he didn't want to participate in high school activities and interact socially. He just felt a tremendous responsibility to his father and a growing commitment to the Dominican priest. Sleep, as noted, was another victim of the daily regimen. Not only did he have to stay awake till all hours of the night to complete his assignments, but now he would find himself oversleeping in the morning, racing around trying to get ready, and arriving late to school. He even found himself in detention for this behavior, where ironically, he would have some time to study.

As for the French, there was a surprising outcome. Joseph used the translation dictionary Father Etienne had given him to construct sentences in English to understand Blaise Pascal's book *Pensées*. It was tough sledding, but after a while, he began to get the hang of how the French language worked and the bonus of finding Pascal to be extremely interesting. Pascal asked and spoke about many questions Joseph had tossed around in his head. He also had Father around to help him with the trickier parts of the language and its usage. Father Etienne would read to Joseph in French at the rectory, gesturing as though that made it easier to understand, and then translate its sense into English. Before long, Joseph slowly began to realize that he could make out most of the translation without using the dictionary. Eventually, Joseph and Father Etienne discussed the finer points of Pascal's observations. Always in English, of course, Joseph never spoke French well.

Pascal was a revelation to Joseph, and it propelled his studies forward. Father would, in time, introduce Joseph to other French writers, philosophers, and theologians. Eventually, Joseph attained a sound reading knowledge of French and prized his accessibility to French writers in their native tongue for the rest of his life.

Joseph's junior and senior years went by quickly. He was becoming a man. He settled into a routine of school, work at the sawmill, and study. His weekends were for catching up on lost sleep, helping Alexandr around the house, and the weekly marketing. The two of them found their rhythm around each other and looked forward to times when they could be together. Joseph occasionally brought up a memory or a question dealing with Maria. Depending on the nature of the question, Alexandr would either talk excitedly about his departed spouse or become subdued. Joseph wondered how his father could bear up day after day without the love of his life being there. Joseph even pondered what Alexandr would do if his son ever met a girl, got married, moved out, and started his own life with someone else. He thought that his father was strong, but maybe not that strong.

~~~~~

Joseph received his high school diploma with his graduating class of 1925. The graduation ceremony, in retrospect, took mere moments, and then there was saying goodbye to all his friends that he had seen so little of over the last three years. Many of his fellow students said, "We need to stay in touch," though how and when that might occur did not generate much thought or discussion. Of course, he had to console Alexandr, who was sobbing after the event. And then, that was it. It was over. The next day he and Martin spent some time together, and then it was back to work at the sawmill. Now that he was out of school, he picked up more hours at the mill during the week, which kept him busy. For whatever reason, Joseph was not motivated that summer to track down friends and try to have a modicum of social life on the weekends.

Vaenko's high school grades had been good, in fact, excellent. He applied for admission to Rainier College, just a few blocks from St. Dominic, and was accepted. He also applied to the University of Washington, and there too, he was accepted. To top it off, his lifelong buddy Martin was also heading for the big university in Seattle. After much agonizing, in the end, and despite his best friend going there, Joseph chose Rainier so he could continue working at the sawmill. Also, by staying in Tacoma, he would not incur the costs associated with living in Seattle. Finally, St. Dominic had a fund that provided scholarship aid for exemplary students to attend the local college. Joseph never considered himself "exemplary," but he understood it helped him stay at home and not have to leave Alexandr alone. He was now set to begin classes in the fall.

14.

Women had always been a struggle for Joseph. He would notice a girl in school and want to talk to her. A conversation would eventually occur, and afterward, Joseph would always feel as though he could have spoken more coherently, with less stammering. The stammering and even stuttering would lead to red cheeks and feeling awkward. He would say to himself, Why am I so hesitant? Why am I stammering? I don't stammer. Without Joseph recognizing it, this state of affairs worsened after his mother's loss. Of course, in his mind, the solution was simply to avoid women. Yet, at this point in his life, he was drawn to and fascinated by the fairer sex. However, with Alexandr's plan, Father Etienne's mentoring, and the sawmill, whether he wanted to be around women or not was simply a moot point. He had no time. He told himself he was not shy, but he truly was. For Joseph, consequential relationships with those of the opposite sex seemed remote.

After high school graduation, Martin, who had seen little of Joseph during the summer, finally tracked him down in early August and invited him to a party a friend from high school was having at his parent's house while they were away for the weekend. Joseph thinking this might kickstart his social life agreed to go with Martin to the gathering. When the big Friday night arrived, the two friends rode the streetcar down to the Stadium District, where the house was located. When they arrived, the party was already in full swing. There were lots of friends from school and many other young people Joseph did not know. After the two of them had entered the spacious living room, Martin was surprised by his girlfriend, Colleen. She had been on vacation with her parents but had come home late the night before. They at once had to talk about what each other had been doing while they were apart. Joseph made his way into the kitchen and was immediately handed a beer by Charles Langley. Charles, or "Charlie" to his friends, had played baseball with Joseph back in junior high school. They shook hands and started making small talk. Like his father before him, Charlie was planning on becoming a doctor. He was headed that fall to Stanford. "Joe, how have you been?"

Joseph replied, "Good, I'm working down at the sawmill this summer. I'm going to start at Rainier in the fall."

"Yeah, I'm getting ready too. It will be fun to get down to California and all that sunshine compared to here."

"I hear you."

Langley, who was about an inch taller than Joseph and about ten to fifteen pounds heavier, had blonde hair that he wore swept over to one side. He and Joseph had been quite competitive when they were younger, each vying for the starting pitcher's job on the junior high baseball team and trying to outdo each other in any sports-related competition. Charlie was popular with the girls, and the fact that his parents had money didn't hurt. There was a lot of traffic in the kitchen, with eighteen to twenty-somethings coming and going, grabbing food and drink. Charlie gestured to Joseph to follow him outside onto the back porch to escape the frenzy. Once there, he pulled out a pack of Lucky Strikes, removed one from the package, and offered one to Joseph. Joseph declined. Smoking had just never been his thing. Langley lit the one he had and took a deep drag. As he exhaled, he asked jokingly, "Joe, what are you going to do with your life? Are you going to get a degree in advanced sawmill processes?"

"I don't think so, funny boy," replied Joseph rolling his eyes. "I was accepted to Rainier. I plan to major in History."

Charlie gave Joseph a thin smile and asked, "Do you still live in that little house that overlooks the bay in Old Town?"

"Yeah, I live there with my Dad," Joseph replied, "Are you still living here in the Stadium District?"

Charlie took another drag off the cigarette, "My parent's house is just two blocks north of here on the left-hand side. It has a view of the water, just like yours. Of course, I will get my own place as soon as possible when I finish school." Looking around, Charlie began pointing at a girl approaching them from the backyard patio where many of the partygoers had congregated. Charlie said, "Joe, do you know Eloise?" Without waiting for a response, he continued, "How would you like to meet her?" The attractive young woman walked up to Charlie. "Eloise, how are you doing?" She smiled at him, and before saying anything, Charlie continued, "I'd like you to meet my friend Joe. He graduated this year with me."

Joseph caught entirely off guard, gave her a cautious smile, and said, "Hi."

Eloise produced a half-smile in return and nodded her head toward Joseph. She turned her back to Charlie. "Can I have a cigarette?"

Charlie said, "Sure," as he broke out another Lucky Strike and lit it for her. "Joe, Eloise graduated two years ago. She was a senior when we were lowly sophomores." Charlie droned on for a while, telling Joseph how he and Eloise had met and so on. Joseph, for his part, tried to act casually but thought he was probably failing miserably. He noticed Eloise was about 5' 6", wearing shorts showing her long and attractive legs. She had long blonde hair, which made Joseph think that she and Charlie looked like they should be on top of a wedding cake together. Charlie's soliloquy was finally interrupted by shouts from a couple of his buddies practically ordering him to join them in the living room for some parlor game they were about to begin. Charlie smiled and said to Eloise and Joseph, "I guess duty calls," and with a quick kiss on the cheek for Eloise and a friendly push on the shoulder for Joseph, he walked back into the house amid cheers and laughter.

Dear God, Joseph said to himself. I'm alone with this attractive girl. His mind raced, trying to think what to do next. Finally settling on a question, he attempted to deliver it slowly and confidently. "So, what do you do now that you're out of school?"

Eloise, wondering if he was ever going to speak, gently smiled at him, which at once relaxed Joseph, and said, "I work downtown at the Chesterton Department Store on 11th and Broadway. I sell women's clothing."

"Really," said Joseph, thrilled that he had thought of something, anything, to ask her. "Do you enjoy it?"

"It's a job. I see all the latest fashions and get a discount if I buy something. I enjoy that part," tilting her head and taking in Joseph, whom she had not really sized up yet.

Good-looking with a great smile and an engaging personality, Eloise made it easy for Joseph to carry on a conversation. He realized that he was less tongue-tied. As the party went on, it became clear that they were attracted to each other, and the alcohol being served didn't hurt. By the end of the evening, Joseph had walked Eloise home. She rented an apartment in the 3 Bridges neighborhood. She asked Joseph if he would like to come in. Joseph accepted.

~~~~~

When Joseph finally got home at close to 5 AM, he let himself in as quietly as possible and went straight to bed. A couple of hours later, with a cup of black coffee in hand, he stared out the front window at the bay. As a rare drinker, he sipped the coffee and nursed a terrible hangover. Just turning to starboard and entering East Passage, a large merchant ship passed closer than normal to a few small fishing boats sitting out a little farther than usual in front of Browns Point and the lighthouse. The waves created by the merchant ship made Joseph appreciate that he was there in the house and not in one of the fishing boats bobbing and rolling around in the swells – not this morning, anyway.

A while later, Alexandr came downstairs, "Joseph, you must have gotten in late last night because I fell asleep around 1 AM, and I hadn't heard you come in yet?"

Joseph nodded in agreement, "Yeah, Dad, it was definitely after 1 AM when I got home. I tried to be as quiet as possible so as not to wake you. I'm sorry I was out so late."

Alexandr made a harumph sound and headed for the kitchen, smelling the freshly percolated pot of coffee.

Joseph, hungover and feeling guilty, thought about Eloise.

~~~~~

On Sunday morning, before Mass, Joseph confessed his sins to Father Simone and avoided at all costs his friend and mentor Father Sauveterre in the confessional on the other side of the church. Even though Joseph was in a dark confessional where the priest could not see him, he was sure Father Etienne would recognize his voice if he had gone to him.

Joseph confessed to Fr. Simone about his encounter with a young woman and that he had been drinking. It was one thing to confess lesser offenses against God. I took the Lord's name in vain, I had impure thoughts, but for sins like straight-up fornication, it was another whole ball game. As he told the priest his sins, he began to realize the gravity of the situation. He wanted to disappear. Well, that did not happen, and after pausing for a moment, Father Simone launched into an explanation of the magnitude of Joseph's sin and its great offense to God. He went on to speak about the personal responsibility of a Christian man toward whomever the woman involved was. Even though Joseph was not arguing or protesting his culpability in this sin, Father laid it squarely on his shoulders that, as a man, it was him and only him who must always respect women. Having sexual relations with a woman to whom he was not married constituted a grave sin. There were no, nor could there be, extenuating circumstances. It was all on him, and to top it off, he had been drinking. Father Simone summed up his counsel by saying, "You are supposed to protect women, not use them." With the completion of his thoughts, Father told Joseph to make a true act of contrition.

For his penance, Father Simone instructed Joseph to pray the sorrowful mysteries of the rosary and additionally to meditate for one hour on the first of the sorrowful mysteries, "the Agony in the Garden," where Christ at one point says to the apostles Peter, James, and John, *"Watch ye, and pray that ye enter not into temptation. The spirit indeed is willing, but the flesh is weak"* (Mk 14:38). With that, Father Simone finished his prayers and blessed Joseph in the name of the Father, and the Son, and the Holy Ghost. He slid the small window shut that separated him from the penitent. Joseph rose, opened the door, and proceeded into the church nave.

Shaken and now really remorseful of his sins, Joseph returned to the pew where Alexandr was sitting. Joseph glanced at his father and thought about how the two of them had managed to avoid talking about the opposite sex and the "birds and the bees," for the most part, whenever the topic in some way or form presented itself in their conversations. Though Alexandr had maybe attempted "the talk" once or twice, Joseph knew that in each of the instances he could remember, they both had retreated from the brink.

Mass was about to begin, so Joseph would have to save the rosary and the meditation for later that day. During Mass, his mind kept returning to what Father Simone had said about his responsibilities toward women. Yet, while walking home from church with Alexandr, thoughts of Eloise stirred within him. Father Simone was, of course, right. What he did was wrong, so wrong, but then he would shift to the question in his head, "Would he see Eloise again?" Joseph was uncomfortable, further complicating his thoughts. He realized he wanted to be with her again, "physically." What was going on? He remembered Fr. Simone telling him that women were not created for his pleasure. He had not come up against this sort of problem before. How could he better understand that what happened was wrong? Yeah, he got that. Yet, at the same time, he was still drawn to thoughts of possibly doing wrong again. Was it just physical? He felt terrible but knew his body ached for that closeness and intimacy he had experienced with Eloise. He was at a loss.

Since his nights were no longer filled with assignments for school and Father Etienne, his mind was occupied in the late evenings with thoughts of Eloise. He had concluded that even though he had been drinking that night, he had not lost his ability to know right from wrong. No way. He knew that they both wanted the same thing when she asked him into her apartment. He knew she was his first and guessed he was not hers. The experience was unforgettable. He thought more about Eloise and quickly realized he knew little about her. Once they had gotten to the apartment, there had not been much small talk. What did they have in common? Likes? Dislikes? He didn't know. What if she wasn't interested in what interested him and vice versa? What were the things she was attracted to? At the party, they talked about nothing he could remember, not because they were drinking, it was more of a situation where they knew where the train was going, and both wanted to keep it moving down the tracks. The physical gratification was astounding, but who was Eloise Turner?

~~~~~

A few weeks later, Joseph ran into Eloise in the Proctor District. She was coming out of the Blue Mouse theater featuring the silent film drama *The Red Lily*, starring Ramon Navarro and Enid Bennet. He watched as two girlfriends of Eloise said their goodbyes to her and hurried toward the electric streetcar. Joseph crossed the street and walked up to her. He removed his cap and said, "Hi."

"Well, Hello, Joseph. What a surprise."

North Pacific

The two moved out of the foot traffic in front of the theater. "Can I buy you a cup of coffee?" Joseph suggested.

"Sure, why not."

They walked to a café a half-block away, where they slipped into a booth. The coffee arrived. Eloise added cream to her cup while Joseph sipped his black. She looks great, he thought. Then, feeling nervous, Joseph said, "I want to apologize for anything that might have happened at your place that maybe you didn't want to happen." He knew instantly that he wanted to take back the words he had just so inelegantly uttered, but his tension had betrayed him, and the awkward apology was out there. He wished he could start again.

Eloise, instead of replying, continued to stir the coffee with a slightly unpleasant look on her face.

"I'm sorry, Eloise. I get a little tongue-tied when I get around you."

"Joseph, I'm a big girl. I'm fine. I knew what we were doing that night."

It struck him that Eloise probably didn't understand his inept attempt at an expression of regret was bound up with his religious upbringing and the admonishing he had gotten from Father Simone during his confession. It also was not any sort of commentary or judgment of her over what had occurred. On the contrary, did she not understand how much he wished to be with her again? Maybe, he thought, maybe not. He wasn't sure.

North Pacific

"Joseph, what happened," she gestured with her arms, "It just happened. I don't believe either of us went to that party intending to spend the night with someone. Maybe the spontaneity of the whole thing and how it played out made it seem like the thing to do. I don't know, and from talking to you now, you don't seem to know either."

Joseph, now entangled in a conversation of his own making, said, "I was thinking those kinds of thoughts over the last week or so. We don't know much about each other. You seem to have a better sense of the situation than I do. I will tell you, nevertheless, that…" he paused and looking uncomfortable said, "Now I'm going to be embarrassed, it was great being with you."

Eloise, getting the slightest hint of redness in her cheeks and her eyes widening, replied, "Joseph, I had a good time, a really good time."

They both laughed. Joseph asked for a refill, and they talked about some of the people who had attended the party. After that, Joseph paid and left a tip. He walked her home, but this time he didn't go in. Instead, Eloise wished him luck at Rainier, and Joseph told her again that it had been great to see her. As Joseph walked home, he thought, I don't know how, but that seemed to go okay. I'm sure she doesn't understand the religious component of the jumbled words I used in our conversation. I don't think what I said precisely matched what Father Simone had to say about my behavior. Conscience and desire, Joseph thought, didn't work well together in this case.

North Pacific

As Joseph approached the house that overlooked the bay, he decided the weather felt different today. There was a suggestion in the air that summer was ending. It was time to start thinking about college. As for Eloise, he still missed her.

It rained that night. Joseph recalled the conversation with Eloise earlier that day. I guess when you get right down to it, I'd have to say that I don't love Eloise. I find her attractive, and, God help me, it would be hard for me to say no to her. But Father is correct about what he told me. Men must respect women. Hell, even though he and Alexandr had avoided the "birds and bees" talk when he was younger, there was no getting around the fact that his Father had always taught him to respect women. Joseph knew that his actions had fallen far short.

15.

A few weeks later, classes began at Rainier College. Joseph was eager to show Alexandr and Fr. Etienne what he could do. From the first day, he threw himself into his studies. He learned quickly that doing this work was preferable to working at the sawmill.

Whether Joseph knew it or not, he had slid back into his learned routine that involved studying for hours on end during the day and at night. And again, he barely noticed or realized, as was the case with his last few years in high school, that he really had no social life. Joseph did manage to meet his friend Martin occasionally for a cup of coffee. Martin traveled from Seattle and the University of Washington back to Tacoma on most weekends to see his girlfriend, Colleen. They were now planning to be wed. Joseph and Martin would discuss what was going on with friends they knew, what was happening in Tacoma, and, of course, world events. Joseph and his father still walked to St. Dominic every Sunday morning, although he did notice that Alexandr was walking slower these days. Father Etienne or Father Simone would celebrate Mass, proclaiming and preaching the Gospel of Christ. Joseph's mind would sometimes drift off to written assignments due in the coming week.

And so it went. Joseph, a good student to begin with, flourished at the college level. He labored with his obligatory classes unrelated to history but treated each of them as a puzzle to be solved and moved smartly through each succeeding year.

In the fall of his senior year at Rainier, there was a break in his very regimented daily routine. One day, Joseph and a young woman accidentally bumped into each other, going in opposite directions while walking down the university's oldest hall corridor. After an eye-lowering "Sorry," and before moving on, Joseph noted that she was pleasing to the eye. After that, he saw her here and there on campus. On one occasion, he saw her and noticed she was also looking at him. Confronted with this social conundrum, at least for Joseph, he managed a "Hi" in her direction. To his relief, she returned the greeting. After a few more obligatory nods, smiles, and hellos in passing, the ritualistic kabuki dance ended on a Thursday in early spring when Joseph crossed paths with her outside and in front of the main hall. It was just the two of them, and he stopped as she approached while continuing to look at her. He said, "How's it going?

"All right."

He took the leap. "Hi, I'm Joseph. Would you be interested in joining me for a cup of coffee?"

After a harrowing moment of discomfort and silence, at least for Joseph, she smiled and said confidently, "Sure, and my name is Diane."

Diane Lassiter was about five foot four and one hundred and twenty pounds of pure energy. With shorter light brown hair and a never-ending smile, she was a whole new experience for Joseph. They hit it off at once, met again for coffee, and then had lunch together. As it turned out, she was in her sophomore year, and Joseph was near graduation. Diane was planning to pursue a Business degree and hoped to begin working with her father in banking upon graduation. She was toying with the idea of eventually getting a postgraduate law degree, but it was still early, and she had not yet made that decision. She lived with her parents and two younger brothers in a beautiful home out in the West End of town near the Narrows Strait that separated Tacoma from the Kitsap peninsula and Gig Harbor. Joseph and Diane laughed about how long they had taken to get together over the last few months. Both wished they had done it sooner. The two dated, going to movies, enjoying after-class walks through the neighborhood surrounding the college, and going out to dinner a few times with Martin and Colleen, who were still trying to figure out when and where they would get married. Spring flew by.

Joseph graduated with honors and a bachelor's degree in history in May of 1929. Alexandr and Father Etienne attended the graduation ceremony - both were incredibly proud.

~~~~~

Three weeks later, at age 64, Alexandr died. Joseph had gone upstairs when his father had not come down one morning and discovered his lifeless body in the bed.

After a few days of standing in front of the window overlooking the bay by day and sleeping fitfully at night, Joseph finally admitted to himself that his father was, indeed, dead. It preyed on his mind that the night of his father's death, Alexandr had said good night as he ascended the steps to the bedroom while Joseph, engrossed in reading Pascal's *Provincial Letters,* failed to return the sentiment. Now he couldn't get it out of his head that had he responded to Alexandr, somehow, some way, his Father might still be with him. Why didn't I answer him? He shook his head and shoulders as if attempting to throw off another emotional weight he didn't want but seemed to be carrying.

Both his mother and now his father were gone, never to return. He was now alone in the house he had lived in his entire life. All of his memories of his mother and father were in that space. The reality overwhelmed him. His parents had spoken of his grandparents, but after they had moved out to the Pacific Coast, all contact over time had been lost. There was no extended family in the United States, at least none he knew of. He thought he likely had relations in the "old country," but so what? He wasn't planning on traveling there anytime soon. He was 22.

He made the funeral arrangements with an extremely heavy heart. The funeral Mass at St. Dominic began with the sung antiphon, "The bones that have been humbled shall rejoice in the Lord," followed by the psalm that began, "Miserere mei Deus" (Have mercy on me O God). Father Etienne said the Mass. Afterward, Alexandr's body was laid to rest next to Maria's in the small Catholic cemetery on the outskirts of town. At the cemetery, Father Etienne sprinkled holy water and used incense on both the casket and the grave. He then recited the words from St. John's gospel, chapter 11, verse 25, *"I am the resurrection and the life: he that believeth in me although he be dead, shall live; and everyone, that liveth, and believeth in me, shall not die forever."* The small gathering, consisting of Fr. Etienne, Martin, a few workers from the sawmill, and two staff members from the mortuary, dispersed.

After the funeral, Martin, who had a car, dropped him off at home. Joseph, still stunned by the tragedy, entered the empty house. As he had done for his entire life, He stared out the window at the permanent but ever-changing waters of Puget Sound. Once again, as had happened after the loss of his mother, Joseph was plunged into despair. All this work, all this effort, what was it for? What was the point? That night he lay in the narrow bed in the corner of the living room. Though it had been almost three weeks, he did not yet feel comfortable with the notion of moving up into what had always been his parent's bedroom. He endured great loneliness. He prayed, Dear Lord, why have you taken my parents? I'm not asking you to bring them back to me. I get that, for whatever reason, it was their time. All I ask is that you give me a sign of some kind that they are okay and with you. You know everything, "Yes, Lord, you know everything, but I know nothing and now have nothing - nothing." He realized that this mental prayer he had just finished had started soundlessly in his head but had ended with him crying out in the empty room. He slowly made the sign of the cross. The house was unbearably silent.

16.

A week later, Joseph had collected himself enough to meet with Fr. Etienne at the church rectory. Father greeted him, and they sat down in the library. Joseph thanked him for all he had done concerning the funeral Mass and the burial of Alexandr. Fr. Etienne rose and poured himself a cup of coffee at the serving table next to the wall opposite them. Then he asked Joseph if he would like some. And even before Joseph said, "Yes, please," the French priest poured a second cup.

After exchanging a few pleasantries, Father brought up their meetings beginning in Joseph's junior year to discuss his progress at Rainier. During those discussions, they both realized the student had done well, better than well. It was back then that Father had broached the subject of Joseph's plans beyond Rainier. It was clear Joseph had what it took to pursue postgraduate studies. Both mentor and student remembered being excited as they considered the possibilities. Father Etienne had even gotten Joseph to submit paperwork for entry into the University of Washington's graduate History program.

There had been no discussions regarding the future since Alexandr's passing, but now Father Etienne pressed Joseph about the subject. Father asked him if he'd thought about it, and Joseph said he had, but now that they were talking about it, he was certainly interested. However, with a tired expression, Joseph added that even if he could get into a university, he did not believe he could afford it.

Father Etienne was well aware of Joseph's financial situation. He had come over to the Vaenkos for dinner maybe a half-dozen times since Joseph had started at Rainier. He and Joseph and Alexandr were more or less a team built around the idea of fulfilling Alexandr's vision for Joseph of achieving the "American Dream." When they discussed it over dinner on those visits, Alexandr would always say to Joseph, "This is what your mother, God rest her soul, would have wanted." Money had always been the obstacle, and now with Alexandr's death, even more so. The priest, looking back, had, upon his arrival in Tacoma, seen the possibilities in Joseph. And now, over six years later, Father Etienne was even more convinced of Joseph's potential.

Father Etienne took a sip of coffee and almost feeling the spirit of Alexandr within him, launched into his thoughts on the topic. "Joseph, I've been researching and talking to some people about your postgraduate studies. I believe we can make this work."

Having raised the coffee cup to his lips, Joseph stopped and returned it to the table. "What do you mean, Father?"

"Well, I think we can send you to the University of Washington, as long as they approve you, to begin your studies for an eventual doctorate in History. That is if you're willing to agree to some terms and arrangements."

"Are you serious, Father? What would it take? I'm all ears," a hopeful smile warily widened on his face.

"I have talked to some wonderful and money-blessed parishioners in Seattle, the Naval Reserve Officer Training Corps (NROTC) program at the university, and a colleague from my studies back in France. I believe we can pay for your education, provide housing at the university for you, and rent your home while you are away in Seattle if you are accepted into the programs." Are you interested?"

Joseph realizing the priest was serious, exclaimed, "Of course Father."

Father, who was all smiles, then introduced the details. The donors would foot the bill for the University. If accepted into the Naval ROTC program, he would be provided with spartan but free sleeping accommodations for himself on campus. Fr. Etienne's colleague would stay in Joseph's home, renting it for at least the first year. This would provide a small income for paying property taxes and other expenses. Father's colleague from France would work on some publishing projects with the now more in-demand Dominican homilist sitting across the table. They would deal with who might rent the home beyond that point when the time came.

Joseph, who had been in such a state after the passing of Alexandr, allowed himself to smile while listening to

Father Etienne explain the details of his master plan. He thought to himself, if only this would work.

The original application for graduate school at the University of Washington that Joseph had submitted at Father Etienne's earlier request came in the mail a few days later, accepting him into the program. Joseph did not hesitate. He quickly applied to the NROTC program at the University the following week. With the exceptional record achieved at Rainier College, and the help provided by Father Etienne, he was accepted into both programs.

This seemed like a point in his life when, with the loss of his father, all his effort had seemed wasted. With the acceptance into the postgraduate studies at the University of Washington, the NROTC program, and the renter arrangement with the house, Joseph believed he was possibly gaining control of his life for the first time. He could not get his parents back. But beyond that, Joseph told himself he could make this happen and have that bright future his parents and he had hoped for. On his walk home from the rectory, as though his parents were right there with him, he thought, we can make this happen, thanks to both of you.

Yet there was a problem that arose simultaneously amid all the good news. What about Diane?

~~~~~

North Pacific

Diane and Joseph sat opposite each other at a table for two at a small restaurant near the college campus. Joseph asked, "How have you been? Did you have a good trip?"

"I haven't seen you in at least a month," responded Diane. "I had an enjoyable time with my cousin Emily in Portland. We shopped, went to a couple of plays, and had dinners outdoors most nights with the gorgeous weather. I think it's warmer down there than up here." Joseph took it all in. He watched her every move, gesture, and smile. He was genuinely happy to see her again. Diane continued, "But enough about that. How has it been for you? How are you doing now that you have had some time since your dad's funeral?"

Just as Joseph was about to respond, the waiter approached the table and asked if he could get them something to drink and if they were interested in eating. They both ordered coffee and accepted menus. As the waiter receded into the kitchen, Joseph explained to Diane what had been going on in his life for the last month or so. He told her about meeting with his parish priest and working out a plan to continue his studies. He said to her that he had been accepted by the University of Washington and was, Lord willing, going to earn a Ph.D. in History. He also told her about the NROTC program and the rental arrangement for the house.

Diane was surprised, to say the least, as the coffees arrived. She poured a little cream into her cup and said, "I'm a little taken aback. I don't know why. I know you talked about this over the final few months of college. But to be honest, Joseph, I didn't think you could pull it off, certainly not because of your grades or anything. My God, you graduated with honors. I just thought the money would be too hard to put together, especially with the passing of your father. I guess I thought that you would not be leaving town." The last words trailed off as they left her lips.

"I'm not going to be gone forever," Joseph replied with sincerity. "I'll be able to come home on some weekends and holidays. Maybe, now that they're married, I can stay with Martin and Colleen once in a while. There will certainly be times during the summer."

"Really, Joseph?" Diane's voice climbed a few octaves. "Do you want to build a relationship around some holidays and weekends?"

"Well, no," exclaimed Joseph, caught off guard. "I mean, what do you want me to do? Do you want me not to pursue graduate school?"

"I didn't say that," said Diane, her voice rising again.

"This is harder than I thought it would be," Joseph suddenly said, feeling and looking uncomfortable. "I guess I thought we could work something out. That's why I wanted to get together today." He rubbed his neck uneasily.

Diane, listening, put her finger in the air, creating a pause in the discussion. Lowering her finger and then pointing it directly at Joseph, she said, "What are we going to do? Did you honestly think we could make this work with you in Seattle and me here?"

North Pacific

"Diane, I don't want to be away from you," as he raised both hands. "But I'm at a loss as to what to tell you. I really thought we might be able to make this work," he placed his hands on top of hers.

She looked down at their hands and then up at him. "There is an innocence about you. You are not very worldly. This has disaster written all over it." With that, she slowly pulled her hands back and asked him, "When are you leaving?" There was a sense of resignation in her voice.

Joseph replied that he thought it would be late September.

With her voice rising just slightly this time, Diane said, "I hear you, Joseph, but what about how we feel about each other right now?"

Joseph replied, "Look, this is not my idea of what I want to do in terms of us right now, but it's like I said, I don't feel I have any other choice." At that moment, he remembered thinking that just a few weeks ago, with the acceptances from the two programs at the university, he had felt as though he was gaining control of his life, at least to some degree. In light of the circumstances and the conversation with Diane, that sense of losing control of his life seemed to reappear. It was difficult to understand, much less explain.

Diane asked Joseph for some details about the UW offers. Joseph told her what he knew at that point about the History and NROTC programs. They drank a little of the coffee and returned the menus to the waiter. The conversation waned. Joseph left some money on the table. He and Diane walked outside. Joseph remembered thinking again how great Diane looked, even though her welcoming smile had turned to one of restraint. The encounter had not gone well.

17.

Joseph spent the better part of a decade achieving his goal of a doctorate in History from the University of Washington. He also graduated from NROTC and took part in summer cruises off the Pacific coast as he became an officer in the Naval Reserve. It was the summer of 1938 when he returned to Tacoma. Joseph's friend, priest, and mentor, Fr. Etienne, had functioned as agent and landlord for young Mr. Vaenko's home that overlooked the bay. Joseph could not thank him enough for all he had done for him.

Joseph's relationship with Diane was a sooner-than-later casualty of his years in Seattle. He had tried to get back to Tacoma from time to time, but hitching a ride or taking the bus from the Montlake neighborhood in the University District of Seattle to the King Street Station downtown and catching the train to Tacoma was an adventure of timing and luck. He would stay at Martin and Colleen's house and then turn around and retrace his steps back to Seattle. This was not something he enjoyed doing. He would study on the train, but it left him exhausted. Even though Diane had genuine feelings for Joseph, the long-distance aspect of the relationship was simply too much to overcome. Time and distance, more than anything, extinguished the flame.

His time in Seattle had been fulfilling. He had worked hard to earn his doctorate with the required coursework, exams, and original research. During this time, he became a Graduate Assistant teaching undergraduate history classes. The work earned him a stipend that provided him with some spending money, for which he was thankful.

Joseph's doctoral dissertation made a case for the geopolitical and military strategic importance of the North Pacific in relation to Japan, the new Soviet Union, and U.S. naval power. He spoke to the technological advances in naval construction that changed everything, militarily speaking, in the Pacific.

To help make his argument, he focused on the history of the so-called "Northern Route" of a potential conflict between the United States and Japan. The U.S. Navy's "Orange Plan" or War Against Japan saw the Japanese making the first move in a military conflict, and then the United States retaliating by taking the fight to the Japanese in their home waters. To get to the Western Pacific and Japan, U.S. Naval forces had to take one of three routes. The shortest of the routes was designated the "Northern Route." It followed the great circle route via Alaska's Aleutian Islands to Japan. Issues abounded. These problems included immense weather systems, harbors that were too small, logistical nightmares, and other difficulties and challenges.

Vaenko analyzed the history of the idea's genesis and the back-and-forth of naval planning debates up to the mid-1930s. He was able to focus on such luminaries as Admiral Alfred Thayer Mahan, who favored the "Northern Route" as a way to take the fight to Japan's doorstep rapidly. Mahan thought it had the best chance of shortening any potential conflict. In his estimation, he believed establishing an American naval force in the Aleutians would "out-flank" any Japanese attempt to take Hawaii and Pearl Harbor. Interestingly, Mahan dismissed the weather problems of the region.

Joseph told the story of how and why the "Northern Route" was rejected in the "Orange Plan" and how it always resurfaced for reconsideration each time the plan was updated. Joseph further examined Japanese military thought and history connected to the North Pacific during those years. He researched the U.S. and Japanese navies' disposition of forces over the intervening years since the original plan's inception showing how each navy might respond to aggression by the other in the strategically critical North Pacific.

All of this, including his literature review, research methodology, findings, context, and implications, paved the way for a unique contribution to understanding the importance of the North Pacific to U.S. military thinking and planning.

North Pacific

The most challenging part of his dissertation was learning how to read the Japanese language. He established friendships with professors who spoke the language and Japanese American students working on their graduate studies. The French language had come more easily to him, while Japanese, on the other hand, had presented more problems. The relationships with faculty and fellow students were the key to his research using Japanese sources. To make it even more challenging, reforms to Japanese script were introduced in the early 20th century, which required another layer of difficulty in learning and understanding the language.

This aspect of his work was incredibly time-consuming and fostered Joseph's inclination to avoid socializing to any meaningful extent. Yes, he made friends, but his workload discouraged the development of close relationships. Yes, a few interactions with women led to meeting for coffee or going to an occasional movie, but they had led nowhere.

Consequently, Joseph's more or less solitary existence remained intact. The problem was, after all that time in Seattle, he had become a man in his thirties. It struck him that his window for achieving a meaningful relationship with a member of the opposite sex was closing fast.

Upon receiving his doctorate, Joseph moved back into his house, even taking the big step of making the upstairs bedroom his own. He placed a desk in front of the somewhat smaller window in the bedroom that surveyed the bay like the larger window on the first floor. For the first time that he could remember, he just relaxed. He spent the summer repainting the house and fixing it up inside and out.

Much to his surprise and delight, he managed to land a job in the history department at Rainier College as an Assistant Professor, with many old friends and faculty welcoming him back to the college. After all the work he had put into getting his advanced degree and joining the history department at his undergraduate alma mater, he treated himself by buying a used 1936 Studebaker, "Dictator." It was a gray two-door coupe. The car sat impressively, he thought, on the street right in front of his house.

Life was good, yet Joseph had no one to share it with, and his loneliness deepened. Of course, he had made some friends in Seattle, but that was there, and now he was back in Tacoma. For what passed as excitement, Joseph, plagued by his seemingly growing introversion, would walk down the steep hill into Old Town, leaving his car at home, on many a Friday and Saturday night, and would have a drink or two at Isaac's Bar (Named after Washington State's first governor Isaac Stevens). He had never really liked alcohol, but he was over 30 now and discovered it helped him to relax a bit. He would spend a few hours conversing with neighborhood friends and old high school and college chums that randomly came into Isaacs and then later would walk up the hill to his house. This routine of teaching at the college, fixing the house up during the summer months, and the Friday and sometimes Saturday night visits to the local bar, with Mass, of course, on Sundays, pretty much summed up Joseph's self-contained existence for the next three years.

Joseph had met a couple of women at Isaacs during this time, but he was never compelled to pursue a more meaningful relationship other than conversation. It was just easier. Yes, a couple of times, the discussions with a woman at the bar would drift towards possibly going to his or her place. However, Joseph never felt it was the right girl. He couldn't explain it. It also brought back memories of Eloise and his mixed feelings after being with her. It also conjured up visions of Father Simone.

It had been almost three years since Joseph had earned his doctorate and settled back into his life in his modest home overlooking the bay in Tacoma. Teaching at Rainier College was the icing on the cake.

While pursuing his postgraduate studies in Seattle, he attended Blessed Sacrament parish in the University District. Dominicans also staffed this Catholic parish. The church was almost twice the size of St. Dominic in Tacoma. Walking to Mass from the UW campus, the church's spectacular towering and now weathered green copper spire guided him to its front doors. As he had done all his life in Tacoma, Joseph often stopped by the Seattle church to spend quiet time talking and praying to the Lord in the Blessed Sacrament.

He had accomplished much in his life to this point. Who would have thought the son of immigrant parents, starting from scratch with few prospects, would produce a son that now held a Ph.D. from the University of Washington and be an officer in the United States Naval Reserve? He knew his parents would have been so proud of his achievements had they lived to see them. Yet, he still had no one in his life to share the good times and bad. He bumped along on these thoughts and his limited social existence until the spring of 1941. It was then that Joseph's life would forever change.

PECATTUM

(Sin)

"But every man is tempted by his own concupiscence…"

James 1:14

Douay-Rheims

North Pacific

18.

The morning Joseph saw that most singular woman at Sunday Mass in the spring of 1941, his anxieties about the opposite sex improved markedly. The confident yet modest way she carried herself made him a little weak in the knees, and those large dark brown eyes were spellbinding. The encounter had swept away Joseph's social hang-ups, which had always found him rationalizing why he should not pursue this or that relationship. He had become a man on a mission.

Joseph kept thinking he must figure out a way to meet her after Mass the following Sunday. He decided he would just walk up to her and introduce himself. But how would he do it with the older woman with her? It must be her mother. What was he supposed to do? Would he walk up to the two of them and say to the older woman, excuse me, I'd like a word with your daughter? That idea was probably dead-on-arrival. Beyond that, he had no idea what he might say. He practiced saying a few words of greeting and introduction in his head, but it always sounded completely wooden and embarrassing. He did not know what to say but told himself he would do it – he had to. And what about that guy he saw her with downtown? He reasoned he would deal with that when the time came. For now, all that mattered was meeting her.

That following Sunday, after not seeing her the week before, he walked into Mass and straightaway saw her, to his relief and excitement. He tried ever so hard not to look at her but caught himself glancing at her way too often. As Mass concluded, Father Etienne, reading from the last gospel, genuflected, and said, "*Et verbum caro factum est*" (And the Word was made flesh - Jn 1:14). Moments later, after the prayers at the foot of the altar for the salvation of the people's souls in Russia, the parishioners began slowly leaving using the main doors. Joseph walked quickly outside and positioned himself at the corner of the church where his mystery woman would have to pass to walk to the bus stop. He noticed he was having trouble breathing, so he took a few shallow, measured breaths to calm himself and waited. At this point, he still didn't know what he was going to do or say. People walked by him. Some said hello or good morning. Joseph smiled and nodded but kept fixated on the church doors. More time passed, and finally, he saw her come out the door and down the steps.

As she headed his way, he realized she was engaged in conversation with - Father Etienne. He froze. Father Etienne saw Joseph and stopped in front of him. His mentor and priest smiled and said, "Good morning, Joseph. I want you to meet Mrs. Ikue Moriya and her niece Miku Shinkai." Joseph, in total disbelief, somehow got the words "How do you do" out of his throat. Miku said, "Hello, Joseph." Her aunt nodded toward him. There was a moment of silence. Father Etienne spoke up. "Joseph, would you be so kind as to talk to Miku for a minute? Mrs. Moriya wants to discuss something in private with me." Joseph, looking more dumbfounded than usual, managed an almost inaudible "Sure" that again sort of stuck in his throat. Father Etienne and Mrs. Moriya walked back to the front of the church and began a conversation.

It was Miku who broke the ice. "Joseph, are you from Tacoma?" She asked in a sure and confident voice.

Coming to terms with what had just occurred, Joseph responded, "I am, and you?"

"I was born and grew up in Seattle. I graduated from Broadway High School."

Joseph's head was swimming. "So, are you visiting your aunt?" Joseph tried to be as natural and relaxed as possible, considering his heart was racing. He wasn't sure he was pulling it off.

Miku smiled and said, "I'm living with her for now. It is less expensive than renting an apartment. My parents have returned to Japan to care for my grandparents, who are getting older. I didn't want to go, much to my father's disappointment. He still thinks I'm his little girl. I'm twenty-eight years old," she proclaimed, raising her hands in a gesture of 'Can you believe it?' "You know how fathers can be about their daughters, and to add to it, I'm an only child."

Lost in her smile, Joseph realized she had completed her thought, and it was now his turn to speak. "I'm an only child also." He began noticing that Miku's manner was making him more at ease. It ran through his head that he was really standing right here and getting to know this woman he had been thinking and dreaming about for weeks.

His thought was interrupted by another voice. It was Father Etienne. The priest and Miku's aunt were back. "I gather, since you're both still smiling, that you got along while Mrs. Moriya and I had our talk?"

"We did, Father," Joseph spoke up.

"Good, good," replied the now jovial Dominican. Looking at Joseph and Miku, Father said, "You both ought to consider coming to my talk I'm giving this coming Friday night down in the church hall. It will be on the incomparable Saint Francis de Sales. Afterward, I'll take questions, and then we will socialize." Father looked directly at Joseph and said, "There will be cake and coffee." He chuckled and added, "It's a good way to get to know others in the parish and an opportunity for the parishioners to talk among themselves about how Father is losing it, has put on weight, or how his hair is graying or thinning, to mention just a few of the comments I've overheard at these affairs."

They all laughed. Then, after a moment of silence, Joseph spoke up. "Thanks, Father, I'll try to make it." Miku nodded her ascent to Joseph's response. Mrs. Moriya thanked Father Etienne for taking the time to talk to her and then looked at Miku and said, "We should be going."

North Pacific

Miku said, "All right," wished Father well, and turned one last time to Joseph, saying, "It was really nice meeting you."

"I feel the same," he replied.

Then the two women headed toward the end of the block to catch the bus.

Father Etienne and Joseph watched them for a moment, and then Joseph turned to the priest and said, "I didn't know you knew that young lady. I've been trying to figure out a way to meet her." Father laughed, "I've known Mrs. Moriya for quite some time. I believe her niece moved in with her about a month ago. She's pretty, wouldn't you say?" Joseph turned to look one more time to see if Miku was still in sight at the bus stop. "Yes, Father, she is definitely pretty." The two men talked for another minute or so, and then they parted. Joseph hardly remembered walking home.

At home, Joseph could not have been more pleased. He had met her. She had a name. He loved everything about her, from her voice to her smile and confidence. Joseph smiled inwardly and thought, I want to get to know her better. Then, he wondered whether Miku would attend Father Etienne's talk the following Friday, as she had intimated when they were talking to Father Etienne. Damn, he thought, she must come. Then a question came to him. If she came, would she bring the guy he saw her with downtown? Was he her boyfriend? Joseph couldn't take it anymore. He put on his jacket and stocking cap and went

North Pacific

for a walk down along the waterfront.

~~~~~

It seemed like forever waiting for Friday night to arrive, but as is the case with everything in life, it eventually came. Joseph arrived at St. Dominic, descended the basement stairs, and entered the church hall. The space was large and well-lit, and many parishioners were already there. Chairs were everywhere, along with some folding tables set up to hold the coffee urns, cups, chocolate cake, plates, forks, and napkins that Father had promised after last Sunday's Mass.

After a few minutes, Father Etienne walked in, and everyone began earnestly looking for a spot to sit. Joseph glanced around for an empty chair when Miku appeared at his side and said, "Shall we sit together?"

Joseph, startled, said, "Absolutely," and pulled up a folding chair for Miku to sit on. He found another for himself and sat down next to this beautiful woman. Elated that the situation had worked out so well, he confidently asked, "How have you been, Miku?"

She smiled and said, "I'm good. I was hoping you would be here." The warmth in her voice and the ease of her manner delighted him.

North Pacific

Disarmed by her remark, Joseph responded, "I was hoping you would be here too." She smiled again and then turned her head toward Father, who offered a prayer for the group gathered there that evening and began his talk.

Father Etienne was a more subdued speaker who did not roil the air with arm gestures but concentrated on his tone and the delivery of his words. He spoke about the Catholic Saint Francis De Sales. He spoke of his life's work and summed up his talk by reciting the great saint's "Complete Trust in God" prayer.

> *"Do not look forward to the trials and crosses*
> *of this life with dread and fear.*
> *Rather, look to them with full confidence*
> *that as they arise, God, to whom you belong,*
> *will deliver you from them.*
> *He has guided and guarded you*
> *thus far in life.*
> *Do you but hold fast to his dear hand, and*
> *He will lead you safely through all trials.*
> *Whenever you cannot stand,*
> *he will carry you lovingly in his arms.*
> *Do not look forward to what may happen tomorrow.*
> *The same Eternal Father who cares for you today*
> *will take good care of you tomorrow*

North Pacific
and every day of your life.

Either he will shield you from suffering or

He will give you the unfailing strength to bear it.

Be at peace then and put aside all useless thoughts,

vain dreads, and anxious imaginations."

Father Etienne was an excellent speaker and knew how to hold an audience. Meanwhile, Joseph, who very much enjoyed Fr. Etienne's talks and sermons, was finding it hard to fully pay attention because his mind was so focused on the slight and wonderful woman sitting next to him.

Father received appreciative applause from those in attendance. The priest thanked everyone and then asked if there were any questions. A few hands were raised, and Father pointed at one of them and said, "Please, what is your question?"

As this was going on, Joseph glanced over at Miku, who seemed attentive to what was being said. Again, he had trouble believing he was sitting next to the person he had been so preoccupied with over the last several weeks. Finally, Joseph heard Father Etienne say, "Thanks again, everyone, and how about we eat some of that special chocolate cake over there." The audience laughed and clapped at the same time. The crowd then stirred, rising, moving chairs around, and making their way to the tables with the cake and coffee.

North Pacific

Joseph looked at Miku and said, "Would you like a piece of cake, a cup of coffee, or both?"

Seeing Joseph was well-mannered, Miku smiled, saying, "Thanks, but no, not really."

Joseph, encouraged by Miku's seeming interest in him, told her, "I've wanted to meet you for the last month or so, ever since the first time I saw you at Mass."

Miku, for the first time, slightly surprised by Joseph's words, blushed, and said, "Well, what took you so long?"

"Well, I don't know, maybe I thought you had a boyfriend or something," Joseph fidgeted a little in his folding chair. There was a din from all the talk going on in the room, which, on the one hand, made conversation a bit harder but, surprisingly, also isolated what they were saying to each other.

Miku said, "Well, that depends upon what you mean. If you mean do I have a steady guy, I don't. If you mean do I go out with guys, the answer is yes, sometimes."

Joseph, embarrassed, said, "I didn't mean to pry. Forget it. It was a dumb question."

Miku said, "That's ok. I started it, I think."

Joseph tried to change the subject by asking if she found anything in Tacoma of interest. She said she liked the downtown area, it felt alive, and it was fun to get caught up in the busy atmosphere. She also said she enjoyed Wright Park, located in the Stadium District, with its wonderful botanical gardens. Miku paused, "I also enjoy Point Defiance Park and especially the Japanese gardens."

Joseph told her that those particular gardens were inspired by the construction of an electric streetcar station in the park, whose architectural design was that of a pagoda. Initially, the station served as the streetcar turnaround from within the park, and though the electric streetcars had been replaced three years ago by buses, the station remained.

Miku said the gardens gave her a sense of her family's heritage. She then proceeded to ask where Joseph lived. He told her it was a small gray and white house near the top of a hill that overlooked the bay. He added that it was about a mile from the church. She laughed and asked, "What do you do when you're not at Mass?"

To which Joseph replied, "I teach history at Rainier College."

"Really," she said, seeming pleasantly impressed. "I work as a travel agent. My father had a travel agency in Seattle, and I learned about the business there. When my parents returned to Japan, my father got me a job working for a friend of his here in Tacoma. It's almost strictly travel between Japan and the States."

The two continued to go back and forth, learning more about each other. At some point, Father Etienne walked over to the couple and said, "It is wonderful to see that you both could make it to the talk tonight." The three of them chatted for a while, and then Father was pulled away into another conversation. Joseph asked Miku how she and her family had found their way to the Catholic faith.

"My family has been Catholic for generations. In Seattle, we were parishioners at St. James Cathedral." She continued, "The cathedral is about a mile from where I grew up." She further stated that her parents' proudest moment had come when she was a teenager. They attended a Mass at the Seattle cathedral, said by Kyunosuke Hayasaka, who had been the first native Japanese prelate to attain the rank of bishop in the Church. Miku elaborated on the importance of her faith and what it meant to her. He was struck by her zeal.

Joseph noticed that the gathering was beginning to break up. He asked Miku, "How are you getting home?"

"The bus," she replied.

"May I offer you a ride?"

Surprised, Miku smiled and said, "You don't have to do that. I'm used to traveling at night."

Joseph said, "I'd love to do it."

"Well, if you really want to, that would be nice."

With that, they headed for the door and Joseph's Studebaker in the parking lot behind the Church. As they drove downtown, they became quiet, yet each extremely aware of the presence of the other. Downtown, Joseph parked the car and walked Miku to her aunt's apartment building. She thanked him for the ride home, and Joseph said, "It was great to get a chance to talk to you. I hope we can do it again soon."

Surprising Joseph, she gave him a peck on the cheek and said, "Me too."

Joseph said, "Good night, Miku." Then he turned and walked to his car. He could not remove the smile from his face even if he wanted to.

~~~~~

For the first time since his parents had been alive, Joseph felt like he was with someone, even though he was not and had only just met Miku. The following Sunday morning couldn't come soon enough. After Mass, he waited outside the church. Thankfully, the weather was good, with no rain. Miku came out the door, down the steps, looked around, saw Joseph, and walked over to him.

"Good morning, Miku."

She responded in kind, as they both seemed a tad anxious. Finally, Miku said, "I must help my aunt out this morning, but I thought, with the good weather, I might ride the bus out to Point Defiance and take in the Japanese gardens this afternoon. I thought maybe you might want to meet me out there."

"What time?"

"I don't know, maybe around two."

"I'll be there. It sounds great."

North Pacific

With that, Miku turned and met her aunt, who had taken a bit longer in the Church. Mrs. Moriya smiled and nodded at Joseph, and then Miku and her aunt disappeared into the crowd leaving St. Dominic.

Joseph walked home and made some coffee. He didn't feel like eating and so stood gazing out the big window at the morning maritime traffic on the bay. He thought to himself, what a turn of events. He could not have been happier or more excited at the prospect of seeing Miku again that day.

~~~~~

Joseph parked the Studebaker not far from the "pagoda" bus station at Point Defiance Park. He looked around for Miku. The weather was mild and comfortable on that summer day, with just the slightest of breezes blowing. Not seeing her, he unhurriedly walked around to the backside of the station, where the gardens were located.

There, Joseph saw Miku looking down over the gardens while leaning against the broad wooden railing that ran the length of the station. Something came over him as he began moving toward her. He realized he did not know what he was going to do next. Miku was looking at the fauna while feeling the warmth of the afternoon sun on her face. She turned toward him as if she had sensed his presence as he approached. Now committed to the encounter, Joseph stood before her and slowly reached out, gently clasping her hands in his. She did not resist. They gazed intently at one another, slowly leaned toward each other, and kissed. It was as if they were no longer in control of their actions. Joseph experienced something entirely unlike anything he had ever felt before. Nothing, absolutely nothing, had ever approached this feeling. As he would remember, it was the most vital moment of his life.

Joseph felt a bit detached from the world. Miku stared up at him. For a split second, he did not know what to do next. However, while struggling to find his voice, Joseph realized that Miku seemed as lost in him as he was in her. They kissed again.

Then they turned toward the gardens. The couple spent the next ten minutes not saying a word. They stood beside each other, shoulders touching, looking out over the beautiful bushes and flowers. At last, Joseph spoke, "Miku, I can't pretend, not even a little, that you are just another person. I must tell you that I'm mesmerized by the idea that you exist." He paused.

"Joseph, it's all right. I feel like you do. It's crazy, for sure, but it's real. I've never been so moved as I was when I first saw you when you held the church door for my aunt and me. We're supposed to be grown-ups, aren't we?" She leaned into him and said, "How do you explain it?"

Joseph hesitated and said, "You say it's crazy, and I say you make me crazy. You're all I've thought about since I first saw you at Mass. Would you like to walk a little through the park?"

North Pacific

Miku said, "No, I like it right here next to you. Let's just stand here and look at the gardens. Doesn't the sun feel good this afternoon?"

"It does," he replied as they continued to lean against the railing. They embraced one more time.

Upon touching Joseph's neck, Miku asked, "Are you wearing a medal?" while twisting the chain gently with her fingers.

"Yes, my mother gave it to me years ago. I told her I would always wear it."

"May I look at it?"

"Sure."

She gently pulled the chain up, revealing the medal. "I think it is beautiful, Joseph," and then returned it to its proper place.

Time passed by quickly, and they reluctantly agreed they must leave. Joseph drove her back downtown to her aunt's apartment. He returned to his house and discovered he was famished, having not eaten all day. After a bite to eat, he gazed out his window and told himself that he had never felt this relaxed. An emerging sense of purpose had replaced his anxiety.

Over the following weeks, Joseph saw Miku as much as he could. Between her job at the travel agency and his teaching, they still managed to get together whenever they could find the time. They went to a couple of movies. He showed her parts of the city she had never seen. Joseph took Miku to Martin and Colleen's house, where he introduced her to the pleasantly surprised couple. They stayed, spent a late Saturday morning with the Linarts, and then had lunch with them while they got to know Joseph's beautiful girlfriend. He also drove her to Browns Point one Sunday afternoon, where they spent some time looking back at the city across the bay while trying to pick out Joseph's house near the top of the hill over in Old Town. The time they spent together seemed to fly by. It was an all-consuming time for Joseph. Being with Miku was all he wanted to do.

Each night while trying to fall asleep, Joseph would reflect on how attracted he was to Miku. She was so beautiful, to be sure, but he fell in love with everything about her. Thoughts backing up those feelings about her flooded his mind. She carried herself with such grace and assurance. Her tone of voice was always perfect for whatever they were talking about. The way she laughed, walked, and made funny faces all combined to make Joseph want to be with her all the time. She had such a way about her. Even the hint of vulnerability she would sometimes flash made him want to care for her in any way he could. He could not get over how powerfully she had moved him.

North Pacific

19.

All was going well with Joseph's newfound relationship with Miss Shinkai. Miku told Joseph she wanted to introduce him to a new friend she had made a few days before when sharing a table for lunch. Joseph thought that would be great and asked if she and her friend wanted to get together Friday night down at Isaacs in Old Town. They could talk, eat appetizers, and have something to drink. Miku agreed, saying it sounded like a good time.

On Friday evening, Miku's friend, Kasumi Takahara, driving her father's beautiful 1938 black Ford sedan with Miku in the passenger seat, arrived at Isaac's Bar just before 8:30. Kasumi, like Miku, was a second-generation Japanese American. She, however, was a native of Tacoma. She had graduated from the same high school as Joseph a couple of years after he had been there.

Joseph had arrived fifteen minutes earlier and secured a booth for the three of them. He stood and raised his hand when he saw the two women enter the front door. Miku and Kasumi then navigated the tables and chairs that marked the circuitous path to the booth. When they arrived, Miku gave him a quick kiss and introduced Kasumi. Both women slid into the booth, one on either side, and then Joseph sat next to Miku. They chatted for a few

North Pacific

minutes, and then Joseph ordered appetizers and drinks at the bar.

The threesome enjoyed each other's company, and they laughed and talked until close to 11 PM. Finally, Miku indicated they would need to get going because Kasumi had to get up to help work at her father's market in the morning. As they stood, Joseph graciously hugged Kasumi and told her how nice it was to meet her. He then turned to Miku and embraced her, whispering in her ear over the din, "I love you." Miku reached up and pulled Joseph toward her, kissing him, and saying, "We've got to get together again soon."

As they all began to leave, a voice from a nearby table rose above the noise in the bar, "Would you look at that, a damn Bohunk with a couple of Japs! What the hell is this world coming to?" Joseph turned quickly to see a guy he recognized from working at the sawmill. His name was Ron Huddleston. The three other guys at his table were laughing about Huddleston's outburst. Bohunk was a term of derision regarding immigrants from the old Austro-Hungarian Empire. Joseph and the two women were now directly in front of the loudmouth whose face displayed nothing but contempt and insolence.

Joseph stared at Huddleston momentarily and then said, "You can call me a Bohunk all you want, but you're not going to insult these two women…." Huddleston interrupted Joseph by bolting confrontationally to his feet, his chair flipping over backward, and slamming to the floor. A hush came over the room. "I'll say whatever I Gawd damn…." Bam! Joseph clocked him squarely in the middle of his face before Huddleston could finish his sentence. He hit him with every ounce of strength he had. Ron dropped to the floor with a thud. Then, with the bar patrons looking on without a sound, Huddleston slowly rolled over and sat up. Blood was streaming from what looked like a broken nose. He was handed a couple of napkins by one of his friends, which he used to try staunching the bleeding nose as he sat there on the floor. The silence in the bar continued as everyone intently watched for what might happen next. As Huddleston struggled to get up, Joseph looked at him disgustedly while simultaneously piloting Miku and Kasumi out of the bar and onto the street. Ron shouted after him, "Listen, you worthless…," His voice trailed off momentarily as he dabbed at his nose. "The next time I see you, I'm going to kick your ass."

Joseph walked the two shaken women to Kasumi's car. He apologized for the racial slur that they were forced to endure.

Kasumi said, "We're second-generation Japanese Americans, we've never even been to Japan, but we've dealt with this sort of thing before. We're okay."

Miku put her arms around Joseph's neck and pressed against him. "Joseph, you were so brave the way you handled that man. Dear God, you mean so much to me. Where have you been all my life?" She kissed him with fervor.

North Pacific

Joseph did not know what to say and instead just shook his head. Kasumi offered Joseph a ride home, but he refused. "I need to walk. I need to cool down. Drive carefully, and thanks for coming." They both waved at him as Kasumi started the engine. Then, as the car began to move forward, Joseph and Miku's eyes locked on each other as the sedan pulled away, heading downtown.

Joseph made his way up 30th Street hill to his house. His hand throbbed. The racial slur used against Miku and Kasumi had really set him off. He had hit that joker with everything he had square in the nose as his father had taught him as a boy. He remembered Alexandr's words to him when he was around thirteen years old, "If you ever have to fight someone, especially if he's bigger than you, make sure to throw the first punch and hit him in the nose as hard as you possibly can." He took some ice cubes from the refrigerator and wrapped them in a hand towel. As he sat in Father's big chair that looked out over the bay, Joseph positioned the towel with the ice over his aching knuckles to numb the pain and minimize swelling. However, the real pain he felt was how the incident must have upset Miku.

The West Coast had always had an element of the population that was particularly racially intolerant to Asian Americans. The situation embarrassed Joseph greatly. Add the fact that the Japanese had been at war with China since 1932 and recently had been militarily threatening U.S. interests in the Pacific did not in any way help matters. Out the large living room window, he saw a few maritime lights moving toward and away from the City's port facilities, but his thoughts were concentrated on Miku. His heart ached for her. Finally, Joseph noticed the time. It was after 1 AM. He also realized the towel was now soggy as the ice had pretty much melted. His fist felt cold and numb. He placed the towel in the kitchen sink, thought once more about Miku, and called it a night.

Joseph awoke just after 5 AM. It seemed to him that no matter what time he went to bed, he would always wake up between five and six in the morning – the curse of an early riser. He felt like hell, as though he had slept little. As he lay there, he remembered a dream from during the night. As he thought about it, more details came to him. In the dream, he and Miku were walking down a series of streets. Joseph tried ever so hard to keep her close, but everything and everybody seemed to be trying to separate them. The harder he tried to be with her, the more situations would arise to frustrate his efforts. Joseph realized he had struggled with this dream as the tousled blankets and sheets attested. Why did he have this dream? Why was it so vivid in his memory? Why couldn't he figure it out?

20.

Later that Saturday morning, Joseph had done the laundry, changed the sheets on the bed, and cleaned up the house. While eating his standard breakfast of one egg with two pieces of toast and coffee, Joseph concluded his hand would be all right, although it was still stiff and sore. He could almost make a fist again. The dream he had during the night continued to trouble him. He couldn't seem to get it out of his head.

Finishing up washing the breakfast dishes, Joseph heard a car idling out front. Looking up and out the window above the kitchen sink, he saw Kasumi Takahara's black 38 Ford sitting in front of his Studebaker. He wiped his hands with a towel, wincing and glancing at the sore knuckles on his hand, and then walked to the front door. When he opened it, there stood Miku waving to Kasumi as the good-looking Ford began pulling away from the curb. There, on his front porch, stood the woman of his dreams. She paused momentarily, almost unsure of herself, something Joseph had only glimpsed in Miku before. She said nothing. Joseph held the door open for her, and she entered. He closed it behind her and helped her with her coat. Miku extended her arms, and they embraced. Joseph said softly, "Miku, are you all right?" She buried her head in his chest and began to cry. They stood in the hallway, holding on to each other as though if either of them let go, the other would be lost. Finally, Joseph said, "Let's go into the living room." He took her by the hand, and they walked over and sat on the sofa in front of the fireplace. As with all the furniture in the house, the sofa had been placed to provide a beautiful view of the bay.

Miku finally broke the silence, "Joseph, I want so much to be with you. Last night frightened me much more than I

North Pacific

had imagined possible. I lay awake much of the night, wondering whether we would be okay. This morning I went to Kasumi's after she had finished helping her dad at the market and asked for a ride here. I hope you're not upset I showed up at your doorstep unannounced?"

"Of course not," replied Joseph. I've always wanted you to see the place. Actually, it's beyond great just having you here."

She looked at his now slightly swollen hand and rubbed it gently. "Life can be so hard," she said in a subdued voice.

The two of them slowly became aware that they had never been truly alone together. The house and view were as peaceful as could be. After a while, Miku leaned into Joseph, and they kissed. Then each slowly became lost in the other. Being alone together became overpowering.

At some point, the two made their way to the upstairs bedroom. Later still, Joseph became conscious of Miku lying next to him asleep. He looked at Miku. He had never known a day like this. She stirred, and Joseph put his arm around her. She turned toward Joseph and nestled in closer to his body. The two said nothing, nothing needed to be said. Minutes passed, and then, with resolve, Joseph said, "Miku, stay with me. Don't leave, don't ever leave."

She whispered, "I can't say no."

They got up about thirty minutes later and found something to eat downstairs in the kitchen. Afterward, they lay propped up on one end of the sofa together, sharing intimate thoughts. Eventually, they went back upstairs and retired for the evening. The next day was Sunday. They did not attend Mass. Kasumi showed up around noon to see if everything was all right. She took Miku back to her aunt's apartment, where she gathered more clothes to bring to Joseph's house.

Joseph and Miku spent the next week juggling work responsibilities and time together. Their need for each other was palpable. Their need for physical contact was insatiate. In the house, as everyone did, Miku succumbed to the remarkable vistas from the bayside windows. She marveled at how the water's surface could change from perfectly ordered and silently still to the starkly contrasting chaotic wind-whipped white caps that would stretch in all directions angrily across the bay. The intimacy of the house, the panoramas of the Puget Sound region, and the snow-shrouded peak of Mt. Rainier towering to the east created a singularly idyllic setting. Being with Joseph, the man she loved, was intoxicating.

In private moments, Joseph surmised that this was what his dream had been about. He couldn't imagine it not being so. Joseph was finally with the woman he loved. All his years of loneliness were erased in a moment. At the same time, Joseph contemplated the dream-like state of his and Miku's relationship. The house now knew the "happiness" that Joseph had always sought.

~~~~~

North Pacific

It was about 7 PM on a Monday, a couple of weeks after Miku and Joseph had become inseparable. She sat in the living room on the sofa, staring at the flames in the fireplace. The small fire crackled, and Joseph, entering the room from the kitchen, said, "Let me stoke that for you."

"No, don't," responded Miku in a tone that caught Joseph off guard. "I need to tell you something." The subdued sound of her voice now made Joseph's brow crease slightly as to the possible weight of whatever Miku was about to say. She motioned to the seat cushion of the sofa next to her. Joseph, with no slight trepidation, sat down.

"I don't know how to say this, Joseph," Miku began. "I've been so happy during this time, happier than I can ever remember." She paused, searching for the words and courage to continue. She sighed. Then, raising her chin a bit and regaining eye contact with Joseph, she said, "I think my conscience has caught up with me." Miku looked for Joseph's reaction. Joseph, for his part, had an expression of concern. Suddenly she wanted to end the conversation but took a quick breath, and said, "We didn't go to Mass for the second week in a row." The statement hung in the air for the longest moment. "I don't think either of us brought up the subject because we didn't want to consider the implications of our actions. That thought and our circumstances stayed with me all yesterday."

"Today, before you returned from the campus, I was drinking a cup of tea, and the house was completely silent. Then, I asked myself, who am I? What am I doing? Our being together this way, as I have been taught my entire life, and I'm sure you also, is wrong. It is sinful. It is a sin in the eyes of God." Joseph continued to look at her. Upon hearing her words, the facial façade he was trying to present for Miku began crumbling badly around the edges. "It's not your fault Joseph," Miku stammered, "I practically threw myself at you, showing up and saying God knows what because I was afraid of possibly losing you."

Joseph finally interrupted, "Miku, what are you talking about?" He paused, his thoughts swirling in too many different directions. Then he continued, "I'm the one who asked you to stay with me. I made the decision that we had to be together."

Miku, with the saddest expression he had ever seen on her face, said in a plaintive voice, "I'm not sure you understand, Joseph. I'm telling you my conscience is practically screaming at me that our situation is deeply offending to God no matter how I feel about our relationship." Raising her voice ever so slightly, as if regretting every word she had just spoken, sadly, she said, "There, I said it."

Joseph realized he had stopped breathing. He tried to gather himself but couldn't. He wanted to say something but realized he had nothing to say that wasn't some sort of rationalization of their circumstances. Joseph leaned toward Miku and drew her close to him. Against his chest, she began sobbing. Joseph, fighting tears back, said, "I'm so sorry, Miku. I didn't mean to hurt you." To himself, he thought, "What have I done?" They were both silent. All either could hear was the faint dying sounds of the fire. They sat there for the longest time. Joseph finally asked her, "What does this mean?" Miku did not respond.

The fire had long since died. The young couple, still fully clothed, had fallen asleep on the sofa. The sun was up, and Joseph rose first and made some coffee. It was 6 AM. While Joseph was doing that, Miku got up and went to the bathroom. When she returned, Joseph handed her a cup of hot coffee. "What are we doing?" He asked.

"Joseph, I think," she paused, "I have to leave."

Joseph turned his head away and said, "I understand." He felt that if she was going to say it, that must be his only response. Again, she leaned into him, and he held her.

They both showered and dressed. When Miku opened her suitcase on the bed, Joseph couldn't take it and retreated down the stairs. Minutes later, she came down and walked over to Joseph, who was standing in the living room facing the bay. As she approached, Joseph turned and said, "I can't believe we're doing this." She started crying. They held each other again, and then Joseph gathered up her suitcase and other things and put them in his car. He drove her to her aunt's apartment, where he unloaded the car, taking the luggage up to the 2nd-floor in front of her aunt's door.

Miku hugged him one last time, kissed him, and in the smallest of voices, said, "Thank you, Joseph."

With that, he turned and walked away. He could hear Miku beginning to sob. He didn't turn back. He got in his car and drove. He drove slowly, aimlessly. He ended up parking down along the waterfront. He wanted to think, but it hurt too much.

21.

If Joseph thought he was alone before Miku came into his life, he was unprepared for the emptiness and solitude he endured after she left. He thought it best to give Miku some space and time to sort things out. This he did to the best of his abilities but after a couple of weeks and not hearing from her, he was devastated.

Joseph went to work each day. He was teaching a class during the summer session but remembered little of it. Students had questions during class, and he would try to let them resolve them by asking other students to answer them. For his part, he would stare blankly at the clock waiting for the class to end. He would go to his office, read his mail, and try to do administrative work, the bare minimum. When someone would knock on his office door, he would at once think Miku was going to walk in, but she did not. He could not concentrate.

Those students who persisted in wanting to ask questions knocked on his office door came in and sat across from him. They would talk about aspects of the coming final exam. He tried his best to explain what the test would cover and what he was looking for in the responses. Many students asked him if he was okay, to which he would nod in the affirmative, smile, and then show them to the door. After looking around for something to focus on, he would give up, put his coat on, and go for a walk on the campus. He would walk from one end of the college grounds to the other at least twice before settling into a chair in the library. No one bothered him there, and he was left to brood in an uneasy quietness.

One late afternoon Joseph left his office at the college and headed home. However, he did not want to go home. It meant thinking even more intensely about Miku. Yet, where else could he go? As Joseph neared his house, he decided he would instead get a drink down at Isaacs, at least delaying going home, a place he didn't want to be for the first time in his life. At Isaacs, he drank a couple of beers, talked to Leo, the bartender, for quite a spell, and then reluctantly drove home.

As he lay in bed that night, he tried again, for what seemed like the hundredth time to sort out the events of the last month. Retrospectively, he now could clearly see he should have had a real heart-to-heart with Miku the day after the incident with Ron Huddleston at Isaacs instead of letting what happened play out the way it did. He had learned about Miku's faith from their many talks and how important it was to her. He talked about his own faith with others. He spoke to God about his faith. But he didn't live his faith. What was wrong with him? Why was he always making these horrible decisions? Why didn't he think about this before it occurred? He remembered confessing his sin with Eloise and how old Father Simone had attempted to get him to see his actions were offensive to God and disrespectful to women. He knew all this in his head. It just didn't translate into his actions. He thought to himself, big shot, graduate degree, beyond selfish.

Joseph had tried to give Miku space. He didn't know what he would say to her when they got together again. He hoped she might turn up at the house unexpectedly as she had that fateful Saturday weeks ago. It did not happen. Also, he still had not been back to Mass, not wanting to confess to Father Etienne his transgressions regarding his inability to follow God's commandments. Joseph finally attended Mass one Sunday morning, hoping to see Miku, but he did not see her or her aunt. Before Mass began, he did not go to confession. Instead, he sat in the back of the church and left just as those about to receive communion walked toward the altar rail. He shuddered, knowing he could not receive communion in a state of mortal sin.

Once back at home, Joseph said to himself enough was enough. He decided he would go downtown to that apartment, knock on the door, and tell Miku how wrong he had been. He would say whatever was necessary so they might have a chance to make things right between them. He had no idea how it would go, but go he would. He loved her, and that was all that mattered.

Joseph's resolve grew as he drove downtown. He parked the car, walked into the apartment building, and with determination, climbed the stairs to the second floor. He knocked on the door. His heart was pounding. No one answered. He knocked again. There was just silence. He returned to the lobby and then walked around outside, killing time. An hour later, he returned to the apartment and noticed the door was open this time. Joseph looked in and saw an older gentleman walking around in the living room.

"Excuse me, sir," Joseph said as the man turned toward the door. "I know Mrs. Moriya and her niece. Do you know where they are?" Joseph noticed as he stepped inside the doorway that the room seemed empty save for a few pieces of furniture.

"They have moved out," replied the man.

"What? Why?" Joseph blurted out.

"Mrs. Moriya did not say. They paid their rent and were gone in a day."

"When was that?"

"Yesterday."

Joseph's head almost exploded. "Seriously, did they leave you a forwarding address?"

"No."

"Damn," Joseph muttered to himself. "Thanks for talking to me."

The man nodded and returned to assessing the state of the apartment.

North Pacific

Joseph left. As he drove home, he turned over in his head all the possibilities he could think of for their leaving. None made any sense.

The next day, while in his office, he tried to track down Miku's friend, Kasumi. He remembered that Kasumi's last name was Takahara from when they had met at Isaacs. There was more than one Takahara in the phone book. From his office phone, Joseph decided to try all of them. He found her on the third number.

"Kasumi," this is Joseph Vaenko. "Do you remember me?"

"Sure, Joseph. What can I do for you?"

"I'm looking for Miku. Do you know where she might be? I discovered that she and her aunt had moved out of the apartment they had been renting."

Surprised, Kasumi said, "Joseph, I really don't know where they are. I talked to Miku just last week. She said nothing about moving."

"Was she okay when you talked to her? Was there anything wrong or something out of the ordinary going on?"

"No, I ran into her Downtown. She didn't say anything was wrong. Maybe she was a bit preoccupied, but all in all, she seemed all right to me. Do you know something, Joseph?"

"No, I don't, Kasumi. Did you know that we broke things off a while back?"

North Pacific

"Yes, Joseph, Miku mentioned it in passing, and I could tell instantly that it was a topic she did not want to discuss, so I didn't."

"So, did she say anything about it, anything at all?"

"She just said it was a difficult situation and asked if we could leave it at that. I didn't press her on it."

"Would you be all right with meeting sometime soon to continue this conversation, Joseph asked?"

"Well, I don't want to get in the middle of something I know nothing about. Affairs of the heart, especially when they involve friends, should probably be resolved by those involved."

"Well, I certainly understand, Kasumi. I just want to learn anything I can that might help me find her, and I get that you want to make sure Miku's interests are protected. Let's follow your thought and not meet. You always know where to find me if you ever want to talk. Thank you, Kasumi."

Kasumi tried to cheer Joseph up a bit, and then the two said goodbye.

That night, Joseph sat in the big chair facing the bay and watched the lights of a freighter as the vessel turned into East Passage, heading north. He had struggled all day thinking about where Miku might be. He deliberated for quite some time about why Miku and her aunt had moved. Where? Why? The more he thought about it, the more the idea came to him that Miku might have returned to Seattle. Yes, Seattle, that's where she was from. I'm sure she has lots of friends living up there. None of this made sense, especially the idea that her aunt would accompany her. Was there something wrong with her aunt? Why would Miku leave and not let me know? Yes, I understand that we had ended badly, and she was distraught, but was it really the end? Was that it? Or was this her way of sorting things out? Joseph's mind darted from one possibility to the next. It's Seattle, he thought to himself. I'm going to drive to Seattle and find her. I will tell her that I love her with all my heart.

Joseph felt alone and lost. He prayed to God to help him fix the situation. He realized that he needed to go to confession about his actions. He also knew it was not going to happen anytime soon. Having Miku and then losing her had shaken him in ways he had not imagined. His nightly prayers had turned into one-way shouting matches with God not responding.

That weekend he drove to Seattle to find Miku. He scoured her old neighborhood in and around the Broadway area as she had described it. He talked to as many people as he could. He actually found some locals who remembered the family, some well, others casually. Everyone he spoke to had not seen, heard from, or had any idea of Miku's whereabouts. All wished Joseph well in his search, but none could help him find her. Driving south back to Tacoma that Sunday evening on Highway 99, Joseph began to slip into a mental depression that felt like falling slowly into a void—an experience reminiscent of his dream after his mother's passing.

North Pacific

22.

In the following days, Joseph rose early and mechanically went to work. He taught his classes. He met with students, many asking the same question, "Are you okay, Mr. Vaenko?" He attended departmental meetings. He did everything he was supposed to do. Yet, upon his return to his house each night, he began changing into casual clothing and walking down the steep 30th Street hill to Isaacs, where he would sit at the bar and drink. He had decided he wasn't interested in a world that did not include Miku. He just didn't care. Joseph would drink slowly but steadily until his head could no longer make sense of anything. Then, late in the evening, Leo, the bartender, would say, "Isn't it about time you head for home, Joe?"

Joseph began to use Leo as an alarm clock that told him it was time to head up the hill so that he would be able to go to work the next day. He never drove his car down to Isaacs because he knew it would be dangerous for him to try to drive home. It wasn't that he was afraid of possibly injuring himself or worse, he didn't care, but he did not want anyone else to pay the price because of how he felt about this damn world.

One night, weeks after Joseph started frequenting Isaacs in the evenings, Leo, concerned about the professor, tried to engage him in conversation to find out what was going on in his life. Joseph, as usual, managed to parry Leo's best intentions through silence and, quite frankly, the inability, because of the alcohol, to carry on a decent conversation even if he had wanted to. No, he was much more content just to let the liquor marinate his brain…slowly. Screw the world. Finally, Leo said, "It's about time you headed home, Joe."

Joseph didn't hear him at first but finally acknowledged Leo's stare, nodded in his direction, and slowly slid off the barstool. He gained his footing, to some degree, and with deliberate steps, walked out of the bar. He felt the breeze coming up from the bay and tried to button his jacket. After a few attempts, he gave up and headed for the ascending 30th Street hill. He was almost to the base of the hill when he heard voices behind him. Joseph could make out a voice he knew as they grew louder and closer. It was Ron Huddleston, the guy he had punched a few months ago for calling Miku and Kasumi "Japs."

As Joseph turned to see precisely where Huddleston was, Vaenko was rocked with a blow to the side of his head that caused him to lose his balance - what little he had - and tumble to the sidewalk. Ron, whom he could see now as he looked up from the ground, kicked Joseph in the ribs. Joseph rolled over slowly into some knee-high grass next to the sidewalk. Stunned momentarily by the power of the blow to the side of his head, Joseph tried to get up. He might have made it, but the punch and his drunken state combined made him lose his balance and tumble to the ground again. A second try at getting up resulted in being kicked in the head and dropping from an almost kneeling position back into the tall grass. From there, it was a free for all, with Huddleston kicking and slugging the helpless Vaenko. Joseph tried in a losing effort to protect his head and the rest of himself. He heard Ron cursing him and his "Jap whores," but Joseph could muster no response. After a few minutes, one of Ron's friends grabbed him and said, "Stop it, you're going to kill him." Huddleston kicked Joseph one last time and then stepped back.

"Bohunk," Huddleston snorted and then walked away.

The laughter slowly subsided as the assailant and his friends made their way back toward the row of shops, bars, and restaurants in Old Town.

Joseph lay there for the longest time. The mixture of the pummeling and the alcohol had left him in a stupor. At some point, Joseph felt he had regained the use of his brain enough to attempt to get up. He failed. He lay there for a while longer and then tried again. This time he managed to stand. He wished he hadn't. He vomited. He hurt everywhere. Joseph realized he could only see from one eye. The other was swollen shut. The taste of blood and vomit in his mouth was awful. His head was bruised and scraped, with caked blood on his face and now matted hair. His jacket and pants were smeared with red splotches and dirt. Every step he took brought sharp pain that emanated from his ribs. One slow step after another, he struggled up the hill. He had no idea if he could make it, but he did. The alcohol and the pain from the beating were a horrible combination to which Joseph was slowly succumbing. The last thing he remembered was being in his house and wanting to clean his wounds. Instead, he collapsed on the hallway floor. He awoke there just outside the bathroom a little before dawn.

It was the worst feeling he had ever experienced. His head was pounding. His side screamed agony. He crawled into the bathroom, slowly removed his clothes, and got into the combination tub and shower. He turned the water on and flipped the toggle that allowed the water to cascade down on him from the shower head. As the water heated, he slumped down in the tub and let the hot water fall on him as he lay motionless. He lay there until the hot water ran out. He turned off the shower and slowly cleaned his scrapes and bruises as best he could. He turned the shower on again and rinsed in semi-cold water. He couldn't believe how he looked.

Thankfully, it was Saturday, and he had nowhere to go. He poured himself a bowl of cereal and percolated a pot of coffee. He spent the rest of the day lying on the sofa in the living room, sleeping and taking aspirin. By Sunday, he felt almost alive. He nursed his wounds and called in sick to the college on Monday morning. By Wednesday, he thought he was almost recognizable.

Some things had not changed. Even more so now, Joseph did not feel as though life was worth living. Again, all he wanted to do was dull the pain. He was back at Isaacs Bar by the following weekend, where he resumed his self-medication regimen to forget.

Thankful that he had not broken any bones, the physical cuts and deep bruises healed. Joseph restarted his routine of drinking away his thoughts about Miku and his loneliness. A significant difference was that now Joseph drove his car down the hill to the bar. He had quit walking down there in the evenings. He made a point of parking his vehicle, pointing up the hill so that all he had to do was drive five blocks up, turn, drive one block, and park in front of his house. Also, while at the bar, on his stool, he was aware of his effort to be a bit more friendly and attentive to Leo and his attempts at conversation. Joseph surmised that this was because he must be building up a higher tolerance level to alcohol. This, of course, was nothing to be proud of, he thought, but it was something.

23.

It was Fall, Joseph thought, as the Pacific Northwest wind and rain moved into the southern and central Puget Sound regions. He couldn't remember all the details, but one night as he was staring at the liquor bottles facing him from across the bar, a woman with steely-looking ash-blonde hair that came down to almost the middle of her back eased up onto the stool next to his and began to make conversation. Joseph didn't say much at first, as was his way with his lately found "dull the senses" program. However, she was persistent and attractive, so he tried to focus on her. She had to be about 5 foot 4, wore dark makeup around her eyes, and one could easily see she was well-proportioned and extremely appealing. Upon further observation, Joseph felt she had a certain tiredness about her demeanor, yet even it had a particular attraction. She looked to be in her early thirties. He remembered them learning each other's names. Hers was Jill something – Conners, he thought. She told him she lived with her father in Ruston, a small company town of sorts built around the smelting plant near Point Defiance Park. They must have talked for an hour. He bought her another drink.

Even though Joseph seemed to drift in and out of the conversation at points, he tried his best to pay attention to what she was saying. It was then that she placed her hand on his leg. She removed it almost at once. She did it again a few minutes later and left it there longer. Joseph remembered looking hard at her. He didn't remember a lot more of the conversation, but at some point, she told him that her girlfriend had had to leave early, stranding her there. She asked him if she could maybe get a ride home when he left. Joseph willingly obliged. Once in the car, Jill asked where he lived. He said just up the hill. She asked him if he had a view, and the next thing he knew, he was standing next to her in his living room, staring out into the darkness at the lights surrounding the bay.

When he awoke the following morning, Joseph had a hazy recollection of the previous evening. As he turned over onto his side, Jill was lying beside him in his bed. She stirred and, reaching out toward him, whispered, "Come here." He obliged. Later that morning, Joseph dropped Jill off at her place in Ruston and then drove to work at the college.

Joseph did not think about it at first, but before long a new routine had developed in what he considered to be his now sorry life. He would go down to Isaacs in the evening, while Jill would get a ride there after her shift as a cocktail waitress at a downtown hotel. The two would drink and eventually wind up at Joseph's, where they would engage in sex and then sleep.

This went on for close to two weeks, and then one morning, Joseph awoke earlier than usual from the previous night's round of drinks and sexual activity. Jill was still asleep next to him. So he tried for the first time in a month to think about what was going on. He found himself struggling to string together actual thoughts through the horrid hangover that was pounding in his head. Why am I trying to think? Isn't the idea, the plan, the strategy not to do that? He turned his head from one side to the other a few times in an attempt to focus more clearly on his thoughts. His head hurt even more. Why was he trying to break the rules he had created to block out his feelings for Miku? And then it struck him. He felt as lonely at that moment with Jill, a real person, right next to him as he had when no one was there. It was a feeling of emptiness, of being very alone.

North Pacific

A few minutes later, Jill awakened. She began kissing Joseph and pressed her body against his. Again, he succumbed to her warmth and sensualness. It wasn't hard.

Later that day, Joseph sat in his office at the college and tried to expand on the thought he had surprised himself with that morning. How could he be lonely? Loneliness was being alone. He wasn't alone. Jill was very much with him. Hell, he could make the argument that he had never been more intimately entwined with anyone in his life. He was not alone, he insisted to himself. Yet, the thought about loneliness had developed into something more concrete that needed to be figured out.

Miku, Miku, Miku, Joseph thought to himself. I'm not trying to equate my feelings for her to my relationship with Jill. I'm trying to figure out how I can feel lonely when someone is with me. To be sure, Jill and I have not had any conversations about our feelings for each other. I'm confident this is the classic definition of a physical relationship. It worked. We were there, each for our own reasons. We stumbled into each other, possibly literally, found each other physically attractive, and followed the happenstance to its logical conclusion. It came to him that this was a one-night stand that persisted because he would not face what was truly happening.

"It is nothing like what Miku and I shared - nothing like it at all." It was then that Joseph realized he was thinking aloud. He looked around a bit self-consciously, got up from his chair, and walked over to the window in his office. He stared for a minute or two at the stands of giant evergreen trees that populated the college grounds. He exhaled. His head still hurt from last night. He rummaged through his desk for the bottle of aspirin that had become a necessary office supply over the previous few months. Joseph poured out a couple and took them, washing them down with the dregs of a cold cup of coffee.

When he got home from work, his routine was to change clothes and head down the hill to Isaacs. Today, however, he changed clothes, but instead of heading down the hill, sat down at his desk in the bedroom and began working on a class lecture. Here in his bedroom, as downstairs, he had a splendid view of the bay, albeit somewhat smaller. Joseph's thoughts that day had been troubling him. So much so that it occurred to him that maybe he shouldn't go out that night. He decided that's what he would do. It was the right thing to do. He would stay home.

Again he thought, what am I doing? No matter how I might try to rationalize or otherwise justify my actions, I know my behavior has been terribly destructive over the last couple of weeks. Who am I? Why is my life such a mess? Yes, I am lonely. Being with Jill is great, but oh so wrong. There's nothing wrong with Jill. It's me. I hate myself. God, I need a drink.

The evening was incredibly hard for Joseph. He really needed a drink. Instead, he took off walking. It was already dark. He headed towards the grocery store a good half-mile away. He picked up some groceries and returned home. He made himself a little something to eat and then retired to the bedroom upstairs, where he attempted to do some reading. He found concentrating impossible and still wanted and needed a drink to stabilize himself. He went to bed early and tossed and turned all night. It was a dreadful night. He was miserable. One drink would be all right, he thought to himself. It's six in the morning, you fool. And you won't be able to just have one. He got up, made some coffee, and decided to walk to the campus. It rained. He didn't care. He was short with colleagues all day. He was a mess. Later that day, he walked home again in the rain.

Upon arriving at the house, he peeled off his wet clothes and showered. Joseph stood under the showerhead until the hot water ran out as it had the night Ron Huddleston had beaten him half to death. He decided to stay home again and not go down to Isaacs. Joseph lasted 10 minutes before putting on his coat and hat and taking a walk. This time he walked back up to the college, through the campus, over to the neighborhood shopping district, and then, finally, headed back to his place. It started raining on the walk home, and he was soaked when he walked in his front door. He ate something and then tried to clean the house to keep busy and not think about the world's temptations. After scrubbing the kitchen, the clock said 10:30 PM. He really wanted a drink. He went upstairs to go to bed. The doorbell rang.

Joseph came downstairs and opened the door. It was Jill. She walked in, took off her coat, and handed it to Joseph. He asked her, "How did you get here?"

North Pacific

"I walked up that horrible hill. What's up with you? You didn't come to Isaacs last night or tonight."

Joseph walked her into the living room. He could tell she had been drinking. She wasn't drunk, just relaxed. He had never really looked at her when he hadn't been drinking, yet she was still a beautiful woman. "I'm sorry, Jill, I felt like maybe I needed to back off on the drinking a bit. It's a bad look for a college professor."

She laughed a little, turned, and put her arms around Joseph's neck. She slowly and softly said, "Did you miss me last night? Do you miss me right now?"

Joseph, aroused, now grudgingly nodded in the affirmative. They kissed. Joseph thought he should stop kissing her and try talking to her about their situation. He didn't. After a few minutes, they went up to the bedroom, the clothes came off, and once again, they had sex. Joseph noticed that the sex was more tactile and much more pleasurable when he was not drunk.

When they had finished and Jill had fallen asleep, Joseph lay in the bed, his conscience gnawing at him. What I'm doing is wrong. This is not the way my parents raised me. This is not what I learned from the teachings of the Church. This is not the way to respect and treat Jill. He slid out of bed, went downstairs, grabbed a blanket and a pillow, and fell asleep on the sofa. The following day was a Saturday. He got up and started a pot of coffee. As the coffee finished percolating, he heard Jill lightly coming down the stairs from the bedroom. "Morning, Jill."

She walked over to him and gave him a very warm hug. "What's wrong, Joseph."

"What do you mean?" Joseph said while opening the refrigerator door and withdrawing a carton of eggs. "Let me make you some scrambled eggs with a little cheese and toast for breakfast?"

Jill smiled, "Sure, but let's talk." She looked alluring as usual, wearing one of Joseph's t-shirts that hung on her in a way that accentuated her great-looking hips and legs. "Tell me what's bugging you and what's really going on, Joseph?"

Joseph had already retrieved the newspaper. He pulled off the rubber band and handed it to Jill. "Here, look at the paper while I fix these eggs." He cracked the eggs into the pan.

Jill nodded and sat at the kitchen table, trying to figure out what was going on with her companion. She sat with one heel up on the chair's seat and her arm around her knee while glancing at the paper. Joseph plated the eggs, buttered the toast, and poured the coffee. Along with silverware and cloth napkins, he put a jar of raspberry jam and a pepper shaker on the table. They ate.

Joseph took the last bite of his eggs and then, looking down at the plate, took a deep breath and said, "Jill, I guess I want to say that our relationship is based pretty much on just sex." He slowly looked up to see how she took what he was saying.

North Pacific

Jill, for her part, looked away from him for a moment and, without looking back at him, replied, "Is there something wrong with me?"

"Of course not," was Joseph's firm reply. He continued, "The fact is, to put it as basically as I can, we don't really know each other. We talk down at Isaacs, but you know, and I know, I've been drunk practically every night down there for weeks. I don't even know what I'm saying half the time when we talk, and for sure, we don't talk once we get here. You know what I mean."

Jill tilted her head and finally engaged him with her eyes. "Do you not like making love to me?"

"To the contrary, I'm completely yours in that regard. Physically, it would almost be impossible for me to tell you no. Didn't last night make that clear?"

"But you didn't stay with me in bed. You went down to the living room."

"Jill, that's my problem. I have been sober for a couple of days and thought a lot about our situation, so I wanted to talk to you. We don't know each other. I think you are a beautiful woman, and I am drawn to you on that account, but what we have between us is wrong." Joseph, raising his voice, slightly frustrated with himself, said, "Do you know why I've been going down to Isaacs and getting smashed every night? It's because of a woman who broke my heart and has disappeared. And now, to top it off, I've taken advantage of you. My plan, my stupid plan, that's what I call it, to drink myself into oblivion so as not to think about that woman, ends up with us getting together. You come along and wow me with your great looks, and I don't know what to do." Joseph got up from the table, ran his hand through his hair, and leaned against the kitchen sink.

Jill stared at him for a few moments and said, "I thought we were just having a good time."

Now it was Jill's turn to move, getting up out of her chair, walking over to Joseph, and again putting her arms around his neck. "Honey, I guess I understand what you're saying, but I'm not certain I understand why you want to give up what we have going," as she lay her head on his chest.

Joseph could feel her body exude warmth through the t-shirt she was wearing. "Jill, you have no idea how much I don't want this to end as he put his arms around her and pressed her body tightly against his, but it's just not right." He gently disengaged and walked out into the living room.

The conversation continued out there as she joined him. "Jill, tell me about yourself."

"Well, I'm from a small town in northern California. When my mom and dad split up, my dad got a job at the smelting plant in Ruston, and I eventually came up here to look out for him. Dad works hard and probably drinks too much. Maybe that's where I got my taste for it. I've always worked. I was married once, but it didn't last. We couldn't have kids. Maybe that was part of it. Anyway, I'm a waitress, I'm a cocktail waitress, but you know that, right?"

Joseph nodded. He did remember at least that much.

She looked out the big window. "Did I ever tell you this is an amazing view? It really is." Again, she moved close to Joseph, and they both sat on the sofa. "What are we going to do? We're not even fighting," she said, starting to laugh. "This gal you've been talking about, you know, the one that broke your heart. She must be pretty special."

Joseph put his arm around her, and the both of them took in the view of the bay. A little later, Jill went upstairs and got dressed. Joseph drove her home. Then on the way to the college later that morning, Joseph, thinking of Jill, decided, and said aloud, "Do the right thing, Joe."

24.

The next day was Sunday, Joseph's third day on the wagon. He wondered how he had gotten himself into this situation. He shook his head and wondered if he should go to Mass. To go to Mass and receive holy communion would obviously require him going to confession beforehand and revealing his sins of fornication and missed Masses to Father Etienne. He just couldn't do it. He instead made breakfast and stood with a cup of coffee, looking out at the bay. It was only later that day that he broke down.

Joseph sat at his desk in the bedroom and struggled with the choices he had made. He had in his heart shamed the memory of his parents. He had shown a great lack of respect for women. He had sinned against the commandments and no longer received Christ's graces in the Church's Sacraments. To top it off, with his decisions, he would lose a friend in Father Etienne. So much had gone wrong for him in so short a time. The problem was, of course, of his own making. How could one guy screw things up so badly?

He finally asked the right question. You can't take it back, he thought to himself, but what are you going to do about it? He remembered his mother asking him that question whenever he had a problem as a youngster. Joseph would explain to her the issue confronting him, whether it be at school or with friends. She always asked him, what are you going to do about it? It would be that kick in the pants to get him out there and do something. He smiled slightly, touched the medal around his neck his mother had given him, and sheepishly whispered, "Thanks, Mom, I think I know what to do."

Later that afternoon, after the Masses were over for that Sunday, Joseph came through the large doors and sat unworthily in the back of the beautiful stone church. He knelt and prayed.

He sat back in the pew and noted that St. Dominic seemed an example of that kind of wonderful old Catholic church that so stirred his spirit. Yet it went beyond its beautiful architecture. He was specifically thinking about how Catholics acted in Church. They were always highly aware of the Blessed Sacrament in the tabernacle on the high altar. People spoke in more hushed tones the closer they might get to the proximity of the sanctuary where the tabernacle resided. Catholics, without exception, genuflected when approaching or passing by the Blessed Sacrament. They bowed their heads when praying, showing, at all times, an "I am not worthy" posture in front of the *real presence* of Christ in the Eucharist.

He knelt again and said, "Forgive me, Lord, for my indiscretions. I am sorry for my transgressions and misdeeds against You, Miku, and Jill. I will be going to confession soon. I promise. Jesus, my Lord, and Savior, I turn to you and ask that you please help me understand what Your will is for me so I may try to live the life you want. I want to do your will, not mine. Slava, na viky!" (Glory to Him forever!)

Again, he sat back in the pew. He listened. After a while, he heard one of the main doors at the back of the church creak. Footsteps sounded as someone came in and knelt in a pew on the other side of the nave. Joseph leaned forward, kneeling one more time, thanked God for listening to his prayer, and then left the silent stone building.

Joseph was going to try to rebuild his life. He discovered that relentless walking helped him with all his physical withdrawal issues and even his personal challenges. So, the new Joseph was forever throwing himself out the front door and walking whenever he had the urge to go to Isaacs or think about Miku or, God help him, Jill. This was all well and good, yet he still couldn't find the courage of his faith and beliefs to confess his sins. The self-inflicted damage to his soul ached within him.

25.

It was Monday evening, just three days before Thanksgiving. Joseph was sitting at his desk upstairs, going over some papers.

Suddenly, he was startled by a powerful flash of light out on the bay. Joseph watched the sudden burst of luminescence as it reflected off the starboard bow anchor of a ship, illuminated faintly by the vessel's navigation lights but more so by the waxing gibbous moon that hung over Tacoma's Commencement Bay.

Continuing to watch the ship, Joseph realized that he had looked up from his desk just before the flash, not because of it. He had been reading and writing when it seemed his head had been involuntarily lifted. He was surprised the ship had escaped his attention, seeing as it had already traversed East Passage coming south from Seattle, cleared Browns Point, all in his line of sight, and was now entering the bay.

The ship gradually turned to port as Joseph watched, presenting more of her silhouette, courtesy of the late fall moonlight. She was a freighter of medium size, dark-hulled, and four-masted – a venerable West Coast transport vessel he had watched come and go from these waters for the last three decades. She was clearly empty, with no cargo in sight, and riding high in the water, exposing her bottom paint. As he tried to make out the ship's name, which remained indistinct in the dimness, he noticed a pair of local green and white dieselized Foss tugs pushing bow waves, heading out from the port to assist the vessel with her docking. Based on her size, shape, and booms, Joseph presumed the freighter was heading for the lumber dock to be loaded with logs, cut lumber, or both.

Yet, as he studied the silent vessel, he was unsure why this ship, this shadowy slow-motion image, held his attention. Perhaps, the glancing burst of light had been caused by an aberration of how the unbalanced moonlight of that late fall evening had inclined upon the vessel in the now dark gray-green waters of the bay. He could not take his eyes off of it. Initially a powerful flash, the light seemed to cling to its existence much longer than one would associate with a phenomenon of this sort, yet it did. It fiercely persisted, almost burning in a sense, for agonizing moments as if a powerful force was attempting to break free of its internment.

The flash's sheer power, the ship's inexorable movement, and the strange, almost otherworldly darkness surrounding the flash's fight for survival left him unexpectedly unsettled. He tried to return to his paperwork, but the strange episode kept returning to his thoughts for the rest of the evening.

North Pacific

~~~~~

Life returned to some measure of normalcy for Joseph. He started coming straight home at night after finishing up at the college. He brought work home with him and, after a quick meal, would go upstairs and be busy at his desk until he could not keep his eyes open any longer and would have to retire for the evening. It brought back memories of his endless hours of studying as a student in that house. His work seemed endless after neglecting it for too long.

~~~~~

Martin had stopped by a few days earlier and invited Joseph for Thanksgiving dinner. Joseph accepted and had an enjoyable evening at the Linarts, playing with the kids and talking to Martin and Colleen. During dinner, the three agreed they needed to get together more often. Colleen asked him if he was seeing anyone, particularly that cute gal, Miku. Joseph smiled and lied, saying Miku had helped her aunt move to Seattle, and he had not seen her in a while. After a big dessert, including pumpkin pie with vanilla ice cream, He thanked them for having him over. As Joseph was ready to leave, Martin told him he had gotten hold of a couple of tickets to the Texas A&M vs. Washington State College football game being played, at what the locals called Stadium Bowl, the Saturday after next and did he want to go with him. Joseph said it sounded great and that he would drive.

~~~~~

Two days later, Joseph was picking up around the house on Saturday morning when he looked out at the bay from the living room and saw, to his surprise, the same ship that had so troubled him earlier in the week. He remembered back to the disquiet the merchant ship had caused him. He never had, to his recollection, ever experienced, what was the word he was looking for - the evil - he felt watching the eerily smoldering dying flash reflecting off the vessel's anchor as it had entered the bay. He shuddered once again at its memory.

The ship was loaded with sawn lumber on the stern and logs from amidships forward. There seemed to be nothing startling about her this morning. She rode low in the water as would befit her cargo. He watched as she angled to starboard to head north up the passage, eventually to enter the North Pacific. As she showed her stern to Joseph, he clearly saw the name, *Cynthia Olsen*.

Imperceptibly, in waters far to the south and west of Puget Sound, incipient storm clouds began to dot the horizon.

26.

On Saturday, December 6th, the inaugural "Evergreen" Bowl was played under the lights of the naturally carved-out bowl that gave Stadium High School and its football field a magnificent presence towering over Commencement Bay. The high school building itself a converted luxury hotel, resembled a French château. Initially built for the Northern Pacific Railroad as a hotel, it was unique, to say the least. There were few venues anywhere that could match the breathtaking power of this setting. Joseph had found a parking spot about four blocks from the stadium in a neighborhood of stately homes that looked out over the bay. He and Martin walked to the stadium and found their seats. Texas A&M had won the National College Football Title in 1939 and was playing Washington State College from Pullman in Eastern Washington. This first-time bowl game for the City of Tacoma relied heavily on nine WSC Cougars from Tacoma's two public high schools to help fill the stands. The game was a sell-out and drew over 25,000 fans. The Aggies were 8-1, had won the Southwest Conference, and had already accepted a Cotton Bowl invitation for New Year's Day. The Cougars were 6-3 but had shut out four of their last five opponents.

North Pacific

The Cougars had a touchdown called back early in the game. They dominated play until just before half-time when an Aggie wide receiver beat the WSC safety for a 38-yard touchdown pass completion.

During halftime, Martin queried Joseph as to his well-being. "How are you doing, Joe?"

"I'm good," said Joseph, staring at the marching band on the field.

"No, come on, you seem even more reclusive than usual. You seem consumed by something. What is it? Is it that woman of yours, Miku? You told Colleen you hadn't seen her in a while. Is that what's bugging you?"

"Aw, Martin, it's complicated."

"So, enlighten me."

"Martin, she's gone."

"Whoa. What do you mean?"

"It means I think she's left Tacoma, and I don't know where she is?"

"I'm sorry, Joe. I don't know what to say."

"Thanks, it's been a rough year for me, but I'm trying my best to figure things out. I've done a poor job to this point, but I'm attempting to turn it around. I really screwed up my relationship with Miku, but I didn't think it might end this way." He decided not to tell Martin about Jill.

"Hang in there, buddy. You have done a lot to improve your life, you know, big shot professor and all. You'll figure it out. Hey, if there's anything I can do to help, seriously, let me know."

"Thanks, Martin."

The teams came back onto the field to start the second half. The two lifelong friends watched the rest of the game. The defenses stiffened, and there was no more scoring. It ended with Texas A&M winning 7-0. Martin and Joseph had a good time, and as a bonus, there was no rain. Joseph dropped Martin off at his place, and they agreed to have lunch the following week.

~~~~~

Joseph went to bed that evening around midnight. He debated whether to go to Mass in the morning. He had felt good about stopping by St. Dominic and praying in front of the Blessed Sacrament, but he had still not gone to confession or talked to Father Etienne. It seemed like he was doing everything he could to avoid confessing his sins to the good Father. He supposed he could go to another Catholic church in town, there were many, but that just seemed wrong. He had gone to Mass his entire life at St. Dominic. Yet, if he did go to confession somewhere else and then go to Mass at St. Dominic, he would have to approach the altar rail and receive communion from Father Etienne. Wouldn't that be an encounter after months of being a no-show at Mass?

North Pacific

Besides his solitary visit to the Blessed Sacrament, why was he not praying to God as he once did? Was it because he didn't feel God was listening to him with all his prayers for real love and happiness? Well yeah, that was a reason now that he was thinking about it. How many prayers and other conversations had he had with the Almighty? He could recall his Mother's death and how terrible that was, and because of her suffering, how, for the first time, he had formulated the question, what if God doesn't exist? If there was a God, he wouldn't, he couldn't allow this to happen, but he did. God, if he existed, didn't seem to care all that much for him in the sense that the things that mattered most to him, his parents and happiness, all ended up causing him nothing but profound grief. He didn't understand it. It made no sense to him and contributed to his lately lax approach to adhering to the tenets of the faith. At least, that is what he tried weakly to convince himself was the problem.

As he tossed and turned, trying to fall asleep, his mind recalled the issues in his life that were not settled, beginning with Miku. What a terrible situation. Where was she? Did something happen to Mrs. Moriya? Was she taking care of her aunt? If she loved me, as she claimed at one point, why didn't she give me a chance to show her how much she meant to me and try to work things out? I miss her so much.

As his eyes drooped, he thought, what about Jill? He decided she was another victim in his sad, sad journey to self-destruction. He closed his eyes and asked God to hear his concerns. Please help me understand my life and what you want me to do to serve you. Of course, he did not hear a direct reply. He contemplated stories of saints and others who had had experiences hearing God speak to them, telling them what to do. From that moment forward, these saints would dedicate their lives to Christ and perform great acts of love and charity. It seemed pretty clear to him that it was probably not his lot in life to have that experience. And with that thought, he finally drifted off into a troubled slumber.

As Joseph finally fell asleep that night, he had no way of knowing that out in the Pacific, the ship that had caused such unrest in his heart upon her visit to Tacoma less than two weeks ago was steaming south toward the Hawaiian Islands as the calendar turned to December 7, 1941.

BELLUM
(War)

"...and the perils of hell have found me."

Psalm 114:3

Douay-Rheims

North Pacific

27.

It was 8 AM on December 7, 1941. The freighter *Cynthia Olsen*, the ship Joseph had watched arrive and depart from Tacoma's harbor a few weeks earlier, was on schedule and making good time on her way to Honolulu. The weather was clear, with only harmless-looking cumulus clouds on the distant horizon. Out of nowhere, an ominous-looking submarine surfaced a couple hundred yards from the *Cynthia Olsen*. From its large deck gun, it fired a shell that whistled across the freighter's bow, raising a column of spray as it crashed into the sea.

The captain, a veteran of the Great War (1914-1918), ordered the engine to be cut, slowing the freighter to a halt. Next, he instructed the stars and stripes to be run up the mast to be clearly seen by the submarine. The captain planned to show that *Cynthia Olsen* was an unarmed neutral merchant vessel wishing no trouble. The captain's first inclination was that the submarine must be German. The German U-boats were sinking ships in the Atlantic and Indian Oceans and possibly had extended their operations to the Pacific. He also spoke to his radio operator and had him send out a distress call.

Meanwhile, the submarine impatiently fired a second warning shot and signaled with flags ordering the freighter's crew to abandon the ship. There was no more time for speculation for the American skipper, who at once ordered the ship's two large lifeboats to be lowered. The crew scrambled into the boats. As soon as they were away from the ship, the submarine opened fire with its deck gun on the helpless freighter.

The projectiles sprang ferociously from the submarine's deck-mounted gun to the merchant ship. There was an instantaneous spark at the point of impact on *Cynthia Olsen*. This time the power of the dark and malevolent flash that had given Joseph such unrest when he had viewed it from his window, erupted into the Pacific and the defenseless *Cynthia Olsen*. This initial attack was followed in minutes by flames and fires breaking out all over the old freighter. Smoke roiled over the decks and lumber cargo onboard. Later in the day, ablaze and riddled by gunfire, she would take on water, roll over, and plummet to the bottom.

The sinking of *Cynthia Olsen* would coincide with the surprise Japanese attack on Pearl Harbor. The submarine was not German but Japanese. In Hawaii that morning, an estimated 2,335 American military personnel were killed in the Pearl Harbor attack. The thirty-three civilian crew members and two military personnel aboard *Cynthia Olsen* were never found. Eventually, they were counted among the deaths that marked the beginning of the War in the Pacific.

The daring sneak attack on the U.S. Naval Fleet at Pearl Harbor started a war that would eventually take the lives of over a hundred thousand U.S. soldiers and sailors. The War in the Pacific would encompass Southeast Asia, East Asia, the Central Pacific, and the North Pacific. It would not end until 1945 and forever changed the lives of all that survived it.

~~~~~

Just before noon, Pacific Standard Time, Martin pumped his car's brakes, making a screeching sound in front of Joseph's house. He turned off the ignition, got out of the car, slammed the door shut, and ran up to Joseph's front porch. He banged on the door and said agitatedly, "Joe, are you there?"

Upstairs at his desk, Joseph said, "I'm coming, I'm coming," as he trampled down the steps and hurried to unlock the door.

As Joseph opened the door, Martin said, "We've been attacked!" He pushed past Joseph and into the living room.

Joseph, closing the door and following behind, asked, "Who? Where?"

"The Japanese attacked Pearl Harbor."

"Are you serious?" Although Joseph could see from Martin's face that it had to be true.

"Damn right. They went after the fleet. It was a sneak attack."

Joseph, eyes widening with each new revelation, said, "So what's happening now?"

"I don't know. I just heard about it on the radio and drove right down here to tell you."

Joseph now went to the radio and turned it on. Turning back to Martin, "You know, this means war. We've talked about it for a year or more, and it has finally happened."

They both took turns fiddling with the dials on the radio, trying to hear more news about the attack and what might come next.

Life as Joseph knew it was turned upside down. The United States declared war on Japan the next day. A few days after hearing of the attack on Pearl Harbor, Joseph contacted the Navy and volunteered for active duty. His closest friend Martin also joined the Navy.

Joseph was an "inactive" naval reservist from his NROTC days at the University of Washington. Earlier that year, most reservists had been called up to active duty because of the Japanese threats in the Pacific. Joseph had been exempted because he was working on a federal grant between the Navy and Rainer College. His involvement dated back to his doctoral thesis dealing with naval affairs in the North Pacific. The grant work related to maritime defense strategy for the Pacific Northwest should Japan attack the West Coast.

The week before Christmas, Joseph received a letter from the Navy informing him that he should report for active duty in Seattle at the 13th Naval District Headquarters on Monday, January 5th. Joseph, for his part, scrambled to plan with Rainier College for his absence. He also worked out a deal with Martin and Colleen where Colleen's younger sister Mary would stay in Joseph's house while he was away. She would also drive his car so it wouldn't become a derelict piece of iron out in front of the house. Christmas that year was a somber affair. Everyone was focused on what would happen next in the new war in the Pacific.

28.

Monday, January 5th, came quickly. Early that morning, Joseph entered the 13th Naval District Headquarters in Seattle after riding the early morning train up from Tacoma. After a few inquiries, he wound up in the office of Captain John Brewer. Captain Brewer shook hands with Joseph after receiving his salute and pointed to a chair on the other side of his desk. When both were settled, he began, "Mister Vaenko, it has been crazy around here since Pearl. There's no stating it any other way. We have had to deal with blackouts, too much radio traffic among our ships, and reports of Japanese submarines everywhere, and I mean everywhere. There have been reported sightings on the coast and here in Puget Sound. Mind you, we've tried to track them all down, and they've proven false to this point. By God, we've even had USS *Gilmer*, the old four-stacker, chasing ghosts around the sound. But enough of what makes my day ever so interesting. Let's have a look at your orders."

The Captain reviewed the documents in the file folder before him and said, "Well, well, what do we have here?" Brewer scanned the papers one more time. "It seems there is nothing but good news for you here." Finally, he looked up and said, "I'll be brief. Those in charge around here think we are living in momentous times. So, you're a history professor, is that correct?"

"Yes, sir," Joseph said with a bit of a frog in his throat.

"Well, that's what is required in the position you are being assigned. You are going to record the history of this damned war," Brewer said with emphasis. "The 13th Naval District handles naval affairs for Washington State, Oregon, Idaho, Montana, Wyoming and all the coastwise shipping lanes from Oregon to Alaska, the whole damn North Pacific. Welcome aboard, my good man."

Joseph thought to himself, well, this sounds like a great opportunity. To the Captain, he said, "Thank you, sir. May I ask, sir, will I be working here at Headquarters?"

Captain Brewer smiled wryly and said, "Mister, you will get to focus on all naval activity that occurs in the North Pacific. In other words, son, you need to be on the water. You need to be a part of what is happening at sea. You need to be right in the middle of it." The Captain paused for effect and then continued, "It also says here that the nature of this assignment will require you to be afforded the rank of "acting" Lieutenant, the idea being it will allow you greater access and less hassle than if you were just a Lieutenant Junior Grade (JG). You'll be flying out of here tomorrow morning for Kodiak, Alaska, where you will join the crew of the USS *Charleston*, the flagship for the Alaska Sector of the 13th Naval District. You are going to get to see Alaska and the Aleutian Islands. You will be reporting to *Charleston's* XO (executive officer). He has been apprised of your assignment and will get you squared away upon your arrival. You'll be part of the 'Ship's Office' onboard. Enjoy your flight," and chuckling, he continued, "Good luck up north with the weather." And with that, the newly minted "Lieutenant" Vaenko found himself out of Captain Brewer's office and in a bit of a daze.

The following morning in the dark at 0600, Joseph was airborne out of Seattle, heading north to Alaska. When he landed in Kodiak, he caught his first breath of freezing Alaskan winter air, possibly better described as his first gasp. He was driven in a jeep to the harbor, where he saw USS *Charleston* tied to the pier. The previous evening, he had read a little about the ship. *Charleston* was an Erie-class gunboat, basically a small destroyer, over a football field in length with mounted 6-inch guns, two forward and two aft. She had a deck amidships that could carry a Kingfisher floatplane. She wasn't as sexy looking as some of the newer, larger ships, but it would be home for him and over 230 officers and sailors for the foreseeable future.

Once aboard, he met the ship's executive officer (XO), who showed him his quarters and explained his expectations. He would help run the Ship's Office and, of course, stand watches. He could devote all time not spent doing ship's duties to his primary assignment of conducting interviews and writing a narrative of what was happening in the North Pacific concerning the war. Later, Joseph was introduced to the captain. The captain sized him up, asked a few questions, and said simply, "We can make this work."

Since *Charleston* was the flagship of the Alaska Sector Force, Joseph was given a letter from the captain to go along with the letter from the 13th Naval District Commandant. Both letters, addressed to all U.S. naval vessels in the North Pacific theatre, explained his task, making it known that Joseph should have access to all officers and sailors. The captains of these vessels were also told to supply any assistance necessary in arranging meetings for the "acting" lieutenant and other aspects of his work. All in all, Joseph was quite satisfied with what had transpired to this point. He was pleased with everything except how damn cold it was whenever he stepped outside.

The next day Joseph spent some serious time talking to the yeoman assigned to the Ship's Office, Henry Bratton. He was a kid from Alabama and shared Joseph's feelings about the weather. Henry brought him up to speed on the scuttlebutt regarding the Alaska Sector Force. For one thing, it wasn't much of a "force." After all, Charleston was the flagship, and she was technically a "gunboat."

Further, she was the only vessel equipped with sonar to detect submarines. The rest of the "force" consisted of two old destroyers left over from the Great War, a couple of Coast Guard cutters, converted fishing vessels, and ten

North Pacific

PBY Catalina aircraft. The PBYs were called "flying boats" because they had hulls that would float and had retractable wheels, allowing the aircraft to take off and land on water or terra firma. Upon hearing all this information, Joseph concluded that the Alaska Sector Force might be able to hold its own against an attack by a Japanese crabbing fleet but not much else.

A couple of days after his arrival, *Charleston* was underway out of Kodiak, providing escort for three cargo ships. Less than twenty-four hours later, the North Pacific weather found them. That night, the small vessels battling the stormy seas could not maintain their positions in the convoy and were scattered in the darkness. In the morning, the small group of ships slowly reformed and then continued toward their destination, Dutch Harbor. Joseph, for his part, even though he had made a couple of trips along the West Coast between Puget Sound and California as part of the NROTC summer cruises, did not have his sea legs and paid the price. After a miserable night, he felt as weak as a kitten.

They had to investigate a supposed aircraft landing at Sand Point the next day, but nothing was found. They passed through Unimak Pass in the evening and arrived the following morning at Dutch Harbor.

There was little to Dutch Harbor before the U.S. Navy and Army arrived. The location had been a small, quiet fishing village with just over 50 permanent inhabitants. With the arrival of the Navy and the Army, the population swelled to over 20,000. There was one bar in the town

North Pacific

known as "Blackie's." Beer was cheap and straight shots were just 50 cents. Joseph, still trying to redeem his life, stayed away.

"Vast" was the word that came to Joseph's mind when looking at a chart of the Alaskan waters. With time he revised his assessment of the North Pacific. It was *"Beyond Vast."* The distance from Dutch Harbor to Honolulu, or Seattle, was unbelievably about 2,000 miles worth of ocean. It just never ended. This immense body of water encompassed one-sixth of the earth's surface. It was as remote as he ever could have imagined. This never-ending space was imposing, stunning, and arresting when the sun was out. It was also like being wrapped in an infinite silent cloud when the waters were still and fog shrouded. Yet when it was cold, when the winds blew and driving snow and ice prevailed, the ocean was fierce, ferocious, and flat-out dangerous as hell. There was no other way to illustrate the North Pacific. No amount of description could ever come close to actually experiencing this incomprehensible part of the earth. Captain Brewer, back in Seattle, had been right about the value of placing the young historian in the world he would be writing about.

Joseph spent his free time re-reading his copy of *Pensées* by Blaise Pascal that he had brought from Tacoma. He had read it before, under the tutelage of Father Etienne, but he was older now and thought he might get more out of it. It had been a gift from Father Etienne so long ago and needed to be read slowly, with Pascal's "thoughts" subject to much reflection. The North Pacific sometimes reminded him of

North Pacific

Pascal's description of the size of the universe. "The eternal silence of these infinite spaces fills me with dread."

Escorting transports of all shapes and sizes between Kodiak and Dutch Harbor was the order of the day, at least for now. There was a mail call early in February, and Joseph received nothing. Later in the month, *Charleston* test-fired her guns. Lots of noise, but everything seemed to work. During March and April, there was more of the same. It was in May 1942 that things finally got interesting.

~~~~~

American naval cryptologists in Hawaii broke the top-secret Japanese naval code. They discovered the plans for the Japanese attacks on Midway Island and the "Aleutian Islands." Chester Nimitz, Commander in Chief of the U.S. Pacific Fleet, quickly assembled a nine-ship North Pacific Force. Elements of that force sailed north from Pearl Harbor on May 21, 1942.

Charleston was assigned to the Patrol Group or Surface Search Group. On May 30th, the Surface Search Group left Dutch Harbor in the morning via Acutan Passage. In the afternoon, a target was deployed, and *Charleston's* main battery of guns each fired two rounds at it. All went well. Some of the newer recruits, who had come aboard recently and were part of the gun crews, had never seen a naval-mounted gun fire before. The waters became choppy as the afternoon progressed, and by evening, the Patrol Group was facing gale-force winds. The ships reached the planned scouting line early the following day and commenced "listening" for the enemy. The patrol group was strung out for miles across the Alaskan waters.

Joseph wondered what would happen should they detect the Japanese strike force approaching them. In his head, the answer was likening the patrol ships to that of the proverbial canaries in a coal mine. He tried not to think about it. The patrol group saw nothing and heard nothing – no enemy surface ships, no submarines, and no aircraft. As for *Charleston's* single PBY floatplane and its aircrew, they had been reassigned, for the time being, to a new Air Scout Group and had been left behind in Dutch Harbor.

Back at Dutch Harbor, the morning of June 3rd began at 0540 with the seaplane tender *Gillis*' radar picking up an incoming flight of aircraft that turned out to be the Japanese Strike Force. Twenty minutes later, the Japanese Zeros, the same fighter aircraft that had ravaged Pearl Harbor and most of the Southeast Pacific, swept down on the harbor. The attack lasted 29 minutes and killed 25 Army and Navy personnel.

The next day, the Japanese again attacked Dutch Harbor from the air. When this follow-up raid ended, the Americans' death count had risen to 43. Additionally, four 6,000-gallon fuel tanks had been destroyed. The barracks ship *Northwestern* was partially damaged, one end of the local hospital facility was destroyed, and enemy shells had also hit a plane hangar. Significantly, the Japanese had not attempted landings in or around Dutch Harbor. However,

North Pacific

a few days later, on June 7th, the Japanese landed unopposed forces on the two most western of the Aleutian Islands, Attu, and Kiska. For the first time in the North Pacific, the Japanese occupied American soil by taking the two islands. Clearly, the Americans were on the back foot, but all expected that this action would not be allowed to stand.

The Japanese had won a tactical victory in the North Pacific with the bombing of Dutch Harbor and the landings on Attu and Kiska islands. But it was to the south in that same timeframe that the war between Japan and the United States turned irreversibly. Although few probably knew it at the time, the U.S. Navy handed the Japanese a monstrous naval defeat in the waters off Midway Island. It put the Japanese, for the most part, on the defensive for the rest of the war. At the Battle of Midway, the US Navy sunk four of Japan's large aircraft carriers (forty percent of their total carrier strength and the loss of most of their best-trained pilots). After that Japan simply did not have the capacity to replace those losses in any meaningful timeframe. It was a stunning outcome when all had seemed lost at one point for the Americans late in the life-and-death naval air battle around Midway.

Aboard *Charleston*, orders were received to remain on station until further notice. "Further notice" turned out to be June 14th. Ordered back to port after fifteen days of picket duty was great news to the small ships that formed the barrier. They arrived in Kodiak on June 16th. The crew aboard *Charleston* was worn out. Two weeks of nerves

North Pacific

always had that sort of effect on men in times of great stress. Three days later, it was back out to sea.

Escort duties resumed between Dutch Harbor and Kodiak. On June 20th, *Charleston* investigated a sighting and found it to be a Russian freighter en route to Petropavlovsk in the Soviet Union. On June 24th, *Charleston* departed Dutch Harbor escorting *SS Lombardi*. *Lombardi's* destination was San Francisco. After crossing the Gulf of Alaska, the two ships headed south to the Strait of Juan De Fuca entrance, which separates British Columbia's Vancouver Island from the State of Washington. There, *Charleston* lowered a boat to take on a passenger and two Alaskan pilots from *Lombardi*. Then the two vessels parted ways, *Lombardi* to San Francisco and *Charleston* to Bremerton. After a night navigating the strait, Charleston turned to starboard the following morning and entered northern Puget Sound at Point Wilson on the tip of Port Townsend, Washington. Orders instructed *Charleston* to proceed directly at slow speed to the Puget Sound Naval Shipyard in Bremerton, Washington, for repairs.

29.

It was in Bremerton that Joseph obtained a 48-hour pass. He took a ferry across the Sound to Seattle and then a bus to Tacoma. He rode a city bus from downtown and was home at 1:30 PM on July 3rd. He had been gone six months. It felt longer. He knocked on the door of his house so as not to frighten Mary, Colleen's sister. She was excited to see him, and they sat down and talked about the war, the house, the view, and Martin and Colleen. Mary insisted that she spend the next couple of nights with her sister so Joseph could feel comfortable in his own home. She then quickly put together a bag of things for herself, and Joseph drove her to the Linarts. Colleen answered the door and, seeing Joseph carrying Mary's bag, screamed and gave him a big hug and kiss. Colleen insisted that Joseph come over for dinner. They negotiated and settled on the following night. Mary, for her part, said she would take her niece and nephew and visit her and Colleen's mother and father during that time so that Joseph and Colleen could talk in peace. Joseph decided right then and there that Mary was truly a saint. It was settled.

Upon returning home that afternoon, Joseph spent an inordinate amount of time looking out windows at the bay he had so missed since shipping out. He realized at some point that his 48 hours were slipping away and tore himself away from that prized activity.

Joseph had asked Mary if she might save any newspaper articles that focused on important things happening in Tacoma while he was away. Sure enough, a stack of papers was on the coffee table in front of the sofa, with particular stories highlighted. He scanned the headlines, and what caught his eye were the articles related to the fate of Japanese Americans. He read where the FBI had begun arresting "Issei" (first-generation Japanese Americans) and a smaller number of "Nisei" (second-generation Japanese Americans), like Miku and Kasumi. Most Nisei were born here in the States and, thus, automatically American citizens. Later, Issei business licenses were revoked, and many bank accounts were frozen.

In February, President Roosevelt signed executive order #9066, which allowed for the forced evacuation and relocation of all persons of Japanese heritage on the West Coast. The first Japanese to be evacuated on March 30, 1942, were from Bainbridge Island, Washington, because of its close proximity (just north) of the Puget Sound Naval Shipyard in Bremerton. By the last week of May, almost 13,000 men, women, and children of Japanese ancestry had been incarcerated at "Camp Harmony" in Puyallup, just outside Tacoma. "Relocation Centers" were being constructed in many places, including Minidoka in southern Idaho, where most Camp Harmony detainees would be transported upon the facility's completion.

Joseph looked around the room and thought of Miku. Was she being held out at the fairgrounds? She was a second-generation American, just as he was. Were these Japanese who had lived in Washington State their entire lives a threat to the United States? It was unimaginable to him. Might not a different approach, conceivably using the FBI, to seek out a handful of possible Japanese American traitors be a more responsible approach to the perceived threat? All of this was so wrong. He spiritually and physically longed for her. He missed her immensely. Joseph wondered to himself, how did this happen? Nothing made sense.

It was summer. The day was warm. He opened a couple of windows to create a cross breeze. He sat back down on the sofa. God, how he loved this place. It was only 1,200 square feet give or take a few, but it was all his. He missed it while he was up north. You appreciate something when you've been taken away from it. It made him think of the Japanese Americans who had lost their homes, jobs, friends, and all but their immediate belongings. He looked out over the bay and just shook his head.

He then closed his eyes and relaxed for a moment. He re-opened them to a knock on the door. He rose from the sofa and said, "I'm coming." When he got there and opened the door, there stood Diane Lassiter, the beautiful woman he had dated in his senior year at Rainier College.

She stepped toward him and threw her arms around his neck. "Oh my God," she exclaimed. "I can't believe you are here. I was shopping up on Proctor Street when I ran into Colleen Linart. She was excited and told me you were back in town for a few days, and so you are." She clung to him tightly, her head alternating between his chest and looking up at him.

Joseph, happily surprised, hugged her back and said, "Can you come in?"

She kissed him on the cheek, "Absolutely, I didn't drive down here for my health." As they entered the living room, the summer marine air from the opened windows moved comfortably and coolly across the room. "This is such a great space, Joseph. I wonder why we didn't spend more time here when we were together?"

"As I remember, we were a bit younger then, and my Father was also living here," Joseph offered with a smile.

"Oh, I know all that. I was wondering why we didn't take more advantage of this to die for view. I remember your Dad. He was a genuinely nice fellow. He was always kind to me. He talked with that "old country" accent of his, her voice quickly dropping octaves trying to imitate Alexandr's."

Joseph smiled and then laughed. It was great to see her. She looked wonderful. In the intervening years, she had grown even more attractive than she was as a college student.

Diane widened her eyes and said, "I just had to see you once I knew you were in town. It's been so long, Joseph. Colleen says you're a Lieutenant on the USS *Charleston*."

"I am."

"Have you seen any action yet against the Japanese?"

"No, to this point, we've been fortunate enough not to have had any encounters. We've investigated many supposed sightings, but none have turned out to be true."

"I'll bet you look great in your uniform," Diane said, smiling again.

"I don't know about that, but I have lost a little weight. Shipboard provisions are not necessarily the best, although our meals are better than our Army counterparts have to deal with. Did you ever get married?" Joseph inquired, not noticing a wedding ring on her.

"Nooo," smiled Diane. "Nothing has ever quite worked out. You know I have high standards, and yes, wise guy," she said with the cutest of smiles, "I'm not getting any younger, yeah, yeah." Then she shot back, "How about you? How's your love life been, Mister Vaenko?"

"Okay, okay, you got me," replied Joseph with a sheepish grin. "By the way, you don't look older. You look great."

She moved over to where Joseph stood and hugged him, "Oh, you feel so good, and you look rather good too. Don't let it go to your head, but I've got a mind to come back here after my parents' pre-Fourth party tonight at their place." She lowered her voice slightly and asked, "What would you think of that?"

Joseph, surprised, put his forehead on hers. Looking deep into her eyes, he said, "Do I know you?"

They stared into each other's eyes for what seemed the longest time. "Shoot, I've got to get going," Diane exclaimed, shattering the silence that had come over the room, figuratively stepping back from the brink. "I've got groceries out in the car going bad, and I have to get over to Mom and Dad's and help with the dinner." They walked back over to the door, and Diane kissed him before leaving. Neither said a word. Joseph watched her walk to her car.

Joseph straightened up the house some. He moved some things around out of habit. He ended up staying at home that evening. There was nowhere he wanted to go. What could be better than being in the space he had discovered he missed so much? It was funny. He hadn't felt like this when he returned from his postgraduate work in Seattle. Maybe it was his age, the circumstances of the war, and now more memories of his life in this house. He played the radio and looked for another book on the hallway shelves to take back to the ship. No one came to the door that evening.

On the 4th of July, Joseph rose from the single bed up against the wall by the staircase. He had slept downstairs since Mary was using the upstairs bedroom. It was another beautiful day. He made himself breakfast and then cleaned up the yard a bit. In the early afternoon, he went for a walk down along the waterfront. It was great to get out and stretch the legs after being confined more or less on that ship for six months. He finally returned home, showered, and put on a change of clothes. He took the Studebaker and picked up some flowers for Colleen.

Colleen was again excited to see him, and after exchanging greetings, they went to the kitchen, where Colleen put the flowers in a vase with a bit of water and then finished preparing salmon for the two of them. "How is it up there in Alaska," Colleen inquired.

"In a word, cold," said Joseph. "It is warming up now, so it's better than it was. It was so dark and miserable when I first got up there. I couldn't begin to tell you how much I wanted a little daylight and warmth. But the days have lengthened, and the nights are almost non-existent this time of the year. It's crazy."

"I wanted to thank you again for letting Mary stay at your place," Colleen said. "It has been a Godsend. She is saving up her money to buy a house after this terrible war is over."

Joseph raised both hands and said, "What's the deal with Martin? How is he doing?"

Colleen looked up and said, "All I do is worry about him. I've started trying not to think about him too much, or I'll go batty. Well, anyway, you know he joined the Navy. You 'probably' influenced him. It's your fault. They made him a Warrant Officer because of his engineering degree and background. Anyway, he is on a heavy cruiser. Is there any other kind?" She smiled. "Oh, it's *Salt Lake City*. Martin said it was an older ship. I went to the library and found a photo of it. What do I know? It's big, gray, and has guns all over it. I wish he were home. I've gotten a few letters from him, and he says everything is going well."

Joseph smilingly interrupted her and said, "That's about the only thing we can write that can get past the censors."

"He tells me he's at sea. That's it. Sure, he asks about the kids and tells me he loves me and all, but this is hard, Joseph. I really miss him." Colleen moved back over to the stove and tended to the fillets. She plated the fish, rice, and asparagus a minute later. Lastly, she spooned a sauce on the salmon and served it. Joseph accepted his plate, and the two slowly ate dinner, speaking less, both more in their thoughts than in conversation. Joseph couldn't remember the last time he had a meal as good as this. It was probably when he had been over here the last time for Thanksgiving before the war. The two spoke more after dinner while she washed the dishes, and kitchen towel in hand, Joseph dried them. After that, she served him apple pie with a cup of coffee. For the rest of the evening, they made small talk. They shared how they couldn't believe how fast time flew by since they were all back in high school. Joseph could not believe he was now 35 and Colleen was 33. Driving home that night, Joseph thought how much better things could have been if there had been no war.

The following day Joseph was up well before dawn, stripped the single bed, got his gear together, and was out the door for the taxi to downtown and the bus ride back to Seattle so that he could catch a ferry back to Bremerton. It certainly would have been easier to use the Narrows Bridge from Tacoma to the Kitsap Peninsula and then up to Bremerton. However, anyone who watched newsreels at the movies knew the "bridge" had rather spectacularly fallen in a windstorm two years earlier and had not been replaced yet. He got back to the ship with minutes to spare.

North Pacific

30.

After the work on the ship was complete, *Charleston* spent some time completing the necessary "degaussing" runs to erase the vessel's electronic signature that could be picked up by enemy sonar detection equipment. She finally left Bremerton only to stop on the other side of the Puget Sound in Seattle an hour later. The Captain wanted to check in at the 13th Naval District Head Quarters. The next day they were back "at sea," headed north to Alaska to resume escort duty.

Along the way, there were stops in Sitka and Juneau, both in Southeastern Alaska. While in Sitka, the base for Russian exploration in North America, Joseph came ashore and toured the small town. He found a Russian Orthodox Church and stepped inside. Russia, of course, sold Alaska to the United States in 1867. U.S. Secretary of State William H. Seward negotiated the deal, and it became alternately known as Seward's Folly and Seward's Icebox. Joseph thought the "icebox' appellation was far more applicable for reasons utterly unrelated to economics. He stood in the center of the round church. It was relatively small. Still, it had high walls that rose to the "onion-dome" at the very top. The walls were covered with beautiful iconography.

North Pacific

Later that day, he discovered the Catholic Church. It looked more like a house on a corner rather than a church. Joseph entered and found himself alone in a pew in the small nave. A white wooden communion rail separated the nave from the sanctuary. He had done some reading and knew that "nave" came from the Latin "navis," which stood for things naval, including ships. Thus, in churches like St. Dominic back in Tacoma, one could look up at the high arching ceiling and grasp the idea that the people were in a small ship, "Christ's Bark," albeit inverted. In Sitka's Catholic Church, it was much harder to gain that perspective.

Yet even here, Joseph found himself as awed as ever because the sanctuary lamp was lit. For him, the modest tabernacle and its contents still signified something vital on the wooden altar. It was a constant. The red lamp burned, and Joseph regretted not stopping by St. Dominic while on his 48-hour pass.

~~~~~

Soon enough, *Charleston* returned to Kodiak and then moved to Dutch Harbor. In a few days, life returned to normal, with *Charleston* providing escort for all shipping in and around the eastern half of the Aleutian Islands chain.

Joseph didn't make a lot of close friends aboard *Charleston*. His time was taken up with research work that required him to move around from ship to ship and meet

North Pacific

with different naval officers and sailors whenever he could. He wrote daily. Of course, he also had to attend to his regular duties associated with the Ship's Office.

The sinking of the Japanese carriers at Midway was easily the most important event since Pearl Harbor. Now the situation in the North Pacific had quieted. The Japanese garrisons on Attu and Kiska Islands at the western tip of the Aleutian Islands chain were being resupplied by Japanese cargo ships from Paramushiro in the Kurile Islands.

The U.S. Army and Navy were working together to build "forward" bases on the islands in the Aleutian chain closest to Attu and Kiska to set up runways from which American fighters and bombers could attack the Japanese garrisons. Winter returned to the North Pacific with its infamous and monstrous weather.

Upon completing a mission to land thirty Army scouts within Constantine Harbor on Amchitka Island, the destroyer *USS Worden* fell victim to terrible snow, high winds, and darkness. After getting the Army personnel ashore, the destroyer was swept onto submerged pinnacle rocks surrounding and dotting the harbor while attempting to withdraw. With the rocks tearing the hull open and leaving her in distress, *Worden* was lost with ten crewmembers drowning in the icy waters. However, the mission was successful, and the airstrips were completed as part of the plan to reclaim Attu and Kiska Islands.

North Pacific

Joseph's work was also on his mind. He had filed weekly reports back to Seattle but rarely heard anything in reply. He had begun to hope to be reassigned to a vessel closer to the action than his current posting afforded. He was aware that a new Commandant had taken over the 13th Naval District back in November, but it was now February of 1943, and it was clear that the Navy was sending more ships north. There was no doubt that something would have to give at this rate in the not-too-distant future.

It was mid-March 1943. One day Joseph went out on deck to walk a lap or two around *Charleston* to stretch his legs. He noticed warships leaving the harbor. He asked some sailors on deck if they knew what was going on. One sailor said, "Sir, I heard they just got in from Pearl yesterday, and now they're off again after refueling and provisioning."

Joseph noticed the largest of the ships and asked, "The heavy cruiser, did you catch the name?"

"She's the *Salt Lake City*, sir."

Joseph peered harder at the ship and thought, "Damn, I'll bet Martin's aboard her."

The heavy cruiser *Indianapolis* had moved up to the Aleutians almost a month earlier. Since arriving, she had caught and sank an unescorted Japanese cargo ship headed for Attu.

The Japanese, however, were determined to resupply and maintain the Army garrisons on both Attu and Kiska. The strategy was to preserve a presence in the Aleutians that would deter the Americans from attacking Japanese forces in the Kurile Islands and possibly threatening the Japanese homeland. Interestingly, this approach or plan used the old War Plan Orange "Northern Route."

An American naval force consisting of heavy cruiser *Salt Lake City*, light cruiser *Richmond* and four destroyers set up a scouting line west of Attu to interdict any more resupply efforts. Subsequently, this naval group and Japanese forces fought a fierce surface action (guns vs. guns) that ended with the Japanese retiring to their base at Paramushiro in the Kurile Islands and being unable to resupply their forces on Attu and Kiska Islands.

The news of the surface engagement got everyone's blood pumping. *Charleston* was being added to the buildup of forces that would be used in the campaign for the Americans to retake Attu and Kiska. There would be no more escort duty. They were going to where the fighting was taking place. It was early May, and now for the first time, the officers and sailors, most of whom had been aboard *Charleston* since before the start of the war, were going to see action. Like so many others, Joseph was glad that something was happening that might help end the war.

On May 11th, 1943, the Americans landed troops on Attu Island. The Japanese were not "dug in" but were "burrowed in," and the Americans found the going tough. On the third day of the assault, *Charleston* provided cover for two transports, *Grant* and *Chirikof,* as they moved in and disembarked their troops. Overall, the operation was not going as planned as the Japanese held positions that greatly hindered the American advance.

On May 22nd, *Charleston* and the destroyer *Phelps* were taking part in a close inshore patrol when nineteen Japanese Mitsubishi Type 01 twin-engine "Betty" bombers (American code names) found a break in the cloud cover over Holtz Bay and swept in on the two American naval combatants. Six concentrated their attacks on *Charleston* and the rest on *Phelps*. Torpedoes dropped in the water by the bombers passed fifty yards ahead of *Charleston*, another torpedo, twenty-five yards to port, while two passed astern. None of them hit home. Seventeen rounds of gunfire hit *Charleston*, while *Phelps* received six hits. Between them, they managed to shoot down or "splash" one "Betty" and damage another aircraft that would prove fatal on its return to Paramushiro using their anti-aircraft guns and throwing up in the air as much "flak" as possible. The anti-aircraft fire also exploded one Japanese torpedo in mid-air.

Both ships were on "call fire" duty a few days later. *Charleston* would wait until receiving information from American spotter planes about where to fire. Those targets mainly consisted of Japanese gun emplacements on the island. This work resulted in *Charleston* firing 99 six-inch shells on May 22nd, 484 on May 25th, and 368 the following day before she was withdrawn. The battle for Attu raged until the end of the month when only 28 combatants of an original Japanese garrison force of over 2,300 finally surrendered. It was a testament to the Japanese soldier's incredible bravery and fighting will.

31.

Charleston had experienced her baptism of fire and proven her mettle. The experience of live combat brought the crew much closer. Everyone now felt they knew their jobs and what to expect. They knew what to do and, more importantly, how to do it when naval combat began. The naval action replaced anticipation for the crew with a resolve that the only way to see this war through was to bear down and make things happen. There was a quiet confidence that they could give their best when called upon.

Two weeks later, on June 11th, *Charleston* returned to Dutch Harbor. Within a week, they were providing protection for the ships involved in the refloating and towing of AP-55 *Arthur Middleton,* a transport that, on the same day that the destroyer *Worden* had been lost in the fierce winds of Constantine harbor on Amchitka Island, had herself dragged anchor and wound up beached. *Charleston* safely took her convoy of ships back to Dutch Harbor, including the refloated *Arthur Middleton*. More convoy work in the Aleutian Islands took up much of the next five weeks. On the 7th of July, *Charleston* was in Kuluk Bay on Adak Island.

North Pacific

Joseph was doing administrative work in the Ship's Office when the XO appeared and shook his hand. "Mister, it has been a pleasure to have made your acquaintance."

Joseph shook his hand, and the XO handed him his new orders. "What's up, sir?" Joseph queried without opening the envelope.

"It seems that District Head Quarters, back in Seattle, wants to get you closer to the action than just riding around with us providing cover for transports. It looks like you're going to be on a Fletcher-class destroyer and go where the action is happening. What do you think about that, Lieutenant?"

"I'm surprised, sir. I've wondered if anyone back at Head Quarters remembered who I was and what I've been doing. I was beginning to think they had forgotten about me."

The XO smiled and said, "Well, they seem to have remembered you, so it's time to pack your things and get ready to go ashore."

~~~~~

Joseph clambered down the gangway with his duffle bag and made his way to town, where he was given temporary quarters out at the naval air station.

His experience of being in combat had made an impression on him. Life is short. It got him thinking. He had not been practicing his faith since before the war. He had prayed less and had not been attending Mass. In the back of his mind, he remembered all the times he had spent praying to God for this or that or one outcome in life over another. He missed praying in front of Christ's presence in the Blessed Sacrament. He missed having God in his life. God gave his life meaning. There were so many rich memories of his mother and her faith, of Alexandr and his. He had learned so much from Fr. Etienne and Fr. Simone. Maybe his combat experience was a wake-up call telling him to become a man and live his faith. Yes, his faith. The beliefs that had taught him that Jesus Christ had lived and died for him. That faith was in his blood, in his being. He had been formed well by his parents and his church. It was the echoes of that faith that encouraged his heart.

On Sunday the 11th, while waiting for his new ship *USS Abner Read* to appear at Adak, Joseph got wind that a Catholic Mass would be said at the Naval Air Station. He thought about it and decided to attend. He was slightly surprised by the number of guys that showed up. His current personal status of a "sinner" who had not confessed his sins kept him from presenting himself for the Sacrament of Holy Communion.

This fact, this sad reality, weighed on Joseph. Whenever he felt good about something he had done, he was always reminded by his conscience that he was still in a state of sin. He was not right with God. The longer this persisted, the more he knew in his heart that he risked his immortal soul. How stupid, he told himself. Fix it.

North Pacific

After Mass, Joseph wandered around Kulak Bay, and Sweeper Cove. The weather was remarkably agreeable, with clear skies and little wind. It was down by one of the docks in Sweeper Cove that Joseph saw the priest who had said Mass earlier sitting on a bench. He walked up and said, "Good afternoon, Father."

The priest, who was around Joseph's age, nodded and smiled. Then the priest asked, "You wouldn't have a match, would you?" Joseph fished in his pocket and found a matchbook. He didn't smoke but had collected the matchbook in a restaurant months ago in Sitka. He handed the matches to the priest, who thanked him and asked him to join him for a few minutes. Joseph sat down, and while the priest lit his cigarette, the two looked out into the cove. The priest took a drag from the cigarette, exhaled, and asked, "Where are you from?"

"Tacoma, Washington, Father."

The priest nodded and said, "Ah, yes, on Puget Sound, a beautiful part of the country. I'm John Considine from Cleveland, Ohio," extending his hand.

"Joseph Vaenko, Father." The two shook hands.

"Who would have thought in a million years we'd be sitting on the edge of the Bering Sea," the priest offered. "The Lord works in mysterious ways, and I know people say that a lot, but it couldn't be more true in this case."

Both chuckled and shared their exploits so far during the war and even some of their pre-war experiences. They enjoyed each other's company. After the priest had finished his cigarette, a thought rushed through Joseph's head. "Father, would you hear my confession?"

Father John responded, "Of course. Does it have to be right now, or can we do it at the Naval Air Station before Mass tomorrow morning? It's completely up to you."

"Tomorrow would be great, Father. I'll be there."

"Perfect," replied the priest.

They both rose, and Father John started to hand the matchbook back. "Keep the matches, Father," said Joseph, "You need them more than I do."

The following morning, after a semi-sleepless night recounting the Ten Commandments and compiling in his head the offenses against the Almighty he had committed over the last two years, Joseph was ready to confess his sins. He had concluded that his echo of faith and remembering how his parents had raised him was not enough. Joseph remembered the Latin saying, *Agere sequitur credere!* (Action follows belief!) He needed to begin practicing his faith. Besides, he surmised, I may be going into action aboard my new ship. It's time to make things right with the Lord.

He found Father John "vesting" in the large room where Mass would be offered in less than an hour. Father John smiled and greeted him while walking over and locking the door to the room they were in. The priest was already dressed in his alb and cincture, so he quickly slipped his stole on (a band of silk worn around the neck and crisscrossed over the chest).

They both made the sign of the cross, and the priest began the penitential rite in a low voice. "May the Lord be in thy heart and on thy lips so that thou mayest rightly confess all thy sins." After Joseph had confessed his sins, which, embarrassingly, took a while, and he had received his penance, the priest said, "May Almighty God have mercy on thee, forgive thee thy sins, and bring thee to everlasting life. May the almighty and merciful Lord grant thee pardon, absolution, and remission of thy sins. May Our Lord Jesus Christ absolve thee, and I by His authority do absolve thee.... I absolve thee from thy sins in the name of the Father and of the Son and the Holy Ghost.... Amen," all said in Latin, of course. Afterward, Joseph thanked him, and the priest wished him well.

Joseph sat in one of the chairs set up for Mass. While waiting for the Mass to begin, Joseph experienced "that moment." There is an instant after receiving the Sacrament of Penance that Catholics experience. It is one of complete and total joy. A penitent knows that if they have honestly and contritely conveyed their sins to the priest, based on the Lord's dictate to the Apostles, *"Whose sins you shall forgive, they are forgiven them"* (Jn 20:23), through Christ's graces, knows their sins are truly forgiven. There is no feeling like it in the world.

At Mass, Joseph received Communion for the first time since before Miku had left him. He thought, was it really two years ago?

After Mass, Joseph shook his head and walked outside into a stiff breeze that was nothing short of bracing. He pushed his hands into the pockets of his three-quarter-length double-breasted-overcoat and mentally ruminated. He thanked God for all he had done for him and began a question-and-answer session with himself as he walked toward the harbor.

Why did you go to confession? Because I have been thinking about it for two years, that's why. I sinned against God with my actions involving both Miku and Jill. Hello, Father Simone. I chose of my own free will to ignore the moral teachings of the faith and do what I wanted instead. I did not show God and those two women the respect they deserved. Vaenko, don't even begin to tell yourself that maybe there were extenuating circumstances. I am solely responsible for my actions and my consequent sins, period.

Damn, I still remember Father Simone telling me men are supposed to look out for women, not to use them for self-gratification. That's what I did, and that's why I went to confession. I was wrong. It's eaten at me ever since.

Can I prove there's a God listening and caring about what I think and feel? No, not empirically. Science is part and parcel of the finite world into which we are born. God is of the infinite.

Then why did you sin? I was searching for happiness. Did you find it? Joseph took a deep breath. I don't even know what happiness is anymore, much less whether I attained it at any given point. The older I get, in many ways, the less I seem to understand. I'm beginning to believe that happiness has always been what I think I wanted, but maybe it's a transitory notion that cannot be sustained.

What about the war? Did seeing torpedoes in the water get your attention? Did you go to confession because of the action at Attu? Sure. A good Catholic boy, which I believe I was at one time, would always want to confess his sins before possibly meeting his maker. Carrying mortal sins around is just playing with eternal fire. I confessed my sins because even though nothing seems to go my way when I pray to God, the Lord is still my great hope. Joseph headed back to his quarters.

32.

A few days later, July 16th, to be exact, Joseph, duffle bag over his shoulder, climbed the gangway of the *USS Abner Read* and reported for duty. The Fletcher-class destroyer was almost 80 feet longer than *Charleston*. She mounted five 5-inch guns and bristled with anti-aircraft guns, depth charges, and torpedoes. Again, he reported to the XO and once again was assigned to the Ship's Office. After asking Joseph questions about the particulars of his unique assignment, the XO said, "So what are we to call you, the fighting history professor?" Joseph was used to these jokes and smiled broadly, saying, "I been called worse."

North Pacific

He stowed his gear and settled into his new "officer's stateroom." It was hardly a "stateroom" by any stretch of the imagination. It was a small compartment for two or even sometimes three officers when they squeezed an extra cot in. There was a set of bunk beds, a sink, a shelf, a couple of drawers, a desk, and a chair. All of this was somehow shoe-horned into incredibly tight quarters with scant little floor space. Still, no one would dare complain if the alternative was the crew's quarters – God help them.

The Officer's Wardroom was forward on the ship's starboard side. The officers paid extra for meals cooked separately from the enlisted men's fare. The tables even had chairs, while cumbersome benches populated the crew's mess.

The Officer's Wardroom also served as the main battle dressing station when necessary in combat. It was here that the doctor was stationed to treat any casualties. The long tabletops could double as operating tables. The wardroom was also equipped with surgical and emergency lighting if and when needed.

Joseph learned to respect this crew as he had that of the *Charleston* because of their professionalism after over a year of service and combat in which they had taken part.

In the ship's office, the yeoman was Benjamin Rappaport, a 26-year-old smallish curly dark-haired schoolteacher from Long Island, New York. "Rapp," as he was known, was of Italian and Jewish descent. He was intelligent, quick, and to the point. He had a degree from

North Pacific

CCNY. Rapp had joined the Navy when the war started rather than risk being drafted into the Army. As he told Joseph that never in his wildest dreams did he imagine he would wind up serving in the North Pacific. They hit it off and spent hours talking while performing their respective duties in the Ship's Office.

One day Joseph walked by Rapp's small desk and saw a copy of *La Nausée* by Jean-Paul Sartre. He picked it up and looked at the publishing date. It read 1938. He asked Rapp, "What's it about?"

Rapp started, "It's about a guy writing a biography, a history, of someone, you know, like you, sir." He paused to smile at the Lieutenant and then continued, "Anyway, he starts suffering from nausea and figures out eventually it's because life has no meaning other than that which you give it."

"Could I read it?" Joseph asked.

"You can see it is in French, right, sir."

"Yes, I can. I do have a slightly rusty knack for reading French. I don't speak the language, not even close, but I get by with my ability to read it."

"Well, I'll be," said the surprised yeoman. "Be my guest."

Over the next few days, Joseph worked his way through the slim novel and returned the book to Rapp, thanking him for it and saying, "It was an interesting read. The author has a whole different take on life that I had not thought about too much before. Maybe we can discuss it sometime?" Rapp's eyes lit up, "Absolutely, Sir, that book has meant a lot to me and my thinking. I would love to discuss it."

If there was one thing Joseph had picked up on from talking to Rapp was that he was knowledgeable. He knew his duties and, for that matter, everyone else's on the ship. You could tell he could do postgraduate work, and Joseph had told him that in an earlier conversation. Rapp was aware of it also, but he had gotten married after earning his bachelor's and now had a couple of kids, and, of course, they came first. As for going to grad school and supporting his family, those decisions would have to be made after the war. Joseph could see the yeoman teaching philosophy someday. That was his strength. I wonder where Rapp learned French. Joseph brought his mind back to the present and asked, "What did you think of the lead character Roquentin?"

"As a protagonist, not much, Sir. He doesn't get the girl and is in anguish throughout the story, but as a conveyor of discovered wisdom, I believe he more than makes up for his unappealing life to that point." Rapp fixed his eyes on Joseph and waited for a response.

"I tend to agree with you about his weakness as a protagonist to whom a reader would be drawn," replied Joseph. "However, I'm not as convinced that he discovered 'wisdom' as you put it."

"Seriously, sir?" Rapp said as he turned his chair toward Joseph. "Forgive my impertinence," he said with a respectful grin, "But Roquentin discovers that ascribing meaning to the past and, for that matter, to the present is an exercise in futility. Sir, I think the book helps explain through Roquentin that life has no meaning. It is pure happenstance, like this damn war. Life is nothing. So, Sartre argues through Roquentin that we must create meaning for our lives through our freedom to make decisions and the actions we take. It is the natural progression of Darwinian thought. Natural selection has proven that humans are not the focal point of the world. Existence for you or me is an unplanned and inconsequential aspect of reality. The only thing man can do to come to terms with this, how can I put it, this "nauseous" thought, is to assert one's freedom by providing the meaning of one's life on his own terms."

Taken aback by Rapp's emotional and firmly held opinion on the book, Joseph smiled and said, "Well, I guess I don't have to ask you how you feel about this story. Has Sartre written anything else along these lines where he advances this position?"

"I believe there is a second book called *Le Mur* (The Wall). I don't have it yet." Rapp continued, "To be fair, sir, I've read some of Sartre's writings in journals after he wrote this book. Sorry if I'm a bit enthusiastic. As you can probably tell, I'm a fan."

"No, no," replied Joseph, "I pegged you as a bright guy when we first met. This Sartre is putting forth an interesting argument. I like that he focuses on people singularly and not the broader theoretical analysis that the British and American philosophers are so fixated on exploring. It's an argument that throws out history, culture, and tradition, yet it shows a way forward if one were to have no belief in a Creator, a God. Besides, it's refreshing to hear opinions and ideas that don't normally come up in the course of a day up here in the Aleutians." A few sailors showed up at that moment with business to deal with, and the discussion ended, yet Joseph kept with him the points and thoughts of the conversation.

33.

As August began, the American build-up for re-taking Kiska, the second of the Japanese-occupied islands, was well underway. Starting on the 12th, *Abner Read* took part in a considerable bombardment effort to "soften up" the island. The shelling continued on the 13th and 14th before troops landed on the morning of the 15th. The landings continued the next day on various parts of the island.

Curiously, however, all the landings had one thing in common. There was no resistance. By the morning of the 17th, the Americans had figured out, to their astonishment, that the Japanese were no longer on Kiska. It was shocking to the U. S. command. Later they would learn that the Japanese Navy, back on the 28th of July, had come in under cover of darkness and fog and evacuated the garrison of nearly 5,200 Japanese soldiers. Attu had been a bloody affair. Kiska was a blessed surprise.

That night there was much celebrating during dinner in the Officer's Wardroom. Everyone had a smile on their face. They all knew it was not the end of the war by any means, but a reprieve, a respite, a pause, was always welcome.

They talked among themselves as to what might be next. After all, the Aleutian Islands were now back under the control of the United States. Would their next mission be somewhere in the South Pacific? Or, God forbid, would it be in the North Pacific? Were they going to take the fight to the Japanese and their base in the Kurile Islands at Paramushiro? Would *Abner Read* be sent back to Puget Sound or San Francisco for maintenance? Joseph wondered to himself, would he be transferred to another ship? That seemed likely. Would there be a chance of obtaining some leave to go home for a few weeks? All these questions and the general relaxation of tension spilled out in the Officer's Wardroom that night. Some officers even stayed in the wardroom when the second set of officers came in for their dinner meal to celebrate with them. Life on a ship is one of routine, and then there is the tension that goes with being in a combat zone. This was one of those few blessed moments that the men could simply exhale. It felt good.

Joseph remembered he had the morning watch, and 0400 hours came early, no matter the circumstances. He had enjoyed his time in the wardroom for dinner and thought he would turn in by 2100 hours. He would be getting up at 0330. Bill, his roomie, was standing the first watch, leaving Joseph to himself in a darkened and empty stateroom. Joseph discovered as he lay in his bunk and thought about all that was going on that he could not sleep. He thought about the house back in Tacoma. It had been over a year now since he had been home. He had to admit that life had changed markedly over the last few years. He had interviewed scores of officers who had helped prepare and then executed the operational plans for the war in the North Pacific. He had interviewed well over a hundred sailors of every rank to this point to bring their perspective of the campaign into play. The weekly updates he sent back to district headquarters now totaled over 80. All of this, he thought, would eventually become the foundation for his work after the war to construct a popular history.

But the end of the war, the historical work, and everything else seemed remote compared to the emptiness he felt when he thought about Miku. It had been over a year since Japanese Americans had been euphemistically housed at "Camp Harmony" just outside Tacoma. Now, all the internees were at camps like Minidoka in Idaho, where they would be kept until the war's end. Whenever Joseph thought about Miku, his spirit felt crushed. He had never loved anyone as much as her. Today's victory was one day closer to the war ending. Would he even dare to hope that the two of them might somehow, someway, be reunited?

Joseph looked at his Hamilton wristwatch with its black face and saw 0050 hours. Bill had yet to return after the end of his watch. The morning watch was a little more than three hours away. He turned over and tried to close his eyes but was confronted by thoughts of Fr. Etienne. He wondered how he was doing. Hopefully, he would still be in Tacoma when this was all over. Joseph frowned and told himself he needed to make that situation right. Fr. Etienne had done so much for him. He could never repay the time and effort the good priest had given of himself so that he could gain the education he had received. He turned over on his other side and then went to his back. He could not get comfortable. He thought again about Miku and then said aloud, "Enough," and raised himself in the bunk. A glance at the watch now told him it was 0115. He wasn't going to fall asleep. He had to get up. He swung his legs out over the side of the bunk and dropped to the floor. Once dressed, he exited the stateroom banging the door behind him.

He leaned over the railing on the ship's starboard side, letting the crisp cold air wake him from his self-inflicted tiredness. Surprisingly, Joseph thought, the cold night air was not alleviating his drowsiness. He thought maybe a walk around the main deck might do the trick.

~~~~~

Earlier that day, *Abner Read* had been ordered to start an anti-submarine patrol close to Blue Jay Rock off Conquer Point on Kiska Island. Not far from there were Sparrow

North Pacific

Rocks and Bluff Cove. Twilight had come at 2045, with sunset arriving at 2130. This was Alaska. An hour later, the moon made its appearance. The broken sky allowed for the moon's sporadic appearance with fog and mist. *Abner Read* moved along slowly at 5 knots. The night could be described as pleasant and calm, with a slight breeze.

Without warning, a fearsome explosion erupted beneath the ship's stern. *Abner Read's* bow plunged heavily down into the cold and dark waters while the stern rose out of the sea amid smoke and fire. The stern, reaching its apogee in the eruptive blast, collapsed into the night water in obvious distress. A rending, tearing sound announced the stern of the vessel, horribly separating itself from the rest of the ship and slipping below the surface to the ocean floor in the icy waters off Kiska Island. It was 0150, August 13, 1943.

General Quarters was sounded from the bridge, and the crew scrambled to their battle stations. Using her "blinker lights," *Abner Read* informed other ships in the area that an underwater explosion had torn her stern off. Word was spread on all the decks, "not" to abandon ship. The Captain sent out a distress call. *Abner Read* was powerless and listing to port with what was left of her stern now underwater. Additionally, the destroyer was drifting toward the rocky beach.

Meanwhile, *Abner Read's* #2 whaleboat was lowered to search for men in the water. The crew members who manned the boat moved to the oily stain of water on the ship's port side. The oil slick extended some 200 yards. In all, 20 oil-befouled sailors were hauled and wrestled into the whaleboat and brought back to the ship.

The medical officer had rushed to the Officer's Wardroom when general quarters sounded. With the whaleboat's return to the ship, the wounded were taken there to join the casualties from inside the ship near the stern. The injured from the whaleboat were covered in fuel oil. The most severe cases, those with serious injuries and deep lacerations, were kept in the wardroom to be treated. Of these, a few men were unconscious. Others drifted in and out of consciousness. Some had internal injuries and or broken bones. One sailor had burns over a good portion of his body. Another young man needed and was given artificial respiration but did not survive.

The ship, drifting toward the rocks that ringed the beaches of Kiska Island, was rescued by the destroyer *USS Bancroft* around 0300. She was able to maneuver close enough to *Abner Read* to pass her a line and pull the stricken vessel away from the shore to safety. The *USS Ute*, a naval fleet tug, then towed *Abner Read* to Adak Island for temporary repairs to make her safe enough to return to the West Coast for extensive reconstruction work.

A report detailing the incident summarized what had happened this way. In the darkness off Kiska Island, as part of an anti-submarine patrol, *Abner Read* was executing a turn to port when it struck a floating Japanese mine. Muster, in the morning, would reveal that 70 crew members were missing and unaccounted for.

North Pacific

Upon returning to Adak, thirty-four casualties were transferred to the naval dispensary – two dozen by stretcher. A handful of them would be air-lifted to the lower 48 for some serious medical attention. One of those was Lieutenant Joseph Vaenko.

VITA
(Life)

"For we are but of yesterday; and are ignorant that our days upon earth are but a shadow..."

Job 8:9

Douay-Rheims

"Behold thou hast made my days measurable: and my substance is as nothing before thee."

Psalm 38:6

Douay-Rheims

34.

Darkness, bright lights, murmuring, attempts at focusing, all coming and going in waves that went on and on. Being sedated, Joseph hovered around the edges of consciousness for days. When he finally arrived at the Naval Hospital in Bremerton, Washington, he underwent surgery for his back and pelvis. Doctors in Alaska had set his broken arm. His pelvis had been fractured. He had crushed vertebrae in his lower back.

A few days after surgery, Joseph slowly began to come around. He was, at last, somewhat successful in centering his thoughts, realizing who he was, and attempting to figure out what had happened. Unexpectedly, he raised his good arm and felt about his chest for his medal. It was gone. He became agitated. A nearby nurse walked over to his bed. "Is there a problem, Mr. Vaenko?"

"Medal," Joseph mumbled. I had a medal," He tried to focus on a figure leaning over him.

"Let me check on that, Mr. Vaenko." She walked over to the nurses' station and conversed with someone. Soon she returned to Joseph and said, "It was with your personal items. May I put it on you?"

Joseph nodded, emotionally relieved. "Thank you," he replied.

The nurses and orderlies were extremely kind to him, and he finally found the strength to respond to a nurse's question about how he felt. Slowly he said, "I'm all right." He thought that was the answer she was looking for, but he didn't know what all was wrong with him. Again, it had seemed like the right thing to say.

"That's wonderful, Lieutenant Vaenko," replied the nurse. "The doctor will be in this afternoon to see how you're doing. We'll try to clean you up some to look more presentable. You've had a rough time, and I'm so glad to see you become aware of what's happening around you. That's a good sign." She smiled and tended to him.

For his part, he started to notice what she was talking about. First and foremost, he was a mess. Bandages, casts, stitches, not to mention bruises, were about everywhere he was able to see. After completing his unscientific and haphazard survey of himself, Joseph swallowed and asked, "Could I have some water?"

The nurse obliged, and so it went that morning as he began to understand his situation more clearly. The more he became aware, the more he felt the pain of his injuries. Joseph was given some medicine, and he slept. Later that day, he met his doctor, who explained to Joseph what they had done to put him back together. The doctor said medicine had come a long way in the previous decades. Without those advances, such as metal plates with screws and other progress, his chances of a reasonable recovery or even surviving the surgeries would have been less. He remembered later that night, thinking back to the doctor's summary of his condition, he had told Joseph that he was "a fortunate fellow."

By this time, Joseph had finally remembered being on *Abner Read*. He even recalled getting up and going out on level 2 of the main deck of the destroyer to take a walk that night to wake up, but nothing beyond that. Maybe more would come to him later, he told himself.

The following day, one of the other doctors told him he had been involved in an explosion aboard *Abner Read* when the ship hit a floating Japanese mine. He had been blown overboard by the force of the blast and had landed in the water, hitting something that had tried to break his back but only managed to fracture his pelvis and damage the vertebrae in his lower back, and break an arm. The doctor continued Joseph's story as it had been told to him, "Once in the water, you managed to get tangled up in some cork netting that had gone overboard the same as you." The doctor had heard that the special cork netting was specifically designed for that purpose. He said, "It worked as advertised and kept you afloat and alive. You were rescued along with a couple of dozen other survivors who had also been in the waters off Kiska Island." He told Joseph that 70 men were unaccounted for in the blast, and, in those waters, most certainly lost. Joseph took it all in.

That night, he thought about how close he had come to being killed. With absolutely no warning, he was catapulted into the extremely cold North Pacific, and, could he say it, did it make sense to say it? Yes, it made sense to him. By the grace of God, he had lived. Tears ran down his face. He whispered "Slava na viky!" (Glory to Him forever!) over and over and over, deep into the night.

As much as he tried, he could not remember what happened on that fateful night in the Aleutians. However, his mind was working better now. As the days passed, he began to look forward to his daily adventure of being pushed around by a nurse or an orderly in a wooden wheelchair through the main hospital building and many of the eight wings that made up the Puget Sound Naval Shipyard Hospital.

After weeks of recovery, Joseph was informed he was being moved to Seattle to recuperate further and begin therapy. When the day came, he and his duffle bag were loaded onto a naval ferry that dropped him off in Shoreline, Washington (really a suburb just north of the city of Seattle). Shoreline was the location of the newly constructed Seattle Naval Hospital. He was moved into a ward with other recovering naval personnel and began to receive physical therapy in large doses compared to the treatment he had been undergoing in Bremerton.

Before he knew it, a new calendar year had begun, and he was told he would be discharged from the Navy. The physical damage done to him would leave him unqualified for active duty. Captain Brewer from 13th Naval District Headquarters, the officer who had greeted him on his first day of active duty in the Navy, came by before his departure to thank Joseph for his work. He told Joseph that the reports and the recorded interviews with the major players in the Aleutian Islands theatre had been essential work and would help immensely tell the story of the war in the North Pacific. Brewer said that Joseph would have access to all his work to write a history of the war in the North Pacific when he was able. Joseph thanked him and shared that "the history" was one of his main motivating factors during his recovery over the last so many months. Brewer told him he believed the fighting in the Aleutians was at an end, so ironically, Lieutenant Vaenko had managed to be a part of almost the entire North Pacific saga. He could even say that he might have even been one of the last casualties of the whole affair. They both laughed and talked genially about the war's overall progress and hoped to see its end soon.

When Captain Brewer left, Joseph, now without his cast and having gained some mobility in using his body, wondered what the future held for him back in Tacoma. He was 37 years old now. Where did the time go? A Catholic chaplain had been around, and Joseph had received Holy Communion regularly. He had not had a heart-to-heart with God about what had happened. Joseph told himself he was saving that discussion for when he got home. During his recovery, the thoughts and ideas of the Frenchman Sartre unsettled him. Joseph also thought of Miku. He wondered whether she was all right. The thought of her being confined in a camp in Idaho, California, or elsewhere repulsed him. Was it beyond hope now that she might ever think about him again?

35.

In April 1944, Joseph and his duffle bag were delivered to his home on the steep hill in Tacoma. It had been almost two years since he had come home on a 48-hour pass. With his new cane, he walked unsteadily into the house and carefully navigated his way over to the sofa. He sat down with his back in one corner of it with one leg up on the cushions and the other on the floor. He carefully positioned himself with his arms and watched his duffle bag be dropped on the floor next to him. He thanked the military driver for the lift and asked him to close the door on his way out.

He closed his eyes. Finally alone for the first time in months, he heard a car drive by the front of the house. Then there was no sound. It was the first time since the mining of the *Abner Read* that he had heard no ancillary noises. There was only blessed silence. Joseph had been in hospital wards for months. The solitude and stillness of the house washed over him. He did not immediately open his eyes and clung to the moment for as long as possible. He knew he would be starting a new chapter in his life when he re-opened them. Was he up to it? What choice did he have? He rested for a few minutes, then got up and sorted his clothing from his duffle bag.

North Pacific

Joseph awoke the following day to Western seagulls making noise as they climbed and swooped up from the bay. He slowly got out of the single bed next to the staircase. It was no easy task. Most certainly, he was not ready to take on the fourteen steps, including the small landing, that separated him from his bedroom. He was actually more concerned about coming down the stairs than going up. Maybe tonight, he thought.

Mary, Coleen's sister, and his house-sitter had moved out a week earlier. He had talked to Mary through Colleen while in the Seattle Naval Hospital, and they had worked out the timing of his arrival and her departure. She had been a godsend to Joseph. She had maintained the house and kept his car running.

That thought reminded him he needed to call on Colleen to see how she was doing and find out what she knew of her husband and the old heavy cruiser, *Salt Lake City*. He looked around the kitchen and in the cupboards. There was some coffee, so Joseph percolated a pot.

He decided that a trip to the grocery store was in order, as the shelves were now essentially bare. Later in the day, he drove to the market in his sturdy old Studebaker. He learned that street curbs and other everyday obstacles slowed his getting around. He did his shopping carefully and slowly, realizing how much effort it seemed to take to do what had been, in the past, easy and straightforward. Store staff helped him carry out his groceries and put them in the car. As this undertaking continued, he realized he would need some help getting the groceries from the car into his house. He considered this as he pulled up in front of his place. He sat in the car, waited a minute or two, and then corralled a neighbor kid walking by and paid him a quarter to lug the groceries into the house.

Joseph learned to sit in the straight-back chairs with firm seats around the kitchen table, as they supported his lower back much more so than the softer cushions of the sofa. This also was the problem with the "big chair," as he and his parents had called it. He made a mental note to purchase a version of a straight-back chair with firm seating and armrests for the living room to replace Alexandr's "big chair." He disliked thinking about it, but his lower back was a mess. Whenever he stood up, you would think the world was ending. His back simply did not want to make that 90-degree adjustment when standing up.

Further, although he hated admitting it, he didn't know how he would get around without his cane. After about a week, Joseph finally found the courage to conquer the staircase, going up and, most importantly, coming down safely. He could finally sit in the solid straight-back chair at his desk and survey the great expanse of water through the upstairs window. A week later, a new straight-back chair with sturdy arms and a firm cushion arrived to replace Alexandr's big (and soft) chair in the living room.

He had to drive weekly to Madigan General Hospital, an Army facility newly opened that year about five miles south of Tacoma, for rehabilitation appointments. Here, he would spend a couple of hours going over and performing stretches and exercises supervised by staff to strengthen his lower back. He enjoyed the drive because it enabled him to put his foot on the accelerator in certain parts of the highway and open up the engine, helping clean out the old Studebaker's carburetor.

Joseph forced himself to take walks. Before the war, he remembered the times he had taken long walks, sometimes twice a day, to stave off the urge to have a drink. Now, with a significantly reduced capacity to take those walks, Joseph understood it was up to him to find a way. However, try as he might, he was unable to walk around the North End and Old Town as he had always done before. At this point in his recovery, the hills were just too much for him.

However, on sunny days, Joseph would drive to the public boathouse along the bay at the city's Point Defiance Park and traverse the "flat and even" walkway along the shore above the breakwater between there and Owen Beach, a beach recreation area within the expansive park. The fresh air was invigorating, and when it showed itself, the sun was always a reminder of how great it was to live in the Puget Sound region. It took him quite a while to cover the distance, but he could feel himself becoming surer of his footing, himself, and his recovery. Would he ever be his old self? The doctors had said probably not. Yet, they encouraged him to work at regaining as much function as he possibly could.

He talked to the administrative staff at Rainier College, and it was agreed that Joseph would resume teaching in the fall. The great news was that he was becoming an Associate Professor. The extra money was welcome. He could now develop course materials for a new class focusing on the U.S. Navy in the North Pacific. Things were working out - slowly.

36.

Not too long after returning to Tacoma, Joseph visited Colleen. After a big hug and both had sat down, Colleen asked for more details of Joseph's situation.

Joseph walked her gently through his story, leaving out parts, and ended by tapping his cane on the floor and saying, "Meet my necessary new friend."

Colleen said, "Oh, Joseph, you won't have to use that forever. You'll be back to your former self in no time. I genuinely believe that."

The conversation shifted to her husband. She told Joseph that Martin was "somewhere at sea." She went on to say that this information was "not helpful," but it got both of them laughing. Colleen told Joseph she hated worrying about him, especially now that the good guys were finally winning the damn war. "Joseph, the more I start thinking of the possibility of Martin coming home, the more I worry something might happen to him. But enough about Martin and me. How is civilian life treating you?"

North Pacific

Joseph wanted to hear more about Martin, but either Colleen didn't have enough information from his letters, as she seemed to imply, or maybe he wasn't writing that much. Either way, it frustrated him. He wanted to hear that his best friend was all right.

"I can't lie. It has been wonderful being home and sleeping in my own bed." As they continued their conversation, Colleen said, "By the way, Joseph, Diane Lassiter stopped by a couple of months ago and asked if I knew how you were doing. I told her I had not heard from you. She seemed disappointed. Anything you want to tell me about that?"

Smiling, Joseph told her, "She stopped by the house back when I was home on that 48-hour pass. You remember you made me dinner. Anyway, she came by the house. It was great to see her."

"Well, I think she's keeping tabs on you. Have you seen her since you've been back?"

"No, I've been keeping to myself and trying to work hard with rehabilitation to lose this cane."

"You should see her, Joseph. It would be good for you, and I'm certain, call it intuition, that she would like to see you very much. She's always had a thing for you."

Again, Joseph smiled, "I'm sure we'll see each other sometime soon."

Colleen laughed, playfully shook a finger at him, and said, "Make sure you make that happen, Mr. Vaenko."

North Pacific

His visit to Colleen's had been pleasant, really nice. For the first time, he felt he was back and living in his hometown. Although he could not get around like he used to, he was comforted by his lifelong surroundings, especially his wonderful home. As he sat at his kitchen table that night, he thought that since it was Saturday and he had gotten around reasonably well that day, it was time for him to return to Mass at St. Dominic. How would that go? He smiled, thinking that the pews were hard, brown-stained wood, but the kneelers had some cushioning. He wondered how his back would hold up during low Mass. He knew kneeling and standing would challenge him.

He had not seen Father Etienne since before the war. Almost everything he had going for him, his education, his job, the house, and much about his faith formation, he largely owed to the Dominican priest. It was time to make that situation right.

~~~~~

Joseph rose Sunday morning about an hour earlier than he might have in the past. He needed the extra time to do his stretches, dress, and generally work out all the kinks that were now a part of his life. As he started the Studebaker that morning, he thought about how he and his parents had walked to Mass each Sunday when he was young. After Maria had passed away, he and his Father continued that enjoyable routine. That morning, upon arriving at St.

North Pacific

Dominic, he parked the car and, using the cane, traversed the parking lot and entered the church. It had been a while since he had been there. As he looked at the altar, the tabernacle, the large crucifix, the pews, the windows, the statuary, and the sanctuary lamp, he felt that everything was still the same. His church had not changed. He felt comforted.

Joseph had told himself going to bed the night before that he would go to Confession before the start of Mass in the morning. That had forced him to stay awake an extra 45 minutes as he examined his conscience and the ten commandments.

Joseph dipped his thumb and first two fingers in the holy water and made the sign of the Cross. Then he walked over to the side of the church and down the aisle along the wall until he reached the confessional, where one person, a younger-looking teenager, was waiting his turn up against the wall. Joseph stopped a couple of feet behind him and became second in line. Standing there, he went over in his head, once again, his transgressions, and in a moment, the door opened, and out came an older woman wearing, as his mother would have called it, a "babushka" to cover her head. The youngster entered the confessional. Again, Joseph waited. This time, it took a while until the young person emerged. The boy, who looked to be in junior high school, looked like he had been given a death sentence. Joseph smiled to himself and thought that the young man had probably been given a full rosary to say for his penance rather than the usual three Our Fathers and three Hail

Marys that most young people of school age received as their temporal atonement for their sins.

He entered the confessional, closed the door behind him, and knelt awkwardly with a wince on the kneeler. He propped his cane against the wall and waited. He recognized that his breathing was shallow and that he was nervous. It had been so long since he had spoken to Father Etienne. Then the little sliding door (about the size of one's hand) was opened, revealing yet another screen separating him from the priest. They each made the sign of the cross, and then Joseph began, "Bless me, Father, for I have sinned…." A moment into the confession, Joseph realized it was not Father Etienne's voice on the other side of the screen. Surprised, Joseph was also relieved. This was not the place to rekindle a friendship, he thought to himself.

When he had confessed his sins, listened to what the priest had to say about his transgressions, received his penance, and said his act of contrition, the priest absolved Joseph of his sins in the name of Christ and completed the sacrament by blessing Joseph. Like so many times before in his life, Joseph made the sign of the cross and exited the confessional. He found a pew further back than he used to sit in. To him, the further back you sat in the church was always a healthy sign of unworthiness. He mused that using that logic might qualify him to be seated somewhere out in the parking lot. He knelt, said his penitential prayers, and eased back off the kneeler and onto the pew seat. With his lower back talking to him, he hoped he would survive Mass.

North Pacific

A look around the church revealed that many men around his age and younger were absent. It reminded him of how many were serving in the armed forces at that time. The small bell was rung, and the altar boys, followed by the priest, entered the sanctuary from a side doorway. Joseph saw that it was not Fr. Etienne. The older priest introduced himself before giving his homily. Father Morris informed those that did not know, including Joseph, that Father Etienne was away providing retreats for Dominican parishes in Southern California. When Father Sauveterre would return was anyone's guess, but until he did, Father Morris promised he would soldier on providing the sacraments to the parishioners of St. Dominic. Father Morris' homily touched on various topics that Joseph quickly forgot, but he finished his prepared remarks with a short, one-line prayer, "O Lord, all my hope is anchored in your great mercy." So true, Joseph mused. He had not reconnected with Father Etienne as he had hoped, but he was pleased to be "home again" at St. Dominic. He said hello to a few people he knew and felt uncomfortably conscious of the cane he held in his hand.

37.

Once in the car, Joseph decided to stop for breakfast at 3 Bridges Café. He hadn't been there since the war began. He parked in front of the little restaurant, entered, and sat back in the corner, leaning his cane against the wall. In a moment, the waitress appeared, carrying a pot of fresh coffee. Raising the pot slightly, she asked Joseph if he would like some. Joseph smiled, turned over his coffee cup, and pushed it gently toward her. She poured the coffee and said, "Breakfast?"

Joseph nodded.

With her free hand, she gave him a menu. The bell on the café door rang, and she turned to greet a couple entering. She showed them to a table by the window and repeated her questions about "coffee" and "menus."

Later, after Joseph had finished his breakfast of pancakes with butter and maple syrup, he reflected that he had not been able to see Father Etienne. Father Morris had not helped much with his vague remarks about when the French priest might return.

In the meantime, Joseph looked over at his waitress. She immediately saw his glance, reached for the coffee pot, and walked toward the table. Joseph smiled and moved his cup toward her again. She refilled it and cleared his breakfast plate and utensils. While doing this, she asked herself why this guy was sitting back in the corner. She looked at him and thought, I remember him. Wasn't he usually a counter guy? Then, she saw his cane propped up against the wall, immediately made eye contact with him, and asked how he was doing.

Joseph, slightly surprised by her attention, told her he was having trouble with his back but was on the mend. He then thanked her for the breakfast and the refill of his coffee. She apologized for asking.

Joseph said, "No, really, it's okay." He felt a bit uneasy and uncomfortable. Looking at the waitress with her slim figure, brunette hair, and intriguing eyes, he said, "Really, I was involved in a situation where I hurt my lower back. The cane is to take a bit of pressure off it and give me some balance and support while it's healing." And, still feeling a bit funny, it struck him, I know this gal. She was here the day I saw Miku for the first time at Mass. I believe I looked somewhat lost and could not speak coherently in front of her. Great. Way to go, Vaenko. You know, she's quite good-looking.

"Well, I wasn't trying to pry, really. I just saw the cane and then remembered you from before the war. You would stop by once in a while."

"I was just thinking the same thing about you, that is, that I recognized you from a few years back," said Joseph, becoming more at ease as they focused more on one another.

"I'm sorry to hear about your back. I hope it heals soon."

Joseph finally looked at her name tag and said, "Yes, I remember you, Denise. I'm a bit absent-minded and get caught up in my thoughts. It's not a particularly good trait, I'm afraid."

She laughed and said, "It's okay. I think it gives you a strangely attractive quality." She laughed again, "I find your way a bit endearing."

"Oh, now you're having too much fun with me," Joseph, amused, responded.

There was an almost awkward pause as both realized they enjoyed each other's company. Then the momentary silence was interrupted by a call from behind the counter that an order was up.

"Joseph," he said, "I'm Joseph," making eye contact with her that he did not want to give up.

"Well, Joseph, I have to get back to work. It has been nice having this little chat. Don't be a stranger."

Joseph said, "Well, you've made my day."

Denise smiled and walked back behind the counter to gather the waiting order. The cook indicated he had yet another that was about ready. Joseph watched her for a minute and then left a larger-than-usual tip. When she seemed engaged with some other customers, he reached for his cane and tried to make his way out the door without being noticed.

That night he thought about Denise. He surmised that she might be a few years older than himself, but not much. He wondered what her circumstances were and wished they could have chatted more that morning. It seemed to him she had a way of sensing things that made him wonder if she knew more about him than he did. She really was an attractive woman. How had he not noticed her before?

38.

In his quest to regain his ability to walk cane-free, Joseph drove to Point Defiance Park and parked his car by the City Public Boathouse. He walked slowly, cane in hand, down to Owen Beach. As he stood looking out across the water at Vashon Island and west toward Gig Harbor on the Kitsap Peninsula, someone tapped him on the shoulder. Joseph turned his head, and there stood Charlie Langley. "Hey Charlie, how have you been?"

Langley grinned, and the two shook hands. Charlie had a great tan and looked as fit as Joseph had remembered him in high school. "I've been great, Joe. I returned from Hawaii the other day on leave. They thought I could use a week or two off. I've performed more surgeries in

Honolulu over the last couple of years than I ever imagined. However, I will have to admit that the experience I've gained will serve me handsomely after the war." Charlie sized up Joseph a bit more and said, "So, what's with the cane?"

Joseph looked down at the cane, "I got tossed around some up in the Aleutian Islands."

"Are you going to be okay?"

"Sure, my lower back needs a little time to heal. I'll be fine."

"Good, I'm glad to hear it." Charlie paused and glanced over at a couple of women reclining up against a log, sunning themselves on the beach. "I drove down here today because the weather was so great. I'll be heading back to Honolulu next Saturday. Have you seen any of the old gang since you've been home?"

"Not really," Joseph said in a voice that might have betrayed the slight embarrassment of his lack of a life. He mentally pulled himself together and focused on Charlie.

"Hey, I saw Diane Lassiter the other day," Charlie said with obvious pleasure. "Can you believe it, she's not married? It blows me away. Anyway, I saw her downtown, and I took her to lunch. She's taking care of her parents and working part-time with her dad. He's an investment banker. I'm definitely going to look her up when this war is over. I even told her so."

"I saw her a couple of years ago when our ship was in Bremerton for some work," Joseph replied, trying to hold up his end of the conversation. It made him think back to the party after high school when Charlie introduced him to Eloise, the first girl he had known intimately all those years ago. Charlie had said he would become a doctor and now was a talented local surgeon. His looks, money, and now his Hawaiian tan didn't hurt his appeal to the opposite sex. Still, he had not married, at least not yet.

"Joe, it's been great seeing you, but I have an appointment downtown in half an hour. So are you still teaching up at Rainier?"

"I am. I'll be back teaching this fall," Joseph added, "And I'm looking forward to it."

"That's terrific," Charlie exclaimed. The two shook hands again, and then Dr. Langley headed for his car. On his way, he stopped by the two women sunbathing, bent over slightly, and said something to them. As Joseph watched, they seemed to listen intently to whatever Charlie was saying and then laughed and giggled. Then both women watched Charlie head for his car, waving at him while still laughing and looking at each other. He waved one last time at them, then jumped in his car and roared up the steep hill that led away from the beach.

It struck Joseph that it sure seemed like Charlie could accomplish whatever he wanted to in life. He told himself he needed to reflect on that when he had more time. Anyway, he needed to get going. As was his new way, he began walking slowly to the path back to the Public Boat House, where his car was parked. On his way, he too passed close to the two sunbathers, only he did not stop to talk to them, and the women, for their part, did not look up at Joseph.

During the trek back to the boathouse parking lot, he thought about his experience in the North Pacific and the mining of *Abner Read*. Who would have guessed that would happen to him? Life is chaotic and uncontrollable, he thought. There are some compelling components to Sartre's existentialist argument. Yet, if true, God and everything he had been taught and learned throughout his life, regarding the meaning of it all, was a lie, or more simply not true. And if it were not true, then as the existentialist case would argue, the world and life were absurd.

He shook his head and then looked again across Commencement Bay at Vashon Island. He saw the stands of trees dotting the hillsides across the island. He could hear the waves lapping the shore, not twenty feet in front of him. This setting was so rich, so beautiful. How could that kind of beauty be random?

39.

Joseph read the newspaper thoroughly. So, the Allies had landed at Normandy a few weeks back, established a beachhead, and were now moving inland. We are in France, he thought, and this damn war is closer to ending. The Soviets were pushing west and the Allies east, and there was nothing Germany could do about it. In the Pacific, the Americans had landed forces in the Mariana Islands on the island of Saipan. It was not over, but the handwriting was on the wall.

It was the first day of summer 1944. Having already met with the Rainier College administration, Joseph began working daily to prepare for fall classes. He was genuinely excited to return to campus.

At this point, Joseph's mind turned to his situation. He lived alone, without a companion to create a shared life. He thought about Miku every day. He realized he should never have asked her to move in. He got that. Man, did he ever get that? But how had that mistake led to this point? It made no sense.

He remembered walking all over Japan Town in Tacoma and searching up north in Seattle for any sign of her, all to no avail. Where did she go? And then, the thought crossed his mind for the first time - should I move on? That, he thought, was easy to say, but doing it, moving on from the most meaningful relationship of his life was quite another. I know I'm not getting any younger. Any chance at a family now is almost zero. Further, who would be interested in a guy who has to use a cane at my age to get around? His nascent thoughts about moving on from Miku gave him pause. He loved that woman. Yet, what if she never came back? Would he sit in his house and talk to himself for the next so many decades? Was it over for him?

North Pacific

I'm still only thirty-seven. Granted, I walk like I'm in my sixties or seventies, but I believe my back will get better, and I will walk without this cane soon. I will. I just will.

~~~~~

Joseph had driven down to Isaacs in Old Town a few times since returning home just to be around people. However, while there, he did not drink any alcohol. At least in that part of his life, he had been steadfast. He sipped on a Nesbitt Orange and even ate a little bar food, a change of pace, and sometimes sadly, a step up from his less-than-stellar cooking at home. During one of those visits, he learned from his friend Leo, the bartender, that Jill Connors had left town shortly after Joseph had stopped coming in. Jill Connors, Joseph reflected, now there was a sensual woman. She was not much of a talker, but she could be mesmerizing when she wanted to hold your attention. I really hope things work out for her.

And by chance, Joseph also learned that Ron Huddleston, the guy who practically beat him to death the last time he had run into him, had joined the Army, and been killed in February in the fighting in and around Anzio in Italy. He shuddered at the recollection of the thrashing he had received that now seemed like ages ago. When Joseph left the bar, he looked up the always steep 30th Street hill and wondered how in the world he used to be able to climb the half dozen blocks to his place without even thinking about it. He looked at his cane and told himself that someday he would be able to do it again. Then he looked up the hill once more and felt less confident.

Spending so much time with yourself made it easy to recycle the same thoughts. You wanted to resolve them, but there seemed no solution, so your brain would set them aside, but never for long, and the whole process would start again. It seemed like yesterday that he was out of high school, enjoying the summer and waiting to start college. So much had happened. He was sneaking up on forty. Was that possible? To this point, he envisioned his life playing out differently than it had. Was there still time to put his life back on track for his now somewhat battered and hazy idea of happiness?

When he was younger, he felt it was just a matter of applying himself to the task like he had to obtain his education, but that wasn't true. Fate was at play, or was it? Fate was a term the Greeks used that spoke to inevitability and predetermination. Maybe "a roll of the dice" better described his life. It sure felt to him that it had been a game of chance to this point, and disappointingly it seemed to fit more with that existentialist talk of Sartre.

Then he thought of Father Etienne and his homilies that spoke of man's free will. He had always believed that he could make decisions that shaped his life, but he also knew forces were at play over which he had no control. He could count his close friends on one hand. That was probably due more to his innate shyness than anything random in the universe. As Joseph mulled these thoughts, he sensed loneliness creeping back into his bones for the first time in quite a while. Because that's where loneliness exists, he thought, deep in your bones and in your soul. His time in the Navy and recovery had blunted the terrible feeling, but now he acknowledged it was trying to return. He remembered Father Etienne speaking of people as social beings who needed human interaction and contact. In general, man was not meant to be alone, hence Eve. These thoughts left Joseph with an empty feeling. Yet, the older he got, the more he acquiesced to its seeming inevitability. Finally, he said to himself, enough. This train of thought was taking him down the wrong track, and he was not up to it, not tonight. He brought closure to his thoughts by asking God to please enlighten and speak to him in some way.

40.

The leaves fell and swirled around Joseph in the parking lot next to St. Dominic. It was late October, and the weather was turning colder. He had just left the college for the day and stopped by the church to visit the Lord in the Blessed Sacrament. He held his coat close to the collar with his free hand and focused on where to place the cane with each step he took as he made his way into the church. Once inside, he walked to the statue of the Virgin Mary holding the Christ child, located two-thirds of the way into the nave in an alcove. In his prayer, he asked if she might pray and intercede with her son for him in his struggles with a silent God.

As he prepared to move on toward a pew, he focused one last time on the statue. Mary used her free hand to point directly at Jesus being held in her other arm. Of course, as Joseph had learned as a child, Mary always directed everyone to her son. After all, was she not the first disciple of Christ? Joseph was moved by the way Mary asked Jesus for help at the wedding feast in Cana and then left it in his hands, trusting that he would deal with it as he saw fit. She never doubted her son. *"His mother saith to the waiters: Whatsoever he shall say to you, do ye."* (Jn 2:5). Joseph walked toward the center of the church and genuflected toward the tabernacle on the high altar.

Once ensconced in a pew, Joseph concentrated on Christ's presence in the Blessed Sacrament. It had made such a significant impression on him as a boy. He had accompanied his mother in this distinctive practice of Catholics, regularly visiting the Blessed Sacrament on so many occasions.

He didn't know what it was. He did not see God. He did not hear God. He did not receive any signal or such thing. However, at some point in his visits with his mother, he began to sense that something, or better put, possibly someone, was truly present in a most special way. And from that point forward in his life, he conducted himself as though he was in the presence of the Lord. When others would enter and exit the church while he was there and act as if it were nothing more than a space used to talk in, he would become upset and pray at once that God would not be offended. He didn't know why they didn't realize it. Having thought about all that, it struck him that it was the nearest he had come to having a sense, a certainty, if you like, of God's existence and presence in this world. It was the closest thing to being in the presence of the transcendent, other than receiving Christ, body, soul, and divinity during Communion at Mass.

As Joseph sat alone in the church, he could hear the gusting wind outside as it rushed through the trees. Yet, at the same time, inside the church, there was a stillness, a hushed and peaceful quiet. Above the high altar was Christ nailed to the Cross, the Cross he was forced to carry to Calvary, agonizingly being crushed to the ground three times by the weight of man's sins in the wood. Jesus, the Son of God, was nailed to the cross, his body viciously splayed upon the wood. When Joseph was little, his mother would always say to him as they would look at the large crucifix above and behind the high altar and the tabernacle, "The Cross is our salvation, Joseph." He missed her so much. It was just one more thing that he did not control in his life.

After sitting and kneeling in the pew for half an hour, Joseph walked to the back of the church, made the sign of the cross with holy water, and pushed open the large door to the outside. As he descended the steps in front of the church, he looked up from where he was placing his cane and, to his immense surprise, came face to face with Father Etienne.

~~~~~

Both men were caught entirely off guard. They viewed each other with incredulity. Finally, they smiled broadly at each other. Joseph finished descending the steps, and the two shook hands and clasped the other's shoulder in greeting.

"How have you been, Joseph?"

Joseph, a bit overcome, said, "I'm good, Father."

Concerned, the priest continued, "Why are you using a cane?"

Joseph paused, again realizing his circumstances, and said, "I'm sorry, Father, I was involved in a mishap in Alaska."

Father visibly made a face of dismay and said he was so sorry to hear of Joseph's situation. "Please, Joseph, do you have a few minutes to spare? Why don't we go over to the rectory where we can talk? It has been so long."

"Yes, I do have time, Father. My classes are over for today, and I was headed home after a quick stop by the church."

"Time with Our Lord in the Blessed Sacrament," Father said softly, then smiling, exclaimed, "Wonderful, let's go over to the rectory."

North Pacific

The mentor and the student of what now seemed like ages ago made their way across the parking lot to the rectory. They settled in at a table in the library, as they had done so many times before, and began conversing.

"So again, can we discuss this mishap that befell you?"

More at ease now, Joseph told Father how his ship had struck a Japanese mine while he was in the Navy serving in the Aleutian Islands. "I wound up in the water and, following repair work to my body, have been trying to strengthen my lower back to be rid of my helper here," twisting the cane in his hand.

Joseph thought, I must make this right with Father Etienne. This is too important to defer until later or to talk around it. Right now is the time. "Father, I want to, umm, I must say something."

Father Etienne nodded, and Joseph began, "Before the beginning of the war, with no help from anyone else, I made some terrible decisions that led to a succession of sinful actions that I have regretted ever since. I didn't want to confess those sins to you, Father. I was certain you would figure out it was me in the confessional from my voice and the sins I would tell you. I guess I didn't want to let you down. So instead, I procrastinated. The initial sins were shameful and eventually led to many others. It was easily the nadir of my life to this point. Then the war began, and before I knew it, I was in the Navy and headed to the North Pacific. Those sins weighed on me morning, noon, and night. I finally met a priest up there in Alaska, and upon reflection, I decided to confess my sins to him."

Joseph began ever so slightly to avert his eyes from Fr. Etienne, but he stopped himself, regained his composure, and refocused on the priest. "I know, I just told you that I avoided confessing my sins to you, Father, but I want you to know that I am truly sorry and most embarrassed I was not man enough at the time to go to you, my confessor, straight away, tell you my sins and with your help sort through it all. Please, forgive me, Father."

"Joseph, Joseph, don't beat yourself up. Of course, as a friend, I completely forgive you. Understanding one's faults and then telling someone about them is not easy, not at all. I cannot tell you how many Protestants have told me over the years that they would have converted to Catholicism if not for the singular idea of having to confess their sins to a priest. The faith teaches that the priest acts *"in persona Christe"* (in the person of Christ) in the Sacrament of Penance. They simply could not confess their misdeeds to another person. Let's call it human frailty. It was always easier to talk to Jesus directly, as they would put it. I always pray for someone who tells me that because they are so close to receiving the powerful graces associated with Christ's Sacrament of Penance. I am more than pleased you resolved your hesitations and confessed your sins to that priest in Alaska. There is nothing more important than your immortal soul. We cannot deliberately, willfully, turn away from the Lord," Father said, smiling and raising his voice in triumph.

Joseph paused, took in Father's words, and continued, "Thank you, Father. Still, the point is, I was ashamed to come to you, and then my actions ended up leading me into further sin, and there seemed no way out." Joseph looked down at the table and sighed.

"Joseph, life is full of trials. The only thing that matters, as I told you, is that you contritely confessed your sins and made atonement for them in the penance the priest gave you, and as the Lord said, *'Go, and now sin no more"* (Jn 8:11).

"Thank you, Father." There was a moment of silence which Joseph finally broke by asking the priest how his trip to California had gone. Father Etienne smiled and began a lengthy discourse on his adventures in Southern California, how the weather was so different from the Northwest, the warm welcome he had received, and how he had tried out some new homilies at different Masses to see how parishioners responded. He told Joseph that he had a book of homilies (what else) in the works and hoped to see it published within the year. Joseph congratulated him and told Father of his plans to author a book about the history of the naval war in the North Pacific.

The two friends, now both relaxed, talked about a range of subjects in which they shared an interest. Then as the conversation began to wind down, Joseph asked Father Etienne one more question. He asked the priest whether he had read any of Jean-Paul Sartre's works and, if so, what he thought of his philosophical ideas. The priest from Orleans paused for a moment. With his elbows on the table, he interlocked his fingers in front of his face in an almost prayerful position, took a breath, released it, and then placed his hands back on the table.

He smiled at Joseph and said, "Yes," he had read Sartre. "Let me tell you this, Joseph, Mr. Sartre is not an English-speaking philosopher who looks at the world from an analytical point of view, that is, scientifically or mathematically. He is a French philosopher. And because of that, he views philosophy in cultural terms. Sartre believes there is no God. There is only existence. It is everything, yet at the same time, for Man, it is nothing because, in the end, Man is finite and will return to nothingness. Each Man will come to an end. With that barren view of life, all Man can do is fall back on his freedom to make choices and decisions and live by their consequences. This, then, is what Sartre is saying, those that use their liberty in this manner define their existence. This is what happens when God is removed from the philosophical discussion."

Joseph went on to share his similar thoughts and ideas related to Sartre. "Father, you wouldn't happen to have a copy of Sartre's *The Wall*, would you?"

Father Etienne rose quickly, walked over to his shelves, looked for a moment, and then removed a book. *Le Mur* (The Wall) Father said. "I only have it in French."

Joseph smiled, "That's no problem. Father, it was you who taught me to read French. I will enjoy reading it in French – always better than a translation. I read *Nausea* in French also."

Father continued to look at his bookshelves for a minute or two. "Joseph, here, read this book also. It is *Etre et avoir* (Being and Having) by Gabriel Marcel. Monsieur Marcel converted to Catholicism in 1929, and this work touches on many of the points of which Sartre speaks. I think Marcel, in this book, shows the beginnings of a Christian approach to existentialism. Marcel asks many of the same questions that Sartre explores."

Joseph thanked him and took the book. Vaenko had been watching Father Etienne look up and down the shelves. The Dominican was getting a bit on in years. He must be 60 by now, he thought. Joseph broached the subject. "Father, how long do you think you will continue to be the pastor at St. Dominic?"

"Oh, I don't know, Joseph. I believe I have a few good years left in me, Lord willing. Many Dominicans are doing their part as chaplains in the war effort. As long as they need me around, I'm up to it. Do you still own that beautiful little home overlooking the bay," Father Etienne asked, changing the subject.

"Yes, Father, I do. I had someone living there while I was in the service. Now I'm thinking about having some work done to bring the house up to today's codes. I'm not interested in it one day collapsing and sliding down the hill. I've lived in that house my entire life, and if I see that it's getting old, what does that say about me," Joseph said with a self-deprecating smile.

North Pacific

Joseph's face then turned serious, and he continued, "I will tell you though, Father, through my experiences of the last three or four years, I struggle mightily with things like loneliness, meaning in my life, and I'm sorry, even sometimes as to whether God is truly out there so to speak. Sartre says no to the existence of God and tells me to get on with defining my own life. Sometimes life seems so dark."

"And yet," Father Etienne replied, "I find you today, Joseph, after all this time, visiting Our Lord in the Blessed Sacrament in our little church."

"I will admit I see the contradiction, Father."

Father Etienne smiled and said, "I would prefer to call it possibly a paradox." "Joseph, remember I am here for you anytime to discuss the questions that trouble you. I consider us great friends even though we have gone a few years without talking. Life can be hard, but great friendships are priceless," the Dominican said while gesturing with his hand and grinning. They both laughed and continued their discussion about the news of the fall of the French "Vichy" government and the liberation of Paris in the second half of August, almost two months ago. Father Etienne was almost tearful with thanksgiving and forcefully stated, "It is only a matter of time now until Germany surrenders."

Father asked a few more questions about Joseph's health, to which Joseph responded as best he could. The conversation made Joseph think about the extent of his injuries and his slower-than-he-had-expected recovery. In all, they spoke for the better part of an hour and then parted with a vow from Joseph to keep in touch and, of course, attend Sunday Mass.

41.

A few weeks before Christmas, Joseph ran into Diane Lassiter downtown at *Peoples'* department store on the corner of 11th Street and Pacific Avenue. He was trying to find gifts for the Linart children, Mark and Darcy. Diane, carrying a couple of bags, saw Joseph first. She set the bags down, threw her arms around him, and gave him a big hug and a kiss. Joseph, definitely surprised, smiled, and tried awkwardly to hug Diane with his cane swinging out precariously. The store was packed with customers, so they moved to a nearby less-trafficked aisle.

Diane spoke first. "It's so good to see you, Joseph. I heard you were home again, and I have been meaning to stop by to see you." She mentally surveyed Joseph and decided that for a man fast approaching middle age, he looked wonderful. "You look so good, Joseph - save for that cane you're using."

Joseph, embarrassed, quickly told her that it was temporary and that he would soon be free of it. She inquired about the circumstances, and he gave her the quick and sanitized version of what had happened. Again, he assured her that it was short-term and that he was receiving therapy to restore his strength and mobility.

As he was finishing his explanation, Diane spoke up. "Do you have time for a cup of coffee?"

"That sounds good. How about here in the store?"

They reached the store's coffee shop and miraculously found a small table for two. Diane piled her shopping bags around her, and Joseph put his cane up against the pony wall next to the table that separated the tables from the customer traffic. They ordered coffee. Upon its delivery to the table, Diane poured cream into her cup. That reminded Joseph of the days back at Rainier College. He noted that she had aged beautifully into a woman in her mid-thirties in the last fifteen or so years since they were a couple. They talked about his return to Rainier and the latest news that the college would soon become a university. She spoke about how the war had thrown her life for a loop. "You know me," she said, "I was so obsessed with making money and establishing myself in the banking world that time just got away from me. Then to top it off, the war started. I wanted to start a family, but now I wonder if it's going to be too late?"

As they spoke, their comfort level grew to the point that Diane finally said, "Joseph, we have to get together after the holidays. We need to spend some time together." She reached across the table, grasping Joseph's hands, and said, "Can we do that?"

Joseph, feeling the warmth of her hands, replied, "Yes, that's a good idea." She seemed pleased and gently pulled her hands back and caught the attention of the waitress, who promptly refilled her cup.

"What are you doing for Christmas?" Diane asked.

Joseph started to make some hand gestures and ended up telling her that, among other things, he would, of course, be going to Mass and that he would be stopping by the Linarts that day with gifts for their kids.

"You could always stop by my parent's place during the day. It's kind of an open house throughout the afternoon. It would be great to see you. You might even get enough finger food to call it a meal," she laughed. Then giving Joseph a matter-of-fact look, she continued, "I would ask you to dinner, but I will be swamped taking care of Mom and Dad, the meal, and all their friends that show up. It is a big deal to them, so it's the least I can do."

Soon after, they decided they both needed to get on with their shopping and other things to do that day.

"I'm going to visit you in your special little house right after the new year. Does that sound good?"

"That sounds great, Diane."

"Perfect."

This time, the two hugged again a little less awkwardly and with more affection, surprising both of them to some degree. They separated, sliding their hands slowly and disappointedly away from each other, and went their separate ways, each looking for Christmas gifts and thinking of the new year.

~~~~~

On the 18th of December 1944, just one week before Christmas, the United States Supreme Court, by a 9 to 0 margin, ruled that those Japanese Americans incarcerated by President Roosevelt using Executive Order 9066 at the beginning of the war were to be released.

In reality, one day earlier, on December 17th, President Roosevelt, after finding out about the High Court's upcoming ruling, made a political decision to release a proclamation rescinding his original executive order. The Camps were going to be shut down.

Joseph read the news and said "yes" aloud while punching the air in front of him with his fist. After all this time, Japanese Americans interned back in 1942 were going to be freed to return to their homes if they still had one or possibly start over again in their old towns and cities or some other location. Joseph wondered where Miku would go. Would she come back to Tacoma? Would she go to Seattle? Since she was in neither city before being interned, or at least he thought she had not been in either, would she go elsewhere? He thought he would try to look up Kasumi Takahara when and if she returned to Tacoma, as she might have updated information or notions about Miku's whereabouts. It was this news that made Joseph's Christmas.

42.

Joseph stopped by the Linart's house in the afternoon on Christmas day to give the children presents. Colleen was extra pleased to see Joseph. After Mark and Darcy opened their gifts, Colleen dragged Joseph into the kitchen for a cup of coffee. She poured each of them a cup and started the conversation.

"Joseph, I've silently stewed about Martin for months now and finally decided I needed to talk to someone about it. I've decided it is you I want to tell."

Joseph, showing some concern in his expression, sat up straighter.

Colleen began, "He called from San Francisco while *Salt Lake City* was at Mare Island Naval Shipyard undergoing maintenance and repair and asked if there was any way I could come down there while they were in port. I, of course, said yes and got my sister to watch the kids. God love her."

They both laughed, and then Joseph said, "Please, continue."

North Pacific

"Well, I've thought about it a lot and have concluded that just m-a-y-b-e (she stretched the word out) something is going on with Martin."

"What do you mean, Colleen?" Joseph imperceptibly moved forward in the kitchen table chair.

"I don't know. That's the thing. It is hard to say exactly what I mean by my speculation. I don't know. He's just a little different. I mean, he's Martin and all that, but…," she paused, "There's a slight bit of distance between us when we're alone."

"Maybe it is because you two have been apart for so long," Joseph suggested. Then he asked, "Can you describe this 'distance' at all?"

"I wish I could, Joseph, but I can't. It's just there, do you know what I mean?" Joseph looked at her and said nothing. Colleen continued, "We would go out to eat. We even went out dancing one night. You know, your friend, my husband, the one who has two or three left feet," she said, quietly smiling. "He seemed like Martin then. It was the times when we were alone and not carrying on a conversation that I would notice him maybe being a little uneasy, maybe his mind possibly elsewhere."

Joseph started to reply, but Colleen added, "It wasn't all the time, just once in a while."

"I don't know what to say," offered Joseph. "As you say, this has been on your mind for a while."

"It didn't strike me as maybe that important at the time, but over the last six months, I've let this thought more or less take over my brain. You know how much I love him, and I don't want him to be different from the guy who left here a few years ago. I want my Martin to return from this God-awful war in one piece, fully intact, ready to resume our lives together."

"Colleen, I couldn't agree with you more. Are you all right?"

"I think so, Joseph, I just needed to drop that on someone, and I figured who better than Martin's best friend."

"I feel for both of you. Maybe you've overthought this thing a little. After all, as I said, he has been gone, and you've been here with the kids. It has been a long time. I'm with you. I want this war to end now. If not now, then tomorrow or the next day. It must end." Joseph sensed his own frustration, and now this.

They looked at each other. Joseph could see that Colleen was about to cry. He reached out and took her hands on the table. Colleen almost instinctively dropped her head down on his hands and cried. After a minute or so, Joseph got up from the table, found a napkin, and handed it to Colleen. She wiped her tears, sniffled, and said, "Thanks, Joseph. I know you are a true friend. I just needed to get that business out of my head. I feel better now. Not all better, mind you, but better."

The two talked some more, and eventually, Joseph left for home. While driving, he wondered whether Colleen had indeed noted some difference in Martin or was it just the length of time and the grind of the war that had Martin lapsing into reflection on the accursed war with that big brain of his.

That night, Joseph, while sitting in his living room thinking a bit about his friend Martin and listening to the news on the radio, heard a reporter ask a question of a military chaplain concerning the war. The chaplain, who identified himself as an Anglican priest, answered the question but added that he hoped and most strenuously prayed that this would be the last Christmas that this terrible war would persist. Joseph looking out toward Browns Point and the lighthouse, whispered, "Amen."

43.

After Christmas, Joseph resumed his weekly trek to Madigan General Hospital for rehabilitation therapy. Upon his arrival that day, he was told that Dr. Wingard, one of his specialists, wanted to speak to him during the appointment. He was shown into a room, where after a few minutes, the doctor joined him. They exchanged greetings and sat on folding chairs, with the rest of the small space empty. The doctor got right to the point. "Joseph, I wanted to chat with you about your condition." Joseph nodded, and Wingard continued, "You're not making the progress with your injuries that we had hoped for."

Joseph thought the Doctor's statement had been blunt but to the point and, he mentally sighed, seemingly accurate.

Dr. Wingard then went over all aspects of Joseph's medical situation and then announced they wanted to run some tests and obtain more current images of the lower back area to see why Mr. Vaenko, as he called him, was not making more progress in his recovery. Joseph, for his part, had puzzled over the same questions himself. Joseph agreed with the doctor. Joseph had noticed that he was increasingly relying on his cane. So instead of therapy that day, Joseph was whisked away by an orderly to have a new set of images taken.

When Joseph returned the following week, he again met with Dr. Wingard. This time, he told Joseph that maybe the original doctors had initially been a little too optimistic in their more hopeful assessment of Joseph's recovery. The bottom line was that the latest information they had gathered indicated that Joseph's progress had unhappily plateaued. He said this was probably about as far as hospital therapy was going to be helpful. On the positive side, Dr. Wingard told Joseph he could still do many things at home on his own to help maintain the most optimal outcome possible.

"In other words," Joseph said, "You're cutting me loose."

The doctor sighed and said, "In a word, yes."

North Pacific

Joseph enquired about a possible follow-up surgery that might lead to a better result. The doctor said that he had talked to some of his colleagues, and for the most part, they thought it was risky, generally fearing the possibility of a worse outcome.

Joseph took it all in and said, "I guess that means I've graduated from treatment to maintenance. Do I have that correct?"

Dr. Wingard, who had been looking a bit apprehensive, smiled, and said, "That's a good way of putting it. I believe congratulations are in order." The two men smiled and shook hands, Dr. Wingard telling Joseph that the day's session would be spent reviewing the maintenance program exercises, stretches, and positions he would use going forward at home.

Behind the wheel of the Studebaker heading home, Joseph vowed he would still beat this thing. He would do what was necessary to improve his back. He just needed to apply himself and make it a priority for his health and well-being. Dear God, Joseph thought, I will be thirty-eight this year. I'm not some old man. He looked over at the cane on the front seat beside him and said to the stick, "I mean it."

~~~~~

By the latter part of the drive back to the North End of Tacoma, Joseph had mentally begun entertaining acceptance of his situation. He stopped by 3 Bridges Café, hoping to catch Denise working, and to his surprise, she was. Of course, he tried not to use the cane or let Denise see him using it. He sat at the bar, and when Denise turned around to see the new customer, a beautiful smile appeared. "Hello Joseph, how have you been?"

"I've been good, Denise, thanks for asking," unable to hold back a grin.

"Coffee?"

"Yes, please, black. Oh, and do you have any pie?"

"Blackberry or strawberry?"

"Blackberry always."

Denise poured a cup of fresh black coffee, cut a beautiful slice out of the blackberry pie, put it on a plate, and presented both to Joseph. "I know it's been about a month, but did you have a good Christmas, Joseph?"

Joseph took a sip of the hot coffee. "It was fine, nothing special."

"Do you have many relatives," she continued.

"I don't know." He smiled again, "My parents were immigrants, and they had no relatives here in the United States, at least that they knew of. I probably have relatives back in Central Europe, but I couldn't tell you. I'm also an only child, and my parents have passed on."

Denise seemed fascinated by Joseph's revelations. From earlier conversations, she knew he was not married, but hearing he had no family surprised her. She started to ask him if he at least had a girlfriend but caught herself and bit her tongue. Instead, she looked over at a couple seated at a table by the window and asked if they needed anything.

Joseph took his first bite of pie and had another sip of the coffee. "Perfect, the pie is delicious." The two continued to chat. In the ensuing conversation, Joseph learned more about this attractive woman behind the counter. She grew up in Seattle, married just out of high school, and quickly had a child. Denise's husband got a job at Boeing, and everything was good. Then he found another woman and left her. She had not heard from him in years.

"Oh, Denise, that's so sad."

"Yes, it was, but it's been quite a while now, and I have decided to live my life rather than dwell on it. My daughter Rose just turned twenty-one."

"How did you ever get to Tacoma?"

"I had a girlfriend from high school whose mother passed away. She left a small home to her down here in Tacoma and now rents the place to me. It's just up the street. Recently, my daughter Rose took a job back in Seattle, so she lives with my parents for the time being. Rose is a very cute gal. I wouldn't be surprised if she doesn't find herself a husband when the war ends."

Now it was time for Joseph to bite his tongue, wanting to say he thought Rose's mother was very cute also, but he let it slide. "I live over near the top of 30th Street hill. It's also a small house."

"You must have a view over there?"

"Yes, actually, it's an incredible view. I've been blessed in that respect," said Joseph, as he thought of his parents and the hard work and good fortune they experienced in coming into possession of that beautiful house that overlooked the bay. "Denise, the pie was delicious." He wanted to add, "Maybe we could take in a movie sometime. What do you think?" But it didn't happen. He had started to say it, but it just wouldn't come out.

Denise, who sensed Joseph was about to say something beyond the comment about the pie, was confused, and it showed on her face. Joseph took a deep breath and asked for some more coffee. The two resumed their conversation, discussing the war and how it would hopefully be over sooner than later. Joseph paid for his coffee and pie and said he would be back soon to continue their conversation. It went well, but as Joseph maneuvered to leave the café, he realized his dependence on his cane embarrassed him in front of Denise. He realized it contributed to his inability to ask Denise out.

Denise, wiping down the countertop, watched Joseph as he left and thought, I could like that guy if he'd let me.

~~~~~

The bedside lamp created just enough light to make out the immediate space in Joseph's bedroom. Joseph laid his head back on the pillow and tried to sort out the day. The news from the doctor had been hard to take. He so wanted to be able to get around like everyone else. He told himself he was serious about using the maintenance therapy program to draw a line in the sand as far as any further physical decline was concerned.

The conversation with Denise that day had been revealing. He realized he had not asked her out because he felt she might be embarrassed by his current physical condition. "That damn cane," he murmured aloud. As much as he did not want to acknowledge it, the fact remained that he would otherwise have asked her out. What did that say about him? It quite clearly showed that he lacked confidence. He believed the most glaring indicator of his life was his being alone. He never imagined this would be his circumstance, but regretfully it was. Then he thought of Miku. He rolled over and turned off the bedside lamp.

44.

Releasing Japanese American internees from the relocation camps across the Western United States took longer than expected. Returning to the cities and towns they had previously lived in became more difficult for many reasons. Fear of discrimination and prejudice was a sad reality in many instances. Another factor was that many Japanese Americans were forced to sell their homes and liquidate their businesses before entering the camps. They had nothing to which to return. Also, The U.S. government's War Relocation Authority encouraged Japanese Americans to move east through brochures and other promotional materials, advocating resettlement in cities that included Chicago, Minneapolis, and even New York.

Japanese Americans began resettlement in January 1945. It was a lengthy process that would last almost an entire year. Slowly, many Japanese Americans returned to the Pacific Northwest, but everything had changed. Anti-Asian racism persisted in many cases, and locally Japan Town in Tacoma would never be the same.

Joseph, on occasion, would drive downtown, park, and slowly walk the streets of the Japan Town area. With his now trusty cane, he would negotiate the ups and downs of the blocks looking for Miku, of course, or Kasumi, or even Miku's aunt. He would ask Japanese Americans if they knew of the whereabouts of Miku Shinkai, to which the response would be a polite no. These fruitless excursions would send Joseph home in physical discomfort and a funk. He would stand for extended periods of time directly in front of his living room window, staring at the bay, saying to himself, where is she?

~~~~~

North Pacific

Joseph settled into a routine. He would get up in the morning and do his stretches and exercises to loosen up and strengthen his lower back. He would make a pot of coffee and have a piece of toast with it. Then it was out the door, fire up the Studebaker and drive to the campus. Depending on his class schedule for the morning, Joseph would stop by St. Dominic, slip into a pew in the back half of the nave, and hear daily morning Mass. Listening to the priest annunciate the Church Latin was soothing to his ear. The prayers asking for mercy recited at the foot of the altar reinforced the proper humility shown toward God by the priest and those in attendance.

"Confiteor Deo omnipotenti," (I confess to almighty God)... followed shortly by the striking of the breast three times while saying, "mea culpa, mea culpa, mea maxima culpa," (Through my fault, through my fault, through my most grievous fault). This prayer and hand gesture set the tone for the Mass. The prayer came from the medieval church and was based on the verse from St. Luke's Gospel, Chapter 18:13, where Christ tells the parable of the Pharisee and the publican praying in the temple. The Pharisee, standing, pridefully praises himself, while *"...the publican, standing afar off, would not so much as lift his eyes towards heaven; but struck his breast, saying: O God, be merciful to me a sinner."*

After Mass, Joseph would head for his office and then on to a lecture hall, back to his office for students and colleagues to meet with him, lunch with friends from on campus, or more generally, by himself. He would read, prepare lectures, and review and grade papers in the evenings. There were also never-ending jobs and tasks around the house to fill up his day. Was it all he wanted? In a word, no. He lacked human companionship.

~~~~~

He and Diane finally connected again when she stopped by the house one Saturday in February. However, it turned out to be a false start to some sort of friendship or relationship when Diane announced she would be accompanying her father to San Francisco to attend to bank business. She had initially told Joseph it would take a couple of weeks, maybe up to a month, before they would return. She said mergers and investment deals needed to be explored and worked on.

Joseph offered to take them to the train, and she accepted. He picked up Diane and her father at the Lassiter residence on the appointed day of departure. Diane's mother hugged and kissed her husband and daughter goodbye while Diane gave last-minute instructions to her aunt. The latter had kindly agreed to stay and take care of Mrs. Lassiter while Diane and her father were in San Francisco.

Joseph drove the father and daughter team downtown to Union Station on Pacific Avenue. He let his passengers off in front of the train station and wrestled their luggage to the sidewalk - no easy task with his back. Then an attendant took it into the station lobby. He parked the car, entered the train station, and found Diane and her father again. They waited for the right train to be called, and then all three made their way out to the platform. After shaking Mr. Lassiter's hand, he and Diane embraced. She whispered in his ear that she could not wait to get back home so they could spend some real time together. Then a whistle blew, and everyone who was going boarded the train. Joseph waved goodbye to them in their first-class Pullman sleeping car a few minutes later as the train eased away from the station. He watched as the Northern Pacific train headed through the half-moon rail yard. The train would continue through Old Town and west along Commencement Bay toward Point Defiance Park. There it would enter a tunnel and reemerge at Salmon Beach, heading south along southern Puget Sound and then eventually on to Oregon and California. Joseph walked back to his car once the train was out of sight. It was then that he noticed the rain falling.

~~~~~

Adolf Hitler committed suicide on April 30th, 1945. Berlin fell to the Soviets a few days later. All German Armed Forces unconditionally surrendered in the West on May 7th and in the East on May 9th. The war was over in Europe. Weeks earlier in the Pacific, the Americans took the island of Iwo Jima on March 26th. The battle for the island of Okinawa, which turned out to be the largest battle fought with the most losses between the U.S. and Japan, ended in late June.

Joseph thought the U.S. and her allies were now poised to strike at the Japanese homeland. He had read about how hard the Japanese had fought, committing suicide in many cases rather than being captured. It reminded him of the earlier struggle in the North Pacific on the island of Attu. The Japanese bravery, as well as that of the Americans, was breathtaking.

It was July. The sun was beating down on the house. Joseph thought, at least here on the side of the hill, I get a slight breeze coming up off the bay. The best two months of the year were beginning in terms of warm summer weather.

45.

"Where does the time go, Speck?" Joseph asked his barber. "I mean, it's been almost four years since Pearl Harbor. So much has happened during that time, yet looking back, it seems like a blink of an eye."

Speck's Barbershop was located downtown on 13th Street, between Pacific Avenue and Commerce St. Now in his 60s, Speck smiled and said, "Time flying by? You don't know the half of it, Joe. Twenty years from now, when you're closer to my age, you'll be asking yourself where your life went?" They both laughed, Speck more than Joseph.

A little while later, Joseph emerged from the barbershop and, with difficulty, made his way up the hill to where he had parked his car on Broadway. In front of the Sears department store, to his surprise and delight, he saw Miku's friend Kasumi Takahara standing in front of the main doors. Kasumi also saw Joseph and the two instantly walked up to each other and embraced.

Joseph, overcome, could hardly find words. "Kasumi, it is so great to see you," he stammered.

Kasumi started to cry. "Joseph, it has been so long." They hugged again.

"Oh, Kasumi, don't cry," Joseph urged as they clung to each other. "Do you have any time?"

Kasumi, wiping her tears and regaining her composure, replied, "I do, I do. But Joseph, why are you using a cane?"

"I hurt my back while I was in the Navy. Yes, I'm using a cane. I'm good. It's not a big deal."

Joseph remembered her father's black 38' Ford and asked if they still had it. "No, Joseph, sadly, we were forced to sell it before having to move to the relocation center in Minidoka, Idaho, and I don't have a car yet."

"Come with me, please," Joseph said, beaming. "My car is right there, pointing at the Studebaker parked just a few car lengths from where they were standing. How about if we get a bite to eat?"

"I would love to spend some time talking, Joseph. That would be wonderful."

Joseph walked Kasumi over to the car and opened the passenger door for her. She slid into the front seat. He closed the door, walked around the back of the car, opened the driver's side door, and pushed his cane into the back seat area. Joseph drove to a restaurant up in the Stadium District. At the restaurant, Kasumi asked Joseph more about the nature of his current disability. He explained what had happened, trying to leave out the drama. She told him of her and her family's experience in Minidoka, Idaho. It broke his heart.

On the other hand, Kasumi looked great. She talked of working as a seamstress doing piecework in her apartment with plenty of business coming her way. Joseph told her he was still living in the same house she had been to with Miku. When the topic of Miku finally came up, Kasumi's eyes became sad.

"I have not seen Miku since before the war. She was not at the Minidoka Relocation Center. I suppose it is possible that she was at another camp, but I know nothing of it, and I certainly have not seen her here in Tacoma since my return."

Joseph explained how he had been searching for her also and had had no luck. This exchange disheartened him as he had hoped that just possibly Kasumi and Miku had been at the same camp. Kasumi remembered well Joseph's attempts to find Miku during the fall of 1941. She told

Joseph she would renew her efforts through friends, relatives, and even strangers to discover what had happened to Miku and her whereabouts.

Joseph, distressed with the thought, changed the subject. "Kasumi, We must have dinner together. Since you don't have a car, I will pick you up at your apartment and bring you over to my place. I will even attempt to make dinner for you. I must warn you, though, that most of my meals are pretty unmemorable," he said with a grin. "How about this Friday?"

"I would love that, Joseph."

"Great, I'll pick you up at 6:00 PM."

The rest of their talk centered around their lives since his accident and her return to Tacoma.

When the conversation ran out, he paid the bill, left a tip on the table, and they returned to the car. Joseph drove her to her apartment.

It was great, thought Joseph, to possibly have a friend like Kasumi. He was so pleased to have run into her that he almost forgot that he needed to go grocery shopping, especially since Friday was just a few days away. What can I make Kasumi for dinner that would not make her wish she was back in the relocation camp?

On the day Kasumi was coming to dinner, Joseph panicked, of course, and finally settled on pasta with, to the best of his memory, the ingredients his mother used to make her spaghetti sauce. He made the sauce ahead of time. He also prepared a salad and some garlic bread. He topped it off with a bottle of Chianti. Joseph had, by this time, gone from not drinking at all to, on special occasions, sipping and nursing one glass of wine. For dessert, he served the chocolate cake with coffee. He had picked up the cake at the local bakery. After dinner, they did the dishes together, with Joseph washing and Kasumi drying.

Kasumi asked him, "In your wildest dreams, did you ever think you would be living the life you are right now? I mean, here you are entertaining a woman whose recent past was that of an internee at a relocation center?" They both laughed. Joseph shook his head, amused, and said, "Absolutely not, but I'm beyond happy you are here." They finished the dishes and then moved to the living room.

The two talked, laughed, and tried as much as possible not to speak of the war or the plight of the Japanese Americans all over the West Coast, trying somehow, someway, to put their lives back together. They also spoke no more of Joseph's disability. They just had fun. It had been too long since they could just be themselves without factors and forces beyond their control dictating their lives.

It was wonderful, Joseph thought, to relax and feel alive with human companionship.

Kasumi, of course, could not get enough of the view out the front window and used Joseph's binoculars repeatedly to identify, if possible, all of the ships, boats, barges, and mystery vessels plying the waters of Commencement Bay. The warm summer night lent itself to this feeling of relaxation. The sun finally set well after 9 PM with its attendant pink to golden hues.

When they decided to call it a night, Joseph drove her back to her apartment near the Botanical Gardens at the Seymour Conservatory at Wright Park down in the Stadium District. During the drive, they both agreed that they should get together again. Kasumi insisted on cooking the meal. Joseph gave her a self-deprecating smile. She laughed and said, "I'll do the cooking but let's do it at your place again. The view is just too incredible to waste. My apartment has a view of the trees close to the botanical conservatory, but it's not your view, not even close." They laughed again and settled on a date in the middle of August.

For the, not by choice, reclusive Joseph, the night had gone perfectly. The companionship had brightened and touched his soul, or maybe it was the glass of wine or both. After taking Kasumi back to her apartment while driving home, Joseph mused that evenings like the one he had just experienced were what life was supposed to be about.

46.

Occasionally, when Joseph would get home later than usual, he would head down to Isaacs for a bit of bar food and a Nesbitt Orange or Soda water. One evening on another of those warm Northwest summer nights, he got into a conversation with Leo. The genial bartender always brought Joseph up to speed on the latest happenings in Old Town. Tonight, he told Joseph about the news that there were plans to open a higher-end restaurant that would include a large dance floor and live music down on the waterfront. The building would be constructed on pilings over the water and resemble an ocean liner. It would be a significant addition to the Old Town waterfront skyline, which at that time consisted of sawmills, docks, and not much else. Leo said it would take a year or two to complete the project, and the restaurant would be called "The Top of the Ocean." Both agreed, after more discussion, that the development would be excellent for Tacoma.

It was a slow night for Leo, with many of his regulars taking advantage of the excellent weather and doing things outdoors. While wiping down the bar's surface, Leo became more serious and conveyed the news to Joseph that Ron Huddleston had been buried at Good Shepherd Cemetery. Joseph knew it well. It was not far from the Catholic Cemetery where his parents had been laid to rest.

Leo said, "I remember you and him getting into it one night in here a few years back."

"Yeah, that did happen," Joseph said, looking down, "I knew who he was, but I did not know him personally. I mean, what I knew of him was that he worked at the same sawmill I did before I went to college. You could say we bumped into each other a couple of times, nothing beyond that."

North Pacific

Leo nodded, "He was a tough guy and seemed to have a big chip on his shoulder. I had to bounce him out of here a time or two. I remember his old man, a tough guy also. He drank too much. They were alike in that regard. Someone told me that Ron's parents divorced years ago. His mother married some guy and moved away. He lived with his dad. As I heard it, he got beatings on more or less a regular basis. The old man died maybe ten years ago, and Ron then lived alone in the family home. He wasn't a happy guy, but he was among the first to sign up when the war started." As Leo finished his thought, a customer appeared at the other end of the bar. He put on his best work smile and moved down the long counter to help him.

Joseph sat there and sipped his orange drink. His mind became focused on the story he had just heard. He remembered back to when he had punched the guy right over there by that booth. He felt so much older now, in the sense that his body was much more worn down than it was back with his first encounter with Mr. Huddleston.

Over the next week, Joseph thought a lot about Ron Huddleston. The beating he had received from him was front and center in his mind. Yes, he had initially hit the guy, but what were his options at the time? If he had not, Joseph was sure Ron would have pounded him right then and there in front of Miku, Kasumi, and the entire crowd at the bar that night. And, after all, Huddleston had deserved it with how he had treated those dear women.

But he could not get Huddleston out of his mind, so much so that he found back issues of the Seattle and

North Pacific

Tacoma newspapers at the college library that told the story of the Anzio operation where Ron had lost his life. The British and American forces had landed on the Italian coast north and south of Anzio. Huddleston had been part of the American 3rd Infantry Division. After landing and establishing themselves, the 3rd Infantry Division attempted to take the village of Cisterna. It was there on January 30th, 1944, that Ron was killed in action. The Americans came within less than a mile of the village but were turned back by the Germans. The 3rd Infantry Division suffered over 3,000 casualties in the battle. And just like that, Ron Huddleston's life had come to an end. Joseph remembered Leo saying Huddleston had been buried at Good Shepherd Cemetery. A day later, while making a quick visit to the Blessed Sacrament at St. Dominic, it struck him that he wanted to visit Ron's grave.

The next day Joseph found himself driving out to the cemetery. He checked at the office, and the older gentleman behind the counter looked through his books and found where Ron had been laid to rest. He gave directions to Joseph, drawing on a piece of paper where the grave was located. Joseph returned to his car, studied the directions and location, and drove toward it. Upon his arrival at what he hoped was the correct section of the cemetery, he pulled over to the side of the road, got out of the Studebaker, and walked through the rows of headstones looking for Ron's grave.

It took a few minutes, but he came upon the marker with Huddleston's name. Joseph stood there for a moment, reflecting upon what he saw. It was a small, inexpensive cement slab that simply read "Ronald Huddleston 1910 – 1944." That was it, nothing more, nothing less. As he stared down at the grave marker, he noticed his shadow overlaying the small headstone. Joseph realized that in each of his three encounters with this guy, including today, one of them would end up on the ground, or now, in their final meeting, in the ground. It was odd. Joseph wondered why Ron had been killed and not him. Was it just dumb luck? How close had he come in the mining of *Abner Read* to lying in repose in his own coffin a mile or two from here in the Catholic Cemetery? While contemplating his fate versus Ron's, he noticed the thin shadow cast by his cane. Joseph saw in it a reminder of how close he had come to joining Ron in death.

Joseph felt an unexpected and surprising bond between Ron and himself as the late morning summer sun bore slowly into his shoulders and back. They had shared life, not in a good way, but life, nonetheless. They had affected each other's lives. Reflexively he felt himself going down to one knee while holding on to the cane with both hands. It struck him that he and Ron were companions in this life in an unusual sort of way.

Joseph realized he was the only person in that corner of the cemetery that morning. He wiped his eyes with the back of one hand while clutching the cane with the other. Then he took his right hand and reached down, touching the grave marker's surface. He ran his fingers deliberately over it. Ron Huddleston had endured a hard life. He came from a broken home with all the consequent trauma that one could associate with it. Yet, when the moment came, Ron volunteered to serve in the Armed Forces. After training, he was sent to Europe in 1943, where he gave his life in service to his country so that others would not have their freedom compromised. He was 34 years old. Did he have any real friends? What had happened between the two of them in the past, Joseph concluded, seemed of little importance in the big scheme of things. He used the cane to lift himself into a standing position. Joseph made the sign of the cross.

"Eternal rest grant unto Ron Huddleston, O Lord, and may perpetual light shine upon him. With your saints forever, because you are merciful. Amen."

Joseph listened to the sound of birds chirping, and it made him feel less alone. He was here, on this side of the grave. He could feel the warmth of the sun. He could breathe in the fresh air. For whatever reason, it was not his time. His life's journey was still to be completed. As he began to walk away, he looked back at the grave, pointed toward it, and made a promise aloud to Ron.

~~~~~

Sunday after Mass, Joseph stopped by 3 Bridges Café to have breakfast and hopefully talk to Denise. Alas, she was not working. He ordered a coffee and a side of toast and instead glanced at a newspaper that had been left on the counter.

North Pacific

Later that day, he sat on his front porch after dinner as the sun started to dip behind the trees on the higher hills to the south. While sitting there, Joseph realized he had not talked to anyone in days.

Over the previous week, Joseph had read the books Fr. Etienne had loaned him. The first was *Etre et avoir* (Being and Having) by Gabriel Marcel. Upon finishing, Joseph thought he was glad he had pursued a history degree and not a physics or, in this case, a philosophy degree.

He followed up Marcel's book by reading *Le Mur* (The Wall) by Jean-Paul Sartre. In the book, Sartre tells the story of three young men during the Spanish Civil War (1936-1939) who are captured and put in a prison cell and told they would be shot in the morning. The three young men spend the night discussing what they are living through. Joseph noted that this presentation of life as experienced was a significant theme in this book and Sartre's earlier work, *La Nausée* (Nausea). He also could see that Sartre and Marcel were both "French" in their approach to philosophy as opposed to British, say Bertrand Russell, and most American philosophers, who were more in line with Descartes' analytical approach, free of actual involvement in the messiness of everyday life as Father Etienne had told him. Both books left him wanting to some degree, and it was then that he realized that he had not read any Pascal in about three years. Again, Joseph made a mental note to break out his favorite Frenchman's *Pensées*.

47.

Diane finally returned to Tacoma with her father from San Francisco. They had spent not up to four weeks but almost three months taking care of "banking business." She stopped by Joseph's house the following day. Diane gave him a big hug and a kiss when he opened the door. She talked about the beauty of San Francisco and vowed to return there someday. Diane, of course, was running errands, and the two of them planned an evening out to catch up. They made reservations for the following Friday night at a swanky restaurant downtown.

~~~~~

When the time came to go out to dinner with Diane, Joseph looked through his "wardrobe" in his closet. He did not have anything new. It wasn't that he could not afford to have a few more nice things. It was simply that there had been no compelling reason to have nicer clothes in his closet. Everything he owned seemed to work well for his current circumstances. He owned a half dozen or so jackets and slacks. Although one of the jackets he still had, he remembered wearing to his father's funeral. He chuckled, tried it on, and surprisingly found that it still fit him. There was maybe a little less room in the arms, but it was doable. Yet, while looking at the jacket in the mirror hanging on the inside of the closet door, Joseph determined he looked right out of the 1920s, which was when he had purchased it. Joseph removed the jacket and set it aside, thinking now was probably a good time to let someone else have it. He looked over the jackets he wore to work every day and selected one he had gotten maybe six months earlier. He studied his ties and picked the one that went best with the jacket. His slacks were passable. He grabbed a belt. The wingtips he picked out didn't look so bad. A good shining would do the trick, he thought. Finally, there was an almost new white shirt that was crisp and helped make it all seem like it worked, at least for the most part. He closed the closet door, found the polish, shined the shoes, put it all on, and decided that he might have to "freshen" his attire going forward.

He drove over to pick up Diane. Her parents greeted Joseph at the door and invited him in. Diane's father went to great lengths to say how sorry he was to have kept Diane in San Francisco for such an extended period. Mrs. Lassiter smiled cheerily and said Diane would be right down. It was then that Diane made her entrance down the staircase. She looked incredible. Joseph listened as Diane and her mother described what she was wearing, a lightweight belted peplum jacket and skirt with continental black pumps. Mr. Lassiter chimed in, "So that's what you were up to when you disappeared for long stretches during those extended lunch breaks in San Francisco." The three laughed. Joseph thought about what he was wearing and quickly interjected, "Diane, we will have to get going if we are to make that reservation." Big hugs were exchanged as Joseph smiling and waving, managed to get Diane down the front steps and out to his car. After opening and closing the passenger door for her, he walked around the back of the Studebaker, thinking Diane was a knockout.

They had a wonderful time at dinner. They ordered a cocktail and a glass of red wine before the meal was served. Joseph explained that he had developed a habit of only having a glass of red wine with dinner. Beyond that, they were able to focus on each other.

"So, tell me more about San Francisco?"

"I loved everything about it, Joseph. It is the metropolis of Northern California. There is so much to do. There are always major events taking place. You can't keep up with it. Tacoma seems so sleepy by comparison."

"So, you would rather be there than here."

"No, no, not at all. I just loved being a part of all that excitement. There was such energy. It was something I had not experienced before. Oh, Joseph, I want to tell you that I learned much more about how money works with my father while we were down there. I'm personally building quite a financial portfolio. After the war, I think there will be much money to be made."

"Money has never been my strong suit, quipped Joseph."

"Oh, stop it. You have a Ph.D. You're not stupid."

North Pacific

"Ok, what I meant by that was that I didn't grow up with money. I've never had the savings I would like. There might be some extra income when I write the book I'm planning, but I'm not complaining. My salary at the university pays the bills and leaves some leftover – not a lot, but some."

Diane smiled at him and said, "I'm not demeaning what you earn or how you earn it, not by any means. I'm just saying that those savings you mentioned could be invested and put to work for future earnings. Oh, listen to me. I sound like an investment banker." They both laughed.

"Like you are," Joseph said, smiling and raising his glass of wine in a toast to his favorite investment banker.

During dinner, Diane mentioned that maybe she could help Joseph update his apparel in the near future. She laughed and said, "You remind me a bit of an old history professor wandering the halls up at the university." Joseph, only slightly embarrassed, laughed a little, not knowing what else to say.

"Joseph, I've missed you these last so many months. I've thought about you a lot, which made me think back to when we were young and in love." She paused, grinned, and resumed, "If things had been different," she paused again, "We could have been together for the last, I don't know how many years." Diane hesitated and then, in a lower voice, said, "We could have had a family."

There was silence between them for the first time that evening.

North Pacific

After dinner and dessert, the couple moved to the lounge. Joseph ordered Diane another drink while he had soda water. A trio was playing, and Diane looked at Joseph's cane and hesitantly asked if he could dance. Joseph had been dreading this moment and replied, "Maybe, if they ever play a less upbeat number." Diane laughed and acceded to his request, seeing panic written all over his face. When a slow arrangement was finally played, the two danced. Joseph remembered how wonderful it had been to hold Diane as he had done so long ago. He also glanced once or twice at his cane dangling over the back of his chair, thinking, I don't need you. Yet, at the same time, he made sure to stick close to the table and not stray to other parts of the dance floor.

It was well after midnight when Joseph and Diane returned to her parent's house. Joseph stood at the door momentarily, and Diane wrapped her arms around his neck and, pulling him down slightly, kissed him. The kiss lasted for what seemed to Joseph a considerable amount of time.

Both looked at each other and wished they were somewhere other than Diane's parents' house. Memories, powerful memories, stirred in each as Diane finally let go and walked into the house, blowing a kiss toward him. Joseph stood there for a moment, then retrieved his cane from up against one of the columns supporting the front porch and returned to the car. He eased away from the parking space, shifting the gears slowly so as not to wake those sleeping. The five-minute drive home found Joseph being borne aloft by thoughts that had been far too infrequent in his life.

48.

And then it happened. News sources reported that the United States had dropped an atomic bomb on Hiroshima, Japan, on August 6th, 1945. Three days later, a second bomb was unleashed on Nagasaki, Japan. Just short of a week after that, Japan unconditionally surrendered. It was August 15, 1945, and the horrible brutality of death and destruction that had reigned over Europe and then in the Pacific was finally at an end.

The news was, at first, hard to fathom, not because anyone thought the war would continue indefinitely, but rather that it might require a full-scale invasion of the Japanese mainland with the attendant loss of too many American lives. The sudden about-face for Japan's military, who up until that time certainly looked like they were going to keep fighting, all came crashing down with the release of the atomic bombs and possibly the declaration of war by the Soviet Union on Japan on August 8th.

When Joseph heard on his radio that the Japanese had surrendered, he sat in his living room chair. His eyes welled up, genuinely surprising even him. Regaining his composure, he breathed. The world in which he lived changed at that very moment. It was as different as night and day. Everyone's lives would change now. Soldiers and sailors would come home. People would try to reestablish their lives. It was an overwhelming thought.

Thoughts concerning the incredible power of the atomic bomb would have to wait, at least for an undefined period of time. Later, it would be estimated that 70 to 80 million people lost their lives because of the war. Future wars, which might include atomic weapons, terrified anyone who seriously considered the consequences of the technological breakthrough. The United States was the sole possessor of this astounding weapon, but how long could that last? But the human mind can only deal with so much at any given moment. For now, it was time to let every nerve relax and even celebrate. The human spirit is like that.

Joseph tried to remember the Introit prayer or hymn from the beginning of the Mass that morning, which celebrated the feast day of the Assumption of the Blessed Virgin Mary into Heaven. He recalled Father Etienne's homily that morning that ended with him re-reading the beginning of the Introit. What did he say? Joseph got up from his chair and walked over to the entrance hall side table, picked up his missal, and read:

"Let us all rejoice in the Lord," for he is our salvation, celebrating a festival day."

Joseph added aloud, "The war is finally over."

He set the missal down on the side table and thought, a suitable hymn indeed.

49.

Joseph and Diane came out of the Rialto Theatre after watching a musical starring Frank Sinatra and Gene Kelly as sailor buddies entitled "Anchors Aweigh." The couple had indulged in popcorn during the movie and were uninterested in stopping somewhere to get a cup of coffee. It was after 10 PM, and they both had to go to work in the morning. Joseph drove Diane to her folk's house, where she continued to live and care for her parents. Her mother was highly forgetful now, and her father was not able to handle well his wife of nearly forty years.

This had been their pattern during the fall of 1945, a movie, sometimes coffee or a bite to eat, and then home. Diane had Joseph over for Sunday dinner with her parents on two separate occasions. Those evenings had gone well, with Mr. Lassiter talking about the end of the war and how there would now be many opportunities in business as the world settled back into a non-war footing. He did warn Joseph that he felt the United States would have to come to Western Europe's monetary aid, which had been economically devasted by the earlier five-plus years of war on that continent.

North Pacific

On a lighter note, Mr. Lassiter was always excited to talk about the University of Washington football season. It had been since 1942 that Washington had fielded a team. George Welch was the coach, and the Huskies were in the midst of the 1945 nine-game schedule. Their most significant win to date was a 13-7 upset victory over the University of Southern California Trojans at Husky Stadium before a crowd estimated at 40,000. Joseph, in the past, had these sorts of sports conversations with Martin. He missed those times and couldn't wait for him to return home so they might resume talking about college football ad infinitum.

After dinner, Joseph would help with the dishes, and then Diane would assist her mother as she prepared for the evening. When that was finished, the two would sit in the living room and talk while Diane's parents padded around the house, speaking quietly so that Diane and Joseph could have a little time to themselves.

During the second dinner at the Lassiters, Diane opened up on the topic of children, which she had only touched on briefly with Joseph before. She explained to him that she was now thirty-six years old, and because of it, "her time," as she put it, what with that accursed war, had probably come and gone, at least in terms of her wanting to raise a small child or children in her forties. She told him the sound of her biological clock ticking was fading.

Joseph listened and thought how the war had indeed been cruel in so many ways. In his case, he thought about how he had envisioned raising a family upon completing his doctorate. That had never materialized. But she was correct. In her case, with all the young men in her father's office going off to war, she had found the opportunity to work more closely with him, learning the ins and outs of the profession. Certainly, she would want to enjoy the fruits of her training and the benefits of making particularly good money. San Francisco had only been a taste of the world opening up to her. Diane then began sharing her thoughts on how she and her "history professor" could travel the world and enjoy a life most would not understand.

They spent nearly an hour talking about how that life together might look and work. At some point, Diane heard her parents' bedroom door click shut. She moved closer to Joseph, and the two of them embraced. "Oh Joseph, hold me, hold me tight."

~~~~~

The following week, Joseph picked up Diane downtown at the bank during the evening rush hour and took her to her parent's place. After a bit of small talk in the car, Diane asked Joseph, "Hey, what's this I hear about you having some woman over for dinner? What's that all about?" Joseph, surprised by the question, asked where she had heard that. "Never mind where I heard it. It's true, isn't it?" Joseph surmised she must have run into Colleen somewhere in the Proctor District. Colleen was the only person he could think of that he had told about Kasumi.

"Yes, it is true," Joseph responded. "Her name is Kasumi Takahara. She is a friend of mine from before the war."

"What kind of friend might that be," Diane now pressed.

Joseph smiled, "An exceptionally good friend. Kasumi is Japanese, and when the war started, she was interned at a relocation center in Idaho. After she returned to Tacoma, I ran into her downtown, and we got together. We have dinner once or twice a month at my place because she loves the view from my living room. We are friends, that's it, really."

"Is she pretty?"

"As a matter of fact, she is very pretty, but I don't have any romantic inclinations toward her. Look, Kasumi is great. You would like her."

"Hmmm," Diane thought for a moment. "Well, I have some news for you."

"What's up?" Joseph said with interest.

"Guess who's back in town?"

"I give, who?"

"Charlie Langley."

"Really. I ran into him down at Owen Beach last year when he was home on leave from duty in Honolulu."

"I did too. I saw him downtown. And now he is back home for good. He has been discharged and will resume his surgical practice here in town."

"Well, that's good news, Diane. I'm happy for him. I'm happy when any of the guys return from having their lives turned upside down."

"Joseph, I wanted you to know that he asked me out for dinner. I mean, after all, we went to grade school together. So I said sure." Diane looked intently at the man across the front seat from her for a reaction. None was forthcoming.

Joseph pulled up to a stoplight and looked over at Diane. "Thanks for letting me know about Charlie's return. I'll have to look him up sometime. I have been looking forward to my friend Martin returning also."

The light changed to green, and Joseph proceeded toward Diane's parents' house. He downshifted as the Studebaker approached the corner of the Lassiter's block and pulled alongside the curb in front of the residence.

"Are you going to come in for a minute?"

"I can't tonight. I've got to return to the university for a meeting about future staffing. We will have to increase faculty and administration personnel in order to meet the demands of the many returning soldiers. In many cases we will have to guess which departments will need the most help."

Joseph got out of the car and walked around it to open her door. Diane got out, and as Joseph closed the door behind her, she turned and looked at him. "So, you and this other woman are really 'just friends,' right?"

Joseph smiled. "Yes, Diane, just friends."

Again, she gave him a "hmmm" and a quick businesslike peck on the cheek and headed for the house.

Joseph watched her walk away and said, "Well, I could tell you to be careful around Charlie. He's always been quite a ladies' man."

Diane, who had reached the front porch steps, looked back toward the car. "Oh, p-l-e-e-e-z Joseph," as she walked up the stairs.

DELOREM

(Sorrow)

"My soul is sorrowful..."

St. Matthew 26:38

Douay-Rheims

50.

It was a dull gray day. Father Etienne walked from the church to the rectory, looking lost in thought. Joseph, driving by, pulled into the parking lot, rolled his window down, and asked the priest if he had time for a cup of coffee. Father Etienne, pleasantly surprised, said, "Why not." He got into the front passenger seat, and the two men drove to 3 Bridges Café.

They took the table in the corner for some privacy, and Denise came over to serve them with a beaming smile. As she approached the table, Joseph looked at her and said, "Denise, I would like you to meet my priest, mentor, and good friend, Father Etienne Sauveterre." Fr. Etienne rose from his chair to make her acquaintance. She nodded amiably, shook his hand, and said, "I am so pleased to meet a friend of Joseph's." Father engaged in a little small talk with her. Denise finally took the order, two coffees and two pieces of pie, both apple. She returned shortly, having heated the pie, and then moved on to other customers.

As both tasted the fresh and slightly heated apple pie, Father asked Joseph, "Your friend Denise, is that right, is a beautiful woman, no?"

"She is Father. I've known her for maybe six years now. I come in here and tell her my problems, just like I do with you," Joseph said, laughing and smiling.

"What's on your mind today, professor Vaenko?" said the priest, obviously proud of his protégé.

"Nothing special. I saw you and thought I would take a chance on you having a few minutes."

"The pie," the priest said as he swallowed his first bite and pointed with his fork at the plate, "C'est merveilleux!" Father looked toward Denise, who caught his glance as he said, "Mes compliments." Denise, now grinning, nodded her head.

Smiling, Joseph said, "I guess while I've got you here, I would like to ask you about philosophy, particularly about the two books you gave me to read by Marcel and Sartre."

"Yes, Joseph, I remember."

"Well, Father, as best I could tell, both authors focus on approaching philosophy based on lived experiences, but they seem to come away with different answers to what seem to be the same questions."

"This is true, Joseph. I expect Marcel to expand on his method in the coming years. It will be interesting to see where he goes with his approach. As for Monsieur Sartre, his approach to philosophy is quite frankly severe and, of course, Godless.

The two talked and ate pie. Denise made a second appearance and refilled the coffee cups. Father and Denise seemed to hit it off wonderfully, with Father promising her he would return to the café for more pie in the future.

Joseph dropped the priest back off at the rectory, thanked him again for the conversation, and drove home on a now cold and blustery late afternoon.

~~~~~

Joseph thanked the installer, closed the front door, and returned to the living room. A brand-new telephone thatced the Bell Telephone workman had just installed was on the small end table next to his tall straight-back chair. He thought, am I the last person in town to get one? The powers at the university had insisted that Joseph avail himself of this modern technology to be reachable by his fellow academics and administration personnel. So much for one's home being the last vestige of privacy in the world. Next to the phone on the arm of the sofa sat the latest edition of the Tacoma telephone directory. Joseph thumbed through it and found the listing for the Linarts. He dialed the number, and Colleen answered. She was excited to hear that Joseph had gotten a phone and asked for his number, writing it down as he relayed it to her. Then, excitedly, she raised her voice and said, "Martin's coming home!"

"When?"

"I think maybe the day after tomorrow or the next day. Martin is catching a ride up from California with a fellow shipmate who bought a car down there in San Diego. The big Walloon is getting out of the Navy and coming home," she practically gushed.

"That's fantastic," chimed in Joseph, who felt himself getting caught up in Colleen's and now his own anticipation. "Have Martin call me once he settles in at home. I can't wait to hear from him." As he hung up the phone, Joseph thought that maybe having a telephone was not so bad after all.

~~~~~

Three days later, his phone rang, and Martin told him that he was home and that they needed to get together. Joseph said he would be right over. He jumped in the old "Dictator" and drove to the Linarts. After a big greeting, Martin told Joseph that Colleen and the kids were gone for a few hours and ushered Joseph into the living room. The two began to talk. Martin was particularly interested in Joseph's cane and the lack of mobility of his good friend. Joseph told him the story. This time he left nothing out as he would always do when others pressed him on the subject. After all, Martin was his best friend. Martin whistled, shook his head, and told Joseph he had been lucky to survive.

After a brief pause, Martin lowered his eyes, not looking directly at Joseph, and said that he, too, had been involved in action in the North Pacific. He said it was a horrific ship-to-ship running gunbattle off the Komandorski Islands with a couple of Japanese heavy cruisers and his *Salt Lake City*. He brought his eyes up to meet Joseph's and said, "It was absolutely the scariest thing I've ever experienced," his face becoming slightly contorted. "Joe, I've not gotten over it yet. I thought telling you about it might help me some."

Seeing that his buddy was struggling, Joseph said, "Stay with me, big guy. We can talk this out. You know I'm here for you."

"I have not talked to Colleen about this to any meaningful degree. When she came down to visit me in California when the *SLC* was at Mare Island for repairs, I think she sensed something. Sometimes I'm fine. Sometimes I feel like I'm my same old self again. But there are other times when things just aren't right. My problem is that whatever is going on has caused me to re-think some of my life-long assumptions about how the world works."

"Really, Martin."

"Yeah, Joe, It's the craziest thing. I was hoping we could discuss this more beyond today when we get a chance. Maybe we can sort some things out. I mentioned the idea to my doctor, and he said if I was interested and trusted our friendship, it might do some good, and so, by all means, pursue it."

"Well, I'm in. Let me know when and where, and I'll be there."

"Thanks, man."

The two lifelong friends swapped stories about life aboard warships and how the Navy had it all over the Army when it came to clean bedding and hot meals. At some point, Colleen and the kids showed up. They all talked for a while like it was old times. It felt good. Colleen invited Joseph to stay for dinner. He accepted.

51.

It had been weeks since Diane had gone to dinner with Charlie Langley, but things had changed. Not only did they have a great time (Diane's words), but Charlie continued to visit her on a regular basis. Diane tried to describe Charlie's attention by explaining that their families had known each other forever and that they had always enjoyed each other's company. But in Joseph's mind, it was pretty clear that Diane was smitten with Dr. Langley. On two separate occasions, Joseph stopped by to see Diane and then drove past the house because Charlie's shiny new black 1947 Chevy Stylemaster was sitting out front. Seeing Charlie's new car made him realize that his 1936 Studebaker 'Dictator' was now over a decade old, and he was now forty.

Matters between Joseph and Diane came to a head when Diane called him one day. She told Joseph she would probably be unable to join him for a fund-raiser pancake breakfast after Mass in the basement at St. Dominic the following Sunday. Diane told Joseph she had accepted an "opportunity" to go with Charlie to Seattle for a medical function gala the Saturday night before the breakfast. She told Joseph that it would be a fantastic chance to meet some important people in the Puget Sound medical community. She "hoped'" that they would be home at a reasonable hour, but she couldn't promise it. Sure enough, Diane did not make it to the pancake breakfast the following Sunday. It was then he knew that "they" were over.

Joseph realized his and Diane's relationship had been, at best, slightly ambiguous. He did run into Charlie days later. They shook hands and talked briefly about how great it was now that the war was over and how much they enjoyed being back in Tacoma. Neither was so inclined as to bring up Miss Lassiter.

~~~~~

Joseph sat in his straight-back chair in the living room at home that evening, as had become his habit, to keep his lower back in line. He thought about Diane and their relationship over time. As he looked out over the bay, Joseph saw more clearly that he and Diane were different in some probably fundamental and important ways. Diane came from strong English roots, with her family coming to America centuries before. She was of solid Protestant stock. Over the last half-century, her family had been movers and shakers in the community. He, on the other hand, was Catholic. His family had come to America in steerage less than fifty years ago. His parents hailed from the mountains of Central Europe and had no money. Diane was outgoing, always thinking one step ahead, and made good sound decisions. He was somewhat reticent about his personal feelings and much more of a loner, although he didn't like using the word to describe himself. She had a good heart. Her politics were liberal in the classic sense. He disliked politics, mainly because some people thought politics were more important than friendships. She was an organizer and a doer while he tended to stare out his window daily, seemingly in a trance. He took his ongoing relationship with God, and his moments of hesitancy or doubt, very seriously. She rarely spoke of her religious beliefs. He and Diane were simply different people, always had been.

What had drawn him to her if they had, as he reasoned, little in common? Well, she was a beautiful woman, of that there was no doubt, and he had always sought companionship, a shared life. He did not like being alone. He and lonely went way back. Joseph paused. He needed to amend that thought. Actually, he was comfortable being alone when he wanted to be. When he was working on history or interpreting the world through the lens of his view of Commencement Bay, he was perfectly happy. It was a distinction Joseph felt, at that moment, he had to make to himself. Yet, he had to admit his definition of happiness had always been to share his life with a woman and possibly have a family. He was beginning to sense that he and Diane, even though she was a brilliant and beautiful woman, probably would not have worked out even if there had been no Charlie Langley.

Then there was Miku. The entire time he had spent with Diane, thoughts of Miss Shinkai were constantly swirling about the periphery of his mind and life. He had not the foggiest of notions as to Miku's whereabouts, none whatever. Joseph told himself that the proof concerning his feelings towards Miku would be tested if and when she ever showed up again. However, that possibility seemed terribly remote to him now with each passing day. If Miku loved him or cared about him at all, she would have contacted him. After all, he had not gone anywhere. He was still living in the same house overlooking the bay. Only God knew where she was, and the "man upstairs" was not supplying any hints.

~~~~~

That night in bed, tossing and turning, Joseph felt his mind entertaining thoughts that always wanted to take him to dark places. Although successful professionally, his life still seemed confusing and not as socially grounded as he would have liked. It was not what he had inchoately planned as a young man. That horrible word "despair" came into his mind. Despair was a word that conjured up visions of standing on the edge of an abyss.

North Pacific

He had been rereading Pascal of late. The Frenchman spoke of the shortness of one's life with eternity on either end of it. Pascal also reflected on how man was the minutest of specks compared to the universe's "infinite spaces." Joseph remembered standing in the stacks in the library the previous week reading some Soren Kierkegaard, the 19th-century Danish Protestant philosopher, speak of despair in terms of being unable to find meaning in the world because all one seems to see is the absence of God. Lying in bed in the darkness of the night with these thoughts crisscrossing his mind, even a sense of hopelessness began to enter Joseph's heart.

To combat this extreme sense of isolation, Joseph propped himself up in bed on one elbow. He looked at the clock on the side table. It read 3:40 AM. He ran his hand through his hair and forced himself to move on to another topic. He lay back on the pillow and tried not to think about the abyss. He ended up replacing thoughts of despair with feelings of loneliness, which was not much of an improvement.

He missed Miku so much. Yet, in the end, he had created the situation that led her to leave him.

He thought back to the time he spent with Jill Connors. Thoughts of Jill and their physical relationship, the sin of his actions, and against God were always with him. Though he had confessed his sins and obtained forgiveness, the memories of what he had done remained. For him, they produced, as he saw it, scars. Yet he thought of them as forgiven scars and decided he was all right with that. When he tried to pray to God, he always remembered Jill and acknowledged his moral culpability and guilt. He remembered how profoundly lonely he had been when they were together and that she had probably been as lonely. The feeling of loneliness was not as terrifying as thoughts of despair, but neither concept was helping Joseph get back to sleep. He looked again at the clock. It was nearly 4:30. He got out of bed and went downstairs to make a pot of coffee. He would be going to work early today.

52.

Later that morning on campus, Joseph was reviewing some notes for a class when he heard a knock on his office door. His first thought was that he had forgotten an appointment with a student. Reflexively, he said, "Come in." The door opened, and in stepped Martin. "Martin, what are you doing here? It is great to see you."

"I was walking by the campus and thought I'd see if I could catch you between classes. Is it a bad time?"

"No, no, not at all," exclaimed Joseph looking down at his desk calendar and up at the clock, seeing he had no appointments this morning and his next class was not for another hour and fifteen minutes. "Please, please, come in and have a seat." Joseph lifted a pile of books off the chair he had in mind and then slid it around the side of his desk to where the chairs could face each other without the desk being between them. "I don't think you've ever been here before, have you?"

"No, I knew what building you were in, but I had to ask somebody where you were hidden," Martin said, smiling at his friend. He closed the door, walked to where Joseph had cleared a spot for him, removed his jacket, put it over the back of the chair, and sat down.

Martin noted that the office probably had as many books as the college library. "Isn't there a policy that requires you to return some of these volumes to their rightful place?"

Joseph smiled and laughed, "Not until the end of the semester, wise guy. Well, have you settled in at home?"

"More or less, it is a big shock to the system after being aboard a warship for the last so many years and then readjusting to family and home life."

Joseph studied Martin as his tall friend related a few stories from home about how his kids Mark and Darcy had grown so much while he was away. He saw his buddy had aged during the war, but who hadn't? Martin's hair was prematurely turning gray. He could see the streaks of age throughout his thick head of hair, especially in his sideburns. Both had turned forty this year. Linart also looked somewhat tired. Though he had been home for a while now, Martin still had dark rings under his eyes that Joseph had not remembered before the war.

North Pacific

Waiting until Martin had finished his stories about his kids, Joseph asked, "What was it like aboard *Salt Lake City*?"

Martin paused, closing his eyes for a moment. Then taking a quick breath, he said, "My time aboard *Salt Lake City* was all right. My fellow crew members were great guys. I have no complaints. I made it home, and for that, I'm the luckiest guy in the world." He hesitated, glancing out the office window and then continuing in a lower voice, "It was up in the North Pacific where my troubles started."

"Do you want to tell me about it?"

"Maybe."

"Well, if you want to, now is as good a time as any. If you don't, I get that too," Joseph said, leaning back in his chair a little.

Martin looked at him intently, and just when Joseph thought this conversation would probably not happen, it did. Martin put his hands to the back of his neck to relieve building or pent-up tension. He swallowed and proceeded to talk about darker things.

"We spent a week or more as part of a picket line west of Attu to interdict Japanese supply efforts from the Kurile Islands. I've never imagined fouler weather than what we endured during that time. The wind howled ceaselessly. They call them "williwaws" in that part of the world. Our ships were tossed in every direction. Snow and rain punished you from port and starboard, forward and aft, even up and down. It would confuse any sense you might have of where you were. After those long days and nights battling nature's incredible raw power, we were ready to call it quits and return to base. However, it was then that we received intelligence that an enemy Japanese convoy had been detected heading for Attu to resupply the Japanese garrisons. So, instead of heading for Adak, we set a course to intercept the resupply effort. Crucially, however, due to an incomplete translation of the coded message, we failed to hear that a powerful escort force was also present protecting the Japanese convoy.

Early the following day, we ran headlong into the enemy. The Japanese escort force consisted of two heavy cruisers, two light cruisers, and six destroyers, compared to our one heavy cruiser, one light cruiser, and four destroyers. We were clearly outnumbered and overmatched. The clash turned into a running gun battle, with both groups in single file firing at the other line. The two Japanese heavy cruisers tore into *Salt Lake City* with their big guns. We traded fire with them for as long as possible. We gave as good as we got, but the Japanese fire slowly overwhelmed us. We were repeatedly hit to the point that we were shipping tons of water, so much so that our boiler fires were doused, and the engines stopped. The old ship, or as the crew affectionately called her, "Swayback Maru," just sat there. The Japanese saw that we were dead in the water and not firing. They charged harder toward us. We had a couple of guns that still worked, but we had used up our ammo. Joe, we fired worthless damned flare shells at the oncoming ships!"

North Pacific

Martin paused and looked down. "It was at that moment I knew we were going to die. There was no doubt about it. My mind raced in a thousand directions. I thought about Colleen and the kids. I thought about the world and what a crazy place it was. I had experienced life, and in mere moments that life would be gone. I could not wrap my head around that reality. In my mind, it felt as though pieces of who I was as a person were fragmenting and spinning away from me, and there was nothing I could do about it. Joe, it was like a large orchestra, all the instruments playing furiously at once, just moments away from the final crescendo that would end my life." Martin sat motionless, not speaking. He closed his eyes and held his hands up. "And then the firing stopped." He paused, "It just stopped. Those damned ships quit firing at us. The entire resupply convoy and all the escorts came about 180 degrees and left the area, all of them. Joe, I'm not kidding. We were done for. There was no chance we were going to survive. I was going to die along with all my shipmates."

Martin pushed air out of his inflated cheeks and wiped an eye with the back of his hand. "We had five feet of water in some of the spaces within the engine room. We had up to a foot of thick cold oil in some other areas. We shipped over 1,000 tons of water," raising his voice. "After about an hour and some heroic repairs, we were able to get underway again and slowly limp back to base. I'm here, Joe, but I guess my punishment for living is that I must continually relive that experience. It is as real for me to tell you the story today as it was when it happened."

North Pacific

Joseph noticed that Martin's brow was dotted with drops of sweat. He had never seen Martin like this before. He was at a loss as to what to say. He slid his chair forward and leaned toward Martin placing both his hands on Martin's shoulders. "I'm so sorry you had to go through that, Martin."

Martin did not move or open his eyes. Joseph got out of his chair and walked to the window that looked out over the campus. In his position of writing a narrative of the naval actions in the North Pacific for the Navy, Joseph knew of *Salt Lake City's* travails in what became known as the "Battle of the Komandorski Islands." But he was unsure what he could do for his suffering buddy. "Martin, is there anything I can do?"

Martin interrupted Joseph and said, "You're doing it now, brother."

"Have you told anyone else this story," Joseph pressed.

Martin remained silent.

"Did you talk to the doctors about it?"

Martin nodded.

"What have they told you?"

"They call it 'combat stress.' They didn't believe it was a major trauma in my case but that it was real. The military shrinks said they had seen this in lots of guys. They tell me it was an event I cannot get out of my head, at least for now."

Joseph waited.

North Pacific

Martin continued. "Remember I told you over at my place that I wanted to tell you about this so that you would know, and it would possibly help me by discussing it. Joe, I have not told Colleen about it, and I don't want to if I possibly can. I don't want her to know that her husband is nuts." Martin pulled a handkerchief out of his pants pocket and wiped his forehead. He was beginning to regain his composure. "Joe, I don't know what to tell you. Maybe we can try to discuss this in the normal course of our day-to-day lives. Promise me, though, that you won't tell Colleen about it. The doctors tell me many vets have this issue much worse than I do. I can't imagine that, but I've seen some guys when I have an appointment with my doctors who are not all there, if you know what I mean. I'm trying not to end up like that."

"Martin, I'll be there for you."

"Thanks, man."

The two talked for a while longer, and then Martin made his exit. Joseph was hurt to see that his buddy had to experience what he had gone through. Yet, on the upside, Martin was here and not with the flotsam in the North Pacific. Joseph was determined to do whatever he could to make Martin, Martin again.

Joseph knew more of the story of the Battle of the Komandorski Islands from his research after the war. It seems that the Japanese Vice Admiral in command had reason to believe American air power was about to arrive on the scene. The flare shells fired by *Salt Lake City* added to this fear as they took on the appearance of aerial ordinance coming down from the cloudy skies. The Japanese fired their anti-aircraft guns. It was then that the Vice Admiral made the call to return to the Japanese base of Paramushiro in the Kurile Islands.

53.

Kasumi and Joseph continued their monthly dinner get-togethers. Without saying anything about it, both parties very much looked forward to each meal and realized the need for each other's companionship. Kasumi needed Joseph to get through her readjustment to life as an American citizen of Japanese descent after the displacement trauma of the camps. Joseph needed her to help him on his bumpy road to establishing some sort of social life after the war.

With over two weeks to go before their next dinner, Joseph received a call from Kasumi. He assumed it was to change the meal, time, or date. Kasumi sounded distant and distressed. She asked if they could meet.

Joseph said, "Sure, where, Old Town, downtown?" After quickly suggesting a few spots they might get together, Kasumi broke in on Joseph and said it might be best if he could come over to her place. Joseph said, "I'm on my way." They hung up.

As he drove to her apartment building across from Wright Park, Joseph worried that Kasumi might have been harassed or, even worse, assaulted in some way. He parked the Studebaker, entered the building, and took the stairs up to her apartment. The cane and the stairs slowed his physical progress, but his mind was now totally focused on Kasumi's well-being. He knocked on the door. Kasumi opened it and hugged Joseph with a distraught look on her face. Joseph hugged her back and felt relieved that she was not, at least as far as he could tell, physically harmed. She motioned for him to sit on the couch. He obliged, and surprisingly, she sat down next to him. Kasumi took his right hand with both of hers, looked at him, and said, "I have some news that I'm not sure you will want to hear."

Joseph arched his back slightly. "What is it, Kasumi? What is it you want to tell me?"

"Today, I delivered some sewing I had been working on to a customer's home, Mrs. Sato. She invited me in for a cup of tea, and we talked for a while. I discovered that she knew Miku's aunt Mrs. Moriya."

Joseph's head snapped up, his eyes now wholly fixed on Kasumi.

She continued, "I asked if she knew where Mrs. Moriya was, and she told me that Miku's aunt now lived in California."

Joseph interrupted and, with a slightly strained voice, asked, "Was Miku still with her?"

"No, Miku was not with her aunt."

"Did Mrs. Moriya know where she was?" Joseph asked with even more urgency.

Kasumi drew in a deep breath. "Mrs. Sato said that Mrs. Moriya told her that Miku had left the United States just before the war started."

"No," Joseph whispered almost inaudibly.

"Yes, Joseph, you know that she worked in the travel business with her father. Miku took maybe the last Japanese ocean liner from Seattle to Yokohama, Japan before the war started. Mrs. Sato thought Miku's aunt had said Miku departed somewhere around the end of October or the beginning of November 1941. Miku told her aunt she was leaving for Japan. Miku helped her aunt contact her brother in San Francisco, and the two moved out on the same day, Miku for Japan, and Mrs. Moriya for California."

Joseph stood up and, not knowing what to think or do, paced about the living room of Kasumi's apartment for a minute but then stopped and steadied himself with his cane. Kasumi watched him intently.

Joseph looked at Kasumi helplessly.

"Come over here and sit down," Kasumi implored Joseph as she patted the cushion next to her on the couch. Joseph returned to where she wanted him, and this time she took both his hands in hers. "Joseph, Mrs. Moriya told Mrs.

Sato that Miku traveled to her grandparents' family home where her Mother and Father were staying in Urakami."

Joseph turned his head slightly. "Where is Urakami?"

Kasumi lifted her head and tried to hold back tears. "Urakami is a, how would I say this, a district, a neighborhood, in Nagasaki.

Joseph interrupted her. "Nagasaki?"

Kasumi continued, "At the center of the neighborhood is the Urakami cathedral. It is the largest congregation of Japanese Catholics in Japan. Joseph, the atomic bomb dropped on Nagasaki, detonated directly above the cathedral that day during morning Mass. The Urakami district lost over two-thirds of its population at the moment of the blast." Kasumi buried her face in Joseph's chest and wept. Joseph held her tightly. He didn't know at that point whether he was holding her for her sake or his, nor did it matter.

~~~~~

The night lights from the bay flickered through the window and onto the ceiling of Joseph's bedroom. He lay fully clothed on the bed, trying not to think, but to no avail. He thought about Kasumi and what a great friend she was and how hard it must have been for her to tell him what she had found out. He was surprised at how he broke down in front of her upon hearing her story. He had no idea that was how he would react, but he did. He remembered sitting in Kasumi's living room as the day darkened, talking about Miku and her family. His thoughts shifted to the bomb. How could one possibly imagine the moment the bomb detonated? All those lives - instantly obliterated.

Then his thoughts turned solely to Miku. He remembered her lying in this bed with him. He remembered the warmth of her body pushed up against his. Who was he kidding? He loved that woman so much. The years since they had been together seemed so many now. He knew from the moment he saw her that she was the one. His hopes of finding her in the Fall of 1941 or after the camps had been shut down were all for naught. He remembered Miku telling him that her father had not wanted her to stay in Tacoma when the elder Shinkais left for Japan. He had wanted her to come with them. She was, of course, as Miku put it, his little girl. Had her father reached out to her and convinced her to come to Japan? Had something happened in her family that she needed to go there? Why didn't she contact me? Why didn't she tell me she was leaving? Had she already decided that we would never make it as a couple? Did her feelings for me fade? He shuddered at the thought.

North Pacific

54.

The following day, on campus with almost no sleep, he talked with a colleague in the History department. Joseph brought up the subject of the atomic bomb and its use by the United States in the Pacific War on Japan. Joseph lamented that it had stolen the lives of so many unsuspecting civilians. He told his colleague that he couldn't imagine how the survivors must have felt and reacted to the enormity of the disaster. His fellow faculty member thought about it for a moment and then suggested that, in terms of magnitude, he believed it paralleled in many ways a natural disaster in Lisbon, Portugal, in 1755. He thought it might be worthwhile for Joseph to read up on it. Joseph thanked him and, that afternoon made his way into the library stacks and got up to speed on the calamity that befell the Portuguese capital city nearly two hundred years before.

The disaster in Lisbon struck on a Sunday, November $2^{nd,}$ 1755, coincidently and ironically, the feast of All Souls Day, during which the Catholic Church remembers the dead. Portugal was a Catholic country, and the churches were full of Mass attendees when the earthquake shook the city that Sunday morning. The quake, originating over 120 miles southwest of Lisbon in the Atlantic Ocean, destroyed or damaged 85% of the buildings in the city and saw massive fires erupt from the devastation that turned into a firestorm, asphyxiating anyone who was near it. Finally, 40 minutes after the earthquake had struck, a tsunami smashed into the city. In all, Lisbon, with an estimated population of 200,000 people at the time, suffered 30,000 to 40,000 deaths in less than an hour. It was, as the saying goes, a disaster of biblical proportions.

Joseph also discovered that the famous French philosopher and commentator Voltaire, a contemporary of the event in the middle of the 18th century, had authored a poem about the tragedy. In it, he spoke of the catastrophe that befell the citizens of Lisbon.

> *"Behold the debris and ashes of the unfortunate –*
> *These women and children heaped in common ruin,*
> *These scattered limbs under the broken marble.*
> *See the thousands whom the earth devours!"*

Later in the poem, as Voltaire contemplates the disaster's meaning, he asks these questions:

> *"Man is a stranger unto himself. He wonders:*
> *What am I? Where am I going? Where am I from?"*

Part of his answer was as follows:

> *"We are atoms tormented in this murky soup,*
> *Swallowed by death by the playthings of fate."*

North Pacific

Joseph closed the book containing the poem. He jotted down a few notes in the small journal he kept in his inside jacket pocket. Then he replaced the book and a couple of other volumes that he had removed that dealt with the historical tragedy.

Walking slowly back to his office, he pondered the comparisons of what he had just read with Kasumi's story of the Nagasaki bombing. Once back in his office, he closed the door and paced back and forth within the confines of his modest space. After nearly an hour of walking back and forth, eight slow steps this way and eight back, Joseph came to see, at least in his mind, the similarities and differences between the two events. There was, of course, the irony of the thousands of churchgoers in Lisbon who were celebrating the souls of the faithful departed that day, only to be counted among them in less than an hour. He juxtaposed that with the civilians in the Urakami district of Nagasaki that fateful morning. Both Lisbon's earthquake and subsequent tsunami, as well as Nagasaki's ferocious atomic blast brutally took the lives of so many completely unsuspecting people. The reality of the two events made Joseph physically shudder.

However, Joseph distinguished between the "natural" evil of what happened in Lisbon and the "man-made" evil of the atomic bomb used on Nagasaki. In part, Voltaire had authored his poem to rail against philosophers of the time who subscribed to fellow philosopher Gottfried Wilhelm Leibniz's theodicy argument that this was the "best of all possible worlds." What was it, Voltaire had said, Joseph thought to himself as he reviewed the notes he had taken while in the library. He translated the French. "Philosophers who deceive, who shout, all is well. Come, contemplate these awful ruins." While thinking over Nagasaki, even now, many were speaking out about the illicit use of atomic weapons. Joseph was not one of them. No matter how an aggressor conducts it, all war is evil and has been that way since the beginning of time. Joseph knew that the use of this weapon heralded the "atomic age," a time that could, in the worst of all worlds, lead to possibly the incineration of mankind. Yet he struggled with how many American lives might have been lost had the United States been forced to invade Japan. He had heard commentators estimate the number to be as high as one hundred thousand.

With time, the natural disaster in Lisbon would allow man to use his unshakable hope and spirit to move on. At the same time, the beginning of the Atomic Age, marked by the events at Hiroshima and Nagasaki, could be conceived as foreshadowing unthinkable man-made horrors. The whole comparative exercise, the disaster in Lisbon, and the bombings of Hiroshima and Nagasaki left him wracked with anguish.

North Pacific

55.

Joseph always wound up at St. Dominic, kneeling before the Blessed Sacrament when things were at their worst. It was late afternoon, and the sun, hidden behind immense dark gray clouds outside the stained-glass windows, rendered the light inside of the church weak and filtered. He went from kneeling in the pew to sitting and back again, repositioning his back, and trying to reconcile his thoughts with his faith. His faith, he told himself, was not up for grabs, but the moorings that held it were being badly strained. Joseph slowly closed his eyes and whispered, "Help me, Lord. Help my unbelief."

He reopened his eyes and began to look intently at the tabernacle. He was conscious of his breathing, heartbeat, and stillness. Surprisingly to him, thoughts of his childhood came to mind.

Joseph remembered his father telling him stories. Alexandr brought many of these stories to America from the "old country." Alexandr's stories were handed down from past generations with a smattering of new narratives sprinkled in. Alexandr would tell the stories using a dramatic and sometimes booming voice. Many were quite amusing, while others carried a more serious tone, weight, and point. One such short story, in particular, now flooded

Joseph's memory. Alexandr had read it in a book of novellas he had received from a friend he had made while working at the sawmill. The author was a Vasyl Stefanyk, and the story Joseph now recalled vividly was entitled "Sons." It was one of the last stories that Alexandr, using gesturing arms, intense expressions, and voice rising and falling, had told him before he had died.

As best as he could remember, the story began with an old farmer walking along, plowing a field with his workhorse. As he remembered Alexandr telling it, the farmer was angry and repeatedly shouted at the horse. Then the old farmer stepped into a rut and twisted his ankle. As he tried to put weight on it, he bellowed all the more at no one in particular. After a few aborted attempts, he finally found a way to limp around and continue to plow the field. He began shouting toward the sky. A small bird started chirping beautiful little noises interrupting the farmer's loud rantings. Hearing the singing, the farmer raised his voice to the little bird. He told the bird to quit chirping and singing around him. He looked right at the little bird and said, in an irritated voice, 'Fly away!' And when the bird did not, the farmer added another thought. Since he, the little bird, could fly, he told it to fly straight up to God and convey this message to him – "Leave me alone." Again the little bird did not fly off but seemed to chirp more quietly and stare at the farmer. He told the bird to tell God not to try to deceive him with songs that didn't mean anything. Songs would not curb the farmer's anger with God. The little bird let out one final chirp and finally flew away.

North Pacific

At this point in the story, Joseph remembered Alexandr telling him that the old farmer was always angry at God because he had lost his only two sons, both killed in a war far from their homeland. To make the farmer's sorrow more extreme, his wife died of great sadness and grief after learning of the deaths of their sons. The old farmer was left bereft of any family, alone to carry on in the world. His anger and resentment at how his life had played out made him intensely bitter toward God.

The old farmer felt the pain of his twisted ankle and the loneliness and sadness of his life. One more time, he looked to the sky and cried out, imploring God to tell him where his sons were buried after they had been killed in battle. He told God he would sell his soul and all his land so that he might travel to where they were buried. He reminded God that he, the Almighty, had resurrected his son. The old man told God he did not expect him to resurrect his sons. He asked that God show him where his sons were buried so that he might go there and lie down beside them. The farmer waited. The wind stirred, but all was perfectly silent. The old farmer broke down, fell to his knees in the middle of the field, and shed tears. Shaking, he cried out to God in terrible anguish, "May your blue dome burst just like my heart." The old farmer then crumpled to the ground, sobbing. Joseph remembered that a few years after hearing the story, he figured out "blue dome" referred to the heavens.

The short story concluded with the old farmer and his workhorse going home late in the afternoon. That evening, broken-hearted, he prayed to the Virgin Mary, "And you, Mother of God,… You gave one son, but I gave two…"

Joseph sat back in the pew with the story completed in his head. The tale resonated powerfully with Joseph when he heard it from his father and now again as he remembered it. He felt exhausted, sapped of all strength. He tilted his head back, and his eyes took in the church's vaulted ceiling. Lord, you are all I have. Please speak to me. Finally, he looked again at the tabernacle and asked God about Miku. Where is her body, Lord? Has it been recovered? Was she afforded a proper burial? Life can be so cruel, so hard. And always, God, you are silent. As he pondered these things, he knelt one more time and, gazing at the tabernacle, experienced the incredible silence and quietness of the setting and thought of the Psalm wherein the psalmist says as a kind of medium, as if spoken by God, *"Be still and see that I am God"* (Ps 45:11).

Joseph made the sign of the cross, rose, and exited the pew. Then it was out the doors and slowly down the steps, a now lonely, useless middle-aged man making his way to his car with the necessity of a cane.

North Pacific

56.

After Mass the following Sunday, Father Etienne was saying good morning and shaking hands as the parishioners filed out the large doors at the front of the Church. Near the end of this pastoral practice, Father caught Joseph's attention and asked if he might wait until he had finished because he wanted to speak to him. Joseph assented with a nod and began saying hello to a couple of his students who attended St. Dominic to meet their Sunday obligation. Once Father finished, he turned his attention to his former student. "Joseph, how are you feeling? You look tired."

"I am Father. I'm actually quite tired these days," Joseph offered without a facial expression.

Father sensed Joseph was in a bad way. "Can we talk about it?"

Without life in his voice, Joseph said, "Sure."

"How about if you pick me up here at 2 PM, and we could go have a piece of that special pie and a cup of coffee?"

That brought out a slight smile from Joseph. "Okay, Father, I'll see you in front of the rectory at 2 PM."

The weather was warm. Joseph went home and made breakfast, one egg, two pieces of toast, and coffee. He straightened up the house and did some laundry. He skipped lunch, knowing he would be eating pie that afternoon. He was not kidding either about being tired. Around noon he sat down in the middle of the sofa, and turning, he put his head on a pillow in the corner of one end and closed his eyes for a moment. He woke up after 1:30 PM. Surprised that he had slept, he shook his head a few times and went upstairs. He changed the shirt he had on, splashed his face, combed his hair, and upon returning to the main floor, grabbed the keys to the car off the hall table and left to pick up Father Etienne. As Joseph drove the five minutes to the church, uneasy thoughts of Miku once again seeped into his being.

At 3 Bridges Café, the two men ordered their coffee and pie. Denise served them but apologized for not chatting as she was preparing orders because they were short-staffed that afternoon. Someone had called in sick.

After making the usual wonderful remarks about the pie, Father Etienne asked Joseph what was troubling him.

"Father, I received some terrible news last week regarding Miku."

The priest frowned. "What is it, Joseph? What do you mean?"

"A friend of Miku's found out that she traveled to Japan before the war started. Her aunt, who I know you remember…"

Father broke in. "Mrs. Moriya, yes, go on."

"Yes, Father, Mrs. Moriya. She told a friend who told a friend that Miku went to be with her family. To make a long story short, It seems that Miku's family lived in Nagasaki, where the second atomic bomb was dropped."

Father Etienne made the sign of the cross, lowered his head, and closed his eyes. A minute later, he raised his head. "Joseph, I am so sorry to hear that news. How do you know Miku was in the blast?"

"Her immediate and extended family all lived right in the heart of the neighborhood above which the bomb was detonated," Joseph replied with a pained expression.

"I will offer a Mass for Miku and her family this week, Joseph. What else can I do for you?"

Joseph did not respond. He tilted his head from one side to the other, showing the physical strain he was experiencing in his neck. He tried to half smile at Father but failed.

Father continued to observe Joseph. He pondered his situation as he understood it. After a minute or two, where there had been no exchange of words, the priest finally said, "Joseph, I can tell from your revelations, physical appearance, and seemingly broken spirit that you are suffering mightily over your news. Let me ask you a favor. Hopefully, it will also help you. Would you please consider driving me to Portland, Oregon, this coming week? I have some Dominican business with the bishop down there. We can talk along the way or just take in the beautiful country between here and there. I also want to share some thoughts about a special place that might help you with your suffering." Father Etienne noticed Joseph a bit bewildered, looking at him and not quite grasping what Father was trying to say. "Really, you must come. It is July, so you are not teaching. This will only take two nights, and then we will head straight back to Tacoma."

"When, Father?"

"Tuesday, Joseph, we will be back on Thursday."

Joseph didn't have anything going on for those three days. "You want to go in the Studebaker?"

"Yes, it will make it." He paused. "Won't it?"

"I suppose. I've just never traveled that sort of distance in her before."

"Well, my original plan was to take the train down there, which is certainly doable. But if you consent to come with me, I believe it would be better for us to drive down instead. It will give us the privacy to talk about things."

The history professor didn't seem to have a spark today, and it showed. Father used a more commanding voice and said, "Joseph, I insist."

Even though Joseph had no interest in driving to Portland, he didn't see how he could tell Father no. "All right, Father, I'll go. When should I pick you up?"

Father smiled. "How about 10:30 AM, after morning Mass on Tuesday? The accommodations are on me and thank you."

"You're welcome, Father."

North Pacific

"And how are you two doing over here," Denise said as she appeared in front of their table with the prettiest of smiles and a coffee pot in one hand.

"A little more coffee would be nice, Denise," Joseph answered with a tired smile.

She poured some coffee into the almost empty cups, and the three of them chatted for a minute before Denise had to move on to other customers.

~~~~~

The next day Joseph took the Studebaker to a gas station up on Proctor Street. Not only did he gas up the old Dictator, but he also had the attendant check the oil, the water, the belts, the air pressure in the tires, the works, to make sure the car was ready for the trip. That night he packed a small suitcase. He saw in the newspaper that the weather would be around 75 degrees all week in Tacoma. Joseph knew that meant it would be 5 to 10 degrees warmer in Portland. Perfect weather, he thought, for the drive and stay.

Preparing for and thinking about the trip to Portland helped Joseph distract himself from thinking about Miku. However, he slept poorly on both Sunday and Monday nights. On Tuesday morning, he was up early and decided to go to morning Mass since he was picking up Father there anyway. After Mass, Joseph sat in his car while Father changed into his traveling clothes and loaded his suitcase into the trunk.

The two friends set off on their journey on a postcard summer day. They made their way to Olympia and then due south through Centralia and Chehalis. After passing through Chehalis, they stopped at a roadside café for lunch, and then it was back on the road. Later they passed through Kelso and Longview. Finally, they entered Vancouver, crossed over the Columbia River into Oregon, and then it was on to downtown Portland. They arrived that afternoon at the Benson Hotel in the heart of the "Rose City."

The two travelers checked into their rooms, Father's on the 3rd floor and Joseph's on the 5th floor. They rested in their rooms for an hour and then met downstairs in the restaurant just off the main lobby. Over dinner, Father laid out the itinerary for the next day that included what he had in mind for his friend.

"Joseph, I have a meeting tomorrow at 10 AM at the Cathedral, which is not that far from here. I have some Dominican business that I must take care of, and it may take a while to resolve some of the issues. That is here nor there. I asked you to come with me to Portland because I know of a special place I would like you to visit. I think it might help you with the sad situation involving Miku and her family. It is called the Sanctuary of Our Sorrowful Mother, but the locals here simply call it the "Grotto." It is only ten miles or so from the hotel. If you drop me off tomorrow at the Cathedral at about 9:45 AM, you can head straight out there. I don't know how long I will be, but no matter what, I have decided that whenever I finish up, I will walk back to the hotel. I need the exercise, and it is only a mile or two. It will do me good, and besides, the weather is going to be fantastic. You can stay out at the sanctuary as long as you wish. You must go. You really must."

Joseph, somewhat revived now from the drive, nodded affirmatively. "Well, I didn't drive all the way down here just to say no to you, Father. I will visit this grotto."

"Excellent," exclaimed Father Etienne.

When they had finished dinner, the Dominican priest gave Joseph a book. "Here, Joseph, I want you to have this book. It is entitled *Le Christ, vie de l'âme* (Christ, the Life of the Soul). Dom Columba Marmion penned this book back in 1917. He was brilliant. He was an Irish priest who became the Abbot of Maredsous in Belgium. No one explains the faith more clearly and concisely than Marmion."

"Thank you, Father. You know I'm always looking for something to read about the faith."

"It will serve you well," Father offered. "I know you need support now, and this book will help immensely. Also, tomorrow, I believe your trip to the 'Grotto' will be well worth your effort."

It was summertime. So when the two had completed their meals and finished talking, they walked up and then back down the boulevard, taking in the evening sights and sounds of downtown Portland.

North Pacific

Back in his room, Joseph felt it was good to have made the trip to Portland with Father. Just getting out of the house and doing something had made him dwell less on Miku. In bed, he looked over the book given to him by Father Etienne earlier in the evening. He fanned the pages stopping periodically to read passages. At the very end of Marmion's work, the Benedictine Abbot quoted the great Saint Augustine (Sermon 123, c. 3.).

"Christ, God, is the homeland to which we go.
Christ, Man, is the road by which we go there."

Joseph switched off the light by the side of the bed and quickly fell asleep.

The next morning, he showered, shaved, and put on fresh clothes. It looked like it was going to be a beautiful day. He went down to the lobby where the restaurant was located, grabbed a newspaper, ordered a black coffee, and read the local news. Father Etienne joined him about twenty minutes later. They indulged in bacon and eggs with hash browns, toast, and small talk.

Joseph dropped Father off at the cathedral as planned. The Dominican priest urged him to fully appreciate the almost "transcendent" feel of the grounds at the sanctuary. The good Father got out of the car and, before closing the door, said, "Joseph, I consider you one of my closest friends. We have been through much since you first showed up with your father years ago and began our

North Pacific

mentor-student relationship. While at the Grotto, observe, listen, and pray."

57.

After navigating his way out into northeast Portland, Joseph found the "Sanctuary of Our Sorrowful Mother." He parked the car and walked into the grounds. He passed through a stand of trees that gave way to a large open plaza-like space. There were outdoor benches with backs that all faced a one-hundred-foot rock cliff. A grotto was hewn from the basalt rock at the base of the cliff. Within the cavern was positioned an altar, and high above it was placed a replica of the timeless sculpture of Michelangelo's "Pieta," imagining the body of Christ, taken down from the cross and placed in the arms of his mother. The Grotto, consisting of the altar and sculpture, functioned as the sanctuary for an outdoor church where Masses were celebrated. It was a spectacular and imposing sight.

Joseph stood staring for a while at the magnificent setting he was in. Then he walked about midway to the altar and hung his cane on the back of a bench. He sat down. The day was incredibly beautiful. The sun seemed to enhance every color and form in the remarkable space. Birds were flying about and singing. It took his breath away to realize that something this beautiful and religious existed within easy driving distance from anywhere in the Pacific Northwest. It could not have been more peaceful. It, indeed, was a place of solitude and prayer.

He placed one arm on top of the back of the bench and relaxed. He sat there for twenty minutes before he realized he had tuned out his thoughts and had just let his senses enjoy the extraordinary sights and sounds of the morning. Joseph's whole body had taken the cue as he let God's creation wash over him.

Not too far from where he was sitting, Joseph noticed a religious Sister in full habit standing by the wood benches. Making eye contact, she smiled and made her way over to him. Standing next to where he was sitting, the Sister asked if it was his first visit to the "Grotto."

Joseph, made to feel comfortable by her manner, replied, "Yes, it is my first visit."

"Could the day be more perfect?"

Joseph concurred wholeheartedly. "I agree with you, Sister. This is a wonderful day and setting."

She smiled and continued her questions. "May I ask where you are from?"

"I'm down here from Tacoma, Washington, visiting your beautiful city with my parish priest," he offered.

Emboldened by Joseph's easy-going manner and friendly demeanor, the Sister asked, "What brings you out to the Grotto?"

North Pacific

"To be fair, I didn't know about it, but Father Sauveterre, my priest, told me I needed to come out here and take it in. So here I am."

Joseph was sitting at the end of the bench. "Do you mind?" the Sister said as she sat in the row in front of him and slid in about six feet so they could continue their conversation. Joseph smiled as she settled in, placing a stack of pamphlets next to her on the bench. Realizing they had not introduced themselves properly, he said, "I'm sorry, Sister, my name is Joseph."

She beamed and said, "I am Sister Ann."

Quite pleased with this turn of events, Joseph engaged the younger woman in conversation. He guessed she was in her late twenties. The two exchanged pleasantries for ten minutes or so.

"What have you got there, if I may ask," Joseph queried, pointing at the stack on the bench.

"Oh, I'm sorry," said Sister Ann, laughing and blushing slightly. "These are pamphlets I'm supposed to be handing out to visitors if they want one." She removed one from the top of the stack and offered it to Joseph.

"Thank you, Sister." Joseph took the pamphlet and saw it was entitled "The Seven Sorrows of Mary."

The weather just kept getting better. The sun now flooded the bench seat area. The two complete strangers, now on a first-name basis, bantered about the setting and the Servite monastery, set back on the grounds on top of the cliff above the Grotto. She told Joseph that the Servites had established the sanctuary and Grotto a couple of decades earlier and built the monastery.

Then, Sister Ann noticed an older woman standing ten yards off to the side, looking like she wanted to ask a question. "It seems as though I am in demand. I must be about my duties." She pulled herself together, collected her stack of pamphlets, and stood up. Sister Ann looked at him with sincerity. "It was a pleasure to meet you, Joseph from Tacoma. I do not mean to be forward, but when I saw you earlier, I sensed that you were bearing a personal cross of some weight. It was just my impression, and please excuse me if I am wrong. However, If I am correct, Joseph, let me tell you, you came to the right spot today. Many people come here to pray and resolve difficulties in their lives. As you know, the prophet Simeon told the Blessed Virgin Mary that a sword would pierce her soul. I am confident you will make some progress by visiting here today. Ask the Virgin Mother to pray for you to her Son. God bless you, Joseph."

Joseph stood and thanked her for the conversation. He also told her to keep up the good work. Joseph sat down again while Sister Ann walked over and engaged the woman waiting for her. He had very much enjoyed her company.

He reached into his jacket pocket and pulled out a currant scone he had bought at the end of breakfast earlier that morning. The waiter had been kind enough to wrap it in wax paper. Joseph opened it now and enjoyed a few bites. It was just after noon, and the day continued to be ideal. When he had finished, he rose from his seat and, cane in hand, made his way to a waste receptacle at the back of the open area where he deposited the wax paper. His back was giving him trouble for having sat too long on the bench, so he walked around a bit and eventually climbed the steps up to the concrete communion railing that ran the length of the niche. He knelt at the railing. Joseph said a prayer of thanksgiving for the wonderful day he was experiencing. Then he got up slowly, positioned the cane, and descended the steps back down to the open area with the rows and rows of bench seating.

Joseph thought about possibly leaving but remembered Sister Ann's pamphlet. He returned to the bench seats and sat once again. He removed the paper booklet from his pocket and glanced at the pages. On the front were listed the seven sorrows of Mary. In order they were "The Prophesy of Simeon," Sister Ann had mentioned "The Flight into Egypt," "The Loss of the Child Jesus in the Temple," "Mary meets Jesus on the Way to Calvary," "Jesus Dies on the Cross," "Mary Receives Jesus' Body," as depicted in the Pieta that towered over the altar in front of him, and "Jesus is Placed in the Tomb."

Joseph remembered all of these scenes from his Saturday morning catechetical classes at St. Dominic, taught by old Father Simone. The pamphlet further contained a small paragraph about each of the sorrows. Under the Prophecy of Simeon, where Simeon told Mary a sword would pierce her soul, was a quote from Saint Alphonsus Liguori. "In this valley of tears, every man is born to weep, and all must suffer, by enduring the evils which are of daily occurrence." Joseph quickly saw in this statement how it applied to him, especially with the deaths of his parents and the likelihood of the loss of Miku. Liguori went on, "Our Lord shows us this mercy. He conceals the trials which await us, that whatever they may be, we may endure them but once. He did not show Mary this compassion...."

As he scanned down the page before him, he came to the fifth of Mary's sorrows, Jesus dying on the cross. In what must have been the greatest of Mary's sorrows, the Apostle John writes in his gospel, *"There stood by the cross of Jesus, his mother...."* (Jn 19:25). And just below the quote, in smaller print, there was a portion of one of the versions of the famous Catholic poem *Stabat Mater* (Grieving Mother).

> *"At the cross her station keeping,*
> *stood the mournful Mother weeping,*
> *close to Jesus to the last.*
> *Through her heart, his sorrow sharing,*
> *all his bitter anguish bearing,*
> *now at length, the sword had passed."*

As Joseph read on, another few verses caught his eye.

> *"Oh, how sad and sore distressed*
> *was that Mother highly blest*
> *of the sole begotten One!*

North Pacific
Christ above in torment hangs,
she beneath beholds the pangs
of her dying glorious Son."

Is there any grief like a mother's, Joseph thought, when she loses a child, regardless of age? He paused and contemplated the Pieta set high above the altar in the niche. There Mary held her lifeless son's body. Joseph, overcome, wiped his eyes. His suffering was not exclusive, he thought. Everyone suffers, even the Mother of Christ. He knew this, of course, but when you are doing the suffering, you tend to think less about others' suffering and more about your own grief.

It was a dichotomy. On the one hand, Joseph was pondering Creation, as present in the glorious sanctuary he was in, pointing to a Creator, Almighty God. While on the other hand, suffering pointed to what seemed to be a meaningless world and an absurd human existence. Catholicism, his faith, taught that God creates every person for a purpose. This purpose, this meaning of our existence, includes physical and mental suffering.

On the very bottom of the back page of the pamphlet, Joseph saw two more scriptural quotes on suffering. The first was from the 2nd Letter to Timothy, chapter 2, verse 3, *"Labor (take your share of suffering) as a good soldier of Christ Jesus."* The second was from Luke's gospel, chapter 9, verse 23, *"If any man will come after me, let him deny himself, and take up his cross daily, and follow me."* This was a hard saying. When the world is right, one says yes, I will take up my cross daily and follow the Lord. Yet, when something happens in this world that devastates one's life, it is entirely another matter of whether one can truly bear their cross.

He looked around the "Grotto" and pictured the benches full of people attending Mass. He also knew that the hymns and the ritual beauty of the Mass could raise one's soul to extraordinary heights. Yet, right there, in the middle of the liturgy, there was always the mystery of the cross made present in the sacrifice of the Mass.

Joseph thought about Father Etienne, Sister Ann, and the incredibly moving natural sanctuary that formed the "Grotto." He leaned forward, placing his head against his hands, holding the bench back in front of him. He closed his eyes. He thanked God for the experience.

He returned to the Benson Hotel, stopping only to fill the tank of the Dictator for the drive back home the following day. Joseph wandered around the downtown area for a while and found a bookstore that held his attention for the better part of an hour. After that, he returned to the hotel for dinner toting two new books. He and Father Etienne shared their stories of the day and dined on the hotel special that evening, Italian Osso Buco, prepared with veal shanks. They checked out of the Benson the following morning and made their way north, returning to Tacoma that afternoon. Father Etienne thanked Joseph for supplying the transportation. Then they both laughed while commenting that they had both separately prayed the Studebaker would be able to make the entire trip without incident. Back at the rectory, as Father was about to get out of the car, the priest looked at Joseph and summed up his thoughts on his friend's mental anguish. "Listen to me, would you say that Christ knows something about suffering? Well, he allows us all to take part in his once and for all redeeming act. At the Sacrifice of the Mass, we can offer him our lives, our Christian lives, and, importantly, our sufferings, in order to more conform our lives with his."

Joseph was worn out when he parked the car in front of his house and went inside. He opened a couple of windows to cool the interior and began brewing a pot of coffee. When it was ready, he carefully unwrapped a scone he had again purchased in addition to his breakfast earlier that day in Portland. It and the coffee would serve as his dinner that evening. After pouring the coffee, he set the cup and pastry down on the side table next to his straight-back chair and ate and drank slowly as Commencement Bay continued to reveal its mood, activity, and surprises. As night slowly darkened the living room, Joseph whispered, "Miku, why?"

DEUS SITAS

(God-Centered)

"And he is before all, and by him all things consist."

Colossians 1.17

Douay-Rheims

58.

Over the next few days, Joseph pondered everything he had experienced at the Grotto. He also thought about his conversations with Father Etienne on the way to Portland and during their return trip. The personal insights he gained at the Grotto had an impact on him. It helped him better understand that suffering has always been a part of man's existence. He was no different from anyone else. He also knew that many people, upon having suffering come to them or to someone they cared about, or even to total strangers, say I won't believe in a God who would condone such suffering and grief. He decided his faith, as passed on to him by his parents and the Church, supplied him with a framework from which to view the world. All that he had been taught, upon years of reflection, made sense, whether he personally wanted something to be different or not. His faith taught him that the answer to his questions all seemed to point to Jesus Christ, his "Good News," life, death, and resurrection. Christ was the translator that unlocked the mystery of God. He knew he needed to focus on what God wanted and not what he wanted.

Understanding also that the world did not exist just for him was helpful in coping with his life. Everyone had to deal with the vagaries of human existence. These reflections, in many ways, strengthened his always ashamedly less than robust faith.

However, he felt the sadness he was experiencing regarding Miku was crushing him physically and spiritually. He told himself that things had to change. He pulled the journal from his jacket pocket and wrote in bold letters at the top of the next empty page, ***#1 I must work on my book.*** He needed to summon all of his inner strength and move forward.

In reality, he had been working on his book for months, just not as hard as was necessary for a project of that scope. The book had to take precedence over everything else. It would tell the story of the war in the North Pacific from his lived experience and the interviews he conducted from January 1942 through most of August 1943. Further, he had his weekly reports submitted to the 13th Naval District Head Quarters during his time in the North Pacific. Additionally, Joseph had begun corresponding with naval personnel ranging from officers to enlisted men, whom he had conducted interviews with, to fill in the blanks after his injury and add any changes in thoughts since the war's end. The correspondence took hours a day to read and ask follow-up questions or request clarifications on points to scores of active and retired officers and sailors. He became a frequent visitor to the 13th Naval District's offices in Seattle and Tacoma. He had to find and read ships' war diaries, action and damage reports, naval interrogation reports, operational analyses, and so on. He was even able to view documents requested and made available to him by the Supreme Command for Allied Powers in Tokyo. Many of these latter documents were in Japanese. He took full advantage of the grasp of Japanese he had learned back while writing his dissertation and the help of a few friendships from his days at the University of Washington, to help with more difficult translations and different aspects of those reports.

Through his work, he became aware of Samuel Eliot Morrison's forthcoming opus covering the full range of United States Naval Operations in the Second World War in multiple volumes that would appear in print over the next decade. Joseph's effort, much smaller in scale, would focus on the vast area of operations encompassing the North Pacific, from the cool and temperate climate of the Pacific Northwest of the United States and Canada to Alaska and the desperately cold and ferociously stormy environment of the Aleutian Islands and the Bering Sea. Additionally, Joseph flew to Washington D.C. and spent much more time there than he initially had planned, doing research at the National Archives and the Pentagon.

During this time, Rainier College became a university. The administration, understanding Joseph's plans and work, helped in any way they could to accommodate his research and writing, thus, at the same time, promoting the new Rainier University. The publication of his book would be a boon to the image the university was trying to project of serious and unique scholarship. The most important news was that Joseph had become a tenured professor.

The sheer amount of work required by the book helped tamp down the lingering disquiet about Miku, her family, and his renewed loneliness.

59.

Joseph parked his car on 26th Street and came around the corner to enter Washburn's Market on Proctor Street when he came face to face with Martin's wife, Colleen. After hellos and hugs, Colleen said, with a slightly apprehensive look, "Did you hear that Diane and Charlie Langley are getting married?"

"Why, no, no, I had not heard that." Joseph tilted his head slightly and looked at Colleen.

"It's true. They are getting married at 1st Presbyterian on the third Saturday in June."

Joseph hesitated and looked at Colleen, not knowing exactly what to say.

Colleen continued. "There's going to be a reception at the Winthrop Hotel in the 'Crystal Ballroom.' It's going to be a big deal."

"I'm not sure what you want me to say, Colleen?"

"Oh, Joseph, I'm not looking for a reaction other than to make sure you are okay."

North Pacific

"I'm good, Colleen. I suspected they might tie the knot. They seemed pretty enamored with each other."

"So, you haven't received an invitation?"

"No."

"Well, it's still a few months off. You may get one yet."

"I don't know why I would get one?"

"I'll be surprised if you don't," Colleen cut in.

"Okay, okay, I will let you know if I get an invite."

"How's Martin?" Joseph asked, trying to change the subject.

"I'll tell you, Joseph, I've decided Martin is a work in progress. My goal is to get my pre-war husband back, and I'm doing everything I can to make that happen."

"That's exactly how I feel, Colleen. I know I am much happier he is here now, back in Tacoma, rather than 'at sea,' somewhere in the Pacific."

"Me too, Joseph." Colleen grabbed him and hugged him one more time. "I've got to get over to the school to meet up with Darcy. Let me know about Diane and Charlie."

"Take care, Colleen, and thanks for the word."

With that, Colleen purposefully headed down the street and toward the school.

Joseph stood there for a moment and watched her disappear down the block. A woman on a mission, he said to himself. He thought about the news Colleen had given him. He took a deep breath and then entered the market.

North Pacific

As Colleen had predicted, upon returning home, he found an invitation to Diane and Charlie's wedding reception in the day's mail. He felt a bit trapped. If he didn't go, it would look like he was a sore loser in the Diane sweepstakes. If he went, he would probably have to actually talk to the bride and groom. God knows what the three of them would have to say to each other. Ugh, what fun. Joseph tossed the invite on the hallway side table and went into the kitchen to put away the groceries.

A few days later, Martin called Joseph to see if they were still on for lunch on Saturday. Joseph said yes, and they agreed to grab a burger at Ryan's, a combination bar, soda fountain, and grocery store a little further out in the North End. They talked a little baseball, with Joseph saying he could still strike Martin out. Martin laughed and told him that he was sure he could crush anything an old man with a cane could throw at him, and that was 'if' he could get it to the plate. Before hanging up, Joseph asked Martin to tell Colleen he had received an invitation to Diane and Charlie's wedding reception but not the wedding itself. Martin laughed and kidded Joseph, saying he was sure they didn't want an ex-boyfriend showing up at the church to interrupt the ceremony with an impassioned plea to Diane not to go through with it.

Joseph said, "Oh, Brother. I think I hear someone at the front door."

On the other end of the line, Martin was now laughing. Joseph thought to himself, that's progress, isn't it?

North Pacific

Martin said, "Just a minute, Joe. Colleen has something to say."

Colleen took the receiver from Martin and said, "See, I told you, you would get an invitation. Are you going to go?" Without waiting for an answer, Colleen said, "You should go. Don't act like a schlub. Be a man and show up."

Joseph, now laughing, said, "What does it have to do with my manhood, Colleen?"

"Just make sure you attend the reception," handing the phone back to Martin.

"You heard her. You'd better go. I do what I'm told. Why should it be any different for you?"

"I'll talk to you Saturday. Thanks for all your help," Joseph said facetiously, smiling as they hung up simultaneously.

~~~~~

It was the day of Diane and Charlie's wedding. Joseph got dressed up and drove downtown for the wedding reception against his better judgment. Did he think of it as maybe the lesser of two evils, seeing Diane and Charlie or facing Colleen? Maybe. He ended up parking down on Commerce St. by the Elks Club and then walked a couple of blocks and then up the hill and around the corner onto Broadway before arriving at the entrance to the Winthrop Hotel.

North Pacific

Inside the hotel, a little winded, he was directed to the Crystal Ballroom, where he at once felt like he needed a drink. It had been a while since those feelings had weighed on him. Per his self-imposed rules, he ordered and received a glass of red wine. The Crystal Ballroom was one of the classier places to have an affair of this sort. Everyone who entered the space was immediately struck by four large Austrian cut-crystal chandeliers that created an imposing and grand environment.

After a sip, make that a swig of wine, he was tapped on the shoulder by a smartly dressed woman who, upon a second glance, turned out to be Veronica Willis, a classmate from high school. Ronnie, as she had always been called, launched into remembering just about everything they had done in school some twenty-plus years ago. Though his memory was not as sharp as hers, she was genuinely fun, and Joseph welcomed the small talk and memories. He had forgotten how much he had counted on Ronnie during accounting class as to the mysteries of that discipline. Joseph was happy to see her after all these years, and their reminiscing brought back good memories of their time in high school.

Ronnie told Joseph that she had known Diane since the two of them had joined the Spanish club, she as a senior and Diane as a sophomore. The two of them had kept in touch and had always exchanged Christmas cards. She had been surprised to receive an invitation but jumped at the chance to see Diane again and have a fun night out. Ronnie's company also allowed Joseph to relax a bit more amid the hubbub of the reception setting. Without her company, Joseph would have felt more self-conscious and uncomfortable.

Minutes later, the bride and groom entered the ballroom and walked to the head of the dance floor amidst clapping and cheering, thus becoming the destination point of the receiving line. Folks began forming to meet, greet, and congratulate the lucky couple. Joseph and Ronnie got into the line and slowly moved forward. When they finally reached the bride and groom, Mr. and Mrs. Langley greeted them. Looking as beautiful as ever, Diane hugged Ronnie and introduced her to Charlie. Then it was time for Joseph. Diane embraced Joseph. She whispered in his ear, "I'm so happy you came, Joseph. I'm so pleased you could be here." Joseph, in sotto voce, congratulated her and looked toward Charlie. Beaming, Charlie made a slight step toward Joseph, and the two shook hands. "Thanks for coming, Vaenko." Joseph thought the newlyweds looked like a dream couple.

Diane broke in, "Joseph, did you see in the newspaper that Charlie and I are honeymooning in San Francisco?"

Joseph had not read the entry in the newspaper. He rarely devoted any time to that section of the paper. "No, but that's great news," Joseph replied without missing a beat.

"We are planning on going to Europe sooner than later after those countries get a bit more back to normal since the end of the war."

North Pacific

Looking at Charlie, Joseph said, "I know you two will have a great time whenever you figure out the best time to go."

Diane said, "Oh, Joseph, did you know we bought a new home?" Now practically gushing, she added, "It is over by the Narrows Bridge. It has a wonderful panoramic view of the straight and Gig Harbor."

Having said the appropriate things, Joseph now felt less comfortable with the conversation. Charlie spoke up, "I see you are still sporting that cane. Are you getting any better?"

Joseph, slightly embarrassed, said, "No, no, I'm good. Thanks for asking." A little more small talk passed between the newlyweds and Joseph and Ronnie. Then it was time to move on so the rest of the line could advance.

Ronnie and Joseph moved across the dance floor to where the tables with the nameplates set at the top of each place setting were located. Ronnie found hers right away. Joseph asked if he could get her a drink. "Yes," she said, delighted not to stand in line at the bar. Joseph returned after about ten minutes, handed her the new glass, and said he was going to track down his seating. They hugged one more time, and he moved away. Joseph had no intention of finding his place to sit. He surveyed the ballroom one last time and slipped out quietly.

As he started the Studebaker and pulled out of his parking space, heading for home, he thought about the affair he had attended. He was happy for Diane, hell, even for Charlie. It was clear that the two of them made a great couple. Diane had undoubtedly been a slightly complicated chapter in his life. Chance, it seemed, had brought them together, separated, and reunited them. In the end, each had figured out they were different people. He mentally wished them the best.

60.

As Joseph drove through Old Town on his way home from the reception, instead of going up 30th Street hill, he pulled over and parked across from Isaacs. He came here less often than he had in the past. He didn't know whether to attribute that to his drinking less or that he could better tolerate his own cooking. However, he was still too mentally wound up from the goings-on at the reception and wanted to ease his mind some before calling it a night. Upon entering, he saw that his old barstool from days gone by was available. He sat down and then thought about what to order. He laughed to himself, reflecting on his rule of one glass of red wine per day as he contemplated what to order to drink. What should he do?

It was then that a woman came out of the ladies' room. He noticed her and became conscious that it was Jill Connors. She saw him too and, smiling, picked up her drink from the other end of the bar and walked toward him. She placed her glass on the bar beside him, and the two embraced.

"It has been so long, Joseph," Jill said with sincerity.

"Jill, you look terrific, the same now as when I saw you last, which was quite a while ago."

"You look good, too," Jill replied, noticing his cane. "What is this, Joseph?"

"Oh, it's a memento of the war, but I'm fine now."

"If you're fine now, why the cane?"

"If I sit too long, it helps me get moving again. I'm not getting any younger. Really, I'm good. Where have you been all these years?"

The bartender Leo, who had been around when Joseph and Jill were together years back, noticed them and walked behind the bar toward them. When he got closer, he said, "I don't believe my eyes!" Jill and Joseph both laughed, and Leo asked if there was anything he could get them. Joseph now clarified his drinking rule to himself. It would now be one glass of red wine *per establishment* per day. He smiled inwardly at his inventiveness, ordered the wine, and insisted that it was on him if Jill wanted another drink also.

As Leo went to fill the drink order, Joseph repeated his question, "So you were about to tell me where you have been."

"Well, when you and I.... wait, I want to amend that. When you decided we were through, I also did some soul-searching and eventually traveled to California to see my ex-husband. We tried to make a go of it again for a while, but there were reasons it didn't work the first time around, and that quickly became evident. So, we split up again. I worked for a couple of years down there, and after the war, I moved back up here. I live again in Ruston and work up on 6th Avenue at the Towers Restaurant. Every time I drive up or down 30th Street hill, I think about stopping by your place to see how you are doing, but based on how it ended for us, I've managed not to go there."

As she sat there telling her story, Joseph noticed that, in purely physical terms, he was still mightily attracted to this woman. Sure, with Jill, it had been a physical thing, a strong instinctual desire, but beyond that, their relationship came down to two lost souls searching for something they could cling to while trying to figure out their lives.

Meanwhile, Jill wanted to know more about what had happened to him during the war. Also, was he still teaching at Rainier? She assumed so but wanted to hear it from him.

They engaged in conversation for a few minutes, something they did not do much of in the past, and then they decided to move to a booth. Joseph told her about his time in the Navy, sparing her specific details of his injuries. Yes, he was still teaching at Rainier, and he even told her he was in the process of writing a book about the war in the North Pacific.

She talked about her 'loser husband' (her words) and how she had settled down since her second attempt with her ex.

North Pacific

They laughed about the changes the war had brought to Tacoma, including the home-building boom, new businesses opening, and even the influx of sailors and soldiers getting out of the service that wound up staying after the war.

They ordered another round.

After a while, Jill, of her own volition, got up, came around the booth table, and sat down next to him. Joseph, who was on his third glass of wine that evening, didn't think about it much at first, but having not drunk this amount in years, he was more or less going along with whatever was happening.

Seeing Joseph's chain around his neck, Jill said, "I see you're still wearing that medal. Why don't you wear it over your shirt so others can see it? It is a beautiful medal. I always loved it on you. It always looked like it meant something to you."

Joseph said, "I'm not trying to make a statement with it. I wear it to remember my Mother. Thanks for the compliment."

Before long, Jill had moved up against him. With her head turned up toward him, she leaned into Joseph and whispered, "Why don't you take me home with you tonight? Maybe we can make a new start or, at a minimum, relieve years of pent-up tension."

Joseph knew exactly what she meant. He, too, was finding it hard to breathe.

North Pacific

What happened next, Joseph never saw coming. He admitted to himself that he wanted to take Jill home with him in the worst way. Yet, Joseph, in what later he would describe to himself as "a moment of clarity from the claret," instead asked himself, what was it that Jill had told him just moments ago? No, not about taking her home, but about the medal. That was it. She said she thought it was important to me. She's right. It does mean something, everything, to me. It is a touchstone to my Mother and my faith. I can't take this beautiful woman home with me tonight. If I did, I would not be thinking of her well-being but only of my desires. If I really care about Jill, I should act like the Catholic man I claim to be and not let this situation go somewhere it ought not.

Joseph lowered his glass and began in a voice only meant for her ears, "Jill, we can't do this. Dear God, you are so beautiful, but you know we will end up where we did before." There was a pause, and then she leaned her head against his chest and began to cry softly. He put his arm around her, and the two became quiet. After a minute or so and regaining her composure, Jill dabbed her eyes with a napkin and sat up straight. Joseph lowered his arm, and they looked at one another.

With only a smidgeon of mascara now out of place, Jill said, "Oh, you thought I was being serious, didn't you?"

Joseph slowly smiled. Then both, laughing lightly, embraced one more time. Then, in a serious voice, Jill said, "You know Joseph, it's been so hard for me to get beyond the disaster of my marriage.

Joseph whispered, "Jill, I'm always here for you. It just can't be the way we were."

She turned and kissed him full on the mouth. "You'll always think about me," and moved back to the other side of the booth.

They talked for a while, and then Joseph walked Jill to her car. As she drove off heading up 30th Street hill, he waved to her and thought, if she were to turn that car around and ask me again, I swear I would say yes. Help me, Lord.

61.

The next day was Sunday. Having stayed out later than usual the previous evening, it had been hard to wake up that morning. He yawned during Mass - not a good look, he told himself. After Mass, he drove to 3 Bridges Café for breakfast. Once again, Denise was not there. This was starting to worry him.

Joseph tried to work a bit on the book at home, but he found himself nodding off. I guess I'm a lightweight when it comes to drinking these days. He shook his head.

Later in the afternoon, he drove to the Linart's house for dinner. He talked with Mark and Darcy about school as Colleen and Martin finished preparing the meal and setting the table. He then sat down to a dinner consisting of a pot roast with potatoes, carrots, and onions. While helping clean up by drying the dishes while Colleen washed, he got the first degree he knew was coming.

"Well, tell me about last night," Colleen casually but deliberately asked.

"The Crystal Ballroom was quite impressive," Joseph began.

Colleen smiled and then, with jest, said, "Skip to the bottom line, Mr. Vaenko. How did it go with Diane?"

"It went well, Colleen. I mean…, I talked to her and Charlie in the receiving line and heard all about their upcoming honeymoon to San Francisco, their future trip to Europe, and even that they had purchased a new home out in the West End that has a view of the 'Narrows.'"

"Come on, give me something," she said with a smile.

Joseph saw she wanted the inside story, whatever that was, and he didn't have it. So, he grinned and said, "I was nervous like I assume you thought I would be. I got through it, and yes, I'm glad that I went, thanks to, let's call it - your encouragement."

"I don't know, Joseph. I expected more. I thought she really had a thing for you."

"She whispered to me that she was happy I came."

"Not going to cut it, Joseph," Colleen said sternly, betrayed only by a broadening smile.

"Come on, Colleen, I went to the reception. I talked to both the bride and groom. I don't believe I could have done much more."

"Did you kiss the bride?"

"Quickly, on the cheek."

"I give up. I guess you did all right, especially considering your boisterous and outgoing style." She laughed. He did too.

While Colleen gave Joseph the third degree in the kitchen, Martin talked to Mark and Darcy in the living room about a planned summer trip later in August. Afterward, Martin asked Joseph to have a piece of chocolate cake and a cup of coffee. When they finished, Colleen collected the empty plates and cups and took them to the kitchen. She reappeared to tell or inform Martin and Joseph that she and the kids were running over to the neighbors for a couple of minutes to discuss some school business about the "teen time" dances scheduled for the Fall at the jr. high school and that they would be right back. As she put it, the "big boys" would be left to themselves for a while. Joseph thanked Colleen for dinner, to which she replied, "Next time, more information." They all laughed while she and the kids walked out the front door.

Small talk ensued between the two long-time friends. At some point in the conversation, Joseph asked Martin how he was doing. Martin said the longer he was home, the better his situation was. The good doctors at Madigan General Hospital were helpful, and friends like Joseph, who would listen to him talk about his condition, made him feel better than he had in the last couple of years. Joseph nodded his assent to Martin's progress.

Martin then launched into a monologue about his treatment at the hospital, complete with digressions regarding other outpatients, their stories, and trials, as they tried to cope with the war's mental scars. He circled back to his thoughts on all that went on at the hospital and decided he was glad the services were available. He asked Joseph what he thought about what he had to say.

"Martin, I don't disagree with you. I also think I've seen a big difference in you between now and when you first returned home."

"Thanks for listening to me ramble, Joe. It seems to make things better when I can unload on you."

Colleen and the kids returned from the neighbor's house. She asked Martin if he would put the car in the garage. Martin obliged, grabbing the car keys and heading out the front door. Colleen asked Joseph one more time if he was really all right with Diane's marriage.

"I am. I thought a lot about the possibility that we might have tried to make a go of it. I know now that it is for the best that things worked out as they did. I'm certain she'll be happy with Charlie, and I'm good with that."

"Well, okay," Colleen closed that part of the conversation. In a quiet voice, she asked, "How are you and Martin doing?"

"Things are going better than I might have thought. I'm quite encouraged."

"Wonderful," she smiled as Martin returned.

Joseph rose from the chair and said, "Well, it's time for me to go home. I've got some preparation to do for a lecture in the morning. Thanks so much for having me over. The pot roast was great, Colleen."

He hugged Colleen, shook Martin's hand, waved one more time to the both of them while getting in his car, and then made the quick drive home. Joseph was always slightly jealous of the family life he experienced at the Linarts that he himself did not possess.

62.

The downside to being a professor at any university was all of the administrative duties that came with working in one's field. Endless meetings, organizing faculty events, even guest seminars, as well as attending constant functions essential to the institution's life. One such occasion was coming up that involved future endowments. Joseph, always the introvert, made the bold decision that he would not go alone to the function. He knew that it would be like all the other events he had attended if he did. He would end up standing around by himself, feeling uncomfortable, nursing a glass of wine, and looking at his wristwatch. Joseph had thought this through and had decided that Kasumi, his wonderful friend, would go as his "date." Of course, the only problem was that she didn't know it.

Joseph called her and asked if they could move up their monthly dinner date by a week because he had something to ask her. She agreed but asked what was going on. Joseph said that nothing was going on and that they would discuss it over the meal, which would be chicken scampi over pasta. She laughed and said she would see him at his place on the appointed day.

Kasumi had been doing very well with her seamstress work and had been able to purchase a car to assist her with the business. When she arrived at Joseph's that evening for the moved-up monthly dinner, she could sense he was up to something. The house was extra clean, and the "chef" was intently cooking the chicken and working on his sauce for the meal. He finally got the pasta water to boil, and in minutes he was making a production out of serving it. The two began eating. Kasumi was unable to restrain herself any longer. "Okay, Joseph, what's going on?"

Joseph feigned surprise and asked her how she liked the meal.

"It is surprisingly good. Now, come on, talk to me."

"Okay, okay, I would like to take you to a faculty event next Friday night at the university."

"What kind of event?" Kasumi asked warily.

"It's a function where Rainier faculty mix with important people and try to line up future funding for endowments and fete those that have already done so."

"Why are you asking me?"

"Because I always go alone to these things, and I want some company and can't think of anyone I would want to go with more than you."

"Seriously?"

"Yes, seriously. I think you could have a good time, meet lots of people, you know, important people and faculty, and besides, you'll be with the most handsome guy there."

Kasumi rolled her eyes and smiled. "I'm probably the only woman you talk to, and so by a quick process of elimination, I'm it."

"That hurts Miss Takahara," said Joseph, grinning.

"What do you wear to these things?"

"Um, nice clothes." Seeing that his answer had fallen a tad short, Joseph offered another solution. "Okay, I can have my friend Colleen give you a call to explain your options. She knows everything."

Kasumi shook her head and said, "All right, for you, I will do it, but you owe me."

Joseph, now excited, said, "Oh, thank you, thank you, I know we'll have a great time."

After dinner, the two friends sat in the living room and talked. "Joseph, should I be worried that anyone at your glitzy affair will be upset because I am of Japanese descent?"

"Oh, Kasumi. I would be shocked if anyone were. This is supposed to be an enlightened crowd. I'm sorry you even had to think of that possibility. The war is over. The government has acknowledged its wrong decision to intern Japanese American citizens. I know many would argue it was about security on the West Coast, but most of it was nothing more than bigotry, bias, and discrimination. Prejudice is a real thing that needs to be defeated. I will say that intolerance is not indigenous to just this country. It is pervasive around the world. You know as well as anyone the ugliness of racism has to be overcome one person at a time, not just by issuing proclamations."

"Oh, Joseph, you are so sweet. I'm not blaming you or Americans in general. Japan started the war with the United States, killing many American soldiers and sailors. Many here who lost loved ones may not ever be able to move on. I get that. Yet I am an American, and this is my country too. I was just nervous about being called out or in any way hurting your image at the university."

"If it came to anything like that, Kasumi, I would gladly leave the university."

Kasumi got up from the sofa, walked over to Joseph's chair, leaned down, and hugged him as hard as she could. "Thank you, Joseph," and kissed him on the cheek.

~~~~~

North Pacific

Joseph picked up Kasumi at her apartment on the night of the university event. They arrived on time, and Joseph felt exhilarated to have Kasumi on his arm as they moved among the gathering. Everyone was extremely friendly to them, and many wanted to know all about the beautiful woman he was with. He also overheard a couple of women enviously commenting on Kasumi's "sheath" style dress and the matching clutch she was carrying. He thought to himself. They obviously did not know that Kasumi was a seamstress extraordinaire.

At some point during the evening, Joseph was waylaid by the head of the History Department into talking to a possible donor who had a particular interest in the naval war in the Pacific. Joseph was reluctant to leave Kasumi alone, but he need not have worried. For as soon as he stepped off to the side to talk with the guest, his "date" was besieged by other guests and faculty who wanted to meet her and talk. They both had a great time.

When the event ended, Joseph drove Kasumi home. He walked her to her apartment door, where Kasumi told him she had a wonderful time and thanked him again for asking her to go. Joseph said he was the most envied guy at the event. Kasumi blushed and kissed him on the cheek. She unlocked her door, and then the two of them embraced. Joseph said, "Thanks again for coming." They looked into each other's eyes, and for the briefest of moments, they both felt unsure of themselves.

North Pacific

Joseph negotiated the stairs of the apartment building and made his way to the car. Driving home, he thought about Kasumi. There was no doubt she had looked stunning that evening. He had always appreciated her beauty, even as far back as when he first met her at Isaacs in Old Town. He remembered that Kasumi had dropped Miku off at his place the day after the fight at the bar. She had taken the time to talk to enough people in the Japanese American community to discover that Miku had gone to Japan before the war started. She was a woman he could talk to and feel comfortable with. He enjoyed her company immensely. As he pulled up in front of his house, set the brake, and removed the key from the ignition, he decided Kasumi was exceptional, and he was blessed to have her in his life.

63.

The Naval War in the North Pacific: 1941-1945 was released in 1950. Authoritative books on the war in the Pacific were few and far between to this point. Libraries worldwide purchased copies, and strong bookstore sales successfully gained Joseph and Rainier University some prominence in certain History academic circles. To his great surprise, because of the response to the publication, the university arranged a speaking tour for Joseph that would take him to other institutions around the county to promote and talk about the book. The trip was hectic as he dashed, as much as one can with a cane, between cities, discussions, talks, luncheons, and glad-handing.

However, one constant during his book tour made him feel more at ease. Joseph was comforted by the knowledge that it didn't matter what city or town he was in on any given Sunday. Mass everywhere was always the same. He would find the nearest Catholic church, hear the Mass in reverential Latin, and listen to the beauty of the Latin hymns sung. There was always a feeling that when any Mass was celebrated, it was like attending a Mass said hundreds and hundreds of years ago. The remarkable continuity and the linkage between generations of believers made Joseph proud of his religious heritage.

Alone in a hotel bed, staring at the darkened ceiling while on the book tour, he thought more and more about Kasumi. He missed her. He had always looked forward to their monthly dinner dates, which he acknowledged were now just an excuse to get together and enjoy each other's company. And then there was the night he took her home from the faculty endowment event. He remembered that hard-to-understand and complex feeling that overcame him right as they said goodbye. He believed Kasumi experienced the sentiment also. The tour took weeks. Joseph lived out of a suitcase and longed to return to Tacoma.

~~~~~

North Pacific

After Joseph's time on the road, he finally arrived home on a Sunday night at Sea-Tac International Airport, located between Puget Sound's two largest cities. Martin drove up from Tacoma, collected the tired, disheveled traveling professor, and took him home.

The next day, finally back in his office on campus, Joseph thought about giving Kasumi a call. He procrastinated and eventually told himself he would call her when he got home that day. He convinced himself it was a much better idea to be home without interruptions or distractions. The day was a bit of a blur, with colleagues stopping by to welcome him back and congratulate him on the book's success. When he arrived at the house that evening, he was genuinely beat, with little sleep the night before and a chaotic day on campus. However, he wasn't so tired to have forgotten one of his tricks for dinner. He opened his briefcase and fished out a scone he had purchased at the student union building earlier in the day. He made a weak pot of coffee. After all, he didn't want anything to impede his sleep that night and settled into his straight-back chair in the living room to eat the small but tasty meal. The view out the living room window was perfect, with the last rays of sun streaking the bay to the west.

He finished his meal and took the plate and cup to the kitchen. He decided it was time to call Kasumi. He returned to the living room, picked up the black receiver, and called her number. He listened as each number he dialed made a clicking sound as it rotated back to its starting position. He thought to himself, steady man, you can do this. The phone began to ring at her end. He thought, one ring, two, three, four, maybe I should hang up and call back later.

"Hello."

"Kasumi, it's me, Joseph. I'm back."

"Joseph," she said excitedly. "How are you? You've been gone so long."

"I know, I know, I would never have guessed writing this book would entail so much of my time once I had finished it."

Kasumi laughed. "It's so good to hear your voice again. We have so much to talk about."

"Well, that's what I was thinking. Are you interested in possibly…."

Kasumi interrupted him, "Joseph, how well do you know David Gates up at the university? Remember, you introduced me to him at the endowment function."

Surprised and a little confused, Joseph replied, "Gates, yes, I know him…."

Again, Kasumi interjected, "Do you like him?"

"Well, yes, I do. He teaches mathematics. He…."

And before he could say anything more about Mr. Gates, Kasumi broke in on Joseph's response one more time. "He called me," she said excitedly. He said he got my number from one of the women that night to whom I had given my business card because she liked my dress and was interested in giving me some work. Anyway, he called, and we went out for coffee, and well, we sort of hit it off. So, we've been seeing each other over the last few weeks."

Joseph was speechless on the other end of the line.

"Joseph, are you there?"

Joseph blew the air out of his cheeks, realizing he had been holding it in. "No Kasumi, I'm here, sorry. I was just surprised about your news."

"I'm so glad you like him, Joseph. It is really important to me that you think he's a good man."

Joseph, now standing, looked around to see if he was somehow taking part in a bad dream. "He's a good guy, Kasumi," he said in a somewhat flat voice and then hoped Kasumi did not catch his less-than-excited tone. She didn't, and the two talked for a while longer before agreeing to get together soon.

Thinking about it later, Joseph realized he did not remember much of the phone conversation after Kasumi burst in with her big news. What had happened? Kasumi seemed over the moon for David Gates. Did she really like him? In all fairness, he had always thought highly of Gates and enjoyed his company at faculty review sessions and the like. They were about the same age. Maybe Dave was a few years younger.

Kasumi had been at the center of his thoughts practically the whole trip, and now this. He thought about it some more and decided that even though he and Kasumi were not a couple, it felt a lot like he was losing "his girlfriend" to someone else. He and Kasumi were close, and both had needed someone like the other in their lives. They had nurtured and grown their friendship to the point of…what? If this worked out for her, they surely wouldn't be able to maintain their current relationship. Also, he asked himself, had he developed different feelings about her since they had resumed their friendship after the war? It was clear he had grown much, much closer to her since the end of the war. He barely knew her at all before the war, he told himself. After getting to know her, as he did now, he knew how much Kasumi meant to him. He certainly wanted the best for her.

Joseph, feeling crestfallen, reflected on the state of his personal life. It reminded him somewhat of the famous film footage of the airship *Hindenburg* bursting into flames and crashing to the ground. It was an apt comparison, he thought.

64.

The book gave Joseph some recognition in his field, making his life more interesting. He received correspondence and phone calls from other academics who were now aware of him and his area of expertise. So now it was time for a modicum of fame and fortune to come his way. His share of the royalties from the book's sale made their way to him. Between the raise in pay upon receiving tenure and the book royalties, Joseph finally decided to remodel his house.

The so-called academic "fortune" had a large chunk of it go to work performed on the house's foundation. After all, it was located on the side of a steep slope and needed shoring up. Then there was a new furnace, lots of wiring, and a kitchen remodel with new appliances. Additionally, he contracted a couple of projects that were of a more personal nature. The first was adding a bathroom upstairs. Joseph's physical handicap made it more challenging to navigate the stairs, especially at night. The second project was the one he liked the most, adding a deck to the north or bayside of the house. The deck was accessed through a door installed in the house's northwest corner by the kitchen table. All in all, the remodel left Joseph worrying about whether he might have to get a loan to finish the work. As it turned out, the bill for the job was covered by his "fortune" with a couple of thousand dollars to spare.

The house needed the work. It was another reminder to Joseph that he was not getting any younger. The house was now a half-century old. He wondered whether his parents would have approved. He was sure his mother would have been as excited about the deck as he was.

The excitement of the remodel was tempered by the loss of his wonderful dinners with Kasumi. She and David were a real item. They did everything together and could not seem to get enough of each other. This reality had led to the gentle fading away of their monthly get-togethers. Kasumi called once in a while to see how he was doing, but he could tell that her important thoughts were on her relationship with Mr. Gates. To help ease the real pain of not spending quality time with Kasumi, Joseph started inviting Fr. Etienne over for dinner to get some life in the place once the house remodel was finished. Father was pleased with the invites, and the two old friends spent many nights discussing Church issues, current events, philosophical questions, and listening to the radio.

And even though the remodel had all but wiped-out Joseph's "fortune," he was badgered constantly by Martin and Colleen, his "so-called" faculty friends, and even Fr. Etienne to consider replacing the old Studebaker. His beloved vehicle was, for sure, on its last legs. Now almost 17 years old, the "Dictator" was well past its prime. Although Joseph thought it still looked a bit rakish, others laughed and told him he looked like he was right out of an old gangster movie. Ever so slightly offended, Joseph spent some time driving back and forth along South Tacoma Way, where most of the city's car dealerships were located. After glancing and blanching at the new car prices, Joseph eventually purchased a slightly used 1950 Chevrolet. Specifically, it was a Styleline Deluxe 2-Door Sport Coupe without the clunky-looking exterior windshield sun visor. What clinched the deal was that it was his favorite car color, gray, just like the old Studebaker. He was surprised by how quickly he adjusted to the new car, and even though he had been nudged, coerced, and shamed by those close to him into updating his mode of transportation, he was happy with the outcome. Joseph's brief flirtation with modest fame and even more modest fortune had ended well.

65.

He parked the new Chevy in front of 3 Bridges Café, grabbed his cane, and walked through the front door. To his delight, Denise stood there looking at him and said, "Hi, stranger." Joseph's face lit up, and they walked toward each other and hugged.

"Where have you been?" Joseph's voice projected his concern.

Denise smiled and said, "Let me get you a cup of coffee, and then I'll fill you in." She walked behind the counter and over to the coffee pot, pouring Joseph a cup. The professor moved to the counter and sat on his favorite stool next to the window. The thought crossed his mind that he seemed to have a favorite place to sit almost everywhere he usually frequented. He smiled and thought, who says men are creatures of habit?

In a minute, after quickly ringing up the only other customer in the café, she brought Joseph his cup of coffee and leaned back against the counter behind her.

Joseph started, "I haven't seen you here for quite a while. So where have you been, young lady? I've been worried about you."

Denise laughed and said, "I've been in Seattle for a spell. My daughter Rose married over a year ago and went and had a baby. Can you believe it, I'm a grandma."

Joseph's eyes opened wide, and he said with a big smile, "Congratulations."

Denise blushed and smiled back at him. "So, I've been up in Seattle meeting and caring for my new grandson, William."

"William, you say," said Joseph. "I remember my mother telling me before she passed away that my name was going to be either Vasyl, a form of William, or Josip, and that she and my father had finally settled on the Anglicized Joseph."

"It had been so long since I'd had a real vacation from this place, so I told the owner that I was going to make the most of it and stay up there as long as I could. He understood, and thankfully when I was ready to return, he graciously welcomed me back into the fold, thanked me for my years of service, gave me the keys to the place, and went on a vacation of his own." Denise laughed again. "I loved every minute of it up in Seattle with Rose and the baby. There's something about a grandchild, at least when it's yours, that makes it more precious than even your own child was. I can't explain it. Of course, I love my daughter, always have and always will, but I have to tell you, maybe it's because I'm older and know how hard life can be and how quickly it passes by, but that grandchild is the most precious thing I've ever come in contact with."

"Well, that's great, Denise, that's fantastic news. I had no idea."

"And what about you, Joseph? What have you been up to?"

"Well, I just finished having my house remodeled and updated. It took longer than I thought, but it is finally completed."

"How is it up at the university?"

"Always the same, young minds and old instructors."

They talked for a bit, and then Denise topped off his coffee and asked Joseph if he was interested in a fresh slice of blackberry pie.

"Is the Pope Italian? I would love a piece of blackberry pie."

"Is that your car? Denise asked, pointing to the shiny Chevy while getting Joseph his pie.

"I just bought it about a month ago. I think I finally had one too many of my friends ask me when I was ever going to get rid of that 'bucket of bolts' I called a car."

"Well, for what it's worth, the new car suits you. I like it."

"Thanks."

North Pacific

With no customers on that late weekday afternoon, Joseph and Denise were able to continue their conversation without interruption.

"So, how is life treating you these days," Joseph asked.

"Well, you know I told you that I've been renting a friend's house for a long time now." She paused, "Well, I bought it."

"Seriously."

"Yes, my friend came to me and asked if I was interested, and I thought about it for a day or so and told her yes. We worked it out with her bank, and now I'm a property owner. I have a stake in the community."

"I guess that means you'll be around for a while."

"Believe it or not, Joseph, and I can't believe I'm telling you this, but I just turned 50 last month, and let me tell you, it gives you pause. You begin to think about your life. The half-century thing has a way of making an impression. I mean, I'm pretty happy with my life in many ways. I have a grandchild, maybe more down the line. It is a real eye-opener, Joseph. I am the first to admit that I have become set in my ways toward many things at this stage of life. When I started working here, it was a job that kept a divorced mother employed and barely paid the bills. Now, after many years, I see this place in a different light. I have people in here all day to keep me company. I hear everyone's stories. It has become my social life. Consequently, when I go home or get a day off, I value my personal time. I enjoy the quiet and solitude of my house. I read, work in the gardens, and dance around the house to my music. It's a great contrast to the person I am around here."

"Seems like you have been thinking about these things a lot," Joseph interjected.

"You know, I have. Being 50 years old is a big deal. Looking back on things, those years certainly went by faster than I would have thought. One never knows when or how it will all come to an end." Denise looked hard at him as if thinking about something. "You're a Catholic, aren't you, Joseph?"

"Yes, I am," Joseph said while being a bit surprised by the question.

"Does your Catholicism, your faith, help you sort out things like I'm telling you about my life?"

Joseph, now engaged with the question, thought for a moment. "My faith gives me a starting point to ask all the same hard questions we all face in life. Without my faith, be it as it may, and no one has ever accused me of being a saint, I think I would be a different person. So I thank God for helping me out. On my own, I'm certain I would make worse decisions."

"I like the person you are, Joseph."

"Thanks, Denise."

At that moment, a group of young men came into the restaurant. Denise greeted them and sat them at two tables she quickly pulled together. They had just finished playing

North Pacific

a pickup game of football and were all interested in her locally famous pie and a cup of coffee. Who would have guessed it? They were boisterous, talking about the great and not-so-great plays that occurred during their game. Denise smiled at Joseph, and he returned it. He left some money on the counter and waved at her as he left. Going out the door, he became conscious of his cane and tried to act as if he did not need it as much as he knew he did.

CONFIDO IN DEO

(Trust in God)

"Have confidence in the Lord with all thy heart, and lean not upon thy own prudence. In all thy ways think on him, and he will direct thy steps."

Proverbs 3:5-6

Douay-Rheims

North Pacific

66.

Looking out the living room window, Joseph saw the large merchant vessel turning to port as it entered Commencement Bay from East Passage headed for the Port of Tacoma. The doorbell rang. Joseph pivoted and, using his cane, walked to the front door. It was 10 AM on a Saturday, and he had just finished his last cup of coffee while reflecting on the marine activity on the bay. Joseph opened the door. Suddenly his brain didn't work. "Mi-Miku." He unconsciously stepped back. "Is that you?"

"Joseph," Miku said as she turned momentarily and signaled to the taxi driver that she was good and that he could leave.

"Oh, dear God, is that really you?" Joseph asked as his eyes welled up. With Joseph shaking, they embraced. Miku, too, began crying. They rocked from side to side, and neither wanted to let go. After an indeterminate amount of time, Joseph straightened up and had Miku enter the house. He closed the front door. Then he held her at arm's length and looked at her. "Miku." They embraced again.

Then as she stepped back, she looked down at the cane lying on the floor where Joseph had dropped it with their last embrace. He quickly picked it up.

"Are you okay? asked Miku."

His mind swirled with fragmented thoughts. Joseph could only muster a "Yes, I'm fine," though realizing it did not explain the cane.

Joseph motioned her to enter the living room. They walked into the natural light of the space with the splendid view. He gestured toward the sofa, and Miku sat down. He sat in the straight-back chair, turning slightly to face her better. They were almost within arm's reach of each other. Joseph's eyes never left Miku's. "How can it be you, here, now, in my living room?" He began to sob slightly again but stopped himself, wiped his eyes, took a deep breath, and just looked at her, now beginning to think that if he blinked, she might disappear.

Miku wiped her eyes also and gave Joseph a look that melted his heart. "Hello Joseph, I'm sorry I surprised you, but I didn't know any other way to find you. I didn't even know if you still lived here. I took a chance."

"Miku, I'm sorry to say this. I don't know how else to say it. I believed you and your family were probably dead."

Miku began to cry again. "Oh, Joseph, that's why I'm here. It has been so long, such a long time. I will tell you everything." She sat there and looked again on the verge of tears.

North Pacific

Joseph got up and walked over to the hallway table, picked up the box of facial tissues, returned, and handed the box to Miku. She thanked him, all the while watching him use his cane. Remaining standing, he asked her if he could get her something to drink. She said a glass of water would help, and Joseph got it for her. He returned to his chair. His head was still swimming, still trying to understand what was happening. Miku was not dead. Dear Lord, how can I ever, ever thank you?

Miku sipped the water and dabbed her tears with the tissue. She said she had, over the years, remembered how breathtaking Joseph's view was, and wasn't that a new deck out front? He told her he had remodeled the old house within the last year and was quite pleased with the results. Miku told Joseph she had flown into Sea-Tac Airport late the day before and had spent the night at the Olympic Hotel downtown on Pacific Avenue. It took a while and a bit more small talk, but eventually, both calmed down enough to resume the main conversation.

"I have rehearsed this a thousand times in my head, Joseph. So, I'll start at the beginning and keep talking until you understand what happened all those years ago."

Joseph nodded. He could not get over how great she looked. It took him back to the Mass at St. Dominic, where he had seen her for the first time. She looked even more beautiful over ten years later if that was possible. She was completely captivating.

North Pacific

"Joseph." Her voice brought him out of his trance-like state. "When we were together, here, so long ago, I had never been so happy in all my life. My love for you, and I believe yours for me, was as great as either of us had ever experienced. It was everything I had ever wanted. Every day, I would sit with my cup of tea, look out over your magnificent view, and thank God for allowing us to be together. Yet, the more I thanked God for our shared love, the more my conscience asked me if what we were doing was what God wanted of us. In other words, you and I both knew we were living in a way contrary to his commandments and our faith. We chose to ignore it for as long as possible, but missing Mass, not going to confession, and persisting in our actions finally overwhelmed me. Ultimately, I knew what we were doing was simply wrong. I remember approaching you and saying we could not do this any longer. It broke my heart, and I believe yours, also. You didn't make it hard for me. I was thankful for that. You were a true gentleman and did what I asked. After returning to my aunt's apartment, I cried and brooded for weeks. I loved you so much." Miku paused, took another sip of water, and proceeded with a deep breath of her own, " Then I got sick. I was pregnant."

Joseph quit breathing.

"Joseph, I was so scared. I didn't know what to do. Eventually, I made a decision that still haunts me to this day. I decided to go to my family in Japan and have the baby. I was not going to burden you with what I perceived at the time as my difficulty. I came to your house those many years ago and asked if I could stay with you. I had been frightened by the fight you were in when you defended Kasumi and me and had to hit that other man. I wanted you to want me, and I came to your house the next morning after the fight to prove I was worth it. Then when I abruptly left and later found out I was with child, I thought I would lose you because you would decide that loving a pregnant girl of Japanese descent and all the war talk was not worth it. All of these memories, how I handled what happened, and my mistakes live deep within me."

Joseph couldn't take it anymore and moved to the sofa beside Miku. "Miku, I'm so sorry. It wasn't you. It was me. I should not have let our relationship go as far as it did when we were together. It was up to me to treat you with the utmost respect. I didn't want to lose you. I believe my insecurities got the better of me. I so desperately wanted you to stay. It was a terrible misjudgment on my part. I've thought about it for over ten years. I am to blame for the dreadful string of events that separated us all this time. What I did to you was sinful in God's eyes, and though I've confessed it and understand that the sin is forgiven, I will carry the deep scars of my deeds for the rest of my life."

They held each other's hands. "Oh, Joseph, this is so hard. Before you say anything more, you must let me finish my story."

Joseph nodded.

"So there I was, pregnant and alone. You remember I was a travel agent. I found that the *Hikawa Maru* was coming to Seattle at the end of October 1941. I booked the trip and arrived in Yokohama almost three weeks later. I never dreamed that Japan would attack the United States – call me naive. I had no idea at the time that the *Hikawa Maru* was the last Japanese liner to make the trip before the war started. Once in Japan, I went to Nagasaki, where all my family lived. It was in Nagasaki, on June 21, 1942, that our daughter 'Tomiko' was born."

Joseph's mind, which had been in turmoil, now slowed to one thought. He, Joseph Vaenko, had a daughter.

Miku began to cry. Joseph still couldn't believe Miku was right in front of him, much less that he was a father. Words failed him. Miku composed herself and said, "She was a beautiful baby. The whole family loved her to pieces. I was as happy as could be as she was our baby. I raised her there with the help of my mother and all the other women in the family. They loved our little Eurasian girl. I would take Tomiko to Mass almost daily, and we, with my help, would pray for your well-being."

Miku paused and asked, "I remember you telling me you were in the naval reserve. Were you in the war, Joseph?"

Joseph moved his hands to his knees and told her, "Yes," he had been in the Navy during the war.

"Was the war the reason you use that cane?"

"Yes, but I'm much better now," Joseph said, being as economical as possible with the truth.

Though not completely satisfied with Joseph's scant explanation, Miku decided to continue her story. "For over three years, we lived in my family's house. I had Tomiko to help me not think about the war and you. In early August of 1945, the terrible destruction of Hiroshima took place. I remember my father coming home from Mass the morning after the news of what had happened in Hiroshima reached us. He had never looked so sad." Miku shifted on the sofa uncomfortably.

"My father took me aside that morning and said, 'Pack a bag for you and Tomiko. You will leave within the hour for your uncle and aunt's house up in the valley to the north. Stay there until I come for you. I have arranged for your transportation. I have a friend who will take you and Tomiko to your uncle's house. I, of course, asked him why, to which he replied, 'Miku, I am your father, and in this instance, I am not asking you. I am telling you to do as I say.' He said it with such sincerity and gravity that I could tell something had come over him. I had never seen him so serious. I swear, Joseph, looking back, I believe he must have had a premonition. So, I packed a bag, and Tomiko and I were taken north by my Father's friend. We did not arrive at my uncle's house until almost 10 PM that evening. I told my uncle what my father had said, and he took us in."

Miku's body and voice trembled. "Two mornings later, another bomb exploded, this one directly over Nagasaki. We all heard and felt the horrible blast and the rushing wind. However, we were protected by our distance from the city and the surrounding hills that caught the force of the gusts. Completely out of my mind with fear for my parents and other family members, I told my aunt to watch

Tomiko and left their house to return to Nagasaki. Yet, as soon as I started, I was caught up in throngs of people leaving the city as fast as they could. They all told me not to go there but to turn around and get as far away from the city as possible. These people were terrified, and I eventually gave up my attempt and returned to my uncle's house." She wiped her eyes with a tissue.

"The next day, after listening to people give their accounts of what had happened and imploring us to move even further away from Nagasaki, I again packed the bag I had brought and left with Tomiko. We headed for Tokyo. It took us, I think, almost two weeks to make our way to the capital. I had to beg for food for the two of us along the way. When we arrived in Tokyo, we went at once to where one of my mother's relatives lived, only to discover they had abandoned the home during the last year of the war. I broke down and began crying in front of this locked, empty, deserted house. We had nowhere to go, our clothes were in tatters, and we were starving. I honestly believed we might die."

Miku halted her story long enough to have a sip of water. "It was then, Joseph, that I remembered that Hiroto Fujisaki lived in Tokyo. You remember him. You asked me once about Hiroto because you had seen us going into a movie theatre together. Anyway, I desperately searched for any knowledge of him or where he lived. After a few days, I was blessed to find a government office where I found his address. We eventually made our way to the house and knocked on the door. He was there and took us in after recognizing me despite my unkempt appearance. We stayed with Hiroto through the winter. When spring came, he took us to Nagasaki to find out what had happened to my parents and other family members. I remembered the terrifying explosion and did not have high hopes. We discovered that the bomb had exploded directly over the Urakami neighborhood where my family lived. There was nothing there. They were all presumed dead. They may have even been coming out of the Cathedral from morning Mass when it happened. We returned to Tokyo, and I grieved their loss for weeks." Again, she paused.

"Are you okay, Miku? I know these memories must be extremely hard to talk about. Do you want to rest?"

"No, I must finish this story," Miku said in almost a whisper. "It has weighed on me all these years, and I want to get it all out." She stood up, walked over to the front window, and stared out at the bay. "I have never forgotten how soothing this view is." She looked at the water for a minute and then returned to the sofa and began to tell her story again.

"From the beginning, I told Hiroto of the circumstances surrounding Tomiko. He was truly kind to her. It was later that summer that Hiroto asked me to marry him. I was surprised, yet I felt I knew he was interested in me. I told him I would consider it and we would talk later. He left on a business trip the next day and was gone for almost a week. I took the time to figure out what I should do. I asked myself what I believed was the most critical question. What would be best for Tomiko? Her safety and well-being had to come first. We had lived with Hiroto for nearly a year. He had been a wonderful man to my daughter and me. As far as you were concerned, I believed you had to have moved on by then. After the terrible war, I also assumed there would be much animosity toward people of Japanese descent in the United States. I prayed about it all night, hoping for guidance and grace to make the right decision. When Hiroto returned, I told him I would marry him as long as he treated Tomiko as his own daughter. He said he would."

Miku sat up straight. "Joseph, life is not fair. We don't control what happens in the world. We can only control what we do when confronted with the world as it is at any given moment. We must deal with life as it comes to us. We must count on our Faith. If I could make life as I wanted, many things would be different. But God gives us our freedom to make our own decisions in life when faced with what this world presents us with each day. As I said, life is not fair, but with our freedom, and hopefully, with God's grace, we make more right choices than wrong ones. And yes, we are living proof that choices impact our lives and the lives of others."

"So, you are married?" Joseph said in a noticeably quiet voice with almost no trace of emotion.

"Yes, Joseph, I am married to Hiroto."

For the first time, Joseph noticed the gold band on her ring finger. Neither said another word for the longest time.

North Pacific

The emotional roller coaster they had shared over the last hour had drained them of their initial intensity.

"Joseph, I also have to tell you that I have given Hiroto two sons since marrying."

For Joseph, the words were now just words. They meant little to him. Finally, Joseph was able to form a question. "Did you get married in the Catholic Church?"

"Yes." There was another noticeable silence in the room. "I always think about you, Joseph. Tomiko's presence every day reminds me of you because she is yours. She is ours. You are always in my thoughts. So much so that a few months back, I went to Hiroto and told him that I had thought about it and wanted to fly to the States and, if I could find you, to have this talk. I told him it was important and necessary to me and for my daughter, and I would not take no for an answer." Yet again, Miku looked out the window at the bay.

Joseph didn't know how to help her, so he just watched her eyes.

Finally, Miku turned back to Joseph and said, "I also decided not to bring Tomiko. My reasoning was, why would I introduce you to your daughter and then take her away from you? Why would I announce to Tomiko that this is your father? And then turn around and tell her that now we must leave. No, it had to be just me. Hiroto was uncomfortable with the idea, but as he thought about it, he saw that I would not change my mind."

Joseph found himself without words.

North Pacific

"Joseph, Hiroto was concerned that something might happen between us if we saw each other again. I swore to him that I would stay only as long as it took to find you and have this talk. So, this, for me, is maybe the hardest part, but I am scheduled to fly home to Tokyo tomorrow. If I had not found you at once, I would have canceled the flight and continued searching for you. But I have found you, and you have now heard my story."

With that, Joseph stood, took his cane, and walked around the living room. He said nothing. Eventually, with Miku watching him intently, he asked her if there was anything else she had to tell him. Again, the words were quiet, drained of intensity, and without life.

Miku rose from the sofa, walked over to Joseph, and embraced him. At first, he did not respond to the gesture other than the mechanical aspects of putting his arms around her. But as she pressed herself into him, he warmed and gently held her more tightly.

She shared a few more inconsequential details, and then they moved to the kitchen and ate some grapes Joseph had bought the day before. She told him as much as she could about their daughter. She related how, once in a while, some of the other children in school would make fun of her because of her partial European appearance. However, Miku told Joseph that Tomiko was an incredibly strong and independent young woman. Little Tomiko would bear these slights with grace and actually wear them, so to speak, as a badge of honor. "Joseph, she is truly special."

North Pacific

As evening approached, Miku confessed to Joseph that the time difference between Tokyo and Tacoma was taking a toll on her, and she felt like she needed to return to the hotel and get some sleep. Joseph said he would take her there. He also asked if he could take her to the airport in the morning. She accepted and thanked him. He asked when she needed to leave, and Miku said 10 AM would be fine. With that answer, Joseph asked if she would be interested in attending Mass with him at 8 AM. Miku was delighted to get the opportunity to return once more to St. Dominic. Then Joseph drove Miku downtown to the Olympic Hotel.

67.

Joseph returned home from dropping Miku off at the hotel. He didn't know what to do - the afternoon had been like nothing he could have imagined. Miku was alive. Miku had been at his house. He had watched her talk. He had embraced the woman of his dreams. He had, once again, seen how beautiful she truly was.

He had a daughter. The family he had always envisioned was a reality - in a sense. Yet, his family lived with another man on the other side of the world.

Yet, all he could think about at that moment was being with Miku again the next day. Forget that she would be flying away from him, most likely forever. He was going to be with her tomorrow.

Joseph knew he was not thinking clearly and went to bed early. As he lay there, his thoughts would start him down a rabbit hole about some aspect of his or Miku's life, or now Tomiko's. He checked himself and tried to think about nothing. It must have worked because the alarm told him it was time to get up. He readied himself for Mass. He looked in the mirror and wondered what Miku thought of him, now a middle-aged man with flecks of gray hair and that accursed cane.

Joseph picked up Miku downtown at 7:30 AM, and they walked into St. Dominic with time to spare. Miku started to go toward the seats she and her aunt used to occupy, but Joseph asked in a whisper if she wouldn't mind sitting in the pew where he had always sat all those years ago. She was fine with that, and Joseph sat there with her, thinking, this is what I always wanted. The Mass began. Much too quickly, it reached the Communion. Joseph stepped out of the pew and allowed Miku to go ahead in front of him. They walked up to the communion rail and knelt side by side. Finally, Father Etienne approached them with the consecrated hosts. As he gave the host to each, his eyes widened. Both Miku and Joseph smiled all the way back to their pew.

When Mass had finished, the couple walked outside and up to Father and said hello. The French priest was astounded. "Father, I know this seems improbable, but it's true. Miku is really right here standing next to us." Father clasped her hands. They exchanged joyous greetings. Then Joseph asked Father Etienne whether he could bless them. Father sensed that Joseph was quite serious and at once blessed the two of them and asked for God's grace in each of their lives.

"Thank you, Father," Joseph said with deep sincerity. He added, "Father, I will get back to you later today to explain what's going on." Father nodded, and then Joseph and Miku stepped aside as other waiting parishioners greeted the Dominican priest.

The 45-minute drive up to Sea-Tac International Airport seemed to take mere moments. They spoke little, both understanding what was happening. As they approached the airport, Miku rubbed Joseph's shoulder. Joseph parked the car, took Miku's luggage, and, using his cane, escorted her to the correct terminal. Miku considered asking for her bag to make it easier for Joseph but sensed this was not the time. She checked in, and they waited by the gate leading to the plane. Again, it was hard to find words. It was happening much too fast. Finally, the call for boarding came, and Miku turned to Joseph, removed an envelope from her purse, and handed it to him. She began to cry. Joseph said, "Miku, don't cry. I love you and always will. You have always been the most important thing to happen in my life. Take care of yourself – and our daughter."

North Pacific

Still crying, she threw her arms around him and gave him a from-the-heart kiss on the lips. She whispered, "I love you, Joseph." Then it was over. He walked to a spot where he could see the plane with the passengers boarding. He watched her ascend the steps, and in a few minutes, the aircraft turned and taxied out to the runway. He observed it take off and then watched until he had to squint as the plane disappeared into the scattered clouds that covered the Puget Sound sky.

68.

It was early afternoon when Joseph returned from the airport. As he set his keys down on the hall side table, he remembered he had had nothing to eat. It was odd because he was not hungry. He walked directly over to the phone and called Martin, telling him he felt under the weather and would have to pass on dinner at their place that evening. Martin told him to take care and get well. Joseph told him he would and hung up.

He realized he still had his jacket on and, while taking it off, removed from his inside pocket the envelope Miku had given him at the boarding gate as she was leaving. Joseph walked over to the kitchen table and sat down. He opened the manila-colored envelope and removed its contents. It was a photograph of a young girl, a beautiful young girl. On the back of the photo, handwritten in English, was one word – Tomiko. So, this was his daughter. Joseph stared at the photograph for the longest time. Eventually, he poked around in the envelope for evidence of anything else being in there. He found a slip of paper. In the same beautiful cursive English, it said, "Dear Joseph, I hope you like the photo of our daughter. It was taken on her 10th birthday. I promise you I will raise her in the Catholic faith. I will tell her about her father and what a loving man he is. Love, Miku."

Joseph felt his strength draining from his body. No, it wasn't from being hungry. He was not hungry at all. It wasn't his strength per se. He looked for the right word. It was his *"spirit"* that was flagging.

He rose from the table and grabbed a blanket that lay over the back of the sofa. He walked out onto the new deck and sat in one of the Adirondack-type chairs. He put the blanket over his lap as it was a bit breezy. Again, he felt weak. He looked toward Mt. Rainier. The mountain loomed large today, the peak seemingly piercing the eastern sky. His eyes returned to the bay before him, and he noticed a slight chop on the water. He continued to stare at the bay. His breathing became shallow, and he remained in that fixed position, with his eyes open but not really recording any sensory input. He had no idea how long he maintained that position, but it was dark when he realized he was still in the chair. It was not that he had fallen asleep. He had not. He reasoned that his mind had just quit working. He had zero interest in what was happening around him or even within him.

He dragged himself back into the house. He slept that night on top of the single bed next to the staircase with the blanket he had used all day outside. In the morning, he was awakened by the phone. It was the university calling him as to his whereabouts. Joseph looked at the time and said he would not be in that day. He pushed the phone deep into the sofa cushions. He again went outside and sat in the same chair. It was Monday, and he repeated his non-thinking existence.

Later that morning, there was a pounding on the door, and Joseph recognized Father Etienne's voice. When he let the priest in, Father asked him if he was okay. Joseph thought about saying he was fine, but he grasped that he was wearing the same clothes as on Sunday, and on touching his face, he felt a couple of days' worth of stubble. "Father, I can explain this." He realized he couldn't, but at the moment, it seemed the right thing to say.

"Joseph," the priest said in a measured voice. "When you didn't get back to me yesterday about Miku, as you said you would, I decided to call you this morning. I couldn't get you, so I tried to call your office. When there was still no answer, I became concerned and drove over to see if you were all right. You look, well, let's say you've looked better. How about I put on a pot of coffee while you clean up a bit, and then we'll talk?"

North Pacific

Joseph, appreciative of Father's concern, nodded and headed upstairs. Twenty minutes later, he returned to the first floor, where the priest had poured two cups of coffee and was seated at the kitchen table. Joseph joined him and took a sip of the hot coffee. "Father, I'm sorry I didn't get back to you yesterday."

It was then that Joseph felt the weakness of not eating since Saturday. Father sensed his plight, walked back to the kitchen area, opened the bread box, and popped two pieces of bread into the toaster. He found some butter in the refrigerator and, after finding a butter knife, prepared and presented the toast to Joseph. "Thank you, Father."

Father smiled. "Now tell me what's been going on, Joseph."

Joseph took a larger sip of coffee. "I don't know exactly where to begin, Father. To my utter disbelief, Miku showed up at my door on Saturday." Joseph told him the whole story, from Miku surviving the bomb blast to her telling him that she was married and that they had a daughter. At that point, Joseph leaned across the table, lifted the manila envelope, removed the photo, and presented it to the good priest. Father looked at the picture. He then got up from the table, picked up the coffee pot from the stove, and poured refills for both of them.

"After Mass on Sunday, I took Miku to the airport. I suspect it is the last time I will ever see her. I sort of lost it with that realization. After that, I guess I shut down. Father, I really love that woman. I cannot begin to tell you how much. Oh, and here is the note she included in the envelope."

Father read the note. "I always thought Miku possessed a real zeal for the faith. She is a lovely woman. She has been through much that could have challenged her faith, but she has remained steadfast in her beliefs," Father said with some emotion. The priest looked at Joseph's wan facial features. "Obviously, Joseph, you've been through many trials regarding this yourself."

Joseph had a couple of bites of toast. It helped immensely.

Father Etienne sat up a little straighter. "Joseph, I would like to share a few thoughts with you. Is that all right? Are you up to it?"

"Of course, Father, please."

"As a historian, you surely recognize that Man and Conflict are practically synonymous terms throughout history thus, whether physical or mental, suffering, pain, and sorrow will always be with us.

Everyone wants to alleviate suffering. No one wants to suffer or have anyone else suffer, but it is a part of the world and our lives. Christ told us so during the Sermon on the Mount. *That you may be the children of your Father who is in heaven, who makes his sun to rise upon the good and bad, and rain upon the just and unjust"* (Mt 5:45). Everything that happens in this world, be it good or evil, touches everyone at some time or other in their lives. Joseph, an old Catholic joke is that if you want to make God laugh, share your plans with him. Mother Cornelia Connelly, an American educator in the 19th century, who started an academy for girls in England and suffered much mental anguish during her life, I think, put it best, "Take the Cross, the good Lord sends you, as it is, and not as you might imagine it to be." Father Etienne paused to let Joseph take it all in.

"As a man, I cannot end suffering. But as a priest, I must do whatever I can to unite people's suffering to Our Lord's suffering.

Joseph listened intently to his priest.

Father Etienne continued. "There is no Christianity without the Cross. There are too many Christians today who believe that truth is relative. They may say otherwise but look at what so many believe. There is only heaven, no hell, and only victims, no sinners. If, as they argue, truth has no borders, is, in fact, boundless, then there is no truth."

Joseph interrupted. "Or, as my Mother would say, 'Your salvation is through the Cross.'"

"Precisely, and amen," nodded the Dominican priest. He looked down for a moment, and then, lifting his head to meet Joseph's eyes, he said, "Joseph, the best possible advice I can give you is to put all your trust in the Lord. The Lord made you, and to him, you will someday return."

"Thank you, Father."

Joseph, now more composed, having eaten a couple of pieces of toast and drank some hot coffee, smiled, and thanked Father Etienne for bringing him back to earth and reality. The two talked about how Joseph needed to pull himself together and get back to living the life he had been given. Joseph then remembered that he had to contact the university about a couple of missed appointments he needed to reschedule for the following day. They shook hands, with Joseph telling Father Etienne he would see him on Sunday.

69.

Joseph was back on campus working the next day, yet he struggled to put Miku out of his thoughts. It seemed as if she was permanently on his mind. What was she doing? What was she thinking? And then there was the matter of their daughter. Once comprehending that she existed, he began to think about her more and more as each day passed.

That Friday, after finishing up early in the afternoon at the university, Joseph slid into a pew at St. Dominic. The glowing red lamp reassured him that he was not alone in the empty church.

He removed a crumpled piece of paper from his jacket pocket and smoothed it out on his leg. Before leaving his office, he had scribbled a prayer on it. He lowered his knees to the kneeler and made the sign of the cross.

"Dear God,

North Pacific

I am but one soul among the countless whom you watch over. Please forgive me for the situation in which I placed Miku all those years ago. Please look after my daughter Tomiko. I cannot take back what happened. I am entirely responsible. I am eternally contrite for my sins. I ask that you guide and sustain these women with every care. Please help Miku's husband always to protect them. I ask this petition in the name of your Son, our Lord, Jesus Christ, who lives and reigns with you, Father and the Holy Ghost, one God, forever and ever. Amen."

He looked up from the piece of paper and pressed his forehead against the back of his hand. Then remembering his mother's words of faith, he whispered aloud, "Slava na viky!" (Glory to Him forever!).

~~~~~

Later that night, at the desk up in his bedroom, Joseph remembered the previous weekend's events. The whole affair had seemed dream-like. Yet, the net result was his intensified and seemingly one-way conversation with God.

Joseph had spent much of his life looking for "proof" of God's existence. He smiled and thought, yes, he, too, was a user of the scientific rationalism of modern man. But he had also learned that science as a method of inquiry and discovery was forever changing with new theories that, in the end, were never the "last word," on any given subject. That was just part of the nature of science. He had also been exposed to many great philosophical arguments, from St. Anselm's Proslogian to the Five Ways of St. Thomas Aquinas. Yet, proof and faith are two entirely different things. One is human and employs reason that helps us better understand our finite world. In contrast, faith is a transcendent gift of the infinite God.

That triggered memories of some personal research on which Joseph had previously worked. He glanced through some of his old pocket journals stacked up against the side of his desk. After going through a few, he found some notes of a thought offered by Benedictine Abbot Columba Marmion, whom Father Etienne had introduced him to when he gave Joseph one of his books on their trip to Portland years before. Marmion explained, "You find some minds which are so attached to their way of seeing things that they are scandalized at the simplicity of [God's] Divine Plan."

Joseph contemplated that thought for a few minutes, then picked up and thumbed through the now well-worn pages of his copy of Pascal's *Pensées*. Of all the Christian writers he had read in his life, this thoughtful and gifted man seemed to get to the crux of some of the most fundamental questions concerning the Christian faith. For Joseph, Blaise Pascal's explanations spoke most clearly and directly to him.

The Frenchman argued that for man to touch the infinite, the transcendent, so to speak, using reason alone was not enough. Pascal contended that "It is the heart which experiences God, and not the reason." Pascal's "heart" is the mind's instinctual perception of a truth. This intellectual apprehension or grasping of truth is found deep within the soul. It allows God's grace and man's freedom to converge. At that point, it becomes man's choice, that is, his freedom, his liberty, to accept or reject God's grace. Reason is used to understand better the physical world we live in. However, since God is infinite, his infinity far outstrips man's limited power of reason to "see" God. Monsieur Pascal understood that finding God is a matter of the heart and soul.

The final piece of the puzzle for Joseph, and his now firm conviction that God was at the center of Man's existence, was to flip to another dog-eared page of Pascal's work and read: "Apart from Jesus Christ, we cannot know the meaning of our life or death, of God or of ourselves."

For Joseph, Marmion's and Pascal's thoughts sufficed. He closed the book forcefully. Removing his spectacles (another somewhat recent addition to his "growing older" look), he rubbed his temples, and let his mind relax for the first time in days as he got ready for bed.

70.

While working on his second book, Joseph reflected on how Tacoma had changed from the days of his youth. The electric streetcars that linked points and neighborhoods in the city had been replaced by buses. The new Narrows Bridge, reconnecting Tacoma to the Kitsap and Olympic Peninsulas, was opened in 1950, replacing the old bridge that had collapsed during a windstorm in 1940. Gas stations, drive-in theatres, and larger retail stores popped up or were in the planning stages. The City's population had mushroomed from around 40,000 in 1900, when his parents had arrived at the "end of the line" of the Northern Pacific railroad, to now over 150,000. Rainier College had become Rainier University. Joseph's beloved waterfront along Commencement Bay, which had once been a long string of sawmills, now saw the slow disappearance of those noisy industrial enterprises and the emergence of restaurants along the shoreline. It had all seemed to happen so quickly. Joseph shook his head and refocused on his research.

The new book, conceived after Miku's visit, kept him from dwelling on the past and what might have been. The working title, *A Naval History of the North Pacific*, was coming along fine. All of his contacts in the field of naval history that he had developed in writing his first book, *War in the North Pacific, 1941-1945*. made this effort much more manageable. They had also provided him with the necessary new contacts for the work's Russian, English, Spanish, Japanese, Chinese, and Canadian elements. The final chapter would speak to the geopolitical importance of this vast area of the globe.

~~~~~

North Pacific

Joseph had become more or less a regular at 3 Bridges Café for breakfast. Thanks to Denise, he would show up most days of the week to find his favorite seat available. And at least once or twice a week, he would stop by when he left campus early and enjoy a piece of fresh pie and a cup of coffee before going home. He and Denise would talk and share the day-to-day goings-on in their lives. Since Denise had bought the house she had rented for years, Joseph found himself helping her around the place and with yard projects on multiple occasions. He enjoyed her company, and she certainly appreciated the labor. He was somewhat limited in what he could do because of his back, but together they figured out ways of accomplishing what needed to get done. She would even fix him dinner when the projects ran well into the weekend afternoons. Joseph had reciprocated by having Denise over for dinner at his place occasionally. While Joseph could never boast of his cooking, he always had his ace in the hole of the view out his bayside windows. Like so many before her, Denise succumbed to the beauty of the breathtaking vistas.

After the Miku "affair of the heart," Joseph had become more reticent and withdrawn with his inner feelings toward the opposite sex. At this point in his life, it seemed clear that he would remain single because of his age and physical limitations. He also knew that he still thought about Miku much too much to entertain serious feelings toward someone else.

North Pacific

Kasumi and Joseph managed to maintain their friendship even though she had become Mrs. Gates. Mr. and Mrs. Gates had moved into a beautiful home over by Annie Wright (Girls) Seminary that, like his own place, had a great view of the bay. Kasumi would pop in to say hi to Joseph in his office on campus whenever she stopped by to see her husband.

During their conversations, she admitted to having a moment, not unlike Joseph's thoughts about her, after that faculty event a few years back. She, too, had wanted to see Joseph again and had to fight against her feelings because of how she sensed Joseph was still, at that time, mourning the loss of Miku. David's arrival in Kasumi's life prevented their "moment" from playing out.

Joseph told Kasumi of Miku's return and her incredible story during and after the war. Lastly and poignantly, he told her about Tomiko. They both commented on the fortunes of life. He was extremely pleased that she was happy and fulfilled as she continued her seamstress work from her new home. Her one regret was that of motherhood passing her by. By the time she and David had married, she felt it was too late. But other than that, she was pleased with her life and also having Joseph in it.

~~~~~

As for Martin, he and Joseph continued to meet when schedules allowed for lunches. They would still go to sporting events together, and then there were the holidays Joseph spent enjoying Colleen's cooking and time with the Linart family. What grabbed Joseph's attention was that Mark, Martin's oldest, had graduated the year before from the University of Washington with a degree in Business while his sister Darcy was finishing up her sophomore year at Rainier. It seemed like only yesterday that those kids were playing in the Linart's backyard on a swing that Martin had built years ago.

~~~~~

Time marched on. Then came the news in the Spring of 1959 that Joseph never thought he would hear. From the ambo at the front of the church, after giving another stirring homily, Father Etienne Sauveterre announced he was stepping down from his post as the parish pastor at St. Dominic. Joseph could not believe it. Well, of course, he could. That was not the point. Everyone in church groaned. No one wanted to see him go. Joseph did the math and calculated that Father had come to the parish in 1922 and thus had been there for 37 years. A further estimation put his age at 82. He couldn't be that old, Joseph thought to himself. At the end of Mass, Father was overwhelmed by parishioners. Everyone thanked him for being in their lives and making them better Christians. They all knew what a treasure Father had been to the parish. Joseph sized up the crowd and decided to find a way to see Father on another day.

On his way home, he decided not to stop at 3 Bridges Café for breakfast. Father's retirement news had taken the wind out of his sails.

As he stood with a cup of coffee and watched the activity on the bay from his living room on that rainy Sunday morning, he remembered Father's homily from the Mass. The Dominican priest said we did not live in a perfect world. No, far from it. Father talked about living in an imperfect or a "broken" world. However, this broken world was full of challenges for man. He said we needed to trust in the wisdom and justice of the Almighty. Joseph smiled and thought he had heard that somewhere before. Father said our individual opinions and standards of fairness and judgment are simply that – our opinions. Even though we think we know it all, our opinions pale when held up to God's providence. God's thoughts are infinitely above man's thoughts. He was going to miss that man. Joseph thought the "broken world" reference Father had used in his homily sounded like Gabriel Marcel, another of Father's French philosophers. Joseph smiled again.

~~~~~

Later that week, he did get in to see Fr. Etienne. They shook hands and embraced. Father told Joseph he was planning to return to Orleans in France to visit with a few extended family members and see some old friends. He laughed and said he wasn't kidding about his friends being old. He said he would also visit some Dominican parishes and monasteries in France, but it had not yet been decided where he would finish out his days. Father Etienne could see on Joseph's face that his protégé was not happy. "Joseph, I propose that we keep in touch via mail, and you never know, I might end up back here in the future. Your new priest, who will be arriving next month, I know from, let's call it, my 'homily tour to California,' that I took a few years back. He has contacted me already and told me he would love to have me live out my days here in Tacoma at St. Dominic. We'll see." Joseph forced a smile and asked where he would get the latest books in French philosophy. Father Etienne laughed and said he would keep Joseph abreast of everything interesting in French-language books.

Joseph had Father over for dinner before he left. They reminisced and became somewhat nostalgic, harkening back to all that had transpired between them. Father laughed and remembered Joseph buying "scones for the road" at the Benson Hotel in Portland. They both laughed about their trepidation regarding the sturdiness of the old Studebaker on that trip. Joseph asked if he might take Father to the airport when the time came. The Dominican accepted the offer. When that day came, Joseph loaded Father's suitcase into the Chevy and drove him to Sea-Tac International. They shook hands one more time before the priest boarded the plane. As Father walked toward the gate, Joseph raised his voice and said, "Come back when you're ready, Father. Tacoma is your home now. Come back to it after your time off for good behavior." Father grinned and nodded. It struck Joseph that this was becoming his new thing. That is, driving loved ones and best friends to the airport to leave him. As always, life was not as Joseph would have planned it.

71.

A Naval History of the North Pacific was released in March of 1961. While it was well-received, it did not achieve nearly the sales of his first book. Nonetheless, the volume was given solid reviews for a not widely known subject. The university was pleased, as was Professor Vaenko.

Thankfully, this time there was no tour scheduled other than a day up at the University of Washington, giving a presentation and answering questions. The only media coverage came from a reporter for the local city newspaper, who interviewed him in his campus office.

~~~~~

Joseph felt like relaxing. The university talked about a sabbatical and authoring another book. Joseph talked Rainier into giving him three months up in Victoria, British

North Pacific

Columbia, at the University of Victoria. He would research the history of the Canadian and American joint naval agreements, treaties, operations, and concerns of both countries regarding the North Pacific. It was the summer of 1961. Joseph rested and thoroughly enjoyed the hospitality and beauty of the City of Victoria. He spent many a fine day in the inner harbor area, with the presence of the majestic Canadian Pacific Railway's "Empress Hotel" and the heavily English-influenced Provincial Parliament Building. His time in this fair city convinced him he could do this regularly.

~~~~~

Upon returning to Tacoma, he scheduled an appointment with his general practitioner because of his growing problems with his lower back from his surgeries over eighteen years ago, reminders of his "swim" in the Aleutian waters. The good doctor checked him out, had x-rays taken, and told him that he was now contending with advancing arthritis in addition to the damage to his lower back. He would have to learn to deal with it and resort to pain relievers when needed. Doctor Harris, himself close to retirement, told Joseph bluntly that he was getting old, and that life would be more of an adventure from this point forward. Joseph thanked the doctor and exited the medical office and onto the street with his cane firmly in hand. As he got in his car, he shook his head, felt the pain, thought about physical suffering, and said aloud, "Father Etienne would say, 'Offer it up.'" He smiled and added, "Lord, give me strength."

~~~~~

A week before Christmas, Martin stopped by the house for a visit. Joseph was pleased to see his buddy, and the two of them sat at the kitchen table and began talking.

"Joe, I stopped by today to ask you a question. Actually, I should be shopping for a Christmas present for Colleen, but you know how I love going downtown this time of the year."

Joseph grinned, "I hope the question is an easy one."

Martin proceeded, "You and I have previously discussed existentialism and read and talked about some of John Paul Sartre's and Albert Camus' books, correct?"

"Yes," answered Joseph, recalling some of their enjoyable conversations and friendly arguments, all the time wondering where Martin would go this time with their ongoing dialogue.

"Give me the kernel of their ideas and yours?"

"Martin, I'm not a philosopher."

Not fazed by Joe's response, Martin continued waiting for Joseph's thoughts.

North Pacific

Joseph closed his eyes briefly and then attempted to answer his best friend's question. "Well, I must say that, for me, Camus' stories are much more interesting to read than Sartre's. His books are more compelling. He's just a better writer," Joseph added.

Martin interjected, "Didn't you tell me that both writers were attempting to make sense of a world that made absolutely no sense?"

"I did," said Joseph, "But they each take a slightly different path to that conclusion. Sartre says there is no God, and the world is meaningless. However, he maintains that man is free and responsible for his actions in this absurd world and can provide his own meaning to his existence through his decisions and actions. On the other hand, Camus says man is limited and constrained by his circumstances. I sometimes wonder if Camus might have changed his thinking some had he lived and not died relatively young in that auto accident. I suspect that Camus and Sartre developed their points of view because of the horrors of the Great War and the Second World War in Europe. So many people were devastated by the atrocities that made up that period. So, in different ways, they both see the world as godless and pointless, thus leaving Man to his own devices."

There was a moment of silence, so Joseph continued. "I also told you I did not believe Sartre's or Camus' interpretation of the world to be correct. If you'll remember, my issue when we started discussing this were related to God, life, happiness, and women. Your interest was linked to your thoughts when you believed you were about to die up in the Komandorski Islands. At that time, existentialism was the new shiny object in the world of philosophy, and the questions posed were worth thinking about." He added, "They're still worth discussing."

Martin nodded assent to Joseph's recollections.

"Anyway, one more time, I am absolutely not a philosopher. To summarize my thoughts in general terms," He paused to see if Martin wanted to say anything. He did not, and so Joseph continued, My take is "Existentialism is a way of coping with a godless world and providing meaning to one's life. The idea fits extremely well with the ideas of modernity, you know, a Man-centered world. Sartre provided a framework for working out one's meaning in life. This is all well and good, and I can see why it appeals to so many people, but the whole thing is predicated on the idea that God does not exist. That just doesn't work for me.

Joseph drew a breath and continued, "Man can use his reason to discover God by contemplating God's creation. The Church teaches that God created the world - out of nothing. 'Ex nihilo,' as the Church would characterize it in Latin. Using reason, science, and faith to better understand nature and revelation leads to a better understanding of the Creator."

For me, while never being able to empirically prove the existence of God, or disprove it for that matter, I believe what I have said to you points to the presence of a Creator

God. I see the Judeo-Christian God at the center of our world, not man."

Martin looked deep in thought, sorting out Joseph's analysis. He began to say something but then started laughing. Then Joseph joined in, knowing they were not philosophers but a history professor with a bad back and failing eyesight and an engineer who had glimpsed death.

Once again, Joseph said philosophical speculation was not something he was trained to do, yet he felt good about his thoughts. "Martin, I'm a second-generation American whose family came from the mountains of Central Europe. At this point, I like to believe, with God's grace, I know who I am and where I stand in this life." Joseph's voice trailed off a bit, and his demeanor became more reflective.

Martin said, "I guess it serves me right for encouraging a 'professor' to give a talk."

"Martin, as for us arguing about this topic, maybe we ought to accept Ludwig Wittgenstein's statement, 'Of which one cannot speak, one must remain silent.'"

"Well, I guess we can agree to that," Martin said as he stood up. "I suppose I should be getting on my way. I've only got so many days left to find something to 'wow' Colleen."

GRATIA

(Grace)

"You have granted me life and mercy; and thy visitation hath preserved my spirit."

Job 10:12

Douay-Rheims

"And he said to me: My grace is sufficient for thee: for power is made perfect in infirmity. Gladly, therefore, will I glory in my infirmities, that the power of Christ may dwell in me."

2 Corinthians 12:9

Douay-Rheims

North Pacific

72.

It was late spring of 1963. Joseph turned the letter over and over in his hands. It had arrived in the mail almost an hour ago, and he had yet to open it. He set it down on the side table next to his chair for the second time and walked away. He knew who it was from. Miku's distinctive handwriting was evident. Of course, the postmark from Tokyo helped also. He went to the kitchen and cleaned up the breakfast dishes. Then with a sigh, he returned to the living room, sat in his chair, and opened the envelope. He removed the two folded pieces of stationary and read,

Dear Joseph,

I know it has been a long time, but, as I told you before, it is difficult to write this letter because of our feelings for each other, our situation, and our faith. Yet here I am doing it.

So first, how are you? I hope you are in good health and making the most of your life. I still pray for you every day. You are in my thoughts more than you might think.

However, let me get to the point of this letter. Has your life changed from when we last met? Are you married? Do you have children? I do not even know if you still live at this address, but I will find out soon enough if this letter is returned to me unopened and undelivered. Knowing you, I'm certain that no matter what your circumstances, if at all possible, you will still be at that wonderful house of yours that you love so much.

Joseph read the second page of the letter.

I need to know this information because your daughter Tomiko wants to travel to the United States to meet you. Are you ready for something like that? Tomiko has grown into a young woman. She is 21 years old and is adamant that she will come to see you and get to know you. As I told you I would, I have spoken of you to her more and more as she has grown.

Most importantly, she now knows the circumstances of her birth and our current situation. As I said, she is a grown-up, although, of course, young, and is strong-willed, maybe a little like her mother. She is resolute about this happening.

Please let me know if her coming over there to visit you might be possible. I would need to know when the best time would be. I know that both of us have been through much because of our actions in the past, but Tomiko is still our daughter, and she is what is most important at this time. I know this is asking a lot, so please reply soon.

You are always in our thoughts,

Miku

Also enclosed in the letter was a current photo of Tomiko. She had grown into a beautiful young woman. As Joseph stared at the photo, he thought he recognized a hint of his mother in Tomiko. He almost cried.

Joseph put the letter back in the envelope and put it down. He took his glasses off and rubbed his temples. It had been so long since he had heard from Miku. The news of his daughter wanting to meet him was beyond wonderful yet intimidating. What if she doesn't like me? Still, he could not pass up the maybe once-in-a-lifetime opportunity of meeting his daughter.

He rose from the chair, retrieved the letter, and moved to the kitchen table to write his response. He drove to the post office and mailed the letter that afternoon. A month later, another letter arrived telling Joseph that Tomiko would be coming in a few weeks.

Joseph contacted Kasumi. He told her what was happening and asked if she could help him. He wanted to change some things around the house to accommodate Tomiko. Kasumi was beside herself with delight and anticipation of the prospect of the two of them finally meeting and told Joseph, of course, she would help. He also got Martin and his son Mark to help out.

73.

The big day finally arrived. Joseph reached the airport with about twenty minutes to spare. He parked the car and entered the terminal. He was visibly nervous as he stood there with a small bouquet of flowers. When the passengers finally arrived, Joseph saw her at once as she slowly walked toward the people waiting. "Tomiko," he said as she got closer. She was a bit apprehensive, but smiled, walked up to him, and said in excellent English, "Hello, Father." Joseph held out the flowers, and she took them. They awkwardly hugged briefly, and he said, "The car is this way." Joseph's heart raced as father and daughter headed for the parking lot. The ride back to Tacoma from the airport was challenging. Joseph could not look at his daughter very much because he was driving the car. He wished he had updated his 50 Chevy. Being 1963, he thought it looked like one of the older vehicles on the road. They spoke haltingly. When they finally arrived at the house, Tomiko was at once taken by the view from the front window. Joseph took her lightweight coat from her, hung it up in the hall closet, and set the luggage on the floor in the living room. He indicated to Tomiko the different points of interest that made up the outline of the bay. Then they sat down, Tomiko on the sofa and Joseph in his chair. They slowly began to converse.

Tomiko, encouraged by her father's gentleness and caring eyes, did most of the talking. She told him her life story in about thirty minutes. She told him she wanted to get to know him and what he was like. Joseph smiled and added a comment or question here and there but mostly enjoyed watching her interact with him.

After about 45 minutes, Joseph stood and said, "Well, I think it's so wonderful to have you here. I don't know what to say. But I do want you to be able to unpack and relax for a while. Let me show you your room." Tomiko glanced over at the bed against the wall by the staircase, assuming that was what he was referring to. Joseph, watching her eyes, laughed, and exclaimed, "No, no, that's not where you'll be sleeping. Let me get your bags, and I'll take you upstairs."

When they reached the second floor, the space had been transformed from Joseph's room with its large desk, with books and papers everywhere, to a beautifully decorated bedroom. Tomiko said, "Is this not your bedroom, Father? I cannot possibly sleep here."

Joseph marveled at her English, smiled, and responded, "Even I don't recognize this room. With the help of some friends, I hope we have made the room into a space you can feel is all yours." He then showed her the upstairs view of the bay. He pointed toward the opposite end of the room and told her she would have her own bath and shower. Tomiko was delighted and much more expressively hugged him. When they embraced, Joseph realized he had not hugged anyone who was his own flesh and blood since his parents had been alive. With that, he left her upstairs to unpack her things, freshen up, and relax from the long trip.

Over the following week, the two attempted to figure each other out. After some fits and starts, they began to develop a rhythm for how to act around each other. This led them to enjoying each other's company all the more. They just seemed to hit it off. Maybe it was because each wanted the relationship to succeed, but just possibly, there was something innate to the whole thing.

North Pacific

After that first week, Joseph asked Tomiko for a favor. Her eyes widened. Joseph reassured her that it was nothing. "Would you be all right with calling me Dad instead of Father? Father seems so formal, and I want us to feel closer than that." She quickly hugged him and said, "Of course, Daddy." They both laughed. "Dad will be fine, smiled Joseph."

After a few months, the Vaenkos, as they called themselves, became closer and closer. They had both wanted this to work out, and it seemed to happen more quickly than either of them in their wildest dreams could have hoped for.

During this "getting to know each other period," Joseph took Tomiko over to meet Martin and Colleen. It went well. The Linarts were as gracious as possible and helped make Tomiko feel comfortable in her new surroundings. Of course, Joseph had Kasumi come over to meet her. Within fifteen minutes, the two women were laughing and jumping up and down, holding each other's forearms. Watching the two of them, Joseph thought to himself, what would I have done without Kasumi as a friend after the war?

Joseph showed Tomiko all around Tacoma, including the Pagoda-style bus station down at Point Defiance Park, where he and her mother first kissed while viewing the Japanese Gardens twenty-plus years ago. Joseph looked at his daughter and said, "I feel somewhat embarrassed telling you that, Tomiko."

North Pacific

"Please don't." Tomiko pleaded. It means so much to me to have these details. She almost cried.

As more time passed, Tomiko instinctively began to help Joseph with some of his physical restrictions. She asked him about his condition, and he had given her a shortened and sanitized version of what had happened to "Dad" during the war and his recovery afterward.

One summer night, as father and daughter were enjoying the end of the day out on the deck watching the sunset over the Olympic mountain range, he told Tomiko about his visit to the "Sanctuary to Our Lady of Sorrows" in Portland, Oregon. Joseph told her how it had strengthened him when he was at his lowest. Tomiko, fascinated by the story, proceeded to tell him that back in Nagasaki, after the dropping of the atomic bomb, at the front of the Catholic Cathedral in the Urakami District, there stood, after the blast, amidst all the devastation and ruin a statue of "Our Lady of Sorrows." They both agreed the coincidence was striking.

August rolled around, and it was time for Tomiko to return to Japan. After breakfast one morning, quite out of the blue, Tomiko declared she did not want to return to Japan but wanted to stay with Joseph if he would have her. Joseph taken aback in a good way, told Tomiko they would have to talk to her mother. Tomiko explained to Joseph that she had thought about him, her missing father, all her life. She loved her mother greatly and had nothing but respect for Hiroto, who had taken both her and her mother in when all had seemed lost. Tomiko explained to her father that their shared ethnic heritage influenced her identity. She paused and asked, "Dad, I've been meaning to ask you about our heritage on the Vaenko side all summer."

Laughing, Joseph said, "Well, if you were looking to find out you are of royal blood and ancestry or anything like that, you have missed the mark by quite a ways and will be sorely disappointed. Tomiko, Your Grandfather, and Grandmother Vaenko came from Central Europe, specifically the Southern Carpathian Mountains. They were of Slavic descent and known as "Ruthenians." I want to argue that's where you get your good looks, but after looking at you all summer, I see too much of your Mother's beauty in you for me to make that claim."

They each wrote letters and mailed them in one envelope to Miku. The response came back with Miku writing that she had considered the possibility of this happening. Although she did not want to lose her daughter, after reading both letters and understanding how both of them felt, she would consent to be "okay" with Tomiko staying longer, always knowing she was more than welcome to return to Japan. She also added that, in the end, because Tomiko was an adult, it was really up to her.

Father and daughter were ecstatic. The fall term was beginning at the university. Joseph talked to some friends in administration and lined up a job for Tomiko in Rainier's student foreign exchange program. With her schooling in Japan, Tomiko had earned the equivalency of a bachelor's degree. She began working at the university immediately, and the two commuted daily from the little house that overlooked the bay.

As time went on, they really felt like they were family. As Martin said with a smile, "They were inseparable and insufferable." Tomiko doted on Joseph. She put much effort into caring for him the best she could. One example was when she bought him a new black, beechwood shaft, "Fritz handle," walking cane to replace the old beat-up one, which was now, after years of wear and tear, a mottled brown, nicked and scratched cane with what was known as an old-fashioned tourist handle. As she saw it, he had probably used the old cane - forever. The Fritz was so much better a cane than the old one, especially with its open-ended styled handle that provided more room for the fingers – particularly Dad's arthritic ones. You could see that he got around much better using the new cane. She also constantly tried to help him clean up his new desk area in the living room, but it was a losing battle, with papers and books piled high everywhere. Sometimes the two of them would eat lunch together in his office on campus, with Tomiko thinking that Dad's office looked much like the corner of their living room at home.

~~~~~

Over the next few years, Tomiko flew back to Japan once for a couple of weeks to visit her mother, Hiroto, and her two half-brothers. Returning to Tacoma, Joseph and

North Pacific

Tomiko confessed that it was awful to be without each other.

Tomiko was also aware that her father tried to be subtle but always wanted her to tell him anything she could about her mother. Tomiko could sense that "Dad" still held intense feelings for Miku. She never spoke of it with her mother or her lately found father. Tomiko bore this knowledge as her personal cross.

~~~~~

It was the spring of 1967. Much had happened during the last four years, including getting Dad to break down and finally buy a television set. Granted, there was really no room for one between the furniture arranged to look out at the bay, the single bed against the wall by the stairs, and the God-awful mess on, in, and around Dad's desk on the opposite wall by the kitchen. But they managed to place the set with cords hanging out of it awkwardly against the wall, sort of in the corner, next to the front window. And then, after all that, they didn't watch it much, but it was good to have it if they wanted to see something special. They did like watching old movies together.

Tomiko, during this period, dated some young men she had met through her job at the university. Dad scrutinized every one of them. Still, honestly, she had trouble imagining leaving Dad behind, moving somewhere else, and starting a family. For now, she decided, she was completely happy living with her father.

They always attended the 8 AM Sunday Mass at St. Dominic. Father Remy, the Dominican who had replaced the beloved Father Sauveterre, was an exceptional priest whom both Vaenkos loved very much.

~~~~~

Joseph and Father Etienne remained in contact, exchanging letters every month. Father hinted in his letters that he hoped to return to Tacoma, but Joseph suspected it might not happen. Fr. Etienne was now in his mid-80s. Vaenko chose not to dwell on missing the good priest but focused all his attention on thoroughly enjoying his now beloved daughter.

74.

It was a beautiful afternoon. The previous two or three days had been foggy, and Joseph's soul had soared when the sun broke through before noon that Friday. It was warm, and he looked forward to sitting out on his deck when he got home. Joseph had finished his work at the university for the day and had made his way over to St. Dominic before heading home.

He entered the Church and slipped into the pew where he sat when he first saw Miku. After sitting for a few minutes, he got down on his knees, made the sign of the cross, closed his eyes, and thanked the Lord for the incredibly precious gift of his daughter. Joseph would do anything for her. She had shown him what joy meant, true joy.

His mind shifted to his parents, now long deceased and long missed. He remembered how their faith had so powerfully informed his own. It made him think of a psalm.

> *The Lord is the portion of my inheritance and my cup:*
>
> *it is thou that will restore my inheritance to me.*
>
> *The lines are fallen unto me in goodly places:*
>
> *for my inheritance is goodly to me"* (Ps 15:5-6).

For Joseph, those verses had always meant to him that his inheritance from his parents was the faith he now possessed and practiced. This was the Sacred Tradition, or as the Church would teach, the "Traditio," the handing on of the historical Apostolic Christian faith from one generation to the next. He bowed his head and remembered Alexandr and Maria. He thanked God for having blessed him with the gift of his parents.

North Pacific

Then, he thanked the Lord for Miku. She had changed his life and had given him their precious daughter. The sun rays, now pouring through the stained-glass windows on the west side of the church, cast a light on a portion of the tabernacle while the red lamp burned on the other side. As always, the red lamp glowed, but he noticed it was exceedingly strong and bright today. Joseph thought to himself that he had seen that intensity of the red lamp once before, but it escaped him as to when. He made the sign of the cross one more time. Then he rose, exited the pew, genuflected, and walked out of the church.

Arriving home, Joseph put his briefcase down next to his writing desk. He noted the desk was a bit cluttered and made a mental note to clean it up some to avoid getting into trouble with Tomiko. She wasn't home yet. So as he had promised himself, he headed for the door to the deck to enjoy the warmth and beauty of the late afternoon. As Joseph stepped out onto the deck, closing the door behind him, he stumbled. He steadied himself by grabbing the railing surrounding the deck and then sat in one of the chairs. "Embarrassing," he thought to himself.

Then Joseph looked to the far shore.

75.

The bay sparkled. Sailboats raced in Quartermaster Harbor between Vashon and Maury Islands. A salmon purse seiner was tied up at the public dock down in Old Town. Seagulls danced against the southwesterly breezes.

"It is everything I remember," said Miku to her daughter. "It was so long ago, but I remember it like it was yesterday. The whole world is in front of your eyes. It is a view without equal." Miku continued gazing out over the expanse of water as the two women stood in the living room.

Tomiko turned back to the view. "When I came home from work that day, I walked into the living room and saw Dad through the window. Tomiko pointed to a chair out on the deck. He was sitting there. At first, I thought he was asleep, but I could tell something was wrong as I got closer. I still can't believe he's gone," she whispered. "He was only 59. We were within weeks of celebrating his birthday. The doctor said it was a stroke."

Miku, moved by her daughter's heartfelt description of discovering her father's body, said, "Oh, Tomiko, I was so in love with your Father. Thank you so much for letting me be with you and attend Joseph's funeral. I know now how much he meant to you."

"I also know how much you meant to him, Mother," Tomiko said, with fresh tears in her eyes.

Miku broke down and started crying, also. They hugged each other and then together tried to recover. "So, what are your plans now, Tomiko?"

"Well, Dad had a will and left me the house and a nice amount of money. It seems his second book sold a few more copies than he let on.

In his papers he left behind, I discovered that he had paid for his funeral and headstone a few years back. I was confused because I also saw that he had also paid for a headstone in another cemetery. I guess that one was for someone else.."

"Well, to answer your question directly, Mother, I entertained the idea of moving back to Japan, but I decided quickly that I love it here too much. I'm going to stay here in Tacoma and make a life for myself. To tell you the truth, I will enjoy and cherish this house for as long as I live. I will also 'attempt,' I have no illusions, to declutter the living room a bit." She grinned. "Otherwise, the rest of the place reminds me of him, and I like that feeling. The Linarts, Kasumi, and Denise, a wonderful woman from the café where Dad and I used to eat, have all said they will help me with any issues that might arise. They are so good to me. I believe they all see me as a daughter.

North Pacific

Mother, I was only able to be with him for these last four years, but we both experienced indescribable joy in sharing each other's lives. I can't explain it. You would think we were father and daughter." Both smiled.

"What if you get married?" interjected Miku.

"If that happens, we will live here, or there will be no wedding." With that thought, both women embraced.

Then, Miku noticed Tomiko's medal on a chain around her neck. "Is that your father's medal?" Miku reached out and took it in her hand. "I remember your father always wearing it."

"He told me it was my grandmother's and what it had meant to her. I will always wear it."

"Oh, honey, now you've got me on the verge of tears again," Miku said, trying to hold up her end of the conversation without breaking down. Miku stood and stared at her and Joseph's daughter, "their" daughter. "Oh, Tomiko," exclaimed Miku, pointing at a paper booklet. "I thought this was a wonderful touch for you to include Joseph's prayer in the funeral Mass handout."

Tomiko sighed, "Dad, over the last few years, developed the habit of writing down little prayers he found in books or composed himself whenever the mood struck him. He recorded his thoughts and other writings in small journals and notebooks that he always carried on him. All of them are there," pointing toward the large stack of journals and notebooks piled haphazardly up against the side of his desk.

North Pacific

"Dad also told me he had spent many an hour in front of the Blessed Sacrament at St. Dominic. He said he had finally reached a point where his conversations with the Almighty had become more coherent and more important to him. That prayer on the back of the handout was the last one he had composed and written in his journal."

Miku looked at her daughter and saw a grown woman before her. "You know I'm leaving for Tokyo in the morning. Are you going to be all right?"

Tomiko replied, "Yes, Mother, I will be fine. I've got a good job at the university. I have made many friends here. Since Dad's passing, I've prayed about it a lot. I've even resorted to trips to St. Dominic at odd times of the day to pray about it. This is where I'm supposed to be. Mother, I am so thankful that you supported me in my pursuit of meeting and getting to know my father. And as Dad would say, Slava Isusu Khrystu!" (Glory to Jesus Christ!).

The two women walked out the door and onto the deck to better view the bay. Miku pointed to a ship that had cleared Browns Point and was now heading north up East Passage. "Can you see the name on the stern of that ship?"

With her younger eyes, Tomiko looked and said, "It's the *Crimson Globe* heading out into the North Pacific." Tomiko paused and then told her mother, "The North Pacific, that was Dad's world," she said proudly. "He was born, raised, worked, and lived out his life on the edge of it. He got to experience it firsthand during the war, and he spent his academic life writing books about it. I can see that ship, the one you just pointed out, Mother. I can picture it taking him home to his beloved North Pacific."

In the living room, on Joseph's side table next to his chair, the back page of the funeral Mass handout lay face up. It read as follows:

Joseph Vaenko's Prayer

Forgive me, Lord, for I am a sinner.
Domine non sum dignus.
(Lord, I am without dignity.)
I thank you for my life, O Lord.
You are too good to me.
I am your servant. I am your servant.
Please help me to do your will.
Please guide me on your path.
Please strengthen my faith, O Lord.
Please fill me with the Holy Spirit.
In the Holy Spirit, I pray.
Lord, calm my fears,
for my faith, hope, and trust are in You.
I ask all of these petitions,
in the name of Jesus Christ,
your Son, our Lord, and Savior.

North Pacific

Thank you, Dear Lord,
for having created me
and for providing me with these
Precious,
and Wonderful gifts.

The End

North Pacific

Author's Note

The novel intertwines history with fiction. I grew up in Tacoma. Much of the story is set in various neighborhoods in Tacoma's "North End," for the most part, before the author was born. The text identifies various buildings, businesses, institutions, and locales in the city. Other sites are given fictitious monikers. There are also locations used in the story that are created out of the whole cloth of the author's imagination. It is a story, a work of fiction. No characters in the story are based on actual persons.

All Old and New Testament references are taken from *The Holy Bible*, Douay-Rheims Version, translated from the Latin Vulgate, Saint Benedict Press, Charlotte, North Carolina, 2009. The Latin section titles in the book and their translations are mine. "Mea culpa," for any errors, I was only ever an altar boy.

Credit and sources for the material used are found below, corresponding to the page number in the book.

Page 4 – **Prayer for Mariners** – based on a prayer from the Gregorian Roman Missal from the early middle ages, 6th to 8th century.

Page 40 – **Exultation of the Cross** – the prayer is taken from the Introit to the Mass for September 14th, in *St. John's Missal,* with an

North Pacific

introduction by Reverend Robert I. Gannon, S. J., Melbourne, Made in Belgium, 1956.

Page 118 – **St. Francis De Sales** – the "Complete Trust in God Prayer" was taken from catholiccompany.com/content/Complete-Trust# accessed on September 1, 2022.

Page 176 - **Cynthia Olsen** – the information gathered about *Cynthia Olsen's* visit to Tacoma in 1941 before sailing to her demise a few weeks later was taken from the following sources: *Voyage to Oblivion*, Stephen Harding, Amberly Publishing, Gloucestershire, UK, 2010. Since the crew of the Cynthia Olsen perished before they could tell their story, the narrative of the sinking of the lumber carrier in this story is developed from recollections of the Captain of the Japanese submarine *I-26,* who corresponded with Bert Webber in the 1970s and 1980s. *Silent Siege – III*, Bert Webber, Webb Research Group, Publishers, Medford, Oregon, 1997.

Page 181 – **USS *Charleston*** – Information related to the "oversized gunboat" was mostly gathered from the *USS Charleston* "War Diary" 1942-1943, declassified by the National Archives and Naval Administration on December 31, 2012.

Page 185 – **Joseph quoting Pascal's "Thoughts"** - *Pascal Pensées,* #201, p. 66, Penguin Books, London, England, 1995.

Page 220 – **USS *Abner Read*** – Sources for the mining of *Abner Read* include *USS Abner Read* (DD-526), Action Report for August 18, 1943, compiled by William L. Swann, March 21, 1998; Samuel Eliot Morison, *History of United States Naval Operations in World War II*, Vol. 7, *Aleutians, Gilberts and Marshalls: June 1942-April 1944*, University of Illinois Press, Urbana and Chicago, 2002; and Robert Sinclair

North Pacific

Parkin, *Blood on the Sea: American Destroyers Lost in World War II*, Sarpedon, 1996.

Page 288 – **Joseph's prayer for Ron Huddleston** – Prayer for a man deceased. *Saint Andrew Daily Missal* from the "Masses for the Dead," p. 467, The E. M. Lohmann Company, St. Paul, MN, 1958.

Page 296 – **Introit to the Mass of the Assumption of the Blessed Virgin Mary** – *The Saint Andrew Daily Missal*, Regular Edition, p. 834, The E. M. Lohman Co., St. Paul, MN, 1943.

Page 324 – **USS *Salt Lake City*** – For Martin's recollection of the naval surface action known as the Battle of the Komandorski Islands and Joseph's post-war research of that engagement, I used Samuel Eliot Morison's *History of United States Naval Operations in World War II*, Volume 7, Chapter 2, pp. 22-36, University of Illinois Press, Urbana and Chicago, 2002; and John A. Lorelli's *The Battle of the Komandorski Islands*, Naval Institute Press, Annapolis, Maryland, 1989; and *Japanese Monograph: no. 88,* 1942-1943.

Page 327 – **Urakami District, Nagasaki, Japan** – The Cathedral and Catholic community that resided in the neighborhood was the location of the second atomic bomb dropped on Japan on August 9, 1945. There are many sources for this event. One I recommend is *A Song for Nagasaki: The Story of Takashi Nagai*, Paul Glynn S.M., Ignatius Press, San Francisco, California, 2009.

Page 330 – **Poem on the Lisbon Disaster by Voltaire** – The version used was found at https://www.studocu.com/en-us/document/the-pennsylvania-state-university/philosophy/voltaire-poem-on-the-lisbon-disaster/21870695 accessed September 1, 2022.

Page 335 – **Vasyl' Stefanyk's "Sons"** – the paraphrasing and retelling of the short story "Sons" is from D. S. Struk's, *A Study of Vasyl'*

North Pacific

Stefanyk: The Pain at the Heart of Existence, pp. 158-162, Ukrainian Academic Press, Littleton, Colorado, 1973. The first quote is on page 161, and the second is on page 162.

Page 349 – **Alphonsus Liguori** – *The Glories of Mary*, "In this valley of tears…" p. 493, by St. Alphonsus Liguori, Redemptorist Fathers, Brooklyn, NY, 1931 (4th Reprint); "He conceals the trials…", p. 493.

Page 350 – **Joseph reviewing the Seven Sorrows of Mary pamphlet at the "Grotto"** – "Stabat Mater" (Grieving Mother), This 13th-century Catholic hymn and its history can be found at wikipedia.org/wiki/Stabat_Mater, accessed September 1, 2022.

Page 403 – **Hikawa Maru** – The last Japanese ocean liner to leave the United States in November of 1941 before the start of World War II in the Pacific. https://www.japan-talk.com/jt/new/hikawa-maru, accessed September 8, 2022.

Page 422 – **Columbo Marmion** – The quote from Marmion, "You find some minds…" is from *Christ, the Life of the Soul,* p. 39, Zacchaeus Press, MD, 2005; Other titles by and about Blessed Columbo Marmion include *Christ in his Mysteries*, Zacchaeus Press, MD, 2008; and *The Grace of "Nothingness,"* Fr. Cassian Koenemann, OSB, Angelico Press, USA, 2021.

Page 422 – Joseph quoting Pascal – *Great Books of the Western World, 33. Pensées,* Encyclopedia Britannica, Inc. Chicago, #278, p. 222.

Page 423 – **Joseph quoting Pascal** – *Pascal Pensées,* Penguin Books, London, England, 1995, #417, p. 121.

Page 455 – **Ruthenian phrases** used in the book are taken from *The Linden and the Oak, A Novel,* by Mark Wansa, World Academy of Rusyn Culture, 2009. Ruthenians today are known as Rusyns and Carpatho-Rusyns.

Made in the USA
Coppell, TX
03 July 2023